Temporary Love

W. Million

STOMILL BOOKS

Chapter One

GAGE

No one has ever taken me seriously. My siblings, my parents, Abby—my on-again, off-again girlfriend—no one believes I can stick with anything long enough to see it through.

Even Hugh, my cousin, who is sitting on the other side of this expensive desk in his high-rise office, the ocean on display behind him, seems skeptical. As a self-made real estate mogul in Bellerive, he's proven to have good instincts—at least about the housing market. His uncertainty about me is unwarranted.

The business degree nestled in my lap from Brighton College in California is real. After this meeting, I'm getting it blown up to cover the entire wall of the cottage I'm currently borrowing from my parents. Every time any of those nonbelievers comes to visit, they'll be forced to read the truth. Gage Tucker can see something through. College degree? Easy.

Or rather, *money* can see anything through, but there's no need for anyone to know how much of my family's money I donated to various Brighton College causes to get this piece of paper. The point is: I got it. The first two years of my degree, I fucked around too much, but once I buckled down, I earned my credits the traditional way, even if it took me a little longer. Sometimes you gotta spend money to make money.

Maren, Sawyer, and Nathaniel—three of my four siblings—bleed money all over charitable endeavors, and at some point, they'll bleed the family dry. So while I might have contributed to the hemorrhage, I have a plan to replenish the funds of our multigenerational wealth. Hugh is the cornerstone of my plan. With his help, I won't be the butt of the family's jokes anymore. They'll have to take me seriously. Everyone will understand that I'm a force to be reckoned with.

Hugh holds out his hand and takes the folder which contains my degree. "Do you have a transcript?"

"A transcript?" I shift in my seat.

"See what kind of grades you got. You're twenty-five. Your four-year degree took you a lot longer to earn than it should have, suggesting a lack of motivation. I'm not in the charity business, which is why you came to me and not Nathaniel, right? Anyone can give away money. Most people, not even most Tuckers, can make it by the truckload anymore."

"I want to make money, yeah." I run my hands down my thighs. Maybe I don't need to be wealthier, but I want the success it represents.

He scans my degree before tossing the folder onto the desk, and it slides across to me. "Is it real?" he asks.

"Yes," I say quickly, genuinely offended. "I earned that piece of paper." *Mostly.*

The edge of the thick page peeks out of the corner, a reminder that I made it this far. Even if I wasn't sure what I wanted to do when I started college, I'm here now. Focused. Determined. Nothing will stop me from ruling the real estate market of Bellerive—a new generation of Tuckers. The Summerset Royals will be coming to *me* for a loan.

"I'm hungry for success," I say. "You won't regret taking me on."

"I will," Hugh says with a laugh. "Of course I will. You'll fuck something up. But you're family, and I always told myself that if you came to me, ready to be a man, ready to lead your family in a way that Nathaniel can't, that I'd help you."

I swallow down my instinctual protest about Nathaniel. Hugh makes it sound like my older brother is doing nothing, and he's done a lot for this island. Far more than I have so far. People love him. Respect him. But no one fears him.

People fear Hugh.

"There can't be any distractions. When I say 'jump,' you really are going to ask how high. And if I don't like what you've done, you'll jump as many times as I want. Over and over again without complaint. That's my price. Absolute obedience."

I fight the part of me that wants to slide down in my chair, take on the stoner voice I perfected in California, and tell him I'll think about it. Nothing in my life has required decisive, immediate action before. But he's my best chance at making my own mark on the island, free of my siblings. I'm so tired of other people telling me who I am, trying to slot me into some column they've dreamed up. Maybe I don't know *exactly* who I am yet, but I know for sure that I'm not the person everyone has invented.

The first step to carving out my own version of Tucker history is being here. No more aimless floating. Learning from Hugh and being part of his organization is exactly where I need to start.

"You're young." He scans the expensive suit I bought this morning for our meeting. "Might want to consider getting a wife. Stability is attractive to investors and clients. The more together you appear, the easier it is to make the sale."

"Marriage?" I croak out. This better not be his first "jump" command. Since he's in his midthirties, marriage might not seem like a big deal to him, but it's a nonstarter for me. The only marriages I've seen have been fucking disasters that people try to paper over—as though the ugly cracks won't show through.

Hugh barks out a laugh. "You should see your face. You'd think I asked you to pilot a spaceship to the moon." His lips twitch in amusement. "Not done sowing your seed across the island, huh? That's all right. You pick the right woman, and you can both have your needs met by whoever you want. Discreet. Effective. Pretty fucking fulfilling, if you ask me."

Sounds like my parents' marriage, or at least my father's side of it. With our ten-year age gap, there are a lot of things I'll willingly learn from Hugh, but how to be unfaithful isn't one of them. I hated what my father did to my mother, and I'd never mimic that. Whenever I wanted to be with someone else, I broke up with Abby, and she did the same. We didn't cheat.

"Yeah, I don't…" But I can't quite bring myself to tell him "*no*" about the marriage idea.

"Think about it. With your legacy, your reputation, people on the island will want to know you're serious. Stable." He rises from behind his desk and buttons his jacket. "I have another meeting. Get your realtor's license. Practice tests are online. When you're ready to take it, come see me. I'll arrange to get you a spot in the next test run on the island. If you pass the first time, I'll give you a junior spot on my team. Let you work your way up. If you fail, don't come knocking on my door. Family or not, like I said, I'm not in the charity business."

I scramble to my feet and hold out my hand. "I appreciate your time."

"As you should." He nods toward the door. "See yourself out."

I sweep my folder with my degree off his desk, relieved he didn't press for a transcript, and that I made it through the meeting without completely fucking up. Hopefully, I can prove myself to Hugh, and the rest of the island, without the false stability of a marriage certificate.

While I might not want to be like my siblings, I always show up for them, which is how I find myself at a charity cocktail party and silent auction later that night. Nathaniel's pet project is something to do with teen homelessness. Bit on the nose, if you ask me, given his past. Though I'm not sure Hollyn Davis was ever actually homeless, just constantly in danger of being on the streets. My parents might have been disinterested, but I never worried I wouldn't have a roof over my head. Hell, we've got lots of roofs all over the world.

My brother Nathaniel and my oldest sister, Sawyer, practically raised me, since none of the nannies who cycled through our mansions seemed able to handle my antics with my closest sister, Ava. Looking back, the two of us took every inch given to us and turned it into five miles. The one time I mentioned it to Ava, she told me I should never regret what made me who I am.

I guess she's assuming I like who I am. She's got enough confidence for the both of us most days.

As the waitress passes by me with a tray of drinks, I snatch a champagne flute off while tugging on the collar of my shirt with my fingers. Flip-flops, tank tops, and shorts are more my kind of attire. Judging by Hugh's designer suit today, I'm going to have to get more accustomed to dressing the part I now want to play. Tonight is like an audition for that. Drop a few worms in peoples' ears about getting into the real estate game. See who's hooked.

Caitlin, my cousin and the family lawyer, sidles up to me, a champagne flute dangling from one hand and a clutch in her other. "I hear you're trying to get into bed with my brother."

I choke on my drink, and I wipe my mouth with the back of my hand.

"Is Hugh really the kind of person you want to emulate?" She peers up at me through her glasses. Her blond hair, the same color as her brother's, is in a tight bun at the nape of her neck.

"He's as good as any." Caitlin and Hugh don't get along, but that's for the same reason Hugh doesn't get along with most of my generation of Tuckers. It's the difference between a do-gooder and a go-getter.

"I suppose if you want to learn how to be an asshole, you couldn't have a better teacher," she says.

"Generational wealth doesn't last forever. If every Tucker keeps spending money and no one is making money, eventually the money is gone."

"Gage, please tell me you understand how interest works. Investing, even? Collectively, the Tucker and Smith families have billions."

I understand her reasoning, but if I don't care about making money, and I don't care about charity shit, what's the point of anything? Which is the realization I came to after college. From childhood, the obvious steps in my path were set: get my high school diploma, get a college degree. But with those accomplished, what do I have? No concrete goal for the first time in my life. Years stretched out ahead of me, listless and unimportant. There has to be something more than *this*.

Hugh is highly motivated and goal driven, things I need to learn. Pick a direction. Aim for something and figure out later if it makes me happy. No one thinks I'm capable of anything, and I'm going to prove them wrong. I'll earn my shark fin.

She takes a sip of her drink and sighs. "You and I have to talk. This girl from Colorado is insistent that she needs to get in touch with you."

"About what?" I swirl my drink.

"You know what. I called you. Left messages. Emailed you. You're avoiding me."

"It's a lie, Cait. Can't be true. I wear my papa stoppers when I'm being a bad boy." I give her my wickedest grin.

"Papa stoppers," she scoffs. "Is her claim possible? That's all I need to know. I'm aware that you and Abby fuck around when you're not together."

"I'm more likely to wear two condoms with a hookup than none at all."

"I genuinely worry about you," Caitlin says dryly.

I down the rest of my drink and ignore her comment. "Besides, the last time I was in Colorado was like a year ago or something. I was on a bender with some guys from college. Barely remember it."

"A year ago? You couldn't have just responded to any of my messages with that? I'm sending the DNA kit. With Maren engaged to Prince Brice, I can get Maren to run the results through the palace lab. If the baby daddy is someone else, at least we can put this to rest."

My phone vibrates in my pocket, and I take it out to see an alert for my doorbell camera. When I click on it, Abby is there in a tank top and shorts. Even from the tiny camera, I'd put bets on her being braless.

"What's the password?" I say into my phone.

She flashes her tits, and I laugh before buzzing her in. Caitlin, who can apparently see my screen, starts coughing.

"You two are back together?"

"I guess so." I wish I'd screen recorded Abby's little show for later.

"What's she going to think if you're a daddy?"

I scowl and close my phone. "Since I'm not, I guess I don't have to worry about that."

"You think you two will ever get tired of the back-and-forth?"

"We haven't yet." I slide my phone into my pocket and grab another drink from the waiter. Abby probably expects me to rush home, but she was the one who broke up with me this last time. She can sweat it out in the house for a bit before I return. By then, she should be naked and needy under the covers.

"You found him," my oldest sister, Sawyer, says as she appears at my shoulder. "Did you tell him about the American?"

I glare at Caitlin. "Lawyer-client privilege?"

"Did I miss the part where you pay me?" Caitlin gives me a falsely sweet smile.

"You're allergic to money."

"I'll take yours." She laughs. "Someone needs to finance my ocean-view office."

"Everyone else in the family gets pro bono but me?" I ask.

"We're all just trying to look out for you, little brother," Sawyer says. "Though, if it's true, I don't know how we break that news to Maren."

"We won't have to," I say, trying not to let her comment scrape across my nerves. "Probably just someone who thinks I'll pay them off rather than getting to the truth."

"*Who's* getting to the truth?" Caitlin asks.

"Whatever." I shrug her off. "It'll turn out to be nothing and then you'll both feel stupid about making a big deal." I set my empty glass on a tray as a waiter passes by. "I'm headed home."

"I'll be in contact either way," Caitlin says to my retreating back.

I wave at her over my head. Whatever those two might think, I know the truth. My hookups might be random, and sometimes frequent, but they're always safe, if forgettable. I don't have unprotected sex, so there's no way this kid in America is mine.

Chapter Two

EMBER

The power is out, which would be fine if it was a power outage and not because I haven't been able to pay the electricity bill in my tiny apartment that I used to share with my sister. Rent is two months overdue, too, but the landlord has taken pity on me, given what's happened. If only the hospital and all the other bill collectors would also back off and let me catch my breath.

Everything was so much easier a few months ago when my sister was alive.

Easier for me, anyway.

Nova, who is strapped to my chest, stirs, and I stop pacing in the apartment to stare down at her, to run my hand along the tuft of hair. She's all I've got left of my sister, and I promised I wouldn't put her in foster care or contact our parents.

But with no power, I can't heat a bottle, much less keep up with the little seamstress work I've managed to cobble together. We're hemorrhaging cash, between formula, diapers, and other basic baby needs. There's just no way to stay on top of everything.

I've been on the verge of poverty my whole life, but I've never sunk so low into the hole that I couldn't see the light. An extra shift or something I created was sold, and I was back in the black. But all I see is red anymore.

I sink down into the old wooden rocking chair, the one piece of furniture I have left in the living room of this dingy apartment. We never had much, but everything else that wasn't an absolute necessity has been sold off, week after week, in an effort to keep Nova and me alive. That's how it feels too. Like we're teetering on the brink.

Finding Nova's birth certificate was a gift. There was someone else out there who might be able to shoulder this load with me. Athena had told me she didn't know Nova's dad. A tourist from Bellerive. A one-night stand. No names exchanged, which had never felt right to me. My sister was the type to at least get a name, and so I wasn't completely surprised that Nova's birth certificate told a different story.

After a million phone calls to some lawyer the Tucker family fluffed me off to in Tucker's Town, I received a DNA kit in the mail. I nearly wept as I swabbed Nova's cheeks. If she doesn't turn out to be this guy's daughter, I'm sunk. We'll drown, and I'll have to do one of the things I swore to Athena that I'd never do. And I can't even be sure that doing the unthinkable will save either of us.

There's a knock on our door, and I hustle into the bedroom to put Nova down in her crib. Thank god she likes her sleep. After I give her a pacifier, I draw the door tight behind me.

I check the peephole because I've been dodging bill collectors and social services for the last week. My middle-aged, balding neighbor is at the door, and his face is flush with what I can only assume is anger or alcohol. With him, it could be either. He's no knight in shining armor.

"Ember," Wally says, "I know you're in there."

I crack open the door, and I offer him a tentative smile. "Nova is sleeping."

"You know who else was sleeping? Me, earlier today when all the people looking for you were banging down the door. I know you were home."

I was, and I'd prayed Nova would sleep through it so as not to give us away.

He shoves a stack of white envelopes at me. "I'm not your secretary. Start answering your fucking door."

"Sorry," I say, but I can't seem to inject the right amount of regret into the word, and he shoots me a dirty look over his shoulder.

When I close the apartment door, I stare down at the final notices and letters from collection agencies. It hits me that I can't keep waiting for some knight to ride to the rescue. Nova's dad may never turn up. At twenty-one, my credit is in shambles, and without that, I can't even leave here to get a cheaper apartment.

One step at a time. I just have to keep putting one foot in front of the other.

From the counter, I grab all the materials to mix Nova a bottle, and I slip out the door, locking it behind me. I hustle down one flight of stairs, and I use my key to enter Mrs. Chapman's apartment. Every time I leave the apartment with Nova sleeping, I feel guilty. My choices are limited.

"It's just me," I call to Mrs. Chapman.

"All right, dear," she replies from what sounds like the bathroom. "Lock up again when you're done."

I heat the water and then mix the bottle. This unit is identical to mine except Mrs. Chapman has utilities, furniture, and a fresh coat of paint on all her walls. Her place feels like a home, like mine used to, before Athena died.

Every time I think about my sister, I want to fall to my knees and weep, but I can't give into my tears. They won't do me any good, anyway.

Nova will be hungry in about half an hour, and the bottle should be cool enough for her by then. Even in all the chaos, I've been able to stick to a schedule. Without saying anything more, I leave Mrs. Chapman's place and take the stairs two at a time.

Back in the apartment, I stare at the stack of envelopes again. I pick them up and sort through them, trying to decide what they'd say without opening them. If I could, I'd avoid all of it forever.

It's becoming really clear that I can't.

My phone is dead, and I'll have to wait until tomorrow to go down the street to the fast food restaurant where Nova and I sit while my phone charges. There, I use their free Wi-Fi to do internet searches on how to survive when you've got nothing. It's a grim way to spend time. But they're busy enough that the employees don't seem to notice that we don't buy anything.

Tomorrow, even though I promised I wouldn't, even though it kills me to do it, I'll have to contact my parents for money. Giving Nova up to the foster system is unthinkable. But I've run out of time and options.

"Forgive me, Athena," I whisper into the dark apartment as I leave the envelopes on the kitchen counter, unopened, and I go into Nova's room to wait for her to get hungry.

The next day, after I've done the lesser of two evils, and then sat in the fast-food place feeling sorry for myself for far too long, I climb the stairs to my apartment. Nova is a heavier weight than usual. Wally will probably be angry if someone else came knocking while I wasn't home, but he can't accuse me of hiding... At least not *in* the apartment.

When I get to the top of the stairs, a tall, built man leans against the wall beside our door. He's on his phone, and his dark hair is artfully tousled. Everything about him screams money from his designer jeans to the T-shirt that costs more than my overdue rent. Something on his wrist glints, and I notice his Rolex watch, which if I'm not seeing things, is worth more than any mortgage I'll ever have.

This can't be a bill collector, can it? Or someone from child services? If they're making that much money, I need to find out how to get into that profession. He doesn't look far off my age.

I squeeze the railing at the top of the stairs, indecision settling across my shoulders. If I step forward and out myself, there's no easy way to back out.

Before I can decide, he seems to sense my presence and glances up. He pushes off the wall, and he ambles toward me, all loose-limbed confidence. He is absolutely the most attractive man I've ever seen in person. His eyes are such a deep blue they're almost the same shade of violet as his shirt.

"Ember Whitten?" he says, cocking his head.

Shit. He knows my name? He *is* a bill collector. I whirl around to escape, and I lose my balance. An involuntary scream escapes me, but before I can tumble headfirst down the stairs, Nova strapped to me, I'm yanked backward into a firm chest.

"If you didn't want me to find you," he growls in my ear, "you shouldn't have fucking contacted me."

"Contacted you?" I squeak out.

He turns us around, so his back is to the stairs and I'm closer to the apartment door. I'm still tempted to make a dash for it. But the way he's looking at me isn't with any kind of menace.

"I slept with you?" There's so much disbelief in his voice, it's almost offensive.

"What? No." I rear back. "Wait, are you..." My brain completely blanks on his name. "Nova's dad?"

Out of his back pocket, he produces a piece of paper and unfolds it, flashing it at me. "DNA says yes. I'm Gage Tucker."

"Oh." Now it's my turn to scan him from head to toe. He must be over six feet tall, and from the flex of his bicep every time he moves, he must work out. My initial assessment that he's likely the most gorgeous man I've ever met still stands. He oozes wealth and authority like no one I've been in the presence of before.

"Did you drug me?" He's still examining me intently. "That's the only explanation. I don't have unprotected sex."

"No," I say, indignant. "I didn't drug you. I also didn't sleep with you. My sister did."

"Right, well, where's she?" He glances around. "I suppose I need to speak to her, not you. Maybe she can explain how the hell this happened."

He's kind of arrogant, and I'm so caught up in trying to decide whether I find his self-importance attractive or a turn-off that I initially skim over his question.

"Your sister," he prompts.

"She died," I whisper. "She died three months ago."

His eyebrows shoot up. "Died?"

"Yeah." My voice is thick.

"So, this isn't some kind of shakedown for money?"

"No," I say, horrified.

"Fuck," he says with a sigh. "This is not at all what I was expecting." He glances behind him. "Do we need to keep standing in your hallway?"

I gesture over my shoulder at the apartment, and I use my key to let us in. Once we're inside, I toss my keys on the counter, and then I notice that he hasn't left the entry.

"Where's all your stuff?" he asks.

"I had to sell it. Babies aren't cheap."

He runs a hand through his hair and seems genuinely unsure of what to do or say. "I need to call my lawyer."

"Okay," I say because I don't have any idea of what comes next either. Nova is his daughter, but the idea of just handing her over to him, a complete stranger, suddenly feels just as foolish as emailing my parents for help or calling child services to have Nova taken into care. He hasn't shown any interest in his daughter at all.

But he doesn't take out his phone, instead he peers at the corkboard hanging on the wall. It's the only thing up, mostly because I couldn't seem to find anyone who'd buy it. The picture frames that used to litter the apartment are all sold.

"Is this her?" he asks, pointing at a photo of me and Athena. She was the opposite of me—blond to my dark hair, dark-brown eyes to my unique lighter shade.

"Yeah," I say, and I try not to dwell on the fact that he clearly doesn't remember her, must sleep with so many women that my sister was just one in a long line. Given how he looks and the confidence he projects, I'm not surprised. But it still makes me sad. Part of me had hoped there'd be some great story attached to Nova, one last piece of Athena I'd get to discover.

"Do you mind if I go into one of the rooms here to call my lawyer?" he asks, peering down the narrow hallway.

"I mean, the bathroom is just there," I point almost straight ahead. I'd rather he wasn't in Nova's room, which I share. And if he went into Athena's room, he might learn more than I'm comfortable with.

He nods and draws his phone out of his pocket before stepping into the bathroom and closing the door. As soon as he's out of the space, I check my phone, which is little more than a glorified clock. Since I haven't paid the bill, I've been cut off from any service.

Nova starts to fuss in the carrier, and I realize I've gone past bottle time. Rather than leaving Nova in the apartment with her baby daddy, I gather everything for a bottle and head for Mrs. Chapman's apartment with Nova still strapped to my chest.

Now that her father is here, I'm not sure what to expect or even what I want from him. I was desperate, and now I'm afraid my desperation might cost me the last piece of my sister that I have.

Chapter Three

GAGE

Caitlin listens to me rattle off my list of concerns, not the least of which is that the baby's mother is dead. Initially, I thought I'd be able to shove money at this problem and be done with it. I can't very well do that when there is no mother.

The apartment is an absolute dump, and it seems like Ember and the baby are living in poverty. When I tried to flick on the bathroom light, nothing happened. Either the electricity has been cut off or the wiring is fried and Ember hasn't been able to fix it. My own mother would be horrified that a Tucker is in this situation.

"Does the baby seem like it's been well-cared for?" Caitlin asks.

"Um," I say, fumbling for a response that doesn't reveal the truth.

"Gage, please tell me you've laid eyes on the baby."

"I have," I say. "The baby seems fine."

"What's her name?" Caitlin asks.

"Nova, I think, maybe." Wasn't that what she'd said?

"Do you need me to fly there? Or I can send Sawyer? I get the sense that you're freaking the fuck out."

I am, but I'm not admitting shit to Caitlin. The last thing I need when I'm trying to prove I can take care of myself is to stumble at the first hurdle. So I have a not-so-secret child. Hugh did say I needed to demonstrate some stability. Being a dad is about as stable as you can get. Though this situation is so far removed from how I thought I'd become a father.

"No," I say. "I'm fine. Just give me the next steps."

"Passport," Caitlin says. "My firm can smooth things over here in terms of the legalities of getting her into the country, ensuring she gets Bellerivian citizenship once she arrives. What are you going to do about the sister or aunt or whatever you want to call her?"

"Ember," I say. It's the one thing I am good at—remembering names, and Ember's had been all over the emails, phone calls, and documents sent to us.

Another thing I'm sure of is that I don't know how to look after a baby. Ember seemed pretty comfortable with the baby carrier strapped to her chest. Other than almost falling face-first down the stairs that is. If I could get her to come to Bellerive, even for a little while, I might be able to convince everyone, including myself, that I know what the fuck I'm doing.

Guaranteed, Abby's going to leave me again—permanently this time. Babies are not her thing.

"Well?" Caitlin prompts.

"What if Ember came to Bellerive?"

"She can be in the country for four months as a tourist."

"Then what?" I have no idea if four months will be enough time for me to feel like I know what I'm doing. Single parenting was not on my *things to do before I die* list.

"A work permit or she'd need to marry a Bellerivian. If she's emotionally attached to the baby, I'd be honest with her about the limitations. Bellerive's immigration policies are strict. There's little chance of the king or the Advisory Council changing that."

"Do we have a fixer close by?" The family has people all over the world who take care of complex problems for us. A passport for a baby with a dead mother that I want to transport to another country seems like a problem.

There's a brief pause over the phone, and I can hear keys clacking in the background. "I can get someone to you. Might not be until tomorrow morning. You'll need the death certificate. How does the sister seem?"

"Sad," I say before I can even consider it. That's the pervading air around Ember—defeated. I've never met anyone who was as pretty as her who seemed like life had kicked them one time too many.

"I'll bet," Caitlin murmurs. "Tread lightly."

"You know me," I say, and I rub the back of my neck.

"I do," Caitlin says with a chuckle, "which is why I reminded you to employ some empathy."

No one has any faith in me, and I used to ignore it, but lately it's pissing me off. Maybe I haven't always said or done the right thing, but I've been making an effort to be more aware since I graduated college. I'm not the same useless, self-absorbed seventeen-year old.

"I'll call you if I need more help." As soon as the fixer gets here, I shouldn't need Caitlin at all.

"Wait. I just heard back from Pamela, the fixer closest to you. She'll meet you at Ember's apartment at ten in the morning tomorrow. She thinks she can get the passport within twenty-four hours if you've got the death certificate."

"Okay," I say. Now all I have to do is figure out how to ask the saddest person I've ever met for a document that's sure to be a source of grief. Fucking amazing.

After I hang up with Caitlin, I take a moment to breathe. I have a kid. My kid is outside this door. Whether I want to be or whether I'm ready, I'm a dad.

Fuck.

I was really counting on riding out fun uncle status for at least ten years before I found myself in this position.

I crack open the bathroom door, and then I walk out into the living room. Ember is gone, and when I call her name, I don't get a response. Scattered across the counter are a series of envelopes. After calling her name again, I peer at the disorganized mail. So many are stamped with Final Notice or Overdue.

Our family has someone who manages all our bills, or at least I think we do, since I've never paid any. My parents set all that up to come out of the trust, and it reminds me that, as a responsible adult, I should probably start learning some of these things.

Even still, any time I received something that looked like a bill, I at least opened it. All of these, piles and piles of envelopes, are still sealed.

I leave them and wander down the hall to open the other doors. A closet. A room with a crib and a single mattress on the floor. No toys or books or extras—nothing I'd expect to see in a baby's room. The claim that she's sold anything of value rings true.

When I open the final door, I realize it must be Ember's. Unlike the rest of the apartment, it feels lived in. The bed is a double or queen, and there are still photos and mementos hanging on the walls. Seems strange she'd have kept all this when she's stripped the rest of the apartment. When I hear the front door rattle, I shut the bedroom door tight, and I circle back quickly so she doesn't catch me snooping.

"You're still here," Ember says, her tone clearly relieved. The baby isn't strapped to her anymore. Instead she's got her cradled in her arms, a bottle propped in her mouth.

"What's her name?" I tip my head at the baby.

"Nova." She bites her lip. "Or I guess you could change it, if you wanted."

Earlier I sensed I'd somehow let her down, and the way she mentions the name change, I can tell that would gut her too. There's something about watching her try to be brave and together that softens me. She's clearly in over her head in just about every area. For once in my life, I can be the one doing the fixing instead of requiring the fixer.

"I don't want to come across as crass and unfeeling, but a lot of this is logistical, and it's probably going to sound like I'm being an asshole." I rub my face because the next question is the most important, but it's also one I feel like I should be asking days from now, not within an hour of finding out. "I'm going to need a copy of your sister's death certificate and a copy of Nova's birth certificate naming me."

"I have the birth certificate," Ember says.

She rushes toward the room with the crib and single mattress, and as she's going past me, I say, "Do you want me to..." I nod toward the baby. "Take her or something?"

"Do you know how to feed a baby?" She eyes me with open skepticism.

"No," I say with a laugh. "Suppose I'd better learn, huh?"

She bites the inside of her lip and shakes her head. "I can handle her. It's just a piece of paper."

"I know it must have been hard for you to be on your own this whole time, but I'm here now. Let me do my part."

Her bottom lip trembles, and I worry that I went too far. It's hard to tread lightly when you don't know someone.

"Sit in the chair," she says.

Since there's only one in the room, that's easy enough. I ease into the rocker, and she passes Nova over to me. She settles into the crook of my arm, and I'm surprised at how natural holding her feels.

"Then you feed her with the other hand. Don't let her suck air, though. When you get close to the end, you need to stop her from sucking air."

"What happens if she sucks air?"

"Bad gas and a lot of crying. Best to avoid." She stares at Nova for a minute without looking at me, and then she rushes off to the bedroom.

I peer down at Nova as she drinks, and I love the little contented noises she's making, as though this bottle is gourmet food at its finest. My mother's insistence that babies were the best part of having children comes back to me.

Ember returns with an envelope. "Birth certificate."

I search her face for a beat, wondering if I can push again for the other necessary paperwork without reducing her to tears. She seems too fragile, as though she's one wrong word away from coming apart.

"I don't have the death certificate," she whispers. "They won't give it to me."

"Why not?"

"I haven't paid any of the bills, so they're withholding it." A stray strand has come loose from the ponytail that's barely holding her hair off her face. "I wanted to, it's just..." Tears pool in her eyes. "There are so many bills. The hospital. Rent.

Electricity. And then all the baby stuff. If I could work... But I can't." She gestures toward Nova.

If there's one thing I can easily fix, it's the money situation. "Go through all those bills over there and make a list of where we need to go and what we need to pay."

"It's a lot," she says, and a tear streaks down her cheek. She scoops it up. "Thousands of dollars in hospital bills and burial costs alone."

I haven't asked what happened to her sister yet, or even her sister's name, but at some point, I'll have to make it painfully clear that I don't know anything about her sister at all.

"Just make the list." Nova reaches up and wraps her little fingers around my pinky. "She's my daughter," I say, testing it out, saying words I thought I'd be able to avoid admitting out loud. "You're not alone in this anymore."

Chapter Four

EMBER

He's taking the whole sudden fatherhood thing well. Or maybe that's why it's taken a few weeks since I mailed off the DNA—he was adjusting to the news far from here. I can't imagine anyone ignoring the responsibility of a child, and I shake my head to clear it.

As I open bills and sort them into piles based on who sent it, I keep glancing over at him. But other than a bit of help with burping her, he seems content to rock her in the chair while he toys with his phone with his other hand.

"Is she sleeping?" I rip open another envelope.

"Yeah," he says.

You'd think having a guy I've never met before invade my life when it's pretty close to the worst it's ever been would be humiliating. And it is, but I'm surprised at how easy it is to have him here too.

I pick up the final bill and add it to the appropriate pile. "Well, I now know all the people who've been trying to knock down my door."

"Bill collectors?"

"And child services. Athena didn't have a will." I snag my lip with my teeth. "I can't pay any of these."

"I have a fixer coming in the morning. Everything will be taken care of. Bills and child services won't matter."

He says it with so much confidence that I almost believe him. Since he's Nova's biological dad, I don't think the absence of a will matters as much. "A fixer?" All the blood leaves my face. "Are you in the Mafia?"

An amused sound comes from the rocking chair, but it isn't quite a laugh. "My parents' generation wasn't far removed, if I'm honest. So many shady stories. My generation is a bit more upstanding. Sort of. It's complicated. Basically, if you have enough money, people will do anything to help you. And, for better or worse, I do mean *anything*."

"What does a fixer do?" While I wasn't able to determine how much money Gage had personally, my brief internet search of the name "Tucker" and "Bellerive" when I was trying to track him down turned up a colorful history for the family. Since I was on free Wi-Fi at the fast-food place, I couldn't really pore over all the details. The only thing I knew for sure was that he could likely help me and create a better life for Nova than what I could give her. Now that we're on the cusp of that, I find it hard to breathe when I have to think about giving her up.

"Whatever I want," he says. "In this case, get child services off your back and by extension, mine. Passport for Nova. And..." He rotates in the rocking chair to eye me. "*You*, if you want."

"Me?" I squeak out.

"I was going to talk to you about it later, when it wasn't so weird for me to ask. But if you want to come to Bellerive for a while, help me get her settled, I can arrange that."

"I can just move there?"

He gives the room a deliberate sweep. "Doesn't seem like there's much holding you here."

Except this apartment is the last place where Athena existed, the place we fled to when we left our parents' place, where we started fresh after Athena finished high school. Nothing about our life here was glamorous, but I don't know if I can just leave it behind.

"I really like living here," I say.

He stands up, and Nova makes a small noise of protest. With what must be some kind of ingrained instinct, he sways lightly back and forth while he makes eye contact with me.

"If you could come back to this apartment later, like if I paid the rent in advance for six months or a year or whatever, would you come to Bellerive?"

"You're going to pay my rent even though I'm not living here?" I can't hold back my disbelief.

"If that's the only thing holding you back, yeah. You're the person she knows best, and I know nothing about babies. Zero."

Which you'd never know by watching him so far. But I guess you can fake anything for a short enough time if you're determined. I've faked holding my shit together for months. The edge of my vision lands on the bills—a very superficial holding it together, anyway.

"It seems like a big waste of money to pay for an apartment I won't be using."

He grimaces. "I'm going to sound like a dick right now, but that money is nothing to me. Not even a drop in a bucket. It's like a tiny mist spray."

"Yeah," I agree, "that does make you sound like a dick." The words are out before I can hold them back, but I've been on the verge of a full-on meltdown for weeks, and he shows up with his fat wallet and makes it sound like money doesn't make or break lives. Money is a *very* big deal when you don't have any of it.

Instead of being offended, he grins, and my heart stutters in my chest. "I like honesty," he says. "Honesty I can deal with."

"Here's some more honesty for you," I say, sweeping my hand over the piles of bills. "I owe thousands of dollars to lots of people. We're talking a high five, maybe a six, figure number. Is that a drop in the bucket yet?"

"Nah," he says, and his playful grin is still there. "Maybe like a full spritz."

I run my hands along my cheeks, and they meet over my mouth. "You're kidding."

"You really don't know?" The amusement is still in his expression, but there's a touch of confusion layering it. "The Tuckers of Bellerive are billionaires. We've probably got more money than even the royal family. My mother would be able to give you the exact totals. I'm a little fuzzy on the specifics."

As if you can be *fuzzy* about billions of dollars.

"Maybe you can just buy the apartment building then. Why rent when you can own?"

"Owning's a hassle," he says, as though my suggestion is serious. "Maintenance. Collecting rent or"—he glances pointedly around the room—"*not* collecting rent. Plus I don't know what the market is doing in this area. Might be a poor investment."

"I want to be too proud to say yes to all of this," I say, staring down at the counter. "But the reality is that I'm just *not*." In fact, his revelation has lifted a massive weight off my shoulders. I'd been worried I would bankrupt him with all my bills or cause some kind of resentment for how poorly I managed everything before he got here. What has been a crushing weight for me is a raindrop for him or a light mist across an ocean. My problems are nothing to him, and it's both amazing and a little infuriating.

"I hate fighting over money," he says. "It's a waste of time. People always take it in the end. Might as well start how you mean to finish." He comes over to stand next to me, and our shoulders brush.

When I look up at him, our eyes connect, and I'm still slightly in awe of how deep and blue his eyes are. I'd say it's an unnatural color except strange colors run in my family.

"Are your eyes two different colors?" He seems to be searching each iris for clues. "One is kind of green and the other is kind of brown?"

"Yeah," I say. "My grandmother had it too. It's hereditary."

The intensity of his eye contact is something I'm used to with other people, but there's another layer to this, and I can't tell if it's one-sided. Never in a million years would I sleep with him; he had a baby with my sister. But it feels like a vibe is developing between us, already, that I'm not sure about. Past experience has taught me that anything that comes in hot is guaranteed to burn me. He's obviously a man who is used to getting what he wants—in everything.

Never, not once in my life, have I picked a decent guy to do anything with, so it makes sense I'd find a fuckboy attractive. Totally on-brand. He probably has babies littering Bellerive and America. Little Gage Tuckers everywhere.

Still, I can't help wondering if he thinks I'm pretty. He's so handsome it's almost disorienting. People who look like him exist in magazines, movies, and TV shows, not in my dingy apartment. Definitely *not* as the anonymous one-night stand my sister had a baby with.

"Bills?" I suggest, forcing myself out of this moment.

"Bills," he agrees, but his voice is husky. He clears his throat and then breaks eye contact to riffle through the piles in front of us. "Start with the funeral home, I guess. If that's okay with you? We need all the paperwork done. I don't suppose you have a car?"

"You suppose right," I say.

"We can't just put the baby in my car, right? Like I can't hold her on my lap."

"We can in a cab," I say. "I've done it for all her appointments. If it's your car or a rental, we'd need a car seat."

He clicks something on his phone and holds it to his ear. "Rusty, can you swing by the nearest baby store and pick up the safest and most expensive car seat and..." He makes eye contact with me. "What else should we have?"

"A stroller," I say because when I see other people with a baby, their lives seem so much easier when they can wheel them around. It's a luxury I haven't been able to afford. Nova is either attached to me or she's in her crib. Our options are limited.

"And a stroller," he says into his phone. "Call me when you're back and it's installed. We've got places to go." He hangs up and closes his phone before slipping it into the front pocket of his jeans.

"Who'd you call?"

"My driver," he says. "I find it annoying to drive in cities I'm unfamiliar with. I always hire someone to do it for me."

I digest this information in silence, but it's becoming incredibly clear that the world Gage Tucker lives in bears no resemblance to my own. Driving anywhere would be a pleasure because *I* have never owned a car. Don't have a license. Never graduated high school. We could not be further apart in our upbringing.

An awkward silence settles between us, and I'm not sure how to fill it. My experience of small talk with billionaires was nonexistent before this afternoon.

"Do you have a job?" I ask.

A hint of a smile touches a corner of his lips. "Worried about whether I can provide for her?" He must see something in my face because his smile disappears. "I have my real estate license." He hesitates for a second. "What'd you do before you took over caring for her?"

He's careful to avoid mentioning my sister, and I don't know if that makes me grateful or resentful. She's just a nameless, faceless woman he slept with once. "I can sew," I say. "I worked at the fabric store not far from here, and I did alterations and whatever else the store wanted. Made some things on the side. The store was still sending me some work until recently—stuff I could do when Nova was sleeping."

He takes stock of the room again, and his brow furrows. "Is there something to sew with somewhere?"

"I sold my sewing machine last week to buy baby formula." If the electricity hadn't gone out at the same time, the loss would have been much harder to take. I sold my last self-made piece the day after my sewing machine was gone, effectively ending any chance of making more money that way.

"You really have been hanging on by your fingernails," he murmurs.

In his pocket, his phone rings, and he slides it out, opens it, and presses it to his ear while keeping Nova steady. It's impressive. I always feel like I'm in danger of dropping something or someone, which is why I keep Nova in the carrier so much. Free hands.

"Rusty's here," Gage says. "Grab whatever you need, including all these bills." He nods at the piles. "Maybe grab enough stuff for overnight. You can't stay here if you don't have electricity. I've got a house outside Colorado Springs, not far from here, and we can buy whatever we need from the store for Nova to sleep in."

He's used her name for the first time since I told him, and the realization triggers something in me I didn't know I was waiting for, as though the use means some level of acceptance—for him, for me.

"Okay," I say, my voice thick with tears, and for the first time since my sister died, it feels like I can take a deep breath. "Okay," I say again, just because it feels like it finally might really be true.

Gage's place in Colorado Springs is huge. It's more of a mansion than a house. I've seen buildings like this on television, but I never could have foreseen being in one. He could put me and Nova on one side of this estate and never see us again.

"Is your house in Bellerive this big?" I ask, taking in the high ceilings, wooden beams, and extremely open space. Four of my apartments would fit in the open plan living room and kitchen alone.

"Nah, it's tiny compared to this place. Only two thousand square feet. Right on the beach, though."

He's got the most expensive portable crib the store sold slung over his wide shoulder, and that trip happened *after* he dropped his platinum card onto the counter of every bill collector as though they were wasting his time by daring to suggest I couldn't pay. If I was into men who defended my honor with money, it would have been a massive turn-on. But I'm not, for like, a billion reasons.

"I should get her a bottle," I say. For the last thirty minutes, I've been holding her off with her pacifier, but I can tell by the way she's squirming and sucking on it that I'm running out of time.

"I'll set this up in the room next to mine." He motions to the crib, but he also bought a baby monitor, and I wonder whether he'll actually take that tonight, too, or if I can ask for it. Having him be solely responsible makes me nervous.

"Where's that?" I ask.

"Upstairs." He points up with his finger. "I'll be back in a minute. Make yourself at home."

I take the diaper bag to the world's biggest island and unpack everything needed to make a bottle, and then I dance around the kitchen trying to keep Nova from having an absolute meltdown. The negative side of being able to stick to a schedule is that Nova can't understand when I have to deviate from it.

Gage reappears just as Nova is finishing her bottle, and he takes me up to the room where he set up the crib. The room is huge with warm walls and décor. My bet is on professionally decorated. There's a queen bed in the room too, and I bite the inside of my cheek.

"You can sleep in here or next door," Gage says, as though reading my mind. "My room is this way"—he gestures to the right—"and one of the spares is that way—" he motions to the left. "There are also eight or ten other bedrooms, I think. I can't remember."

"Right here, if that's okay."

I take him through Nova's bedtime routine, and he seems to feign interest. At no point does he offer to do any of it himself. He's completely content to watch me.

"You're really good with her," he says when we're leaving the room.

"Not much choice," I say.

"Do you mind...?" He rubs the back of his neck. "What happened to your sister?"

"An accident," I say, quickly.

He nods his head and doesn't ask for more details. My shoulders drop with relief.

Downstairs, my overnight bag is still by the door, and when I go to pick it up, Gage puts a hand on my arm.

"This is probably happening too fast, and judging by your debt, also not fast enough. But we need to figure out what you want or what you're willing to do for Nova." He runs a hand down his face, as though the weight of these decisions is finally hitting him.

I can sympathize. I've spent months with that feeling living inside me too. It's kind of nice that someone else is sharing it now.

"Can we sit down and talk for a minute? Tomorrow, Pamela, the fixer, is going to ask what we're doing. I'll need an answer."

I sit in the armchair, and he lies on the couch, staring at the ceiling. It makes me feel like we're in some televised therapy session.

"I'll pay your rent for a year," he starts. "All the bills. Everything will be paid in full."

"I really don't—"

"Technically, you can live in Bellerive on a tourist entry for four months without needing something else."

"Like a work visa?" I haven't done any traveling, but I've watched enough television to understand the complication. Most countries only let you stay there for so long.

"Exactly." He sits up and looks at me, and I realize his other position took the pressure off me to answer.

"Four months..."

"That's right, and your apartment will be paid for a year. There's no downside, is there? Is there anything stopping you from coming?"

Other than the fact that I don't know him, no. Though, that in itself is probably a reason to go—I don't know if Nova is going into a good situation. A rich one, for sure. But a good one? I'll always wonder if I don't go.

And the idea of giving Nova to him, even if she's his by blood, makes my stomach roll. It feels a bit like I'd be giving up on Athena, too, and I already have enough regrets where my sister is concerned.

"What would I do in Bellerive?" A few internet searches at the fast-food place turned up picturesque landscapes and oceans alongside rolling hills. Gorgeous, but I've also never left America.

"Be her nanny?" He gives me a hopeful look. "I know nothing about babies or being a dad. That's not to say I can't learn or won't, but it's going to be a stretch for me. A big one. My siblings would probably tell you that I'm incapable of looking after someone else." He winces at his last claim as though it pains him to admit it.

He's done a stellar job of taking care of everything since he showed up on my doorstep, so whatever version of him they know isn't the one he's showing me.

"I just passed my real estate license before coming here. Next week, I start working for my cousin, Hugh, at his real estate company. While I learn all there is to know, I'm going to be busy."

He must think I'm not sold yet because he adds, "I'll pay you."

"Oh, no, you don't need to pay me." I wave my hands in a crossing motion. "She's my niece."

"I'd be paying someone if you weren't there." He shrugs. "Might as well make your life a little easier for when you come back here. The money doesn't matter to me."

Those words cut deep, though I'm sure he doesn't mean for them to. The root of all my worry for months has been money, and he's right, I'd be foolish to turn down the opportunity to make money while being in Bellerive. My stubborn pride that keeps trying to surface needs to be permanently buried while I'm with Gage. Wherever my inner gold digger lives, she needs to step up to the plate. He doesn't care about money, but the more I can amass before I leave Nova with him, the better.

With money, I can visit her later. With money, I don't have to take the first shitty job I find. With money, I might be able to afford some design classes. With money, I can have a consistent internet connection so I can sell my designs online.

He was right earlier. There is no downside. At the end of four months, or however long I stay, my life will only be better. It's practically a guarantee.

"Yes," I say in a firm voice. "Yes, I'll go to Bellerive for four months or however long you need me, and I'll take care of Nova while you build your real estate empire."

A slow smile spreads across his handsome face. "You really think I can build an empire?"

"Yeah," I say, and I find I actually mean it, even if I don't know him that well. Today, I watched how many doors his money opened. It's hard to believe it won't open just as many in Bellerive. "I'm positive."

Chapter Five

GAGE

Normally, I sleep like someone shot me full of tranquillizers, but last night I think I woke from every sound. In the next room, I could hear Ember get up with Nova, and I laid there wondering whether I should go next door, offer to help.

At the moment, I'm a dad on paper, and I'm sort of okay with that. I'm not sure at what point she'll feel like mine, but right now, Ember and Nova are visitors to my life, not permanent fixtures.

Early this morning, Ember took Nova and went back to the apartment to pack up. I had a video meeting with Hugh and the rest of the sales team in preparation for my start next week. Once we get back, there's a bunch of odds and ends I need to complete before I have my first official day on Monday. For the first week, Hugh has me shadowing Martin, who is one of the top sales agents. The week after, I'll be with Hugh learning all the other parts of the business. The perks of being a relative, I bet. But I'm not going to complain, and no one on his team dared to say anything. I did catch a few raised eyebrows before they schooled their expressions.

They can call me a nepo baby to my face, and I won't even flinch. I'll own it.

As soon as my meeting is over, I text Rusty to come get me. I've got twenty minutes to get to Ember's apartment to meet with Pamela, who'll be collecting the documents to get us on Bellerivian soil in the next day or two. Just the thought makes me feel more settled. Once we're back in the seaside cottage, we can get things set up for Nova, and maybe then I'll feel like a parent.

Jesus, I'm a dad.

I cannot force it to sink in or plant itself in my psyche.

When we pull up to the apartment building, which is clearly in the poorer side of Pueblo, Colorado, Rusty asks if I want him to wait. There's no point since I don't know how long it'll take Ember to pack her life into suitcases.

When I open the rusted door of the front entrance, I honestly don't even know how I ended up sleeping with anyone who lived here. We must have gone back to my house, or maybe she was someone who tagged along after the bar closed. The fact that I don't remember is embarrassing, and it's not going to get easier as Nova ages and wonders about her mother. I won't be able to tell her anything, not even a first impression.

Keeping Ember in her life is the only way Nova will have a chance to know her mom, and it's an important reminder to stay on Ember's good side.

At the bottom of the stairwell, I hear loud arguing, and when Ember's voice becomes distinct, I take the stairs two at a time. Without assessing the situation, I wade through the small crowd that's gathered outside the door until I'm standing in front of Ember, who is being shouted at by an older man.

"Whoa, whoa." I hold up one hand while my other finds Ember's hip, squeezing myself between her and this irate man. "Hold up. You should not be in her face like that. Whatever your problem is, you have no right to speak to her like that."

"I wasn't in her face," he says, eyeing me with obvious suspicion. But he's taken a step back. I've got at least half a foot on him, and I work out regularly. If he wants rough, I can give it to him.

The crowd behind him seems to sense a change, and they disperse back to their apartments. I can't tell if they were trying to support Ember or tear her down along with this man.

"You *were* in my face, Dad," Ember says as she peeks around my side, an edge to her voice. Her hand has landed on top of mine on her hip, but she seems to be drawing strength or comfort from it rather than trying to push me away. At least I haven't fucked that up by touching her.

"To keep my daughter's death from me is truly evil," he says without missing a beat. "I would never keep something like that from you."

"You just told me that Mom died last year," Ember says, and her voice is thick.

"I didn't know where you were. Athena kept you from me." There's venom in his voice when he mentions his eldest daughter.

"Is there a reason why you're here now?" I ask, trying to figure out whether I should be escorting him off the property.

"Ember emailed me. She wants me here."

"I emailed *Mom*," she says.

"It's the same." He stares at her. "What else are you keeping from me? I know there's something else. There was always something else with you girls."

This guy makes my parents look a hell of a lot better than they normally do. Ember hasn't invited him in, and she doesn't have Nova strapped to her. Her dad must not know.

"All right," I say, making an executive decision, "you need to leave."

"The hell I will," he roars, fists clenched at his sides, and the apartment door across the hallway cracks open.

Hit me, old man. I dare you.

"Is there a problem here?" A tall, heavyset, late-middle-aged blond woman appears at the top of the stairs. She's got an air of authority that I like immediately. We've only spoken on the phone, but I'd know her anywhere. Pamela, my fixer, to the rescue.

"This gentleman was just leaving," I say.

"I'm not going anywhere." He crosses his arms and almost visually seems to dig in his heels.

"If Mr. Tucker has asked you to leave the property, you're now trespassing. He owns the building. I can easily make a call to law enforcement to have you charged and removed," Pamela says.

"You don't own the building." Ember must be on her toes, and her lips skim my ear.

"I do." I glance over my shoulder, and our lips are far too close for an instant before she drops down. "As of this morning." Pamela sent me the comparable properties late last night, and with the growth in this area, it made sense to purchase the building. A numbers game—both in terms of how much I offered and what I got in return. Made me realize I might have learned a thing or two in studying for my real estate exam.

"You bought the building," Ember says from behind me, and I can hear the awe in her voice. It's not the first time it's happened to me in relation to something financial, but it's the first time I remember my wealth giving me a zing of pride. A surge of power, always. But pride? That's a new one. That's at least twice now that she's made me feel good about myself, like maybe I might be capable of being a useful human in the world.

"We're not done." Ember's dad points at her before turning toward the stairs.

They're *so done*. At this point, I'd move heaven and earth to keep that man away from Ember and Nova. I watch him go down the stairs, and when the front door gives an audible click, I shift toward Ember. "Are you okay?" I run my hand down her arm.

She gazes up at me, and another blast of protectiveness rushes forward. A little red warning light flickers to life inside me. I could be navigating unfamiliar waters when it comes to this girl.

"He seems..." There are so many things I could say, but since that's her father, I can't voice them.

"Terrible? Athena made me promise I'd never let Nova anywhere near him," Ember says, and she bites her lip. "But I was really desperate yesterday morning, and I emailed my mom. I thought she might be able to give me a little money without telling him, anything to tide me over. I didn't expect my dad to track me down."

"I'm sorry about your mom." Even now when she mentions her mother it's clear that, while her parents might have been a package deal, she had something positive or nostalgic for at least one of them.

"Thanks, yeah... I can't... It's hard to process. I don't even know how she died," Ember says.

"I can find out," Pamela offers, "if you want. Shall we go inside? The whole apartment complex doesn't need to know Tucker business."

Ember steps back, and I slide past her, Pamela hot on my heels. In the tiny kitchen, Pamela checks through all the documents Ember gathered together before I got here.

"This all looks good," she says. "I can get your passport and Nova's without any issue. Mr. Tucker made it clear your entry into the country would only be good for four months?"

"Yes," Ember says, and she glances toward the bedroom where Nova must be sleeping.

"Photos," Pamela says, pulling a tripod and a bunch of other equipment out of a small backpack I didn't even realize she was wearing. "We'll get yours and when Nova wakes up, we'll see if we can get her picture ready."

While Pamela snaps photos of Ember, I can't help the brief flare of attraction that ignites in me before I snuff it out. I'd have to be dead not to notice. Long dark hair. Gorgeous eyes. Hard to get a true sense of her figure from her ill-fitting clothes, but there's something going on under those layers. From the photos on the corkboard, if I'd met her and Athena on the same night, Ember would have been who'd I'd be drawn to based on looks alone.

Finding Ember cute is not helpful for anything right now, but it's a vibe I think I can deal with for the next four months. My instinctual desire to protect her based solely on how sad she looks is a bit worrying. I'm not usually the protective sort, but first she loses her sister, and now her mother.

That thought drags me right out of my worry spiral. I've never had a thing for women who hang back, play hard to get. Straightforward has been my go-to. You want me and I'm single? You can have me. Ember doesn't seem like the type to pursue me, and I certainly won't be pursuing her.

"Can we get the baby up?" Pamela asks. "Will that be awful? If I can get these applications submitted before noon, we'll have the passports by the same time tomorrow." She checks her watch.

"She's pretty easygoing," Ember says, rushing into the bedroom to get her up.

The next twenty minutes are a struggle. Nova has two modes after being woken up early—a wide smile or crying uncontrollably, and neither is suitable for her passport photo. In the end, I have to hold her pacifier over the camera lens to get her looking and concentrating in one direction without either smiling or crying.

When Pamela leaves with the paperwork, Ember makes Nova a bottle and passes both my daughter and the bottle to me when it's ready.

I rock in the chair with her, and it's the first time since yesterday that I've been in charge of her. I appreciate Ember easing me into this whole thing. If she'd passed me Nova and walked out of my life, I'd have failed miserably. Nova deserves a good dad, not the man I've been up to this point.

"Was your dad always like that?" I ask.

There's a heavy silence behind the rocking chair from the kitchen, and when I twist to try to see her, she's biting her lip.

"Yes," she answers. "My sister and I ran away from home when she turned eighteen and finished high school. He never touched me, but he put his hands on Athena and my mom a lot. Athena thought if she left without me that I'd be next."

"Must have been a tough childhood." My dad was a philandering asshole, but he never laid a hand on anyone in anger. He drinks too much sometimes, but even then, he's more sloppy than mean.

"Athena and Mom protected me from a lot of it, I think," she says, twisting her hands.

There's something she's not saying because she's gone almost ashen in color, but I don't want to pry too hard. We hardly know each other, and the last thing I want is for her to burst into tears. Liquid leaking out of a woman's eyes makes me go all wobbly inside, and I say things I don't mean.

"Did you pack?" I ask.

"There's not much. Clothes, mostly."

"Can you bring any photos you have of your sister?" I stare down at Nova who is close to finishing the bottle. Before she starts sucking air, I've got to get it out. "I'll get copies made for Nova."

"Mm-hmm."

I glance at her over my shoulder, and she's wiping tears off her cheeks. She shakes her head when I raise my eyebrows. Nova finishes the bottle, and I pop it out of her mouth, throw the burp cloth over my shoulder, and I stand while I pat her back, making my way to Ember. Words are not my specialty, but I hate that I made her cry. I draw Ember into my side, and I'm surprised that she curls into me willingly. A baby on one shoulder and a woman crying on my other one. Feels strangely right. Maybe Ember and I will even be friends—good friends by the end of this.

"You don't have to be in this alone, you know," I murmur into her pineapple-scented hair.

"My sister is—was the only person I've ever been able to count on." The words are garbled by her tears. "There's just me now."

I'm hesitant to say anything in response because I haven't historically been someone anyone could count on. While I hate that reputation in my family, I also understand that at least some of it has been earned—which Maren pointed out to me when she gave me the DNA results. She thought I took her ex-husband, Enzo's, side in the divorce, but the truth is much worse. I wasn't paying enough attention to even realize they were divorcing. My brain has been hardwired to look after myself first and everyone else second.

"You can count on me." I run my hand along her back in a soothing motion. "We don't know each other very well yet," I say, "but you can count on me. For anything."

And that's one promise I intend to keep, no matter what.

Chapter Six

EMBER

Bellerive is stunning. It's lush hills and ocean views, and I'm fairly certain I've been transported into a fairy tale. The plane ride was both thrilling and terrifying. It didn't even feel like we were moving, much less incredibly quickly. And we were so high up that every possible doomsday scenario looped through my brain until Nova became fussy and I had to worry about whether all the first-class passengers were annoyed. Everyone in our section of the plane smelled like money, and the one time I got up to go to the bathroom, I caught a glimpse of the people sitting in another section—squished seats, harsh lighting—nothing like our area.

Now, my knees are almost pressed against the dash because it was the only way we could get Nova's car seat squeezed into the back of Gage's fancy car in the right position. As Gage cruises along the highway that'll take us to his beachside bungalow, I think I could get used to this place, this life.

"Sorry," Gage says, staring at my knees. "I should have brought the SUV. Not sure what I was thinking." He runs a hand through his hair.

"It's fine." It's probably the nicest car I've ever been in. The seats are automatic, leather, and they have both a heating and cooling function. Objectively, I knew people lived like this, but it's strange to realize I'll be steeped in it and still feel like an outsider. Since I'll only be here for four months, I'll likely never feel like I fit.

"As soon as we're settled, I'll give you my card to go get whatever Nova needs. You can charge everything—clothes, diapers, formula, furniture. I only have that fold-up thing from the house in Colorado for tonight."

He turns off the highway onto a paved road that has farmland on either side. "You live on a farm?" I can't keep the surprise out of my voice.

"No." He laughs. "God, no. A lot of the interior land is farmland. Most of the development across the island has happened so as to guarantee an ocean view. The coast is crowded, for the most part, and the interior is sprinkled with developments, unless it's a legitimate town or whatever. Works out okay, I guess. Bellerive needs the farmland, or we'd be completely reliant on imports, which just jacks up prices."

"I have no idea why anything is built or not built in America."

"I didn't know anything about it until I had to take my real estate exam. So many fucking laws in Bellerive. Island and all, I guess. Anything happens too fast or in the wrong way and we screw ourselves and all the generations that come after."

"You're really passionate about real estate, huh?"

"I'm really passionate about being successful. The mode and method don't matter as much."

"Gage, you're a billionaire. So much money that my brain screams '*does not compute*' whenever I consider those zeroes. If this isn't successful, my world just flipped upside down."

"That's not my money."

When I raise my eyebrows at him and gaze pointedly around the car, he chuckles.

"I didn't say I was above *using* the money." He pulls into a wide driveway, and a beautiful white stucco bungalow stretches across the land in front of us. "I didn't earn any of this." He sweeps his hand across the view.

As someone who has struggled for years to have anything, his justification seems weird to me. So what if you didn't earn it?

"If you think earning it is so worthwhile, why not give it all up and start from scratch?" I'm a bit annoyed, to be honest. Being successful off the back of previous success isn't the same as clawing your way up from the bottom. The two paths aren't even comparable.

"Give it all up?" He lets out a laugh of disbelief. "There's a difference between seeking a purpose and being an ungrateful idiot. Despite what you might think, I know what I've got."

No, he doesn't, but it's not my job to try to teach him. Unless he really did turn his back on his wealth, he can never truly understand what it's like to scrape together enough change to get one last canister of baby formula or what it's like to stand in front of the various diaper options and try to calculate the costs of cloth versus disposable. There's nothing romantic or noble about struggle. All of it sucks. Brings you down in ways no one can see.

"All right." Gage sucks in a deep breath and runs his hands along his thighs. "We're doing this." He's staring at his front door, and dusk is falling around us.

It's a bit late for him to have second thoughts about anything. I had to present my return flight when I landed, which is exactly four months from today. I've got four months to figure out how to let go of the last piece of Athena that'll ever exist.

"Here we go," I whisper.

The house has clearly been professionally decorated in colors and tones to complement the beachy vibes and ocean view. Calming blues and grays and whites dominate all the open spaces. There are windows everywhere, but the curtains are drawn. Nova is strapped to me as I go out the sliding doors to take in the ocean view. There's a wide set of stairs down to the beach to the left with a fancy wood-and-metal railing. Kayaks, paddleboards, and surfboards litter the sand, and there's a shed down there that's likely meant to house them. Because an ocean isn't enough, there's a gated pool in front of us with an edge that makes it feel like it's part of the vast expanse of water. I can't even imagine how much it must cost to have a view like this.

"You live here." It's more of a statement than a question, but I have to be dreaming. There's no way my life goes from what it was two days ago to *this*. My best-case scenario had Nova's dad throwing some money at us to make us go away, not changing my entire life.

"We do, yeah," he says.

His shoulder brushes against mine, and when I glance up, he's searching my face as though the answer to some unasked question lies inside me. But I'm not the solution to anyone's problems.

"For now," I say, turning back to the ocean view.

Letting myself get used to anything here would send me spiraling when I have to leave. Gage is off-limits. All this wealth is off-limits. I'm on a vacation from real life, that's all. After this, I go back to my apartment, back to my city, and I try to piece my life together. No family, just me.

The thought is deeply depressing.

But as long as I haven't put too much stock in this place, this life, I'll be okay. Temper my expectations. Nothing will ever be as good as being here, but it doesn't have to be for me to be content. My entire life so far has taught me that happiness isn't achievable, but I'll take this sliver of an easier lifestyle and hold onto it with both hands while I can.

No matter what happens to me, Nova will have a great life, and I'm going to make sure that nothing will prevent her from achieving the happiness Athena and I haven't found. Nova will never know the misery we've felt.

Chapter Seven

GAGE

It's a chorus of ringing in my dream, and I can't locate the sound. Whatever I hit doesn't seem to turn it off.

"Gage," a female voice calls.

I'm dragged out of the depths of sleep, and I rub my eyes before sitting up. At the door to my bedroom is Ember, dressed in a skimpy pair of shorts and a tank top. It's a view I could definitely get used to. Then I realize the doorbell is going off over and over.

"What the fuck is that?" I ask, throwing back the covers. I sit on the edge of the bed for a second to collect myself before I stand up.

"That's what I was wondering. I peeked out the window, and it seems to be a group of guys and a woman?"

"What day is it today?"

"Wednesday."

"Ah, fuck. It's poker night. I can't believe I forgot." My boxer shorts don't cover much, and I grab my jeans off the floor to tug them on.

"It's one in the morning."

"Up until two days ago," I say, "one in the morning was just a time on a clock. Meaningless."

She huffs out a breath, and I realize it's probably not an answer she likes. Most of my responses have elicited a hint of annoyance from her, but I'm choosing to ignore it. I can't help that I grew up with money and privilege and she didn't. She's going to have to figure out a way to get over it because it's not my problem to solve. As long as she's with me, she's got both of those things too.

"Are they all rich assholes?" she grumbles as she follows me down the hallway.

"They're all rich," I admit. "You can decide on the asshole part. I wouldn't want to deprive you of that."

"Sorry. I shouldn't have... I'm just so tired."

When we get to the junction for the front door, I turn around to face her. "You can't wear that to meet my friends." I wave a hand in the direction of her barely-there outfit.

She glances down, and in the faint light streaming in through the windows, a flush creeps into her cheeks.

"I forgot I was wearing this."

"Is Nova still sleeping?"

"Somehow, yes. She'll need a bottle in about half an hour."

"Throw on some clothes and come join us," I say.

"You're going to play poker?"

"Next week I become a responsible adult. Might as well live it up for a few more days."

She stands there for another beat while I pass her to go to the door. I open it and lean into the frame.

"You are a persistent bunch of assholes," I say in a cheerful tone.

"Best kind," Seth says, shoving me out of the way to enter the house. He flicks on my lights on his way past. Two of my other guy friends trail behind him, slapping me on the shoulder, and Abby hangs back, bringing up the rear. She's tucked one side of her long glossy brown hair behind her ear, but the other side hangs loose, partially concealing her face in the moonlight.

"You didn't call," she says. "Did you get rid of her?"

"Not quite," I wince. "Long story."

From inside, Nova lets out a frustrated cry, and Abby's eyes widen. "You brought the baby here?"

"Yeah, it's..." But I don't know what to say. I should have called her, but I was so focused on fixing Ember's life that I forgot the rest of the world existed for a few days. Not exactly something I can admit out loud to the woman who's been in and out of my bed for the better part of four years. Ember will be inside, mentally tallying me in the rich asshole column. I think I've mostly avoided it up until now.

"Look, do you want to come in?" I ask, half of my mind already on Nova and wondering whether my friends are harassing Ember.

"I didn't really have 'stepmother' on my bingo card," Abby says, sliding past me. "You couldn't have just left the baby with her mother?"

As soon as she's in the door, she tenses, and I realize I am actually the world's biggest idiot. At no point have I mentioned Ember's existence, but there she is, in the open plan kitchen, baby in her arms, while Seth helps her mix a bottle.

The rest of the guys are setting up the poker table as though Ember and Nova aren't even there. I didn't tell any of them I had a one-night-stand baby. The plan was for no one to *ever* know, but they're all acting as though it's not life-changing.

"Are you fucking kidding me?" Abby whirls on me, fury in her eyes. "You brought *her* here too? What is this? Is she *living* here?"

"I mean, yes, but..." Fuck. What can I say? Does it even matter? It doesn't seem possible to keep Abby *and* Ember happy. Abby is hot, but she's a viper. She's never bitten me, but I've seen her go after plenty of people she considers competition. "The baby's mother is dead, Abby. That's her sister."

She eyes Ember with open skepticism. "She can't stay here. If we're together, she can't stay here."

"Then I guess we're not together," I say, throwing up my hands. "She's helping me with Nova. Are *you* going to help me with the baby?"

"Fuck you, Gage. I'm not your *nanny*, and I'm not the one who went out and got some trailer trash pregnant because I couldn't keep my dick in my pants. I've had to have a full STD panel done because I have no idea if you've been riding bareback with a bunch of side pieces every time we've broken up."

Seth clears his throat loudly from the kitchen, and I realize Ember probably heard every word of Abby's vitriol.

"Get out, Abby," I say, pointing toward the front door. "Figure your own shit out. I don't have time for your drama."

"*My* drama?" Her eyes practically bug out of her head. "How is this—"

"Okay," Jarod, her twin brother says, appearing at her side. "Let's get you home." He widens his eyes at me, and I know he's telling me to expect trouble. Abby wants everything to happen on her own terms, which never used to be a problem.

"I don't know what's going on right now," Abby says, glancing at Ember again, "but I know one thing with absolute certainty. You *always* regret letting me go." She lets Jarod lead her out of the house, and he must put her in their car with their driver because he's back quicker than I expect.

When I glance toward Ember, she's feeding Nova and refusing to look in my direction. Can't say I blame her. My ex-again-girlfriend just shit all over her and her entire family. I really wish I hadn't opened that door tonight.

Seth goes to the card table, and I head in Ember's direction, but she glances up, and there are tears in her eyes.

"I'm just going to..." She nods toward the hallway.

"Don't," I say. "Stay. Abby was mad at me, and she lashed out at you. I'm sorry."

She shakes her head. "I don't belong here." Then she rushes off, leaving me with my friends.

I slump into my seat at the table and gaze around at all their faces.

"You've been in some fucked-up shit over the years," Jarod says, "but you're a dad? What the hell, man? You didn't tell any of us?"

"I didn't intend to actually *be* a dad," I say. "My plan was to pay her off. But Nova's mom is dead." I gesture toward where Ember disappeared. "The two of them were living in an apartment with no furniture, no electricity, and on the cusp of being homeless."

"What would that even be like?" Reggie asks, shuffling the cards. "I get pissed when I don't get the best suite in a hotel."

The two situations aren't even comparable. Perhaps Ember has a point about the level of privilege I've been raised in.

"I couldn't leave them there." More importantly, I found that once I was in their company, I didn't want to. It didn't even occur to me to keep my original plan. Despite our obvious differences, Ember is easy to be around, and god help me, I've got a soft spot for her obvious trauma. I want to fix it or soothe it or do something, anything, to make it better. For the first time in my life someone needs me, and it turns out that I like being needed. Who knew?

"What's the plan now?" Jarod asks.

"Ember is going to stay here for four months, help me get used to being a dad. Then she'll be out of her tourist visa and back to America, and I'll be on my own with Nova. A single dad."

"You and Ember aren't..." Seth leaves it open-ended.

"No. She's great, but no."

"Will you?" Seth asks.

"You don't shit where you eat," I say. For the next four months, I need Ember's help more than I need to get laid. It's that simple. Beyond that, I want Nova to know her mother someday, and I can't do that for her. She'll need her aunt in her life.

Seth nods and checks the cards Reggie dealt without commenting.

"Is poker night still on next week?" Jarod asks.

Poker night shouldn't even be on tonight. "Might have to shift to a Friday or Saturday or put it on hold. Grown-up responsibilities are creeping in. I start working for Hugh on Monday."

"You're so dead," Reggie says with a laugh. "Hugh will eat you alive. I have heard stories, man, from so many people tougher than you. Your lazy ass is going to get fired."

That's where he's wrong. I'm turning over a new leaf. Monday, my life will flip like a switch. Drifting, irresponsible billionaire turned real estate shark. People will write stories about how epic this transformation is going to be.

"I give him two weeks," Jarod says.

"Three," Seth says, tossing a chip into the middle of the table.

"I'll split the difference," Reggie says. "Two weeks and one quarter."

That's not the middle between those two numbers, and I exchange a glance with Seth, but neither of us correct him. We could explain how he's miscalculated multiple times, and he wouldn't get it. I sometimes wonder if Reggie's family took the whole selective inbreeding of the uber wealthy a little too seriously for a few generations. He's at least one brick short of a load. Nice guy, but really fucking dumb.

Works out well for all of us in poker, which is why he's here. He makes the rest of us feel smart, and we line our pockets with his family gold.

"What's going to come first?" Jarod asks. "Will Gage be back with my sister or sleeping with his nanny?"

"She's not—she's Nova's aunt." I can't keep the frustration out of my voice. Hopefully, Ember is too busy getting Nova back to sleep to hear any of this. Otherwise, she's going to be booking herself a return flight for tomorrow, having decided I'm unfit to parent Nova. That might be a fair assumption, but I'd hate for her to think it.

"It'll be Abby," Seth says with authority as the rest of us organize our cards. "She was right. No matter what, you always end up back in bed with her."

A couple weeks ago, I would have agreed with him, but the last few days have started something ticking inside me that feels different. And I don't know yet whether that's wishful thinking or the whole truth. But the idea of getting back together with Abby doesn't appeal to me at all.

"We all grow up sometime," I say.

"To Monday," Seth says with a laugh. "To adulthood."

The others raise their shot glasses, and we all throw them back. In four days, my path will be set.

Chapter Eight

EMBER

Eavesdropping is a bad habit. I'm sure the delightful Abby would call it a lower-class or "trailer trash" habit, but I call it a tool of survival. When you grow up in a violent household, you learn to listen and listen well.

The good news is that, despite the warm vibe between me and Gage, nothing will happen between us. He's hung up on Abby, and even if he wasn't, he doesn't "shit where he eats," which was a crude but effective way of saying he'd sleep with me, but it'd probably fuck everything up.

I should be grateful for the clear lines. In my head, there's an ick factor in being with Gage, the last man my sister was with, like that. But I also can't deny how attractive he is, and if he's going to wander around the house with no shirt on like he did last night, I'll have to start doing some baking to fatten him up. The guy is cut, lean, so fit I wonder whether *that's* been his job. He's a walking temptation.

I change Nova's diaper on the bed, and then I get her day bag ready. Gage wants me to get everything she needs to live here, and I made a list last night when my brain wouldn't shut off and let me sleep.

The weirdest part about meeting Abby wasn't even that Gage has a girlfriend he never mentioned. It's that she's an awful human being, nothing like my sister. Maybe personality doesn't matter so much for a one-night stand—I wouldn't know—but if Abby is his idea of a perfect woman, I'm surprised he and I even get along at all. She was sharp and mean, and while I might be a little prickly sometimes, I wouldn't deliberately hurt someone.

Hearing Seth proclaim that Gage and Abby always find their way back to each other even when they break up stopped me from going back into the room once I got Nova to sleep.

As much as it's possible to have some distance from Gage in this house, that's probably the right thing to do. But it bothers me to think of Abby being in Nova's life, a role model. Ultimately, it's not my decision, though, and I need to let go of things I can't control, or I'll never want to unstrap Nova from me in order to leave Bellerive.

"Gage?" I call as I come out of the hallway, Nova in my arms. When there's no answer, I check his room, but he isn't sleeping either.

I wonder whether he's gone to smooth things over with Abby when I notice the sliding door to the beach is open, just the screen door across it.

Rather than cradling Nova the whole time, I slip her into the carrier that I automatically put on every morning like a normal piece of clothing. Once she's secured, I follow the breadcrumbs of Gage's sandy footprints down to the beach. Out in the ocean, someone is surfing.

I shield my eyes against the glare of the sun, and I can't help being impressed at how easy being upright on a wobbly board looks with him in charge. He rides the wave into shore and then hitches the board under his arm to wander closer to me and Nova. Water cascades down his body, and under different circumstances, there's a chance I'd be drooling or considering dropping my pants. Things would be falling from me at his feet.

"Shopping?" he suggests, running a hand through his wet hair.

"I guess so." I shrug, and I force myself to meet his gaze instead of noticing every ripple of muscle. "We don't have much for Nova, but I don't know where to go."

"I'll have a car pick you up. Have anything big like a crib or whatever delivered to the house."

"You're going to put it together?" I ask, and I can't keep the amusement out of my voice. For the life of me, I can't picture him with any sort of tools. It just seems beneath him.

"I could," he says, and he tilts his head. "Or there are people who do it for a tiny spritz of money."

"Ah, yes," I say with a knowing nod. "The money fairy is very generous, I hear."

"I didn't say a sprinkle of fairy dust," he says, tossing the surfboard in the direction of all the other water sport items littering the beach. Someone else must clean it all up, put it away. "The money is clearly an endless well. It's not magic."

"An endless well isn't magic?"

"Not in my world—which, I might remind you—you're now living in."

I am, and it'll never stop being weird. None of this money is mine, or at least not yet. Gage said he'd pay me, and while it objectively makes sense to take his money—he doesn't care about it—accepting it doesn't quite sit right with me.

So many things I'm going to need to learn to deal with or get over for my own good. I'd have to be very stupid to leave Bellerive worse off than when I arrived.

"I'll grab you my card with the endless well," he says as he leads us back up the stairs.

"People won't wonder why I have your card?" I ask.

"They don't care. They'll take it. I'll give you my pin—but memorize it. Can't write it down. The money's all the same to them. No one will question anything."

Everything about his life is so foreign to me. I cannot wrap my head around how easy the world is all the time.

"Hugh has me doing stupid health and safety bullshit at the office today, so I won't be around."

"Oh, okay," I say, and I can't explain why that sends a little frisson of fear down my spine.

I'll have a driver and a credit card. What else could I need from him?

In the kitchen, he fishes his wallet out of a drawer, passes me a platinum card, and then rattles off a six-digit pin. He has me say it back to him four or five times before he lets me get ready to leave.

"Buy three or four car seats," Gage says when I'm on my way out the door. "Then we don't have to switch them in or out of vehicles."

"You have four cars?"

"Ten," he says without missing a beat. "But some of them would never fit a car seat."

"Endless-well problems," I say.

"You got it." He winks at me before biting into an apple. "I'll see you at dinner."

Dinner. I'm almost afraid to ask what that'll involve.

"Oh," he says, as though it's just occurred to him. "Just a sec." He jogs over to where Nova and I are standing at the door. She's already strapped into her car seat, and Gage told me the driver switched over the base to the SUV this morning. He crouches down in front of her, and he stares at her for a minute before giving her a kiss on her temple and then shaking his head. "I don't know when this all feels real."

Honestly, I'm right there with him.

The elderly driver, Bill, takes us into the center of Tucker's Town, the biggest city on the island. First, he gives me a tour, relaying all sorts of historical facts about how the city was constructed and how the periods of history are clear in the architecture. As we loop through the various streets, I can see exactly what he means from the cobbled streets to the Victorian steepled or gabled roofs. Then he transitions into royal gossip, including the recent coronation of King Alexander and the death of King George. The tale of King Alexander and his now-wife seems to be a delicious soap opera fit for a romance novel. Living an experience and hearing about it are two very different things, though, and it's a reality I'm all too familiar with.

While he drives and talks, Nova gets her morning nap in, and I get to finalize my list of what to buy. Gage's card is tucked securely into my wallet in Nova's diaper bag, and the more Bill talks, the less anxious I am about using it.

Money is money. No one will care.

"Mr. Tucker said to take you to this store." He pulls up in front and helps me get the stroller from the rear. "Would you like me to wait?"

It's a multistory storefront, a department store or a mall. I check my watch and shake my head. "Can you come back in two hours?" By then, Nova will need a bottle and a nap.

"I'll be here in two hours," Bill says, waving to me as he climbs back into the car.

It's only once he's gone that I realize I have no way to contact him or Gage if anything goes wrong. My phone didn't even work in America, let alone here. Even if there's free Wi-Fi, I have no email address or contact details for anyone.

All I have is a credit card and a pin number that I'm repeating in my head over and over.

Deep breath. It'll be fine.

Inside, I check the store listing and take the elevator to the second floor where all the kids' clothes and toys are.

As I wander the aisles, I keep checking price tags and wincing. The card weighs heavy in my bag, and I don't know if I can bring myself to use it when I know I could get twenty outfits at Goodwill for the cost of one outfit here. I don't even know if Bellerive has thrift stores, but it seems silly to spend this much when there are bound to be more affordable options.

I take out my phone, and I stare at it, wishing I could call Gage. There's absolutely no doubt in my mind what he'd tell me. Money grows on trees or it's an endless well of cash or whatever other phrase would make me hold back an eye roll.

With a deep breath, I start piling some of the cuter outfits in strategic places on the stroller. The next time I check my phone, I realize I need to pay for everything before Bill's stuck waiting for me. I line up for the register with the outfits and little ticket stubs for the bigger items that I'll need to pay for and have delivered.

But as I stand there, I realize I don't have Gage's address. If I just tell them to deliver it to Gage Tucker's house, would they know where I meant? The island is small, but is it *that* small?

When it's my turn at the cash, the woman scans all my items and bags them, and when she gives me the total, I try to act like that amount of money is totally normal. I saw Gage do it enough when he went around paying all my bills.

Then I make the mistake of glancing at the clerk, and I must look like a thief caught with their hand in the cookie jar because her eyes narrow, and she checks the name on the card.

"Gage Tucker?" She raises her eyebrows. "I am well aware of who Gage Tucker is, and he's not buying baby things. His brand is more dating Barbie than buying them."

"He gave that to me," I say. "He said I could use it."

"You know the pin?" She clearly doesn't believe me.

"Yes," I say with conviction only to realize the numbers have completely left my head. "Or I did, but now I'm like..." I'm nervous, and I can't quite remember what order the numbers go in. Visions of the police being called and me being hauled off to jail if I put the numbers in wrong dance in front of me. What would happen to Nova?

"I'm sorry, but I could lose my job for processing your credit card fraud. I know he's got more money than sense, but there's no way Gage Tucker is out here paying for some poor woman's baby supplies. It's just not a reality we live in."

I could tell her the baby in question is his, but I suspect she'd laugh in my face. Whatever she thinks she knows about him doesn't seem to be either good or charitable.

"Okay," I say, tears coating my eyes. "Okay." Except it's not okay because Gage told me to get everything, and he made it very clear he'd be too busy to help me. I'm here to do these things so he doesn't have to worry about it, and I can't get any of it right.

"Look," she says. "If you've got his number, I can call him and clear this up." She picks up the receiver and waits for me to rattle off digits I don't know.

I shake my head.

She sets the receiver down with a sigh. "I can't help you." She wags the credit card at me. "And I'm keeping this, and my manager will return it to Mr. Tucker or destroy it if it's counterfeit. I won't call the police or anything. You've got a baby. And I've been there. You know. Broke. Making hard choices." She gestures toward Nova. "But you're all over the cameras in the store, so I wouldn't try this again here or anywhere else. You've obviously already gotten a stroller out of this scam."

My face is so hot I think I might overheat and die on the spot. In all my years of being poor, I don't think I've ever felt so dirty, and I know she's not trying to be mean, but it just feels so vicious. And untrue. But I have nothing to back up what I have or don't have. Having seen Abby last night, I certainly don't look like someone Gage Tucker would associate with. My clothes really are from a thrift store, or things I cobbled together myself from odds and ends. I'm not wearing a thousand-dollar T-shirt and Gucci jeans.

Without saying anything, I wheel the stroller around and practically sprint to the elevator. I take it down, heart racing, and I can only get a complete breath once I'm outside the store.

Bill pulls up within seconds, and he jumps out of the car, coming around to flip the stroller closed and get Nova locked into the base.

"I must say," he says, "I'm surprised you aren't weighed down in bags. I've been circling for a few minutes in case you had a lot of heavy things."

I just shake my head, unable to speak for fear of bursting into tears. Instead of sitting in the front beside him, I get into the back beside Nova, and I fuss over her the entire ride back to avoid having to speak to Bill.

As soon as I'm in the house, I set down Nova's car seat, and I burst into tears.

Chapter Nine

GAGE

When I got to the office, I found out they wouldn't have a desk available for me to use until Monday. Hugh's secretary took me through all the online training modules I have to have completed before I start. Slip and fall. Workplace harassment. Workplace health and safety. The list feels endless, and part of me wonders if I could pay Ember to complete some of these for me. Since I'm not even doing them at the office anymore, who the hell would know?

I've only just gotten home and set up at the kitchen island, the ocean view behind me so as not to be a temptation, when Ember comes in the door, sets down Nova's car seat and releases an inhuman sob.

For a beat, I sit at the island unsure of what I'm supposed to do, but then I notice she doesn't have any bags or boxes. Bill isn't struggling behind her to bring anything in.

"What happened?" I ask, and Ember jumps, hand flying to her chest, and that only seems to make her cry harder.

I leave my place at the island and go to her, and after hesitating for a second, I gather her into my arms, and she clutches onto the back of my shirt, crying so hard I'm not sure there will be a tear left in her body.

"Em," I whisper. "Talk to me. What the hell happened?" It's clear Nova is okay. She's in her car seat sucking on her pacifier. The way she's sucking makes me think she's going to need a bottle soon. The fact that I am pretty sure I recognize that, warms my chest. I can totally do this dad thing.

"They—they—they—" She takes a deep, shuddering breath. "Kept—kept—kept your card."

"What?" I try to back up so I can see her face, but she just holds me tighter.

"They thought I was trying to steal from you," she wails.

"Why didn't you call me?"

"I don't have your number or even your address." She hiccups. "If I was her, I wouldn't have sold anything to me either."

I keep one arm looped around her, and I rub my forehead with my other. The few times I've given Abby my card, no one has even questioned it. But we've been together on and off for years, and her family is also wealthy. If I put on my objective lens, Ember doesn't look like someone I'd give my credit card to, which makes me feel like part of the problem.

But it also really pisses me off that whoever made her feel like shit didn't just call me or my mother or really anyone in my family who could have cleared up the charges.

"I'm sorry," I murmur. "That's my fault. How can I make this better?"

She doesn't say anything, just keeps crying, but at least it's not quite so full-bodied and soul-crushing anymore.

"I'm going to fuck up a lot, partly because that's what I do, but also because I've never done this before or anything like this with anyone. I haven't had any practice," I say.

"I don't want to go back to that store."

"Oh, no, we're going back, and I'm making it very clear that whatever you want, you get. Always. No matter what."

She backs away from me and runs her hands down her tear-streaked face. "You don't understand how she made me feel. Credit card fraud? No matter how broke I've been, how desperate, I've never stolen from anyone."

I frame her face, and I search for the best thing to do here. *God, she's adorable.* Even all puffy from crying, she makes me ache with the desire to keep anything bad from landing at her doorstep. It's almost like her sister is sitting on my shoulder telling me to take care of her, if I was the type to believe in that sort of thing, anyway.

"If you don't come back with me, it's harder to make it right." It's the old 'get back on the horse' analogy. If she doesn't face what happened in the store, it's more likely to follow her during her time here. Word spreads fast on the island, and I don't want anyone to think she's stealing from me or that I'm not aware of what's happening under my own roof.

"You have things to do." She throws her hand in the direction of the island.

"It's all online training, and honestly, boring as shit. I was on the verge of falling asleep before you got home. I can do it later." I meet her gaze and calculate whether she's going to be pissed off or find my next comment cute. Odds are fifty-fifty, but at least she wouldn't be crying anymore. "Come be a rich asshole with me."

She lets out a strangled laugh and steps away from me. Reluctantly, I let her go.

"She needs a bottle," she says, glancing at Nova, who is frantically sucking on her pacifier like it possesses her lifeblood.

"Teach me how to mix it," I say, walking toward the island.

Ember hesitates at the entrance, and I'm not sure if she's deciding whether to get Nova out of her car seat or whether she wants to teach me some bottle-making skills. Though I've been avoiding it, I need to learn, do my part, be the parent. Whether I pay Ember or not, at some point I'll have to take full responsibility for Nova, and I need to be ready.

"Then you can teach me how to change a diaper," I say as I gather everything I've seen her use for the bottle.

That elicits another watery laugh.

"No," she says. "I'm saving that lesson for when she has an explosive poop. All up her back"—she gestures—"and in her hair."

"That is probably the most disgusting thing a woman has ever said to me."

"Hang around with me long enough, and I'll take you to new heights." She purses her lips and glances toward the ceiling. "Depths? Talking about baby poop might be a depth, not a height."

"In either case," I say, "it stinks."

She laughs and comes over to stand next to me, hands splayed on the island, mirroring my pose. "Thanks," she says, glancing up at me.

"For what?"

"Trying to make me feel better."

"Does it really work if you know I'm doing it?"

"It does." Her eyes are soft, and she's incredibly cute.

Not the right thing to be thinking, but I can't help myself. There's just something about her that makes me want to be someone I've never been before. Her sister on my shoulder whispering, "Make her happy." But god help the both of us, I am *so not* the guy to make anyone happy.

"That bottle." I sweep my hand over my gathered ingredients.

"You ready?" A small smile plays at the edges of her lips.

"As I'll ever be." Which is true. Even people who plan to be parents probably just have to jump in, immerse themselves in the experience. I've let myself stay on the outside the last few days, and I need to recalibrate my thinking.

"All right," she says, and she starts showing me how to measure, check the water temperature, and shake to get rid of chunks.

By the time I'm done, I realize how lucky I am that she agreed to come, how lucky Nova has been to have such a caring aunt.

And when I'm done with those fuckers who made her sad at the store, they'll all understand that Ember is a Tucker now.

Instead of getting Bill to drive us, I load Nova and Ember into the SUV. Ember is jittery, and I'm not sure what she expects to have happen when we get to the store, but there's no way she's feeling bad again. Whatever I have to say or do to make it clear the employee made the wrong choice, that's what I'll do. Get a manager, have her written up, whatever.

"Don't get her fired," Ember says when we get closer.

"She made you cry," I say. "If she deserves to be fired, she'll be fired."

"I couldn't remember your pin. I didn't know your address, and I didn't have your phone number. What would you think in that situation?"

"She made you feel like shit. That deserves a response. Nova is a Tucker. That makes you a Tucker by extension."

"Be all arrogant, hot, rich guy. That's fine. But don't try to take her job."

I'm not sure whether to respond to the hot or arrogant first, but both make me feel strangely warm. Even though I know one of those isn't supposed to be a compliment, I think it might be?

"I don't look like I belong with you." Ember huffs out a breath. "And, like, I'm not with you, but I had your credit card. Obviously, that's going to raise some eyebrows. And I was nervous. It was just... It was a mess."

"You could belong to me." As soon as the words are out, I realize I mean that, but not in the way that it sounds. I've known her for less than a week. "I mean with me. I mean..." I shake my head. She's family now, that's all. "Why would you say you don't belong?"

"For starters, my clothes." She gestures down her body. "Goodwill special today. Tomorrow, it might be stuff I've sewn together myself from scraps."

"That's easy to fix. That's superficial shit. I'll send you with my sister, Ava, tomorrow. She loves to shop."

She bites her lip, but she doesn't say anything. So far her instinct has been to say no, and I bet she's fighting it hard right now. Looking the part *is* half the battle in this country, this world, even if it's only on the surface.

"I just don't fit," she says, but she doesn't look at me. "I don't blame the saleswoman, Gage. And I don't want you to either."

That's nice of her. Very charitable. It's unfortunate that I have a vindictive streak a mile long, and a newly discovered desire to protect her at all costs. The two probably aren't going to be a good combination.

We arrive at the store, and I use my VIP parking pass to get us valet. Start how you mean to finish, right? No expense spared. No luxury turned down. We're going full Celia Tucker. My mother will be proud when she hears about it, and some of my siblings will likely be disappointed. Can't win 'em all, but you can go out in style.

"Whatever I do," I say to Ember as I push the stroller toward the elevators, "just go with it."

"Should that worry me? That worries me." Her lip is between her teeth.

"I might embellish the truth." *A lot*. My mouth sometimes runs away from me when I'm heated, but at least I've sort of warned her. "Where was my card last time you saw it?" I ask as we ride the elevator up.

"With the checkout person. She kept it." Ember massages her temples.

"She's the one who made you feel like shit?"

"Gage."

My name is a warning that I'm going to ignore. She doesn't understand this world yet, but she will.

The elevator settles, and the doors open. I loop one arm around Ember's waist, and the other hand I keep on the stroller to steer it. She glances up at me.

"Just go with it," I say.

"I'm not kissing you," she says.

I fight a smile. "I didn't ask you to, but can't say I'm upset you considered it."

"You have no shame." Her cheeks are a pretty pink.

"Shame? Why would I need that?" I wink at her.

I take us straight to the register, and since there isn't someone there, I ring the bell several times, obnoxiously.

"Gage," Ember says again.

"You know, I'm not even sure my mother has said my name that many times in a row in that tone. Probably a nanny did, though. I wasn't listening."

"Can I—" The click of heels behind us slows, and I rotate to face a woman not much older than me, and I feel like I might have seen her before, but I can't quite be sure.

"Oh," she says, glancing between me and Ember. "Oh, no."

"I'd like my credit card back," I say. "And I'd like you to find whatever Ember already had picked out, and I'd like it comped for the inconvenience of having to come here myself."

Her cheeks are bright red, and she hurries around the counter. She fishes my credit card out of a drawer and passes it back to me.

"For all I know, you could have been keeping the card for yourself," I say, wagging it at her.

"I would *never*." She rotates her shoulders back and stands up straight. "I apologize to your... Girlfriend? I had no idea."

"Why would *you*, someone who works at a store in Tucker's Town, know anything about my life? I wouldn't expect you to know anything other than that I'm a Tucker." I cock my head. "This is my daughter." I shift down the canopy of the stroller to show Nova sleeping. "And this is Ember." I loop my arm around her waist again. "If you had some questions regarding the card being used, you had other options. Humiliating her was not your best or even most logical choice."

"I didn't mean to humiliate her."

"No? So you didn't accuse her of credit card fraud? Imply that this stroller was obtained illegally?" My tone is icy.

"I can't remember exactly what I said." She meets my eyes, and I can almost see her calculating. "She's not your usual type, is she?"

"I think I'd like you to explain that comment." I narrow my eyes. "If you dare."

"Okay," Ember says from beside me. She snatches the credit card back out of my hand. "Just those clothes from earlier." She goes to pass the card over, and I steal it out of her fingers before she can.

"We're not paying for them," I say.

Ember wraps her hand around my shirt and almost drags me a few feet away. "The money means nothing to you. You've told me that a billion times."

I smirk. I see what she did there.

"If we don't pay, it probably comes out of her wage. Everything is expensive here."

"She made an expensive mistake. Commission by being nice to you, or nothing by being an asshole. And, might I remind you, that comment back there"—I point toward the register—"was either an insult to me or to you, and neither is acceptable."

"What do you care what some shopgirl thinks?" Ember raises her eyebrows, a challenge.

"You're playing me like a fucking fiddle."

"I've learned every note."

"An impressively quick study." I grimace.

The money doesn't actually matter, and she's right that I'll never again wonder what this store clerk thinks of either me or Ember. If Ember hadn't come home sobbing, I'd have collected my card and told her to go fuck herself and walked back out. But that just doesn't feel like enough.

"She's not winning," I say. "She made you feel bad, and I won't have it. I won't. If I have to call her manager, I will. If I want to go full atomic bomb, I'll sic Celia Tucker on her."

"I'm really starting to think I don't want to meet your mother," Ember mutters and walks back over to the register. "Do you get commission on these sales?" Ember asks.

The clerk eyes me warily and then purses her lips before nodding at Ember.

"We'll take what I picked out earlier, but you need to discount it to match the price of your commission. You're still going to be out money, I guess, but it's better than Gage going full Hulk and raging out to your manager, which is what he wants to do. He'd prefer you lost your job, and I would prefer you did not." Ember seems to make very pointed eye contact with her. "I wouldn't want you broke and making hard choices again."

The saleswoman flushes, and her jaw works. This is far from the best deal I've ever gotten for a fuckup, but it seems to be making Ember feel better to be taking charge. She's got an inner bad bitch, and I kinda like it.

"Fine," the woman behind the cash register grits out. She digs a bag out from behind the sales area, and I watch as she scans each item before refolding it and placing it to the side. At the end, I ask her to turn her screen so I can see the amount of commission she should get, and then I watch as she takes it off the price of the clothes.

She can explain that to her manager later when they're trying to get all the math to make sense.

The screen in front of me lights up with the new total, and I insert my card and punch in my code. When it beeps that the transaction cleared, I take the bag off the counter, and I peer at the saleswoman's name tag. "Thanks for the service, Janessa." Then I wheel the stroller around, grab Ember's hand, and I say, "There's a much better store in Rockdown. Let's go there. Fewer entitled assholes."

This makes Ember laugh, and she looks up at me with a twinkle in her eyes. "You're not going to be there?" she whispers.

"Hush now," I say, leaning down. "I just defended your honor."

"Is this the part where I swoon?"

"Yes." I chuckle and tug her into the elevator behind me. "At least pretend to be a little impressed? My ego needs to be stroked regularly."

"As long as it's just your ego," she says, and her cheeks go pink.

"What else would you stroke?" I feign confusion. Her slip of the tongue and obvious embarrassment is adorable.

"I didn't want to come back here," she says, quickly changing the subject and spoiling my fun, "but I'm glad I did. Thank you. It felt good to stand up for myself a little."

"I've got your back," I say, and I squeeze her hand. "You're Nova's aunt. For the next four months, we're a team. Someone goes after you, they go after me."

"I like that sound of that," she says, her tone quiet and shy.

Me too. Far too much.

Chapter Ten

EMBER

Flirting with Gage Tucker is a bad idea. I reminded myself of that over and over on the way to Rockdown on the other end of the island. We cruised along the central highway, right down the middle of the country, but it still took over an hour to get there. This island looks tiny on a map, but it's not *that* small. Once we were at the other high-end department store, Gage got a cart, and no expense was spared. Five car seats, a crib, another playpen, a change table, bedding, mattresses, more clothes, and the list went on. If I could think of it, he was adding it to the cart. He even got some big tent shade thing so Nova and I can hang out on the beach without worrying about a sunburn.

But the whole afternoon made us feel a little too close for comfort, and the last thing I need is to be too reliant on him. Even when I'm no longer living on the island, I want to be part of Nova's life in some way, and forming any sort of connection with Gage beyond friendship puts my relationship with Nova at risk. At the very least, things could get awkward, at the most, he could prevent me from seeing her again. If there's one thing men have consistently proven themselves to be, it's untrustworthy. They think of themselves first, and everyone else is secondary.

But there are some appealing aspects to Gage. I can't lie to anyone about that. Unfortunately, he's the same guy who slept with my sister and doesn't seem to remember it, and the same guy who's been in a long-term on-again, off-again relationship with a woman who seems like someone I'd never be friends with. I don't agree with pitting women against each other, but I doubt Abby shares my belief. Everything about Gage and his life screams, *"He's not like you, Ember,"* at full volume in my ear. Impossible to ignore, but it also doesn't eliminate the things about him that feel... A little *too* good. The money is obvious—who wouldn't want to be rich? So is his extreme level of attractiveness. Wealthy and good-looking should be an outlawed combination.

Nova cries, and I fly out of bed to lift her out of the playpen before she wakes up Gage. Diaper change or grab her bottle first? I settle her against me, and I open the bedroom door before realizing that she's peeing through her diaper while I'm holding her. So gross.

As I toss down the protective mat for the bed and set Nova on it, I can't help drifting back to my favorite muse.

Gage.

This protective vibe he has going on is the real gold dust, and I can't help thinking that my sister's life might have been completely different if he'd been around to sprinkle even a tiny smidgen of that in her direction.

Living in the same house with him for four months is going to be an emotional tightrope walk. Too friendly or not friendly enough. There has to be some balance somewhere, but flirting is out. Ogling him is out too. I just need to convince my conscious and unconscious selves that he's hideous. Horrendously unattractive. Pretend he has vile body odor and bad breath. How can I trick myself into believing it?

Hypnosis, maybe? Gage would pay for it if I asked, I'm sure. The thought makes me laugh a little as I start stripping Nova for a diaper change. All the furniture is being delivered and assembled today, and I'm hoping this is my last day of diaper changes on my bed.

"You're just in here giggling away to yourself?" Gage is leaning against my bedroom door, shirtless, and more awake than I'd expect for this hour of the morning. My heart leaps at the sight of him.

Apparently, I also need to convince my body that he's hideous, which would be much easier if he wore more shirts. He can certainly afford them.

"My inner voice is pretty funny," I say.

"Your outer voice has had a good line or two." He watches me for a beat and then says, "Do you want me to do that?"

"She's a bit fussy," I say. "Would you mind getting her bottle? I was going to do that first, which is why the door was open, but then she started peeing on me."

"Peeing on you?" He scrunches up his face.

"It happens." I gesture to my damp shirt. "I've had worse."

He scans me for a beat, impossible to read. "One bottle, coming up," he says, and he pushes off the frame, and I hear him pad down the hall in his bare feet.

By the time he gets back, I'm just zipping up Nova's new onesie. He takes her from me and settles on the bed to feed her. I cross my arms and try not to feel self-conscious. Whenever I'm at the store next, I need to buy a shapeless nightgown or flannel pajamas if we're going to keep meeting in the dead of night. Then I remember I need to strip the sheet off her playpen and change my own shirt.

"Sorry if we woke you up," I say as I put on a new sheet. "I try to get her before she cries too much or too loudly, but it's hard when she's up every few hours."

"I was thinking that we should take turns when the nursery is set up. You a night. Me a night. Switch back and forth. Then hopefully, you're not so exhausted, and I'm not too tired for my new job either."

"No, it's okay. You're paying me. This is *literally* my job."

"Whether you know it or not," he says, focused on Nova, "I've been up with you every night, every time for the last few nights. I don't get out of bed, but I'm awake, and I can't believe how tired *I* feel." He tears his gaze from Nova to stare at me. "And you've been doing it alone for months." He swallows. "I can't keep avoiding my responsibilities."

Tears fill my eyes, and I have to look away from him. I *am* tired. So freaking tired. All the time. But it's not just Nova, it's been everything.

"If it helps, you'll be saving me from feeling guilty," he says.

"You'll just be sleep deprived instead."

"Better than sleep deprived *and* guilty. It's a terrible combination. Would not recommend."

Anything combined with sleep deprivation is the worst. Part of me thinks that's why I had such an intense reaction to the credit card debacle. Lack of sleep coupled with emotional overload.

"I guess I see your point," I say.

"It's a deal," he says, and he pops the finished bottle out of her mouth, switches the burp cloth to his shoulder, and stands up to burp her like someone who's been doing it a lot longer than a few days. "Now show me how to get her back to sleep."

So I mime or outright illustrate all the ways I've learned to coax her back to sleep, and he watches me with undisguised amusement before he chooses to rub her back in circular motions until her eyes flutter closed and she's sleeping again.

"Easy," he whispers as we both stare down at her in the playpen.

"Sometimes," I say with a soft laugh. "And sometimes it's really freaking hard."

Our gazes meet for a beat, and the air charges around us. *He is hideous. Not at all attractive. And even if he was, men cannot be trusted.*

"I'll get out of your way so you can change your shirt," he says, his voice rough as he heads for my bedroom door. "See you in the morning." He draws the door closed behind him, and I breathe a sigh of relief.

We've got four months, and I'll have to pray every day that this tiny spark between us fizzles and dies rather than catches and burns both our worlds to the ground. Nova and her well-being have to come before any flare of attraction. Otherwise, I'm a terrible aunt.

I owe it to Athena to be better than succumbing to some base, primitive attraction. While I've never been one for casual affairs before, temptation has never looked so good or been so close.

Ava blows into the house like a hurricane the next morning. Gage mentioned she was "a lot" when he told me she was picking me up to take me shopping. He said no one would take me seriously as a Tucker until I looked like a Tucker. I'm both excited and terrified about what that might mean, but it definitely sounds expensive.

"Don't even look at the prices," Gage says to me as he takes his smoothie from the housekeeper. Once again, he's not wearing a shirt. If I bought him one today, would he get the hint? It's distracting to have him all muscled, tanned, and always within my line of vision.

Ava lounges on the couch with some sort of highly caffeinated beverage in a square to-go cup that Gage already made fun of her for having. She smells like expensive perfume, and every inch of her is highly stylized. Make-up, hair, clothes—not a smear, line, crease, or stray hair anywhere. With her long dark-brown hair and light-blue eyes, she's as strikingly beautiful as Gage is ruggedly handsome.

"I'll use my card," Ava says.

"I gave her mine." He takes a gulp of his drink.

It's hard for me not to say that I don't want either of them to pay, that I can scrounge together enough to get a shirt and some shorts.

"I heard your card stopped working." Ava shoots him a sly grin.

"That's not what happened. Nothing wrong with my card. Service was sub-par." Gage sets his empty glass on the island, and the housekeeper takes it off and puts it in the dishwasher while she continues preparing food for the fridge and freezer.

Apparently, Michelle comes twice a week to clean and prepare several days' worth of meals. She works for the Tucker siblings, rotating through them. Gage explained that the number of events and opportunities to eat out meant most of the family didn't really need a daily personal chef, and I thought my head might explode at how normal he found his own explanation. Then I really thought I'd entered an alternate dimension when Michelle gave me a survey on my likes and dislikes so she could prepare appropriate food. I can't even remember the last time someone made me a meal.

"Are you sure you're going to be okay here with Nova?" She's in the swing we bought yesterday, and while she's typically been a good baby, I've never seen her so smiley before.

"Michelle is here all day." He gestures to the housekeeper behind him. "My mom is stopping by this afternoon, and she likes babies."

"The only stage of humanity that Mother enjoys," Ava says, rising off the couch. "Let's go. Ticktock. Shopping waits for no one."

She heads for the door, and I follow her. Once we're close, she gives me a once-over.

"Where's your purse?" Her eyes are narrowed.

"I don't have one. I usually use the diaper bag," I say, flushing. "I have Gage's card in my back pocket."

Ava holds out her hand, and I set Gage's card in it. She slides it onto the side table near the door. "You really are a blank canvas," Ava says, opening the door. "This is going to be fun."

I'm not sure why, but that statement makes me nervous.

Chapter Eleven

EMBER

Ava drives her hot-pink Audi R8 Spyder like a race car driver on cocaine. We zip in and out of traffic, completely oblivious to other cars and lanes of travel. The wind whips through my long hair, even with a high ponytail securely fastened.

When we sail past a police car, and Ava merely waves and blows the officer a kiss, I think I might die for a different reason.

"You're not worried about getting pulled over?" I ask as she makes another dramatic lane change well above the posted speed limit.

"No." She laughs. "I've slept with him a few times."

She says it so casually that it takes a minute for me to absorb it.

"Even if Stephen pulled me over, I'd either pay him off or offer him a blowjob. I'm not going to jail or losing my license for driving a little fast on the highway."

A *little* fast?

"If you're going to be a Tucker, you have to realize that rules don't apply to us." Ava goes across all three lanes of traffic, a series of honks following us, to take the exit. She pumps the brakes. "We make the rules."

Gage is arrogant, but Ava is a whole new level of entitled, and I'm not sure what to make of it. The notion that nothing matters or that everything can be easily solved is so far removed from my life experience that I'm wondering if I may have entered another plane of existence. People don't really live like this, do they? Zero accountability?

Somehow, we arrive at the center of Tucker's Town at some exclusive boutique clothing store in one piece.

"What size are you?" Ava asks as she tosses her keys to the valet attendant outside the store and rounds the hood.

I tell her, and scurry after her, suddenly self-conscious of my cut-off jean shorts and plaid, oversized shirt with the sleeves rolled up. My running shoes were used two years ago. They're practically worn through now.

Ava blows in the door ahead of me, and despite the vicious wind, she still looks immaculately put together. She rattles off my size to the saleswoman and then leads us to a sitting area outside a suite of changing rooms.

On a low table off to the side of the plush chairs and couches is a coffee maker and pastries.

"Help yourself," Ava says, gesturing to the food. "It's all included."

In the probably astronomical prices. One way or another, someone is paying for this spread, so I help myself to a pastry with strawberries and drizzled with a cream cheese sauce. It's quite possibly the best thing I have ever eaten.

"What is this?" I ask, amazed.

Ava glances away from her phone to take in the tiny square of pastry still left in my hand. "There's a rumor that the queen makes those. Don't know if it's true. Wouldn't surprise me. How we ended up with Betty Sue farm girl as our queen, I'll never understand."

"The queen of Bellerive bakes? For other people?"

"She did, yeah. She was the pastry chef at the palace. Quite the scandal. King Alexander stuffed more than a bun in that oven." Ava smirks. "According to my mother's sources, when she can't sleep, she still bakes, and then the palace gives the food away as goodwill gestures." She waves her hand at the table. "Or if you're connected, you just get a platter to highlight your status with the royals."

The saleswoman returns loaded with clothes, unlocks one of the changing room doors, which is the size of a bedroom, and hangs up each item. When she's done, she leaves the door open and addresses Ava. "If you need anything else, don't hesitate to ask."

"I won't," Ava says with a smile. "All right, Ember, get your ass in there and try some things on. We've got all day, but I have a list of stores as long as my arm to take you to. If we don't find much, we can always drive to Rockdown. Gage said to get you a full wardrobe. He mentioned that you didn't bring much from America."

There wasn't much to bring, so that's true. "A few things might be good," I say. "I'm only here for four months."

Ava waves me off and takes a sip of the coffee she's just made herself. "Normally, I ignore my brothers... and my sisters, actually. But this will be fun. And who doesn't like fun? We're getting you at least a month's worth of outfits. No arguing."

I slip into the changeroom, and I put together my first ensemble. The material of the shorts and shirts are smooth and weighty, and likely a bazillion dollars. I search for a tag and don't find one. That'll be a problem at the register.

When I step out, self-conscious, Ava nods her head, and then stands up to tug on various edges of my shirt and shorts.

"You have a good eye for pairing colors," Ava says to me. "But these fits aren't great. Not your fault." She calls the saleswoman over, and then they're deep into conversations about sizing for various brands before I'm given new sizes, and told to try again.

When I come out the second time, Ava claps her approval. "Yes, we'll take that outfit."

"There are no prices on these. How do we keep track of how much we're spending?" I whisper.

"If you have to ask, you can't afford it," Ava says, and then she laughs. "I forgot this store didn't advertise their prices on quaint little tags." She shoos me back into the changing room. "Set those in the 'yes' pile and then try on something else. There's no budget, Ember. There's just a yes or no pile. If it's a maybe, it's a no."

Back and forth we go through countless outfits. Sometimes I come out and it's an immediate no. Most of the time, her instincts match the ones I have when I look at myself in the mirror. Other times, we ask for more color choices or a different size.

By the end of the first store, our shopping trip is more collaborative and less one-sided. I've never had a budget-less trip in my life. Most of my clothes came from Goodwill or other thrift stores where I've been lucky to find a few items that mostly fit or that I can make fit with a few small alterations.

We spend all morning and most of the afternoon hopping from one store to another. Then when she asks if I've heard from Gage, and I mention I don't have a working phone, she stops into a store and has a second phone, for me, added to Gage's plan. The salesperson's expression is neutral during the entire transaction, and she never implies Gage wouldn't want me on his phone plan. There is definitely something magical about being a Tucker. I imagine hanging out with Ava is like being with a celebrity. No one questions any of her choices and behaviors, and she just pours more money out of her card and into whatever she wants.

The endless fucking well.

Once we have enough clothes to satisfy Ava, she declares that we now need handbag and shoe options to go with the clothes we selected. Warmth spreads across my chest for the first time since we started the shopping trip. Handbags, I can do.

She opens the door to Franza's, one of the most expensive and coveted handbag designers in the world, and I can almost feel the drool pooling in my mouth. While I've seen these bags on the internet, I've never seen one in real life.

"Finally," Ava says, shooting me a sly glance, "I found something you seem to be excited about."

"I love purses, handbags, anything like that," I admit. As we wander the store, Ava picks up various items before setting them back down, but I can't bring myself to touch anything. Then, I see one that I really like. The black leather has the distinctive PP design for Petra and Paul Pascal, the brother-sister team who run their handbag empire. The asymmetrical look reminds me of something I designed a few months ago for a client I had. Of course, my leather had been reclaimed from a thrift store leather jacket, but the concept is so similar that I'm a little stunned. "This one," I say.

"That's a good day-to-day bag," Ava agrees. "Now we need a few clutches and smaller ones for events and parties."

"I won't be going to any of those," I say. "I'm the nanny. The aunt, but also the nanny. That's the deal Gage and I have."

"You do not want to be caught unprepared, and as Tuckers, we're often forced to attend charity functions with Sawyer or Nathaniel. And with Maren now dating Prince Brice, it's a whole thing. We'll buy the stuff, and if you never end up needing it, it's whatever." She waves her hand.

"I could just…" I hesitate because I don't want to seem cheap, which appears to be a cardinal sin in Gage's family, but I also don't want to buy something I won't use. "I used to make and sell handbags and purses and things as a side business at the fabric store I worked at."

"But you didn't have *anything* when I came to pick you up today?" Ava eyes me with open skepticism.

"Nova and I were…" The words are hard to get out, even if they're true. "We were on the cusp of being homeless. I had to sell everything."

"God," Ava says, rolling her eyes. "My brother is such a dick. It took him weeks to come to terms with being a dad. *Weeks.* It was a whole midlife crisis. He was *not* okay, but you *really* weren't okay."

"I get that Nova was a surprise," I say, and I try not to dwell on the fact that he knew for so long and didn't come. The important part is that he did show up, and once he did, he made sure everything was okay. He never made me feel like I didn't try my hardest to keep Nova's life together, didn't push me about what happened to my sister. I can be angry that it took him so long to arrive, or I can be grateful he came at all. On a rational, reasonable level, I know which one serves me better.

I can't help the little pinch to my heart, though. If he'd come sooner, I might not have been living in a dark apartment, might not have had to run down to Mrs.

Chapman every time I needed to heat a bottle, might not have contacted my dad, might not have felt so deeply, epically alone.

"He's been pretty firm," Ava says, leading us to the register to pay for the one bag, "about not getting married or settling down or any of that until he's really old. Like fifty or something."

"Oh?" I say. "He and Abby seem like they've been together for a long time."

"Oh yeah," Ava agrees, sliding her credit card into the slot. "Years. On and off like a light switch. Which is why I'm sure it really burns Abby's cookies to see you living with Gage. Even if you're not living-living with him. I'm sure those cookies are black with rage."

"She wanted to live with him?"

"My brother has this phobia of becoming like our parents."

"Who are still married?" Following this conversation is like being in the middle of a storm. The information is coming fast and furious, but the direction keeps changing.

"Yeah, but not happily. Or not really happily? I don't know. I try not to think too much about our mom and dad. My dad cheats. My mom puts up with it. If she cheats, she's much better at keeping it under wraps. For a lot of years, it was obvious that Dad's affairs made Mom miserable. Maybe she has her own side piece now. She doesn't seem to care what he does anymore."

"Couldn't they just get divorced?" I suggest.

"Then Mom wouldn't be a Tucker anymore. Someone else might take her place in society. To her, that's worth everything, I guess. She comes from a wealthy family, but not Tucker-level wealthy. Millions versus billions."

"Right," I say, following Ava back to the car with my new bag. "This is a lot to take in."

"My family is fucked," Ava agrees. "Hey, can you take your hair out of your ponytail?" She stands at the driver's side and gestures to me before getting in.

I tug the elastic out, and my long dark hair tumbles halfway down my back. It's been months since I've done anything other than wash it and pull it off my face. My priorities have been elsewhere.

"Can I do something with that?" Ava points at my hair and makes a swirling motion with her finger.

"Like cut it?"

"Layers, maybe some highlights, give it some dimension. Make you look less *poor girl* and more *rich girl*."

I wince.

"Yeah, you probably don't like being reminded you were so poor. Sorry. My sensitivity chip is a bit broken sometimes."

Probably because no one ever makes her use it. It doesn't seem to matter what she says or to who. People take whatever she says in stride.

"It's just weird to be someplace where I don't fit in at all," I say. "Where I come from, everyone looks like me. Has what I have." *Or don't have.*

Ava laughs. "I highly doubt everyone looks like you. Otherwise, fashion designers would be slumming it to find their next top model. I guess you're kind of short for that. Maybe more catalog than runway. But you're very pretty, Ember, and if my brother hasn't actually said that to you, I guarantee he's thought it." Ava gets in the car as though Gage finding me attractive is no big deal.

The truth is, I don't want to consider what Gage has thought about me. My own imagination has been in overdrive when it comes to him, and the last thing I need is any sense that the attraction might be mutual. Even if being with him in any way wouldn't screw up my life forever, he slept with my sister. And even if I don't want to hold it against him, can even understand why he did it, he didn't come get Nova as soon as he found out about her.

It's better if I file him in the untrustworthy and unstable column, the same place I put most men. Keep my guard up and my expectations low. That's really the only way I'm going to survive the next four months living in the same house with him.

Chapter Twelve

GAGE

"**S**he's a gold digger," my mother declares as soon as I tell her where Ava and Ember are. She scooped up Nova the minute she walked in the door, and she's hardly set her down. It's strange to put this version of my mother together with the one I know. If she carried me around like that as a baby, as though I was the most precious thing in her life, I never felt that a moment after I could walk.

"She's not a gold digger. Shopping was my idea." I don't hide my annoyance. This isn't an argument I can win with her. If I'd left Ember in her thrift store clothing, my mother would have been embarrassed that I let someone associated with the Tucker name go around the country like that.

"Good gold diggers do that, Gage. They make their desires feel like yours. Next thing you know, you'll be marrying her, and you'll swear to me then that it was your idea."

"I'm not getting married," I scoff. "You and Dad have put me off of ever doing that."

"Desperate people do desperate things, and if she was as poor as you're making her sound, that's a powerful reason for her to try to hitch her cart to yours." She floats around the kitchen preparing a bottle for Nova as though she hasn't missed a day in the last twenty-plus years. "As a Tucker, you have to be aware of these things. I've been telling you this since you hit puberty, and look at you"—she gestures to Nova—"a surprise baby. Obviously, you didn't listen to me, but you should now. If the mother was alive, you'd have been roped into some sort of relationship. Now it's the sister doing it."

"You haven't even met Ember, so this conversation is stupid." Everything that's happened between me and Ember so far *has* been my idea. Mine, and I'm not having my mother plant ideas in my head because she believes everyone in the world wants to be a Tucker. I take a bite of my apple and watch her... Be a mother. "You really do like babies."

"I love them," she says. "Why do you think I volunteer at the neonatal unit three times a week?"

I didn't know she did that, but I'm not going to say that out loud. She'll accuse me of never paying attention, and I suspect she'd be right. Not the first time I've had that accusation leveled at me recently. It's something I'm working on changing with Ember and Nova, though. I'm going to notice everything. Be so observant. Anticipate their needs.

The new and improved Gage Tucker will become a stable, reliable father and a hardworking member of the Bellerive community. No more surfer slacker who only cares about himself.

A solid plan, but it makes me a little nervous. The businessman thing I was totally on board with weeks ago, and I even did the stupid online training today while Ember was gone. Most of the answers I found in online forums, and I don't know if that's cheating, but the course didn't say I *couldn't* do that. I'll call it being resourceful and count it as a win.

But Nova is a whole other road to navigate. She's not a multiple-choice question or a set of laws in a document. Screwing up another human being just by being myself is a little terrifying.

If it wasn't for Sawyer and Nathaniel, I'd be a lot more fucked-up than I am. Nova doesn't have any older siblings to steer her in the right direction when I make a mistake, and I don't have a partner to turn to once Ember leaves. Maybe she'd still let me call her? She can give me advice.

"When do you start with Hugh?" my mother asks, sticking the mixed bottle into Nova's mouth.

"Monday," I say, and I lean against the counter, watching her sway gently with Nova in her arms. This whole thing is like the twilight zone.

"Your father is just thrilled you're going to be working with Hugh. He really thinks highly of him. A great representation of the Tucker name."

Hugh only has the Tucker name because he has a double-barreled surname. My parents sold off all their companies and no longer do much of anything, so their interest in what represents the Tucker name seems weird. Mom, apparently, volunteers at the hospital, and then she collects and sells gossip like currency. It's her favorite thing to do. And Dad? As far as I can tell, he fucks women who aren't my mother and travels the globe.

"She's going to call you Grandma," I say to avoid talking about Dad or Hugh in depth.

"We might have to come up with a more modern name. Glamma. I'm too glamorous and young to be a grandmother."

She's not *that* young, but she dyes her hair black and is terrified of a gray hair being spotted. The dermatologist is on speed dial for when her skin even *thinks* of forming a wrinkle. "Whatever you want, Celia."

"Glamma, it is."

She doesn't even clock that I didn't call her Mom.

"Ava and Ember should be back soon," I say, though I suspect that's a lie. "I should put Nova down for her nap." Ember left a written schedule for me to follow, and I've been doing okay so far. It's been good for me, I think, to be alone with Nova. It's definitely made me appreciate how tough the last few months must have been for Ember, and how much of an ass I was to wait weeks before going to Colorado. Even then, I showed up assuming I wouldn't have to be a dad. Throw some money at this anonymous woman and our baby and keep living my life. Be a dad if and when I felt like it.

I've never admitted that out loud to Ember, and I don't think I will.

"I'm still surprised you brought them back here," my mother says, setting the empty bottle on the island and then burping Nova. "You're sure she didn't talk you into it? You were so set on washing your hands of this mistake."

"You can't call Nova that," I say. If Ember was here, I can only imagine what she'd think. Even if it's true, you don't say that to a kid, but I'm not surprised my mother doesn't realize it. "I guess I have more of a parenting instinct than I thought." It's not so much that I saw Nova and realized I had to do the right thing, but that I saw Ember and realized I couldn't do the *wrong* thing.

I take Nova from my mother, and I walk her to the door to wave to her before putting Nova down in her newly constructed crib. As soon as Ember left this morning, I had a team of people in here putting things together, rearranging furniture, and getting Nova's room *just right*.

In the room, I lie Nova in the crib, and I rub her back. She can roll over, which is apparently why she's fine to sleep on her stomach or her back, and she cries a lot less when I start her on her belly. Ember warned me about that last night, but I tried my luck earlier. Not making that mistake again. Nova was pissed at me for setting her on her back first, and it took her a long time to settle.

Her breathing evens out, and I'm still in awe, as I stare down at her, that I'm her dad. My phone buzzes in my pocket, and I sneak out of the bedroom with the baby monitor before retrieving my phone as I head to the living room.

There's a text from Seth asking if we can grab a beer, and a second text from an unknown number. I click on the unknown number, and it's a selfie of Ember and Ava with the message, *New obsession unlocked—sending you random messages about my day.*

I enlarge the photo, cutting Ava out of it, and I examine Ember's face. She's gorgeous, so beautiful that it's almost painful. But what really catches my attention is how relaxed she looks. Normally, there's a tiny bit of tension around her eyes or in her expression. A wariness or uncertainty, as though she expects the rug to be pulled out from underneath her or the loss of Athena pokes through in unexpected places, painful and fresh. She often looks like she's one wrong word away from bursting into tears or fleeing the house.

I have to reply, but I'm not sure what to say. Texting is new territory, and so I go with something simple.

You got a new phone.

Gage Tucker got a new phone, actually. I'm just borrowing it for a few months. How's parenting?

Surprisingly excellent. How's shopping with my sister?

Surprisingly excellent.

The three little dots appear and disappear, appear and disappear, and then they don't come back for a few minutes. I stare at my phone wondering if I need to say more when another message arrives.

Ava wants to take me out for dinner.

My sister wants to wine and dine you? You should say yes. If you want to make me proud, order the most expensive bottle of wine on the menu and then don't drink it all.

OMG. No.

I chuckle at the horror I'd likely hear in her voice if she was here. Then she'd probably either imply or explicitly call out my privilege in being able to do something like that. Then I text back, *Pictures or it didn't happen.*

It's not happening.

Let me talk to Ava, and it'll happen.

You can text her yourself. I'm not getting involved in your sibling one-upping. She already left your credit card on the side table at the door.

What? I get off the couch and go to the front door to find my card shoved under the dish where I place odds and ends like money or keys. Ava is such a brat sometimes.

Rather than letting my annoyance get the best of me, I decide to take Ember's advice and I text Ava. *Where are you eating dinner?*

Rainforest Bistro. Don't worry, I won't keep your responsible adult out too late.

I can't decide if the implication that Ember is the only responsible one irks or amuses me, but either way, I'm about to put that notion to the test. I call Bill to see if he's able to swing around to the Rainforest Bistro to take Ava and Ember home after dinner. He's available, so I call the restaurant, and I order two of their most expensive bottles of wine—one red and one white—to be delivered to their table upon arrival.

Then I text Seth to come over for a drink since I can't leave the house. Ember and Ava will be a while.

Three hours later, I'm feeding Nova when the doorbell goes off.

"Want me to get that?" Seth offers.

"Yeah," I say, keeping an eye on the level of Nova's bottle. "It's probably Ember. She doesn't know the code yet. I usually buzz her in with my phone. Guess I should change that."

He ambles over to the door, and when he opens it, Ember says, "Gage Tucker, you got me drunk! Oh, you're not Gage. Gage!"

I can hear Bill and Seth talking in the entrance, probably about all the various bags Bill is trying to haul in from the car.

Ember rounds the front entrance, and I glance at her over the couch, Nova is still drinking in my arms. Ember's shorts and shirt are new. The shirt fits her in ways that should be illegal, and her long dark hair isn't in a ponytail for the first time since I've known her. Her hair is thick and dark and halfway down her arm.

My sister has turned Ember into some sort of goddess. I should hate the transformation. It's going to make it so much harder to be in this house with her and not want to fuck her, but the way she's weaving toward me, loose and relaxed, is just too goddamned adorable.

"I told you not to drink the wine," I say with a grin.

"Well, then you clearly don't know your sister." Her eyes are bloodshot, and she slumps into the couch beside me. Whatever they did to her at the salon, she doesn't smell like pineapples anymore.

Seth trails behind her from the door, amusement coating his expression. "Ava's tricky like that," he says.

"At least you had Bill there," Ember says. "Sober Ava is a horror show on the road."

I bark out a laugh. Drunk Ember is highly entertaining. "Tell me some more truths."

"Nope." She mocks sealing her lips. "I'll get in trouble." She reaches over and smooths Nova's hair before planting a sloppy kiss on the top of her head.

"I'm going to go," Seth says. "I'll see you around, Gage. Nice to see you again, Ember."

"Bye, Seth!" Ember waves to him, and I give him a head nod.

From the couch, the lock clicking into place is audible, and then I realize how quiet the house is. Before Ember got home, Seth and I were talking about surfing and rock climbing while I looked after Nova.

I glance at Ember, and then I immediately regret it. She's staring at me with open curiosity.

"You don't remember sleeping with my sister, do you?"

The way she says it makes me think it's been bothering her. I can't bring myself to say it, so I just shake my head.

"Because you've slept with so many women?" She cocks her head to the side, as though she's trying to puzzle something out.

"I don't know about '*so many*,'" I say. In my friend group, I'm probably in the middle ground in terms of women I've slept with. Some of my friends have been with the same person since high school, others have a new woman every night, and then there's me—somewhere in between. When I'm with Abby, I'm only with her. But when I'm not, I sometimes lose track, obviously.

Nova finishes the bottle, and I take it out of her mouth before rising to burp her. "I'm going to put her down again," I say, more to avoid talking about my sex life than because Nova needs to go back to sleep right this second.

"Yeah, sure." Ember rests her head on the back of the couch.

It doesn't take long to get Nova to sleep, but I half expect to return to Ember sleeping on the couch or her having gone to bed. Instead, she's clearly still awake, and the crease in her forehead suggests she's deep in thought. I take a seat on the couch again, and I wait for her to say whatever is on her mind.

"Ava thought it was weird that I've only slept with one guy. Do you think that's weird?" Her head falls to the side, and our gazes connect.

"You and Ava had girl-time confession, huh?" My heart kicks at the realization that Ember is that inexperienced. It's not the craziest thing I've ever heard, but it's surprising given how she looks—I'm sure she's had offers. But I'd really rather not pass any kind of judgment on whatever "*normal*" is. Typically, with the life I've had, I'm not an accurate judge of what the majority has experienced. Learned that in college, more than once.

"I haven't had, like, the best experiences with men. You know? My dad being abusive, and then I seemed to pick really controlling boyfriends when I was younger. And then I just... didn't want any boyfriends at all after I saw Athena go through hell with more than one of them. Just not worth it. Someone could seem really great and then flip—like Jekyll and Hyde. Men can't be trusted to be who they say they are."

"You can trust me," I say.

"Can I?" A hint of a smile touches her lips, but it isn't filled with humor. "Did you really wait weeks after getting the paternity results before coming for Nova?"

Fucking Ava. The people you can't trust are your family. *That* I can get behind.

"I had a hard time processing the results," I say, carefully. "The fact that I can't remember... If I'd known how badly you were struggling, I would have kicked my own ass and come sooner."

Tears fill her eyes, and she nods.

"I didn't know, Em. I promise. I wouldn't have left you like that if I'd known."

"I don't want to be mad about it. It feels stupid to be mad because you did come, and you did save us. How can I be mad about that?"

"I don't know." I sigh. "Two things can be true, can't they? You can be happy I came, and you can be pissed off I didn't come sooner. I don't think one has to cancel out the other—as much as I'd like for that to be the case."

"That's a very mature response."

"I'm trying it out—maturity. I'm a dad now, you know." We stare at each other across the small distance of the couch. The air around us heats, and I'm pretty sure bad ideas are on the horizon. If she doesn't have them, I certainly do. "I should get to bed." I stand and swoop the baby monitor off the table and shove it into my back pocket. "I'm on Nova duty tonight. You can sleep off that wine."

She grabs my hand before I can leave, and when I gaze down at her, she merely says, "Thank you. For everything."

Unable to resist, I smooth the strands of her hair back behind her ears. "You and me. We're just figuring it out together. No need to thank me."

She stares at me wordlessly with her big multicolored eyes, and I have the strangest urge to pick her up and carry her to bed, but it doesn't feel sexual, not really. It's something else, something I've never felt with a woman before.

"Night, Em." I trail my fingers down the strands of her hair before heading for my room.

We're only at the start of the four months, and I can't keep my hands to myself. I've got no idea how we'll stop ourselves from doing something stupid.

Chapter Thirteen

EMBER

Somehow, Gage and I made it through the weekend without calling off this whole arrangement. I wouldn't have blamed him after I probed his sexual history and gave him mine. Talk about embarrassing. How many women he's slept with is really none of my business, but I am a little glad I mentioned that I knew he didn't remember my sister. No point in pretending, and he'd been stepping around the truth for days. Even if the truth makes me sad, it just solidifies that I'm the carrier to Athena's memory for Nova—Gage will never be able to tell Nova anything.

The next morning, I was relieved to discover a bottle of aspirin and an extra-large bottle of water next to the bed. My forced sobriety the last few months definitely meant I needed both to cope.

Surprisingly, Gage never said anything about how drunk I was or how personal I let things get. Maybe because he was too exhausted after being on baby duty all night. I hadn't heard a thing in my alcohol-induced slumber, but he took naps at the same time as Nova the next day.

The uninterrupted sleep did me a world of good, and I took both Saturday and Sunday night so Gage was well rested for the start of his job today.

It's strange being in the house by myself this morning, even though Gage made sure I had Bill on speed dial in case I needed to go anywhere. The house is a little lonely after the nonstop company the last few days. He also left me cash, not his credit card, and I suppose I could go somewhere, but I have no idea where to go.

Besides, tonight, his whole family is coming over to meet Nova and to celebrate the start of his job. I wouldn't want to go somewhere and end up getting back late because I didn't know any better.

Although the house is practically spotless, I still go around with the vacuum and then use a cloth to dust the nonexistent dirt. After months of feeling like I couldn't do enough, be enough, it's hard to be still, to take in my good fortune. Other than tending to Nova's needs, there's nothing I *have* to do. Working at the fabric store dominated my life for years, and then I added my side business of making bags for people, which was mostly through word of mouth. And I had my sister, my constant companion, my best friend, my biggest protector, and champion. Having all this time just makes me miss her more and regret so, so many things.

When Nova wakes from her first nap, I have to get out of the house, and I take the sun shelter, her diaper bag, and her play mat, and we go to the beach. There, we watch the people surfing and enjoy the nice weather. Anything to avoid the too-quiet house.

At her second nap time, I gather everything from the beach and trudge up the stairs. I've just put her down in her crib when the doorbell rings.

She seems reasonably settled, so I leave her to see who's at the door. When I peek out the side window, my heart kicks. *Abby.*

Her annoyance is clear through the glass, and she seems to be talking to someone, but I can't figure out who. It looks like she's alone. Then I catch a voice through a speaker, and it's definitely Gage. They're fighting without him even being here. Great.

I don't think Gage would want or expect me to open the door to that, and I head to the living room, but only a minute or two later, Abby is standing at the back sliding door, knocking on the glass. She can see me, and I can see her. We stare at each other, and then she rattles the locked door as though to make a point.

I consider texting Gage to see exactly how bad it'll be if I answer the door, but she's already distracted him from work once. Since nothing in Gage's world seems to work like mine, I don't know if he can get fired, but I wouldn't want to be responsible for that if he can be. First days are usually a little chaotic.

"Just answer the door," Abby yells through the glass.

Girl drama is so exhausting. With a repressed sigh, I get to my feet and pad to the door, flipping the lock and pulling the sliding glass open.

"I just need to get some things from Gage's room," Abby says, eyeing me.

"Okay," I say with a shrug. "Gage knows you're here?" I already know he does, but I have no idea if he knows she's going to be *in* the house.

"He does." She breezes past me, confident and disdainful.

A few minutes later, she comes back with a sweater in her hand. It doesn't look like her size or style, but I don't say anything. Poking the bear when I don't have a gun behind me seems foolish. Instead of going back out the sliding door, she takes a glass from the cupboard and helps herself to the leftover smoothie from Gage's breakfast that's still in the fridge.

I turn on the TV and ignore her, flipping through the limited local channels, not really paying attention to what's on, mostly just trying to avoid the confrontation that I can feel brewing in the air. She's making a point, whether I'm willing to witness it or not.

"You know, Gage and I have been together since the summer before freshman year of college. We're endgame. I wouldn't want you to get your hopes up. No matter what happens, no matter where he dips his dick, he always comes back to me. Always. Doesn't matter who else catches his eye; I'm the one that holds it."

"Okay," I say, and I keep cycling through the channels. If they keep breaking up, I don't see how she's actually holding his attention. Saying that might lead to a physical fight, and her fake nails look tough and sharp.

"You probably think you hit the jackpot with him. Someone like you, living here. But all of this is temporary." She flings her hands out. "Don't get too comfortable." She chugs his smoothie. "As soon as your four months are up, we'll hire a real nanny to raise his kid, and he'll be mine again."

The insinuation that Nova is nothing more than an inconvenience gets my back up. She can threaten me or mock me all she wants, but she better not be going after my niece. I'm not having some wicked stepmother situation on my watch.

"Gage wants to be a dad," I say.

"No, he doesn't. He feels sorry for you. Feels bad that she lost her mother. He has no interest in being a parent."

"Sounds like you're working off of outdated information," I say, even though this feels like new information to me. Not completely unexpected. He slipped into Dad mode fairly quickly, but if I think back to his aloofness, his attitude when he saved me at the top of the apartment stairs, he didn't give off *"give me my kid"* vibes. More like *"here's some cash, I gotta go"* vibes.

"We'd already agreed we weren't ever having kids," Abby says with a sneer. "Don't you get it? We've talked about these things. That's how close we are. People don't change that fast. He made a mistake, and he's prepared to pay for it."

My phone rings on the table, and I can make out Gage's name from the call display. Also, he and Ava are the only ones who have my number.

Because I'm tired of Abby's bullshit, I swipe to answer and put him on speaker phone. She's acting like I've stolen Gage from her, and that's so far from the truth. As an outsider, it looks like her attitude is the problem in her relationship with Gage, and that's got nothing to do with me.

"Hey, Gage, Abby's here, in the house," I say when I answer.

"I'm aware." The frustration in his voice is clear. "Am I on speaker?"

"Yeah, sorry. I can take you off."

"No, don't. Abby, like I already said, you don't have anything at my house. You don't keep things at my house. You need to leave before I call Stephen and have him escort you off the property for trespassing."

"You're not going to do that," Abby scoffs.

"Yeah, I will. You don't want to test me, Abs. I'm fucking pissed you're in my house when I already told you no. We're not together right now. You've gotta let it go."

The "right now" gives me pause, as though they might have already discussed a scenario in which they *would* be together again.

"We're not done talking about this, Gage," Abby says, sweeping the shirt she stole off the island and storming toward the sliding doors. "This isn't over."

She opens the sliding door, but she doesn't bother to shut it, just strolls out as though closing a door is beneath her.

"Sorry, Em," Gage says through the speaker.

"She took your sweater."

"I'll buy another." He chuckles. "I saw her leave on the cameras, and I know which one she has."

"Is it expensive?"

"What do you think?"

I take a minute to consider what someone like Abby might do. Vindictive. "It's either the most expensive one you have, or it means something to you."

"Yeah," he says, but he doesn't clarify which one it is. "Next time just let her rage on the other side of the glass."

"Got it," I say.

"Caterer should be there in half an hour to start setting up for dinner tonight."

"Okay." I move to the sliding door and shut it, relocking it again. "How's your first day going?"

"I've been trailing Martin, and it's been okay, I guess. Hugh says I'll be selling properties by the end of the week."

"That's good, right?"

"I'm going to be working on commission, so yeah."

I don't point out that he doesn't need the money.

"I gotta go," Gage says. "Another meeting. Another chance to hear people here tell me how great they are."

"Your kind of people," I say with a little laugh.

"I'm gonna be great," he says, and I can hear the smile in his voice. "But I'm not there yet."

After we hang up, I can't help thinking that he's a lot closer than he thinks.

Ava came to the house early because she said first impressions with her parents are critical. She's taken me through a whole beauty routine that I'll never be able to replicate, but maybe that doesn't matter once Celia and Jonathan Tucker have met me once.

With the first impression over with, I can go back to being me. She tugs on my hair as she drags my strands through the straightener, steam coming off the ends. My hair has never looked so glossy.

"I feel like this is going to be false advertising," I say. "I'm never going to look like this again."

"Sure you will." Ava sprays my hair with some kind of shine sheen and then draws another section through the straightener. "You're on the learning curve. In four months, this will all be second nature."

Except I don't need or want it to be. Once I leave here, these skills she's so sure I'll acquire will be useless. A relic from another time.

"Has Gage told you anything about our family?" Ava asks.

She told me a little while we were out for dinner the other night, but I drank so many glasses of wine, the details are a bit fuzzy. "Not really," I admit. "We've mostly just been figuring out stuff with Nova."

"Nathaniel is the oldest. He's just started getting into producing not-for-profit documentaries. Talking about those is his favorite thing. Ask him about those. He'll love it. Sawyer is a physiotherapist who, as far as I can tell, mostly works for free. She serves anyone on the island who can't afford care. Very noble. She's very good at pretending to be interested in anything you say to her." I catch her rolling her eyes in the mirror. "Sawyer has always acted more like a mother to me and Gage than a sister. It's super annoying."

My mind drifts to Athena, who did the same for me. But I was always so grateful for her. She carried all the weight so I didn't have to, and I didn't realize how heavy it was until it was too late. Tears prick at my eyes, and I blink frantically.

Ava just finished my makeup, and I get the sense she wouldn't be sympathetic to me ruining it.

"Then there's Maren—the middle child. She's a professional philanthropist. All she does is charity work. She's recently divorced. Dating a member of the royal family now. And there's some weird tension between her and Gage because he magically fathered a child when Maren would love to be a mom. It's a whole thing."

"She's upset about Nova?"

"Not really. But maybe? It's complicated. Sawyer probably knows, but Maren and I aren't tight like that. I'm closest to Gage in age and attitude."

"Gage is after Maren and then you?"

"That's right. Mom and Dad saved their best for last." She winks at me in the mirror. "Unlike my other older siblings, Gage and I aren't interested in giving away all the family money. We're interested in making it. He's getting into real estate, and I'm working on developing my own perfume line."

"Must be nice to have all the money behind that," I say without thinking, and then I slap a hand across my mouth. "Oh my god! I'm sorry."

"None of us are offended by nepotism." Ava laughs. "But I wish it was as simple as having the money. The rules of the trust state that we can't use that money to fund business ventures. We can use trust money to maintain our lifestyle, that's it."

I frown and consider how I can ask why without seeming either nosy or stupid. Then I remember she said Nathaniel and Sawyer have businesses.

"Your older siblings..."

"Worked for someone else for a while and saved up the cash to get started. Takes a while, but it's easy enough to do when your day-to-day funds come from the family trust. And there's like a loophole. If you set up a not-for-profit, you can fund whatever projects you want. Nathaniel and Sawyer might have done that. I haven't asked. But Bellerive has really strict laws around what qualifies. My perfume line can't be not-for-profit. I want the success of making heaps of money. It'll take me a while to get things up and running—I'll need investors—which is annoying, but fine. It's not like I'm starving."

Like Nova and I almost were. Even when the odds are a little stacked against the Tuckers, they really aren't.

"That's why Gage is lucky to get in with Hugh. He can have his own success and make lots of money and not have to worry about the trust rules. You can't tell anyone, but Gage's actual goal is to compete with Hugh, not work for him. That's years from now, though."

"Because he needs to save the money?"

"Yeah, and—"

"Sawyer's here," Gage calls down the hall.

Ava tugs the last piece of my hair through the straightener. "Right on time. Okay, get dressed. I put your outfit on the bed, and then come meet the fam." On her way out the door, she turns back to me at the last minute. "And whatever my mom says to you, just ignore it. She has a really hard time believing that not everyone is a terrible person like her." Then she draws the door closed behind her, and I'm left with that warning, which makes me a little worried about the family I've chosen to immerse Nova in.

Chapter Fourteen

GAGE

When Ember comes out of the bedroom hallway in a wispy purple dress that makes her tits and ass look full and tight, my breath catches in my throat. In Colorado, I knew she was pretty, but it wasn't the gut punch that's started happening to me since Ava took her out and gave her a makeover. I spent all weekend adjusting to the change and avoiding her by pretending to nap in my room.

Gone are her ill-fitting clothes and messy hair. She's no longer pretty in a wholesome, small-town way. That was something I could cope with—occasionally looking at her and finding her cute or adorable—totally doable. Ember was a puppy you didn't want anyone to kick. Protective, best friend, or big brother vibes. All acceptable ways to treat Nova's aunt who I'll need to have contact with for years. Cute Ember was a situation I could navigate for four months without a problem. My libido would be firmly in check with my right hand and some cold showers. No other women, but not her either. Easy.

Unfortunately for me, she's left cute and adorable far behind in favor of becoming an absolute smokeshow, and that's bad news for our living situation. Cold showers and my right hand don't seem like nearly enough when she looks like *that*.

From beside me, Nathaniel squeezes my shoulder. "You're going to live with her for months and not fuck things up?"

I resent the implication that I'm likely to screw up, but I also can't tear my gaze away from Ember. Some sort of magnetization has been switched on between my eyes and her body. Even if I wanted to look somewhere else—which I don't—I can't. My eyes have decided that Ember is not a snack, she's a whole fucking meal. God, I might be drooling.

I'm totally going to fuck this up.

"Yeah." My voice is rough, and I clear my throat. "It'll be fine. She's a good girl. Too good." One sexual partner when she looks like that? She's got standards I'd never meet. "Ember wouldn't have any interest in someone like me."

"I notice how you didn't say you wouldn't have an interest in her," he says.

"I'm sure you're seeing what I'm seeing."

"You drooling over her and Mom clocking you from across the room? Yeah, I'm seeing that."

Against my better judgment, I glance in Mom's direction and sure enough, her eyebrows are raised at me as though Ember's appearance has perfectly illustrated her point about Ember manipulating me into wanting her. Little does she know, what's happened to Ember is all Ava's fault. I scowl at her to let her know we're not on the same page.

Ember crosses the room, and when she gets to my side, the nerves are practically vibrating off her. I'm careful not to touch her when I lean close and whisper, "You look gorgeous." Goose bumps rise across her bare arms, and her hand lands on my forearm. Simultaneously, I wish everyone would leave, and I'm also really glad everyone is here. "It'll be okay." And if it's not okay, I'll kick anyone and everyone out. "Do you want a drink?"

"Just water," she says.

"Nathaniel, this is Ember, Nova's aunt. Ember, this is my oldest brother. Nathaniel spends his time—"

"Producing not-for-profit documentaries," Ember says, her voice a little stronger. "Ava told me about it. What's your latest project?"

She gazes up at Nathaniel with undisguised interest, and a twinge of jealousy pinches me. Nathaniel is probably the kind of guy someone like Ember would like. Unwaveringly loyal. Doesn't sleep around. Reserved. Polite. The epitome of the good breeding my mother wanted with her firstborn. She'd given up by the time she got to me, I think.

"Prince Nicholas and his wife, Julia, have started a not-for-profit education program in Tanzania, and I've been working with their team to help produce a documentary. I'm just dipping my toes into producing. Haven't done much of it before. I have some ideas about other things I'd like to do a little closer to home."

I slip away before I can catch Ember's response. The sooner I grab that water for her and come back, the better I'll feel. The last thing I need is Nathaniel swooping in and charming Ember, making everything even more complicated.

At the temporary bar set up near the sliding doors, I order myself a drink and Ember a glass of water. While I wait, my father ambles up beside me, his whiskey sloshing around his glass.

"You'd better be careful with her." He nods toward Ember. "You already have one illegitimate child, and I could see how she'd be tempted to give you another. Secure her place in your life."

I can feel my jaw clenching, and I have to will myself to relax. My parents' default mode is to assume everyone is trying to swindle us. It's always been like this, so it shouldn't be a surprise.

"She's helping me transition Nova to life in Bellerive, to me as her father. That's it. You and Mom are always worried about some Tucker doomsday, like the worst thing that could happen is a loveless marriage with someone more interested in our money and status than us as a person." I've got some news for him about his marriage to Mom, if that's the case.

"Divorces are expensive." He visibly bristles. "Children are expensive. Combine the two, and you'll be paying out of pocket for years."

"Here's all I'm going to say on that." I pick up both my drinks from the bartender table. "If either you or Mom make Ember even a little bit uncomfortable tonight, you'll both be out the door on your asses."

"Jesus, she's already got you wrapped around her finger?"

"She's a good person," I say, meeting his gaze. "She doesn't deserve your distrust or Mom's. Say whatever you want to me, but you say *nothing* to her."

As I walk back to Ember and Nathaniel, I watch Dad tell Mom that I laid down the hammer. She just rolls her eyes in response. While Dad might listen, Mom will do what she wants. She always does. Celia Tucker is more of a Tucker than any of us. Sometimes I think she railroaded Dad into marrying her, and that's what's made them both paranoid. They know what a bad marriage looks and feels like. I would say their concern for their children is admirable, but it's clearly more about money than happiness. God forbid anyone get a piece of the Tucker pie who wasn't deserving in their eyes.

Prince Brice has joined Nathaniel and Ember, and he's already got Ember laughing. It's not the first time she's laughed, but in the week since we've known each other, it's been a rare sound.

The only thing Brice and Maren's ex, Enzo, have in common is their ability to be the center of attention. While Enzo's persona felt a tiny bit false or put-on, there's not a disingenuous bone in Brice's body. He's a certified good dude. We've even gone surfing together a few times.

Maren and Sawyer are fawning over Nova, who is in her swing, and I hope that means Maren's attitude toward me has thawed a little now that I've come back to Bellerive *with* Nova. My decision to be a money daddy instead of an actual father caused a massive fight. When I'd argued that not everyone wants to be a parent, she'd told me I shouldn't be sleeping around if I'm not prepared for the consequences. Given that she's gone from one long-term relationship to another, we were never going to see eye-to-eye on that. She's never had to worry that her inability to be completely satisfied with a partner might mean she's a little too much like Dad.

Me, on the other hand? I'm convinced that whatever faulty gene runs through his blood also runs through mine. In the years Abby and I have been together, I've never cheated, but we've broken up a lot. Sometimes it was my idea, sometimes it was hers, but the breakup never bothered me. There was no way I was turning down a chance to sleep with someone else. As much as I'd like to think otherwise,

I'm not sure I can be anyone's forever. Or if I am, I need someone like Abby, whose idea of happily ever after includes frequent breaks from each other.

"If you'll make your way into the dining room," the head caterer says, "dinner will be served shortly."

I pass Ember her water, and she gives me a grateful smile, and then she falls into step with Nathaniel while Brice is beside me.

"You're going to have to be careful with her," Brice says to me in a low voice.

Him too? Unbelievable.

"There are a lot of wolves in this world," he continues, "and she's very much a lamb. There are people on this island who'd love to take a bite out of a Tucker."

"I'm not going to let anyone hurt her." She doesn't know it, but I'm standing at her shoulder with a gun pointed at anyone who might dare to come after my family through her.

"If you ever need anything, call me, call Maren. We're family." He pats me on the back before moving around the table to take his seat beside Maren.

Then I notice that my mother has wrangled the seat beside Ember, but Nathaniel is on her other side, and Sawyer is across the table. I was too slow, and I've somehow been relegated to a place out of earshot. That's not going to work with my mother right there. Disaster is written all over that.

"Sawyer, switch me seats," I say when I get to her shoulder.

She glances at me, and I think she might protest, but then she must see something in my face that tells her I'm not taking no for an answer. She pushes back the chair and goes down the long table to sit near Dad.

When I take my seat, I mouth to my mother to behave. A hint of a smile tilts her lips. While the waiters come around with the first course of soup, my mother turns to Ember.

"So tell me," she says, "what were you doing before you came here?"

I tense, expecting my mother to immediately go on the attack, but she surprises me by slipping into charming socialite. For the rest of the meal, she peppers Ember with softball questions that make her seem interested and almost—dare I even think it—*kind*. It's a façade, and I'm tempted to lean across and tell Ember it's a trap, but by the time dessert is being served, my mother hasn't said or implied a single terrible thing.

At one point, Nova starts to cry in her swing, and when both Ember and I scrape back our chairs at the same time, it's Brice who leans back, takes her out of the swing and starts charming her as though it's second nature. Ember's smile is uncertain at first, but once she sees how comfortable Brice is, she brings her chair close to the table again. My parents might be train wrecks, but I've always been able to count on my siblings, and now their partners.

The evening winds down, and my parents are the last to leave. I escort them to the door while Ember puts Nova down for the night.

"I appreciate the small talk you made with Ember."

"Hearing her answers only solidified what I already believe," my mother says, airily. "No one that poor would ever willingly go back to it. Her ideal career is designing handbags, for god's sake. As if that doesn't have '*Use a Tucker*' branded across it."

Apparently the high road is just too steep for my mother. She can't even manage it when she's already halfway there.

"And there's something strange about however her sister died," she continues. "An accident? With no details? Not even when I pressed a little? What has she told you?"

I stare at her, unsure how to answer because I haven't pushed Ember for the details. Why would I? "Talking about Athena makes her sad."

"I bet it was a drug overdose, not an accident at all," my mother says. "She could have done drugs while she was pregnant with Nova. Have you considered that?"

"You know, if you keep up this judgmental bullshit, you won't get a chance to know your granddaughter, *Glamma*."

"You sell anything today?" my father interjects.

Silence sits heavy between the three of us before I decide to go with the topic change.

"It was my first day," I say. "Kind of impossible. But Hugh said I should have some listings by the end of the week."

"Don't let him down," my father says. "He's giving you a great opportunity."

I open the front door to usher them out. The last thing I want is another lecture from my father about responsibility. The script never changes, just the circumstances. *Be better. Do better. Stop fucking up.*

Their lack of faith would be stunning if it wasn't so consistent.

They might not realize it now, but the Gage standing in front of them is the new and improved version. Screwups are a thing of the past.

Chapter Fifteen

EMBER

The rest of the week passes like a tortoise ambling toward a finish line. Except I know that next week will look exactly the same. The finish line is four months from now. Every day, every week, stretches out ahead of me in a vast line of sameness. I don't ever remember having the luxury of being bored before, and that's what I am, but it's more than that.

Gage goes to work, I look after Nova, and when he gets home, we eat dinner together, and then if it's my night with Nova, I put her to bed and then retreat to my room. If it's his night, I leave her with him, and I go to my room.

It's a strange, lonely existence, but I don't want to lean on him too much or take too much comfort in his presence. Everything I have right now is temporary, and it's better if I treat it that way at all times.

To pass the days, I go to various stores and pick up odds and ends to make Gage's house feel more lived in. A pillow or a blanket. A mug or two. At a print store, I make copies of the photos I brought from Colorado. I get frames for pictures of Athena, and I scatter them around Nova's room. Even when I'm not around to tell her stories, at least she'll know what her mom looked like.

Then, on Thursday, in a fit of annoyance and creative boredom, I decide that the flow of the house doesn't seem quite right, and I rearrange the furniture while

Nova naps. I'm fully prepared to put it all back if Gage hates it, and I'm on tenterhooks at the kitchen island the minute Gage walks in that night.

He stops at the spot where the entrance widens into the open concept living room, dining room, and kitchen, and he doesn't say anything for a moment, just looks around with a furrowed brow. After seeing him in a suit for the first time on Monday, you'd think I'd be used to it by now. But each day, he somehow gets hotter. *So, so hot.* Not a good sign.

"Is it bigger in here? Did you blow out a wall while I was at work?"

"I rearranged all the furniture." I give him a small smile. "I can't tell if you like it or hate it from that comment."

"It's different." He shoves his hands into the pockets of his suit pants and walks around the space, seeming to take everything in. "Can you do this with other spaces? Like if I took you into any room, does your brain automatically rearrange furniture and accessories?"

Now it's my turn to frown. This is the first time I've had this kind of space to work with, but in our small apartment, Athena and I were always looking for ways to maximize space, to make the little we had seem like a lot. "I—I actually don't know."

"I've learned this week that my brain doesn't work like this." He makes a circling motion with his hand to encompass the room. "Obviously." He laughs. "I've lived in this house for months, and I never once thought to rearrange anything."

"It just came to me today." Though maybe it had been percolating in the back of my brain all week because once I started, I didn't even second-guess myself.

"Hugh gave me three properties that have been on the market for months. Said if I could sell them in the next four weeks, he'd give me some of the big deals. The real moneymakers."

"Tap into that endless well."

"Exactly," he says with a hint of a smile. "Thing is, I'm not completely sure why these properties aren't selling. I have ideas, but I could be totally wrong. Do you want to come take a look at them with me this weekend?"

"Oh, I don't... What would I know about real estate?"

"Who knows?" His smile broadens. "Before today would you have said you knew anything about maximizing space?"

Well, *yes*. Just not on this sort of scale. "I don't know anything about how billionaires live." I shake my head.

"Excellent."

"Excellent?" It's the first time I've had an inkling that my poor background could be a positive.

"None of these houses are owned by billionaires. Average Bellerivians looking to sell their homes. Your kind of people." He takes off his perfectly tailored, and likely very expensive, suit jacket, rolls up his sleeves, exposing his forearms, and he goes over to the play mat to lie on the ground beside Nova, swinging the dangling bits lying over her head. She makes an excited noise in response and kicks her feet. My chest warms at how comfortable he's become with her over the last week. Despite what Abby said, I think he'll be a good dad. He's done his night shifts without help or complaint.

"How was the peanut today?" he asks.

"Good," I say with a small smile. "A happy girl. Do you want me to get you a drink or something?" He often cracks a beer as soon as he gets home, but it's always just one.

"You don't have to wait on me," he says from the floor as he turns on his side to run his big hand along Nova's stomach.

"Your first listings are normal homes?" I lean against the kitchen island.

"The billionaire houses come after I learn how to sell everyday houses. Hugh says I have to learn to walk before I can run, whatever that means. Commercial properties and farms are another lucrative branch, but Hugh already has *'a team for that.'*" He uses his fingers as air quotes. "Like I'm going to let that hold me back from learning it all. Island-wide real estate domination is the ultimate goal."

The preheat alarm goes off on the stove, and I put the shepherd's pie in the oven, and then, even though he said I didn't need to, I crack open a beer and take it to him. He gives me a half smile and holds the bottle away from Nova when she tries to get her hands on it.

"Hey, I was thinking," he says, and then he seems to wait for me to face him. When I do look at him, he's sitting up, long legs stretched out, one hand behind him, the other holding the open beer bottle. "Do you want me to get you a sewing machine or something? There's a fabric store in Rockdown, and we could go there this weekend, if you want. You don't have to put your life on hold by being here, and you mentioned you used to make things."

"If I'm only going to be here for a few months—"

"Em, stop being so fucking accommodating all the time. It's okay to take up space in the world, in my life, okay? I didn't invite you here so you could hide out in your room like... like some paid help. You're family. You're Nova's aunt. I know this might all feel too quick or feel like too much—*I get that, trust me*—but it's okay to ask for what you want. I'm not going to say no. Don't wait until you're mad about something to be assertive."

His assessment of me is shockingly accurate, and I stare at him for a beat. "Yeah, I want the sewing machine, and I'd love to go to the fabric store. And... And I'd like to do things with Nova that aren't just shopping and hanging out here."

"Like a spa or something?" Gage raises his eyebrows.

"No!" I laugh. "No. Like... Some kind of baby group or parent-and-tot classes or something like that. Do they have those here?" In Colorado, I was too busy staying alive with a roof over our head to worry about growth charts and keeping Nova on track with her mental development. But hours of free time this week and a lot of internet searches has led me to believe I've been slacking.

"I have no idea if those things exist. I guess they do?" He shrugs. "I've never had a kid before." He raises his eyes to the ceiling and seems to be thinking. "I think Seth's sister has a kid. I can text her." He shifts to slip his phone out of his pocket. He sets down his beer bottle, and his fingers fly over the keyboard. "Done. Tell me what else you need."

"Nothing."

"Bullshit. You've got unlimited resources, unlimited funds. Seize the opportunity." His phone buzzes on the floor beside him, and he flips it over to check his messages. "Okay, Felicity says there's a parent-and-tot swim at the big outdoor pool on Mondays, another thing that the queen hosts on Tuesdays at the palace, some sort of open gym thing on Wednesdays, and the children's museum in Tucker's Town is half price on Thursdays."

He's staring at his phone, frowning at whatever else is coming through, and I'm still stuck on one of those options.

"I don't know," he says, glancing at Nova. "She doesn't seem ready for the open gym."

"That's your biggest take away? The queen hosts a children's event on Tuesdays at the *palace*, and your biggest surprise is the open gym?"

Amusement coats his expression when he glances up at me. "You got a thing for royalty, Em?"

"No, I mean, I don't know. Shouldn't I? Aren't they important?" At the very least, they're famous. The newspaper headlines I've seen in the shops make it seem like the royals still have something to do with island politics, too, but I don't understand the whole system.

"They're just people." He sets down his phone and takes another swig of his beer. "You already met Brice. He's just a guy, like other guys. Rich. Privileged." He points to himself with his bottle. "Exceptionally handsome."

"Yeah, I mean, I guess he seemed normal enough? He was great with Nova."

"Knowing Queen Aurora, the palace thing will be for everyone in the world to attend. It won't be some exclusive rich-people thing, trust me. She grew up on a cow farm. With *real cows*."

The way he says it makes me laugh, as though the scandal of a working-class person in the palace is too much for him. Maybe it is. I don't understand much about the island's social or political hierarchy, but I like the idea that she's welcoming, down-to-earth, maybe someone I could even relate to on some level as a fellow outsider to this whole world.

"She's my kind of people, huh?"

"Just saying you might not feel as out of place as you expect. By all accounts, Rory is a gem."

"Can I get Felicity's number? I wouldn't want to show up in overalls and plaid if I actually need a ball gown and a tiara, despite what you might think." The oven beeps, signaling that the shepherd's pie should be ready.

"You think I'd lead you astray?" Gage's hand is splayed across his chest. "We're a team, Em. I'll be the last person on this whole island to fuck you over. In fact"—he points his bottle at me—"I'd murder anyone that did."

"No need to murder anyone. And let's be real. You'd hire someone to do that." I slide my hand into an oven mitt and take the food out of the oven.

"Fair," Gage says, setting down his bottle and picking up his phone. "I wonder how much that costs?"

"You don't care about money." I set the container on the countertop.

"True, but it's good to know the fair market value for a service you'll likely need."

"Gage, you're not hiring a hit man."

"*Hit person* is probably the correct term. And I might." He glances up at me. "I just might."

"Can you just send me Felicity's contact?" I let out a huff. "First impressions are important here, and I don't want to screw up one that feels kinda huge."

I grab the plates from the cupboard, and my phone lights up with a message from Gage. Hopefully, that's Felicity's number. With a finger, I flick open my phone and nod my head. Exactly what I needed. When I glance up, Gage is staring at me. "What?" I ask.

"Don't go hang out in your room tonight. Stay out here with me. We'll watch a movie or something. Or read books. Or watch makeup tutorials. Or whatever girly shit you want to do."

"Girly shit?" I laugh. "Did that really come out of your mouth?"

"Well, I don't even know what you like to do. Read? Watch TV? Paint your nails? What have you been doing in your room every night?"

Mostly I've been staring at the ceiling trying not to be miserable—thinking too much about my sister, wondering too much about Gage, second-guessing all my life choices. The usual.

"Sleeping," I say.

He tilts his head, clearly unimpressed with my answer.

"I don't know. I just play on my phone or whatever. It's fine. If you want me to stay out here I can."

"We're working on being assertive tonight," he says, getting to his feet and coming toward me with his bottle. "You were doing so well. Now, tell me the truth." He sets his bottle in the sink.

"I hate when you set your bottle in the sink instead of putting it where it belongs," I say, and I cross my arms.

He plucks the bottle from the sink, tugs open the bottle bin, and drops it in with a clatter. "Done." He mirrors my pose and meets my gaze. "If you could do anything tonight, knowing there's a tiny person sleeping in the house, what would you do?"

Make out with you on the couch until we were both breathless and incoherent.

The thought pops up automatically, as though it's been hiding in my brain just waiting for an invitation to surface. My cheeks start to heat, and instead of answering him, I dish up the food. What am I thinking? That's the last thing either of us needs to be doing *any* night. I shake my head to clear it, but Gage misinterprets it.

"Come on. There must be something you'd want to do." He accepts the plate I slide across to him.

Think. Think. Think. I cannot tell him what I just thought. "Okay. Fine. Two things. I'd love to sit outside and have a drink, listen to the ocean, and look at the stars."

"Or?" he prompts getting out silverware for both of us.

"Have you ever watched the Interflix series with your sister and Prince Brice? The race one? You probably have. I've never seen it, and people were talking about it at dinner on Monday. I haven't been able to figure out how to get Interflix to work on your TV. I can only get the local stations, and they kind of suck."

"I saw the first episode, but then I didn't watch anymore."

"Why?"

"Truthfully? I haven't always been the best, most supportive brother." He grimaces and stirs his shepherd's pie, still standing at the island, spooning up a mouthful. After he finishes chewing, he says, "The good news is that we can do both those things. The pool house has a TV that can be swiveled outside, so you can view it from the patio."

"Of course it does," I say before I can reconsider my words.

He chuckles. "You're going to get used to this."

Part of me really hopes I don't. I'm not sure I can take the loss of something else I love.

Chapter Sixteen

GAGE

It's really fucking early, but I should be used to that by now. A week of semisleepless nights and early mornings should make Saturday's wakeup a breeze. Strangely, sleep deprivation doesn't work like that.

The houses we're going to see are supposed to be empty of people when we arrive, so our schedule is tight. Get in, assess, get out. I clip Nova into the base in the back seat before climbing into the front of the SUV.

"We're picking up one more person on the way," I say to Ember as she clicks in her seat belt.

"Who's that?"

"Posey Jensen," I say. "She's an interior designer. I figured two sets of skilled eyes are better than one."

"You and her?"

"No, *you* and her," I say with a chuckle. "I'm useless. I just can't see it. The space doesn't open for me that way. No creative spark in me. What's in front of me is what I see. That's it."

"I really don't know that I'm going to be any help." She peers out the window.

Last night we spent hours on the patio, drinking a few glasses of wine and watching the Interflix series my sister was part of and that aired almost a year ago. It was a bit weird to literally watch my sister fall in love on camera, but I definitely enjoyed how into the viewing experience Ember was. She guessed outcomes, speculated strategies, asked about editing decisions (which I knew nothing about, but suggested she ask Maren), or raved over the skills of the adventure race participants.

The show was good, but Ember was highly entertaining. This morning, as though it was the wine that loosened her up and not the relaxed atmosphere, she's closed up. I get two steps forward with her before sliding three backward.

I've got less than four months to get her to warm up to me, but maybe it's better if neither of us warms up *too* much. The smokeshow just keeps smoking, and I'm already choking on the fumes. From the top of her head to the tips of her painted toes, her body sends subtle signals to my dick. Normally, I like that feeling, but with her, I don't think I should. In fact, I think it might be bad.

If she loosens up to what, based on the brief glimpses I've gotten, might be her authentic self, being around her could be the equivalent of setting myself on fire. Dangerous. Painful. All the bad things. Because even the biggest forest fires burn out, and they leave a swath of crispy, damaged land in their wake. That's not something either of us can afford when we've got Nova to think about.

After the late nights and early mornings this week, I'm starting to feel less like a stranger or a fun uncle and more like a dad. I can't even begin to describe how strange it is to look at Nova and realize I'm responsible for her *forever*. No flaking out or taking a break or considering myself first or any of my other previous coping strategies for close personal relationships are allowed. Real mind-bending shit.

We're not in Posey's driveway long before she slides into the back seat of the SUV, makes a fuss over Nova, and then sticks her hand out to Ember in the front seat.

"Posey Jensen. You must be Ember. Gage thinks the world of you." She grins. "He did not tell me how pretty you were, which is progress for him."

"Oh, um…" Ember glances at me. "I'm not sure what to say."

"You'll get used to Posey," I say. "She's blunt in a good way." I steer us toward the first house.

"The plan is for the brain trust—you, me, and Ember—to figure out how to sell these unsellable houses?" Posey asks as she picks up Nova's pacifier, which is resting on her chest, and pops it back in her mouth.

"If we can, yeah," I say. "Martin's consulted on these places for other agents, and they still haven't sold."

"Martin Garneau is too cocky for his own good," Posey says. "I'd love to see him taken down a peg or two."

Most of Hugh's team suffers from an abundance of confidence. While I can see how that strong internal belief that you're the shit would be helpful to sell anything, I'm hoping that it also means they've missed some easy solutions.

As I turn into the neighborhood of the first property, small and condensed, Ember peers out the window. "Definitely my kind of people," she whispers.

"The price point on this house," Posey says from the back seat, the sale sheet in her hand, "is totally unrealistic."

"It's not far off comparables," I say. "A bit high, but it shouldn't stop offers."

"Have prices gone up that much since Brent and I bought?" She digs her phone out and seems to be doing an internet search. "Wow. They have. That's unreal. How are people affording these places?"

Ember seems engrossed in the view, and I try to step into her shoes, imagine what this area would look like from an outsider's perspective. This section of Tucker's Town is the poorest in the city, but even still, the prices are on the rise. Many locals are actively moving out to cheaper areas of the country or at least considering it. Sell high, buy low. All of that is information I got from either Martin or Hugh this week as I shadowed them.

Most of the houses in this district are a thousand square feet or less, and the land lots are close together. There are no driveways, and everyone parks on the street. Each house is either well-maintained or is on the verge of needing massive repairs. There's not much in between. This section of the city represents the Great Depression, and it shows.

"Are people buying these cheap only to knock them down and rebuild?" Ember asks. "That's what happens in a lot of poor neighborhoods where I live, assuming everything around it is good. Rich people buy the shitty properties, knock them down, and then rebuild. Do it enough times and a poor neighborhood isn't so poor anymore."

"Bellerive has a lot of bylaws and countrywide rules about tearing down buildings. Unless the structure is no longer sound, it's almost impossible. You can add on, but tear down? Not really. Especially in Tucker's Town. Everyone wants to preserve the integrity of the building eras." Posey passes Ember the sale sheet.

"Which is why I was so impressed the other day with what you did at my house. If I can just rearrange things in someone else's place—change the perception of the space—maybe I can sell the unsellable," I say.

I parallel park in front of the right unit, and the three of us get out. Nova is sleeping, and I unclip her car seat to bring it with us. At the door, I set her down to key the code into the lockbox to get us into the property.

Posey and Ember enter the house first, and I follow behind them with Nova, who I set on the ground just inside the entrance. She's sucking gently on her pacifier in her sleep, so I know we've got time before a feeding or a changing meltdown.

"Well," Ember says, looking around. "It's cluttered. Way too much stuff."

"Definitely," Posey says. "Do you think you could convince them to store some things in a Tucker warehouse, free of charge?"

"I don't know. Martin and Hugh didn't tell me much about the listing, which is probably part of the test. I'll ask the sellers." I take out my phone and open my notes to make a list of things to do.

As we walk through the two bedrooms, bathroom, kitchen, and living room, neither Posey nor Ember says much. The place is crammed with things, not a hoarder level of packed, but a good clear out would make the available space more obvious. Whoever lives here has kids, which I've learned even in the last week, means a lot of toys and various gadgets.

"Well?" I ask when we get back to the living room.

Ember's lips twist, and she shrugs.

"Assertive," I remind her.

Ember glances at Posey and then gestures to the furniture. "I'd completely change the layout of the furniture, and I'd move the TV to a different place. Maybe there." She points to a corner.

Posey nods her head. "What else?"

"Other than clearing out about eighty percent of their stuff?" Ember asks. "I'd repaint the bedrooms to neutral colors, throw a few splashes of color into cheap accent pieces—pillows or throws—and I think that would go a long way. I could even make those pretty easily. You'd want the place to feel homey rather than lived-in, right?"

"I'd say she's spot-on," Posey says to me. "She has good instincts."

"I told you." I grin at Ember, and she smiles back.

"Did you work in real estate or interior design at home?" Posey asks Ember.

"No." Ember lets out a little laugh. "Just years of doing a lot with a little."

"Not everyone can see space and know what to do with it," Posey says. "It's a particular skill."

I take rapid notes in my app of the suggestions Ember made, and then we all hop in the car to head to the next property. At the second one, Posey and Ember work together to pick apart the slightly more upscale property in a better area of the city while I feed Nova a bottle. By the time we leave there, I have another list of action items. The third property is much of the same, except now Ember has more confidence, and the minute we're in the door, she's rattling off things she'd change.

Once we're done, I take Posey home, and while we're sitting in her driveway, I turn to Ember. "You still good to go get whatever you need to make you happy?"

"I'm not unhappy, Gage," Ember says with a hint of a smile. "Bellerive is gorgeous, and it's not like I'm working hard. You don't have to buy me things that I'll only use for a few months."

"Ship it all back home with you. I'll pay to have it delivered to your doorstep." I put the car in reverse. "I'll take that as a yes."

We drive for a while before I decide I'm going to pry for once. All week, I've let her set the pace of what she wants to say, but I'm starting to wonder if she'll ever tell me anything important if I don't ask. It's good for us to know each other—at least a little—since we'll be in each other's lives for a long time. No harm in becoming friends; that's a safe zone. Might even help me get over the urge to sleep with her.

"My mother said you want to design purses or something?" When she doesn't answer right away, I glance at her and see her flushed cheeks.

"Silly, right? It's not like I'll ever be a Franza." She hugs her purse to her chest. "But god, I just love it, you know? Everything about it. The lines and the textures and figuring out dimensions. I earned a bit of money at home, making them on the side."

"Why didn't you scale up? No one becomes who they are overnight."

"Scaling takes money. Most of the time, I had enough to use the profit to purchase materials for the next design. Anything leftover bought me a coffee." She shrugs and seems lost in thought for a minute.

"I'm already paying you to help with Nova," I say, "but if you're willing to consult on properties I can't seem to move, I'll pay you for that too. I'm paying Posey for today, assuming the properties sell. You should get some of that too."

"I don't mind helping," Ember grumbles.

"You need to learn to take what's yours. When your boss at the fabric store offered to pay you overtime, did you ever say no?"

"Obviously not." Ember rolls her eyes. "I needed the money."

"Then take what I'm offering. You can say 'thank you,' but you can't say 'no,' deal?"

"Okay," she says with a resigned sigh. "Okay. Thank you." She turns to gaze at me. "It's just hard. Out of one side of your mouth, you keep calling me family, and out of the other side you keep shoving money at me. I don't know—maybe I'm wrong—but I don't think family should be like that. Athena and I did all kinds of things for each other without expecting anything in return."

Her last statement causes a sheen of tears to enter her eyes, and she looks away, back out the window.

"Do you want to talk about your sister?" I ask gently, and I reach across the console to run my hand along her leg. She grabs my hand and squeezes.

"No," she says, but the word is choked out. "I just... I can't."

"I don't know what I'd be like if something happened to any of my siblings. Maren had a bad fall while rock climbing in Chile. She could have died, and that was close enough for me."

"Athena was everything to me," Ember whispers. "My only real family. Now I've got Nova, but she's not really mine. She's yours."

"You can play as big of a part in her life as you want," I say.

"For four months," she says, and when our gazes connect, I don't know how I didn't see this earlier. Of course four months is never going to feel like enough for her. Leaving Nova must be like letting go of her sister.

"Do you want to stay longer?" I ask. "I can find out what we can do."

She lets my hand go and runs her fingers under her eyes, scooping up the tears that fall. "I don't know. I've only been here a week and a half. Maybe leaving won't feel so huge, so impossible, in a few months."

The big-box craft and hobby store looms ahead of us, just on the outskirts of Tucker's Town. My online search said this was the best place on the island for everything Ember might need.

"The offer is there," I say before putting the SUV in park at the front of the store. "If you decide you want to stay longer, I can make some calls. There has to be a workaround."

She searches my face for a beat and then she nods, but I have no idea what's going on behind her expression.

"Let's go get you everything you need."

Ember grabs the stroller out of the back while I unclip Nova, and the three of us walk into the store, and I can't help thinking how normal it all feels.

Sell some houses, look after Nova, keep Ember happy. It's a simpler life than I expected to have, but I'm surprised at how much I'm enjoying the change. Now I just have to make sure that nothing from my old life tips this new one into the wrong direction.

Chapter Seventeen

EMBER

The next three weeks pass in a blur of watching Nova grow up, helping Gage reconfigure and stage houses, sewing my own creations, and dipping my foot into Bellerivian society. Despite Gage's assurances, today is the first day I'm brave enough to go to the queen's Tuesday baby group at the palace. Last week, we did the pool, and the week before was the children's museum, a multistory experience. For most of it, Nova still seems too young, and I'm hoping that today feels more social and not overwhelming.

I'm in the SUV with Bill and Nova when my phone rings and Gage's name flashes across the screen. I slide to answer, and before I can even say hello, Gage says, "The last property just sold, Em. I signed the paperwork five minutes ago. We did it. We sold those fuckers in the four weeks Hugh gave me." He lets out a triumphant laugh, and my chest warms.

"That's amazing," I say. "You must be so proud."

"I am," he says. "I couldn't wait to call you. We have to go out tonight to celebrate. I'll ask one of my sisters or my brother to watch Nova. Do you like Mediterranean? I know a great place. I'll get us a table."

"Uh, maybe? I don't know if I've ever had it." Athena and I didn't eat anything that wasn't cheap or homemade.

"You'll love it. Hugh's at my door, so I've gotta go. I'll see you at home later. Good luck at the palace."

"Okay, thanks," I say before Gage clicks off in my ear.

He definitely worked for those sales, which sort of surprised me. The two of us cleared out the three properties of clutter and stored everything in shipping containers at the marina, after Gage called in a favor with a friend. Then I made the accent pillows and blankets along with picking up a few wall décor pieces at thrift stores. For once, Gage didn't mind my cheaper instincts. He's on a tight company budget until he can prove his worth. The whole experience was a frantic but fun few days of juggling Nova and a bunch of other moving pieces.

Bill drives up to the palace gates and speaks to the guard there. They have a friendly banter which makes me wonder how many times the Tucker family has entered the estate. Lots, probably. Billionaires with, now, family ties to the royal family.

We glide through the metal gate after it slides open, and Bill seems to know exactly where to go, even though this is the first time. We're driving back to a two-story building to the left and near the back of the property. There seem to be several units, and each one has its own staircase to a doorway. Just outside one of the ground-floor units is a huge playground, and there are already children running around. Tables are set up with drinks and snacks, and there are mothers and fathers milling about.

Gage offered to take the morning off to come with me, but I didn't want him to do that. He brought me here to fulfill this role and making him tag along is more for me than Nova. The number of men is surprising. Are these men nannies or dads or what is this? Does everyone in Bellerive have flexible hours?

"All right," Bill says, hopping out of the car. "Let's get the little miss sorted."

Once I have Nova in the stroller, Bill stands with his hand on the door to the driver's side, watching us.

"Mr. Tucker suggested I wait here, just in case you're uncomfortable. Is that also what you'd like?"

The thought of Gage prewarning him that I was so far out of my comfort zone that I might flee makes me laugh a little, but I'm glad Bill can stay and that Gage already smoothed that path for me.

"Yes," I agree. "Please wait."

With a deep breath, I head toward the small crowd of people. They're chatting as though they've known each other forever, and I stop at the outside edge to take stock. I don't have a kid I can just let loose, as some parents seem to have done, and I haven't brought my sling to tie Nova to me. Indecision eats at me.

"Ember Whitten?" A lithe blond woman emerges from the crowd. She reminds me of a Rapunzel with her blond hair and big green eyes. "Maren said you might be coming today. I'm Rory." She extends her hand, and I realize I'm meeting the queen as though we're two normal people on the street.

I tuck my freshly straightened hair behind my ears, and then I meet her handshake. "I can't call you Rory, can I?"

"Of course you can." She gives me a gentle smile. "We're family adjacent, and I remember how lonely this island is when you feel like an outsider."

My shoulders sag with relief. "It *really* is."

"Do you have your phone?"

I dig it out of my diaper bag, and I pass it to her. She types something in and returns it to me. From my screen, I can see she added herself under Rory and texted herself from my phone.

"Now you're not so alone," she says. "There are all sorts of people here today. Who would you like to meet? People Celia Tucker would approve of, or people Maren Tucker would approve of?"

The fact that they aren't the same is interesting, and I can't decide if it's a test or an honest assessment of my tastes. I'm not sure either of them associate with people Gage would approve of, but maybe Rory doesn't know him as well as she knows Celia and Maren.

"Maren," I say. While I've talked to Celia more and she's been nice to me so far, I've heard enough of Gage's comments to realize her kindness probably has strings I haven't seen yet. Maren's kept her distance from me, Nova, and Gage, but she seems to have a good reputation on the island.

"Excellent choice," Rory says with a hint of a smile. "I'll introduce you to Nick. He brought Amelia today because Jules is working on some funding issue in Tanzania."

"Oh," I say, connecting the dots. "He's Brice's brother, and Nathaniel is working on a documentary with them."

"That's right. You're getting the lay of the land."

"Six degrees of separation from a Tucker is a real-life game in Bellerive."

"That is a quality reference," Rory says with a laugh. "You will find the Summersets and the Tuckers have their fingers in almost every pot. My husband is currently trying to convince the Tucker family that an arena that'll house an ice rink is a solid Tucker investment."

"How's that going?"

"About as well as you can imagine on a tropical island."

"What's with the ice rink?"

"I used to figure skate." She gives me a wry smile. "And my husband has a serious case of trying to make me as happy as possible to counteract all the negatives of this job and role on the island."

"Sounds like something Gage would do," I say without thinking.

She gives me a sideways glance. "Is that so?"

"Oh, it's not... Nothing like *that*."

"The ice rink and arena aren't a terrible idea. Alex has designs on luring a big league hockey team here or international skating competitions. Increase island-wide morale, boost tourism. We've got the land near the Olympic pool. Make it a whole sports complex."

"I'd love for Nova to learn how to skate," I admit. "It was one of the few things my parents did with us as kids. Took us to the free skate."

"See," Rory says with a grin. "I just need to encourage more foreigners to move here. Then we'll be able to teach all the locals how to skate."

"I'm only here for three more months," I say, thinking of Gage's offer weeks ago to look into other options. The thing is, I don't know where I'd live or what I'd do. He can't keep paying me to look after Nova. That arrangement already makes me squirmy, so I did some research on apartment rental prices. If I could branch out and be completely independent, I could stay. But living here on my own doesn't seem like it will happen in this lifetime. The wages versus the cost of living just don't make sense. The things I could buy, the life I could have in America with the money I'm saving, is worlds away from what I could afford with the same money here.

So I just need to find a way to cope with the timeframe I have. Nothing says I can't come back to Bellerive to visit.

"Make sure you use my number while you're here," she says as we draw closer to a tall, athletic man, who I'm pretty sure used to do some modeling. His brown hair and hazel eyes are certainly striking.

"Nick Summerset, this is Ember Whitten. She's Nova Tucker's aunt, and she's living with Gage Tucker at the moment while they get Nova settled."

He juggles the baby in his arms, switching her to his other arm while he extends one hand to me. "How old is Nova?"

Even though I get asked this question all the time, I always do a quick mental check, and the counting never fails to make me sad. "Just turned six months the other day."

"Amelia here is about five months. I think you've met my wife's sister, Posey? How are you finding Bellerive?"

"I have, yeah. She was great," I say, and then our conversation flows freely from there. It's clear, much like Gage's family, that Nick was raised on small talk and being able to make anyone feel at ease. When our conversation peters out, he gives me his wife, Julia's, number and then introduces me to a set of moms nearby. Rather than having me explain the awkward situation with my sister and Gage, he breezes through the facts in a straightforward way that doesn't allow for too much curiosity. It's a skill I would kill to learn.

By the time the playgroup is finished, I'm buzzing. My phone is full of new names and contacts, and I'm amazed, as Gage predicted, at the variety of people at Rory Summerset's gathering. While I did meet bankers and socialites, I also met a hairdresser on maternity leave and the wife of a car mechanic who waits tables at a diner in Tucker's Town.

When I get home, I pop Nova out of her car seat to get her ready for her nap, and I'm surprised to see Gage at the kitchen island. He must have parked his sports car in the garage. Each week it's been a different car, so I'm not even sure which one he has.

"Hey," I say.

"How was it?" he asks. "Decided to come home for lunch so I could hear all about it."

He's drinking another smoothie. I swear if Michelle didn't make meals for the fridge and freezer, Gage would starve. Smoothies are his go-to. I've never even seen him make a sandwich.

"It was *so* good," I say. "I met so many people." I flash my phone at him. "I have all these numbers now."

A hint of a frown floats across his face. "Like who? Let me see. Wouldn't want you getting in with any mean girls."

Like Abby?

I pass him my phone, open to the contacts, and he scrolls through the list.

"Was Hugh excited or mad that you sold all three houses within the first month?" I ask as he keeps scrolling. I really did talk to a lot of people.

"That's an interesting question." He glances up at me, lost in thought. "Now that you mention it, he was not thrilled. I think, despite the fact he hired me, he expects me to be a total fuckup."

My phone buzzes in his hand, and he peers down at it with a frown. "Dirk Churchill is excited to have met you?" He cocks an eyebrow at me. "What's this about?"

I can feel my face heating, and I snatch my phone back to read the message. "A dad I met at Rory's thing."

"I know who Dirk Churchill is. Banker. His parents should have named him Dick. So close to the truth, and yet, so far."

"He was very nice to me today."

"I bet he was." Gage takes a swig of his drink. "He's married."

"Was, yeah," I say, and I pass Nova to Gage while I start making her bottle. "Divorced now. He has kids. Little kids. They were cute."

"Did he ask you out?"

"He asked if I wanted to get coffee or dinner sometime."

"Hmm." Gage shifts Nova to his other arm and starts fussing over her, zooming her around and avoiding me. "Are you going to go?" he finally asks.

"Yeah, I guess?" I shake her bottle, and I hate how my heart is pounding, as though admitting to coffee is a cardinal sin between us. We aren't dating, and if Gage went out with someone, even if it was Abby, I'd just have to suck it up and watch him. We're roommates and sort of co-parents, but we aren't together in any sense.

He takes the bottle and tilts Nova back in his arms, holding her close with one hand and the bottle with the other. Watching him care for her is one of my favorite things to see, and it always completely centers me, as though there's nothing in the world better than seeing Gage with his daughter.

Every day, she looks more and more like a Tucker and less like Athena. Her light hair is darkening, and it seems like her eyes might even end up being a shade of blue. They definitely aren't brown.

"He has to be at least ten years older than you." Gage tears his gaze away from Nova. "That doesn't bother you?"

"All I do is hang out with you and Nova. Before you came along, she was my whole life for months. I just—I just want to live a little. Do something, anything, that's just for me."

He searches my face, and he nods, but he doesn't seem happy about it. When Nova finishes her bottle, he burps her and disappears into her bedroom to put her to sleep.

Before leaving the house, he grabs his glass and drains it. He slides it across the island to me, and he seems to think for a moment before he says, "Tonight, we live a little."

Then he's out the door before I can say anything, but I'm not sure whether I should be excited or terrified at his proclamation.

Chapter Eighteen

EMBER

When Gage summons baby reinforcements for the night, I never expect all three of his sisters to answer the call. But thirty minutes before we're supposed to leave, Maren, Sawyer, and Ava arrive on our doorstep.

Ava immediately sweeps me away, making a fuss over my hair and makeup and then flicking through my closet for the perfect outfit.

"My brother is taking you on a date," she says, holding up a green dress she watched me try on a few weeks ago before putting it back.

"It's not a date," I say. "It's a celebration. He did something Hugh didn't think he could do."

"Hell," Ava says with a laugh, "I didn't think he could do it either." She turns to me with a thoughtful expression. "I never would have thought Gage would be good at *any* of this."

"Any of what?"

"Living with a woman and not sleeping with her. You're not sleeping with him, are you?"

"No!"

"Not yet, huh?" She plucks a blue dress with an asymmetrical line out of the closet and hangs it up. "This one." She goes to the bed and sits down. "Or raising a kid. Holding down a consistent, steady job where he has to wear a suit every day."

He looks so good in those suits that every day I have to remind myself that developing a crush on Gage Tucker would be a colossal mistake. At some point, a man always lets you down. It's science or psychology or just the way the world works.

Besides, I can't think of one reason why someone like Gage Tucker—incredibly hot billionaire—would ever give someone like me a second glance. We aren't people who make sense together.

"A year ago, Gage was more likely to become someone's pool boy than he was to sell houses under tight timelines. Then it's like this switch flipped in him about six months ago, and he's just been steadily plodding toward a version of himself I would have never suspected he had in him."

I don't know what to say to that, but I am grateful for the Gage I'm living with. Other than tidying up after himself, and his inability to make even the simplest meal, he's been a thoughtful, caring partner who pulls his weight with Nova. His privilege shows, but it hasn't overwhelmed me so much that I can't relate to him.

I slip on the dress Ava picked out, and then she makes me stand in front of her while she checks my makeup and smooths my long hair.

"You are fucking gorgeous," Ava says. "Go make him beg for it."

"Ava," I say with a scandalized laugh. "We're not—it's not—"

"I'm not kidding. If he ever asks, make him beg. *Please*."

I give her arm a light slap and step around her, grabbing the clutch I made this week off the table by the door.

"Ohh." Ava takes the bag from my hand. "You made this?"

"Yeah," I answer, suddenly shy. It's burnt orange and pops next to the blue of my dress.

"I want one," Ava says, passing it back to me. "I'll be around this week to pick out my color. I'll be your first influencer, and together, we'll make each other famous." She winks at me before leading the way out the door.

In the front foyer, Ava waves to her sisters. "I'm off! Have fun."

"You're not staying to babysit?" I ask. Gage is nowhere in sight.

"God, no." She lets out a laugh. "I came to play dress-up. That's more my speed." Ava must see Gage behind me because something sly enters her expression. "On his knees, Em. Pleading."

"What is it you think I should be begging for?" Gage asks as he comes flush with my shoulder.

"Getting in her panties." She lets out an evil cackle at Gage's frustrated expression and then gives us a finger wave. "Toodles. Enjoy your date."

"I'd apologize for her, but..."

"You'd spend your whole life doing it?" I suggest.

He laughs and the sudden tension eases between us. "You look gorgeous, by the way," he says, and his hand skims across my lower back and waist.

Outside, a low-slung sports car I've never seen before sits, and Gage opens my door before sliding into the driver's seat.

"You ready to live it up?" he asks.

The answer should be yes, but the truth is, I really don't know.

The restaurant is all dim lighting and curved leather booths. Surprisingly realistic and oversized candles hang from the ceiling. Even though it's packed, the restaurant isn't noisy. The atmosphere is pretty and romantic and intimate—the opposite of something we should be doing together. My heart skips at the notion that Ava might be right, and I don't even know what to think about that.

Do I want this to be a date?

It would complicate things so, so much, but at the same time... I glance at Gage with his expertly tailored suit which highlights how well he takes care of his body. The idea of being with him is not nearly as repulsive as it once was, and if I'm completely honest, the real ick factor was my sister and had very little to do with him as a person. He's not so much the guy who slept with Athena as he's become Nova's dad. Which is the same in some ways, but also very different. Every day he moves farther away from someone she knew for one night, the fuckboy I saw that first day, and becomes the complicated man I'll have to associate with for all of Nova's life.

Gage orders us wine and then he goes through the menu, pointing out dishes he thinks I'd like, others he encourages me to try. When I'm indecisive, he orders sample platters of a bunch of things, even though nothing is listed as sample size on the menu we have. As Ava told me, the Tuckers make their own rules. Every time it happens, it never fails to stun me, but the waitress doesn't even bat an eye at his request.

"Do you come here a lot?" I ask before I can consider how that might sound.

"One of my favorites," he says. "I should have brought you here sooner. When you agreed to come to Bellerive, I promised myself that I'd be more observant than I normally am. That I'd notice if you were unhappy, which is why we got the sewing stuff, right? But then today, I realized I might have put on my blinders again." He searches my face from across the table. "Did I miss it? Are you really fucking miserable, and I missed it?"

My heart aches for a moment at how earnest he is, at how much the thought seems to bother him, and not for the first time, I consider how different my sister's life and fate might have been if he'd been a real part of her life. Tears fill my eyes.

"Oh shit," he mutters. "You are."

"No." I shake my head, and I will my tears away. "That's not it." I take a deep, shuddering breath. "Did my sister contact you at all? I mean, was I the first person to tell you about Nova?"

"I found out about Nova through Caitlin. Your sister never contacted me. Maybe she meant to and then she had her accident?"

"Maybe," I agree, though I know that's not true.

"How did you track me down?"

"I called every Tucker I could find online until someone gave me Caitlin's number. Then she confirmed she was your lawyer, and that seemed almost as good as getting you. At least you'd know." I hesitate for a beat. "Then I hoped you'd care."

He rubs his face and looks away. "My original plan was just to give your sister money and be done with it." His voice is rough, and he can't meet my gaze.

"I figured," I say, quietly. "The guy I met at the top of the stairs didn't seem that interested in being a dad. You changed quickly, though. You are a *great* dad."

"Do you think so?" He squints at me. "My parents were so hands-off that it's hard to know what 'good' looks like. And she's still so little. Other than the big smile and kicking feet that says she's happy to see me, I've got no clue if I'm doing anything right."

"My mom tried to be a good parent. As best she could. But my dad was so volatile. Unpredictable. Whether he was drinking or not, my father had two personalities, a little mean and fucking terrifying." A shiver runs through me at the memory of all the times I cowered behind a door, hoping not to be noticed, unlike my sister, who'd storm out like a lioness, fierce and protective. As a kid, it didn't seem like anything could keep her down.

"At least he won't be able to find you here," he says, taking a sip of his wine. "And I can make sure he can't get near you when you go home."

"You don't have to do that." Thinking about going back to America on my own only makes the sadness bubbling in me threaten to boil over.

"Nova connects us, Em. From now on, you need something, you call me. Today, tomorrow, years from now, doesn't matter."

He says it, but he can't mean it. It's easy to make grand gestures and proclamations when I'm sitting in front of him, when time and distance haven't made it possible for him to push me to the back of his mind. There's no Abby sitting on his lap telling him that I'm not *really* a Tucker. Tucker-adjacent doesn't make me part of the family.

And if that woman on his lap isn't Abby, it'll be someone like her who he'll be just as keen to see happy. I'm not Nova's mother. He doesn't have to have a relationship with me. With a single snip, he can cut me off from any and all contact.

"I don't understand how I keep saying the wrong thing." Gage tries to catch my gaze. "What did I say? Talk to me."

"You have no obligation to do anything for me, to keep me in Nova's life."

He leans back into the thick leather of the booth, and instead of contradicting me, he seems to really think about what I've said. "You think I'd cut you off at some point?"

"You could. That's all I'm saying."

"That's not *all* you're saying. Say what you mean."

"Fine." I take a deep breath. "I think if you get married or have another woman in Nova's life who's... who's like a mother figure for her, a partner for you, they might convince you that I'm not needed."

"They'd be wrong." He shrugs. "And I'd never agree."

The waitress brings our food, setting multiple platters on the table all around us. It's more food than I can imagine us eating, but Gage doesn't seem at all surprised by the excess.

There's no point in arguing with him about this. Neither of us will really know what he'll do until he's in that position. What I've found with people is that they can tell you anything you want to hear in the moment, only to realize later that they can't be or do or fulfill whatever claim they made. Words are easy.

He scoops up food off the plates to put on his, and as he does so, he explains to me the heat level and taste. For someone who doesn't cook, he's very specific about flavors, and I wonder if that's from eating at upscale restaurants most of his life, where the menu probably lists the notes people are meant to taste.

Once we both have full plates, he makes eye contact with me. "I get that you're in a difficult position. You don't have a legal right to Nova, but if you want that, we could probably figure something out. Draw up paperwork with Caitlin. I can give you that security, if you need it. You don't have to exist in her life on my word and honor—we're not in medieval England."

"You'd do that for me?"

"What makes you think there's anything I *wouldn't* do?" He glances at me before slicing through a piece of meat with his knife. "I haven't found anything yet."

A whoosh of something unexpected lights within me, and I stare at him across the expanse, unsure of exactly what this feeling is. Gratitude? That doesn't feel big enough for whatever this is. Gage is the only man I've ever met who understands that words aren't enough. That words are easy to give out, easy to change. I need concrete, stable actions to back up whatever is said.

"That would mean a lot to me," I say, barely able to get the words out of my throat where they're lodged beside a lump.

"Consider it done," he says. "I'll call Caitlin tomorrow and find out what can be finalized."

We eat in silence for a few minutes, mostly because I'm too overwhelmed to come up with something else to talk about. The guy sitting across from me is nothing like I expected, and in so many ways, everything I've needed. And that, the reality of that thought, is unbelievably scary. The only guarantee I'm getting is a spot in Nova's life, and I need to keep reminding myself that's all I want or need from him.

"After this," he says, "I want to take you somewhere else. Are you up for it?"

"Where?" I ask, patting my mouth with the napkin. Gage was right about the food. Everything from the chicken shawarma to the falafels to the tabbouleh to the soft baked pitas and hummus is delicious. If we're going somewhere else, I need to stop eating before my dress is straining at the seams.

"Wino Wine Bar," he says. "Posey and Brent are going tonight. Posey thinks you'll love it."

"We can't leave your sisters with Nova all night."

"Maybe not my sisters, plural. But Maren and Brice already agreed to watch her as late as we want."

"On a Tuesday?"

"Is that a yes?"

I scan his patient expression for a moment, indecision swirling. We already feel so much closer tonight than we have in a while, as though we've purposely stepped toward each other, outside the comfort zone we've established over the last month. Nothing about tonight is about business or Nova or any of the other topics we've established as safe over the last month. I should say no, go home, let the distance widen between us again.

Whether it's the wine or the way he's gazing at me with such open affection, as though my indecisiveness amuses him, my decision becomes clear.

"Yes," I say, "let's go."

Chapter Nineteen

EMBER

Bellerive has a thing for dimly lit, expensive experiences. Wino Wine Bar brims with deep reds, blacks, and grays. The leather furniture is plush, and I bet there's not a speck of pleather in the place, even though it often wears better and washes easier. If I hadn't been here for a month already, the opulence would stop me in my tracks the minute we emerge from a secret VIP hallway.

Gage takes my hand, and we weave through the crowded tables. Over the speakers, slower paced, sensual music plays. It's the kind of sound I'd hear coming from Athena's room whenever she had a boyfriend over once we moved in together.

"There they are," Gage says, and he raises his hand to wave to someone.

When we get to a curved booth, we're overlooking a long, wide dance floor that's crowded with couples. They all seem to be dancing a similar style that I do not recognize and feel vaguely scandalized watching.

I slide in beside Posey with Gage on the outside, across from Brent. Once all the introductions are done, I lean into Posey.

"Are they literally having sex on the dance floor?" I ask.

Posey throws back her head, clearly delighted. When her laughter fades to amusement, she says, "It's Bellerive's version of the bachata. Has a loose relationship to salsa, maybe? Full on grinding on the dance floor is what it becomes once everyone has had enough to drink. But on Tuesdays, they have a lesson starting at ten. I thought it might be fun for you to try it."

"By myself?"

She laughs again. "We'd all do it." She gestures to herself, Brent, and Gage. "You with Gage, me with Brent."

"I'm not sure dance-floor sex is the best idea for me and Gage," I say, and I realize I might have had a bit more wine with dinner than I realized.

Two more bottles of wine arrive at the table, already uncorked.

"It's a dance lesson," Posey says. "A lot of it will probably be individualized instruction." She glances at Gage who's busy chatting to Brent about something sports-related, might even be the feasibility of the arena being built. "Besides," Posey continues, "sexual tension is like the best part of a guy-girl friendship when you think the other person is hot. No chance of following through, just the delicious, delicious possibility."

Spoken how I imagine someone in a long-term committed relationship would view angst and heartache. It's probably a lot of fun to watch, like seeing Maren and Brice dance around each other on the TV weeks ago. As a spectator, the drama of will-they-won't-they was fun. I'm not as convinced that uncertainty is as delicious to experience. Angst is best enjoyed in small doses through someone else's reality.

"Let me live vicariously through you," she says with a wink.

"You could just find yourself a guy friend to have inappropriate thoughts about," I suggest as Gage pours me a glass of wine.

"Don't give her any ideas," Brent says, clearly having overheard me.

I flush, and Posey laughs. "Don't let him fool you. Brent is very, very secure." Posey flashes her engagement ring. "No other man has even slightly turned my head in years."

"But she really loves inserting herself into other people's romantic entanglements," Brent says, leaning closer to me. "Her own real-life reality TV."

I'm momentarily struck dumb at the implication there's anything going on between me and Gage. There isn't. For all I know, when he has to leave in the evenings to show a house, he's meeting other women.

Except I don't really believe that. It'd be easier if I did.

For the next hour, the wine flows, and Gage slips out at one point to check on Nova without me having to mention it. I didn't want to be the nervous one, but I've never left her for longer than a few hours, and every other time, Gage has been the one with her.

When he returns, he tells me that everything is good, and Brice and Maren are going to stay the night. One of the Tuckers owns Wino Wine Bar and there's a room above the bar we can crash in.

My stomach flutters with nerves at the idea of staying here with Gage tonight, but he doesn't seem bothered. Knowing how off my expectations have been so far, the "room" is probably a multistory apartment or a giant space where I can barely see Gage, let alone come close to touching him. We might be sharing, but not in the way my brain automatically assumed.

After a bottle of wine, the speaker crackles and a woman speaks over the microphone, inviting anyone to come to the dance floor who wants to learn the Bellerive Blue Bachata. Posey lets out a whoop and practically pushes Brent out of the booth. The house lights come up a little over the dance-floor area.

"You two," she says, her finger waggling between me and Gage. "Come on. No excuses. Let's have some fun!" She drags Brent down the small flight of stairs.

Gage glances at me, clearly hesitant. "Do you want to try it?"

"Do you?"

His eyes light with a mischievous glint. "Oh, sweetheart, I grew up here. I already know how to do it, and I do it *very* well."

"So you could teach me?"

"Oh yeah," he says with a cocky grin. "I can teach you. Probably more than you want to know." He grabs my hand and leads me out of the booth and down to the dance floor, on the opposite side of Posey and Brent.

The instructor starts talking about a shuffle step and a hip sway, and when I glance at Gage, I find he's already doing it effortlessly. He wasn't lying or being overly cocky. His movements are fluid and confident. My body heats in response, warmth pooling just below my stomach. Thankfully, the instructor goes slow enough that I can follow, even when I'm distracted by Gage's rotating hips beside me.

Next, we go through a back and forth step, a step tap, and then left and right turns. When I struggle with the turn movement, Gage stops what he's doing to walk me through it slower.

"Imagine it's all happening on a line." He gestures beside us. "Shoulders start in the opposite direction you're going to turn in, then you turn"—he rotates slowly—"one-two, step, three, and then four brings you back to where you began."

I follow his lead, and it makes a little more sense. The instructor suggests we pair up, and Gage draws me close without hesitation. She goes through each set of eight counts over and over until I think I might actually pass as somewhat competent. I'm a little out of breath by the time she calls the last beat.

"That's it for our lesson tonight, folks," she says. "Next week, we'll go over the front and back crossovers and work on some partner-based turns."

"They do this every week?" I ask, and when I glance up at Gage, he's staring at me as though I'm the most interesting person in the room.

"Sounds like it. You want to come again?"

"Could we?" I ask.

"We can do whatever you want," he says.

"We can't ask your sisters to babysit every week."

"Pay enough money, and someone will take the job." His eyes gleam with a familiar certainty. "Not something you need to worry about. You want to learn how to dance on Tuesdays, we'll be here."

When our gazes connect, the same rush as earlier floods through me, and I feel like I should say something, but I don't have the words.

Around us, the lights dim again, and a slowed down, sensual version of a popular song spreads across the dance floor.

"Want to put your new skills to the test?" Gage asks, his voice rough. He holds out his hand for me to take.

Yes and no. I bite my lip, but I take his hand. He draws me tight against him, molding my body to his, so I'm straddling one of his legs. This is much closer and tighter than when we were learning a minute ago.

If I want to come back again, I need to be okay with the close contact. Learning the steps solo would get boring, and as erotic as watching this dance was from up above, I can't imagine how it's going to feel on the dance floor with Gage with no instructor calling the beats, taking up space in my brain.

Combustible. Sinful. Downright dangerous.

"Stay relaxed," he says, his hand on my lower back. "The more relaxed you are, the easier it is for me to lead."

Easy to say, so hard to do when he smells like expensive cologne and moves like a man built to deliver orgasms. He catches the beat, and then we're off. His lips are close to my ear, and he keeps time, counting so low that only I can hear. But it gives me something to focus on beyond the way his athletic frame feels against my more petite body.

He's a good dancer, a really good dancer, and I wonder why he hasn't had me here every night, hypnotizing me with his moves.

Song after song, we dance. Time loses all meaning, the wine buzz I developed starts to wear off, and I'm breathing heavily. But I don't want this connection to end. Every time he wants to do something more complicated, he whispers the next direction in my ear, and a shiver races down my spine.

Dancing with him is magic, and it makes me wonder where else he'd lead, how else he could help me to achieve maximum pleasure. I've never been able to move on a dance floor like I am tonight, and I'm sure he's the reason. His hand is on my back, guiding me, drawing me close and letting me drift away, but he's always in control.

I've been avoiding eye contact because I can feel myself getting progressively more turned on. I'm absolutely soaked, and it's not from sweat. If he suggested it, even hinted at it, I think I'd ruin everything tonight for a chance to be skin-to-skin with him. And that's not like me, which should be terrifying, but it's exhilarating. The idea of feeling these things for any guy has seemed like an impossibility before. Even these past few weeks with Gage, I could acknowledge he was hot, but I didn't necessarily want to sleep with him. When his hand slips below the curve of my waist to my ass, I don't just tolerate it, I want it. I imagine his hand going further, sliding down, underneath my dress, teasing between my thighs to feel how much I want him, how eager I am for him to touch me.

When I dare to glance up at him, he's staring at my lips, his eyes dark with the same desire I feel coursing through me.

"Fuck, Em," he mutters.

And I know exactly what he means because I'm also on the cusp of losing control. Whatever sense of right and wrong I might have had before where he's concerned has been obliterated by so much close contact and too much alcohol.

I lean into him, and our noses graze, our lips a hair's breadth apart. His hand slides into my hair, but instead of drawing me closer, he seems to be maintaining the small distance.

"I'm not a good enough man to say no, Em. If this happens, you have to mean it."

I want it to happen right now, in the moment, but I don't know if I'll mean that tomorrow. If I'll wake up and wish I hadn't thrown away my safety and comfort. Because that's what Gage is right now. He's comfortable and safe and stable.

If I kiss him, if we do what my body is begging to do, none of that will be true anymore. Men you sleep with are none of those things.

I suck in a sharp breath and back away. "I have to go to the bathroom."

To my retreating back, he calls, "I'll meet you back at the table."

He doesn't seem to mind that I teased him, ground myself against him for song after song, and there won't be any follow-through. The few times I went out with Athena, guys would try to hit on me, and when I didn't respond how they expected, they'd call me a tease or frigid or a bitch.

In the bathroom, I brace my hands on the counter, and I stare at myself in the mirror. A stall door opens, and the last person I want to see anywhere struts out. She drops her clutch on the counter and examines herself in the mirror with a critical eye.

"He's always had a thing for boring, plain girls—like your sister," Abby says, taking lipstick out of her small clutch and uncapping it. "Never takes him long to get his fill. One night. Maybe two. Nobody knows more tricks in bed than me. Someone like you could never satisfy him, not for long."

I just stare at her in the mirror because I don't have the energy to respond.

"Enjoy it while you can," she says, and then she coats her lips before pressing them together. "It won't last beyond your time here. You and your body are a convenience, and when it's not convenient, he'll come back to what he really wants." Then she grabs her bag off the counter and she's out the door before I can even formulate a complete sentence.

Like every other time a mean girl has said something shitty, a thousand responses come to me the minute the door clicks closed. Whether anything happens between me and Gage is beside the point—I'm not going anywhere. Gage is going to make sure I have a right to be in Nova's life forever, but I guess bragging about that before it happens wouldn't be wise. I have no idea how much sway Abby has over Gage. It doesn't seem like much because he never talks about her, but it could also mean the opposite. He doesn't talk about her because it hurts too much to do it. I know that feeling all too well.

Once I've gathered myself, I leave the bathroom and find Gage at the table, sipping a glass of wine. Brent and Posey are nowhere in sight.

"They're gone," Gage says. "Stay? Go?"

"Go," I say with decisiveness. One close call with a bad decision is enough for me, and if I keep drinking and keep dancing, I can't be sure I'd have the willpower to resist the call of my body. Even now, as I watch Gage while he drops a tip on the table, hands me my clutch, and takes my hand, my body is sure of what it wants.

Him, all over me. Between my legs, the length of him thrusting into me in the same way and in the same rhythm as he dances. The ache between my thighs is almost unbearable. I'd probably come within seconds if he touched me.

He seems completely oblivious to the dirty thoughts I have on repeat as he leads me to a coded door near the back. Then we're climbing a narrow set of stairs. At the top, there's a three-piece bathroom and a double bed. The room is not huge; it's tiny. Neither of us could sleep on the floor, even if we wanted to.

"Did you know this was so small?" I squeak out.

"Yeah," he says, and he glances at me over his shoulder. "There are extra toothbrushes and mini tubes of toothpaste under the sink, if you want one."

I put a hand over my mouth, assuming he means that I need one.

He lets out a little laugh. "It's fine, Em. Your breath smells fine. It's just a courtesy for anyone who stays here, that's all."

I use the bathroom first, and when I come out, Gage has stripped down to his boxers. He hands me his shirt, and his muscles ripple.

"I doubt that dress will be comfortable to sleep in." Then he goes into the bathroom without another word.

While he's gone, I frantically strip down into his shirt and my underwear, and then I get under the covers, just as he's coming out.

He clicks off the overhead light with confidence, and the room is pitch-black. There is a window in the bathroom, but there's nothing in here. The bed doesn't dip with his arrival, but I can sense he's closer, and I catch a whiff of his minty breath. My heart thrums in my chest.

"Did you set an alarm?" I ask. The last thing we need is to oversleep.

"Yeah," he says, but he doesn't elaborate. "I hope I didn't..." He sucks in a sharp breath. "If I made you uncomfortable, I'm sorry. If you don't want to do this next Tuesday, I get it."

I don't exactly know what he means and why I'd have been uncomfortable. I was practically climbing his leg on the dance floor. If anyone should be sorry, it should probably be me. Even now, in my head, I'm going through all sorts of scenarios that would ease the ache between my legs, and all of them involve him touching me.

And the thing is, I know I could ask, and I know he'd do it. There's not a doubt in my mind.

But I also know that if I ask, we can't come back from that. And Abby's words are too fresh in my mind. Even if I don't believe her, it still feels like there might be a grain of truth in her claims. Once or twice and he'd be tired of me, and we'd have created all this weirdness between us for nothing.

"I want to come back next Tuesday," I say. "Maybe just without the alcohol."

"Those lowered inhibitions are a bitch."

Not the word I would have used. That one I'd reserve for his ex-girlfriend in the bathroom, but she's a problem for another day.

"Hey," he says, "can I... I liked being close to you. Would you mind if I held you for a bit? I promise I won't let it get weird."

I know what I should say, but I also know that word isn't in my vocabulary with him tonight. There's only one word I can say. "Yes."

"Turn your back to me," he says, and his hand slides across my hip, and when I'm on my side, he drags me across the bed and tucks me into his embrace.

It's the coziest, safest place I've ever been in my life, and I breathe a deep sigh of relief and satisfaction. Then I burrow deeper, and he chuckles against my ear.

"Cold?" he murmurs.

"No," I whisper. But I can't explain how I feel.

The darkness envelops us, and his big hand spans my rib cage. My instinct is to wiggle, to get his hand to either drift lower or higher, land somewhere I want him to touch, take that safety and satisfaction and burn it to the ground with my desire.

"Can I ask you a favor I've got no right to ask?" Gage says, his voice hushed.

"Anything," I say, and I mean it. At this point, he could ask me for the moon, and I'd do my best to deliver.

"Don't go for coffee or dinner or whatever with Dirk Churchill. You can do so much better than him."

"Okay," I say, unable to get anything else past my lips.

He tightens his hold on me, and then we both lie there in the dark until his breathing evens out, and his arms grow slack, but even then, I don't move away.

Chapter Twenty

GAGE

Ember and Nova have been in my life for two months, and I can't really remember a time when they weren't. It's the weirdest thing about the before-Nova and the after-Nova time period. When I look back, I don't recognize the person I was before, the guy who took weeks to show up for his daughter, to show up for Ember.

This guy goes to Wino Wine Bar on Tuesdays with Nova's aunt who doubles as a nanny and tries not to get a hard-on that lasts for days. *This* guy gets paperwork drawn up to have said aunt exist in Nova's life through the end of time—invitations to birthday parties and other special events are now a guarantee. *This* guy sells low-and-mid-income properties, even though his boss promised him bigger fish.

Of all the things this guy has become, that last one is the only one that's causing me to lose sleep. The lack of sleep is a side effect of me constantly thinking about or analyzing other sales agents' success in the company and grilling them on their divisions, sales histories, problems they've faced and overcome. Whatever morsel they'll feed me, I chew on the details.

Those first three sales made me hungry, so fucking hungry that I'll work any angle to sell the properties I have, to land more, and to outwork every other member in the company. No showing is too early or too late. No house is too big of a project. When I pick up a listing I don't know what to do with, I take Ember there and we rearrange furniture, tweak the décor, declutter. She'll listen to me bounce ideas off her at all hours of the day or night—on the phone, via text, or after Nova has gone to sleep and we're watching some shit reality TV show that she consumes like her favorite candy. She's my secret weapon, and sometimes it feels like I would never be where I am without her.

If I left my real estate education to Hugh, he'd have me on a trickle feeder, the smallest morsel at a time. Whether Hugh senses I could be better than him or he's just trying not to overwhelm me, I don't know.

But I can guess.

Hugh doesn't seem like the type to arm his competition, and while it might take me years to truly stand toe to toe with him, I'm learning fast. So fucking fast that it gives me a jolt of pride every time I realize how much I already know. Turns out I might have sucked in college because I didn't care enough to succeed, not that I was dumb. That truth might seem obvious to some people who know me, but it's a revelation to me. I've always been the slacker in the family, the one who couldn't get things right. The one my siblings had to rescue from poor or impulsive decisions. Not anymore.

Parenting is the same—every day I feel more confident with Nova. She's starting to hold her own bottle, pull herself up on furniture, and she's so excited and happy to see me. To her, I matter, a lot. It's strange but empowering to realize I'm one of Nova's core people around which her world revolves, that I'll always be that person.

Ember has been working on getting her to say "Da-da," and she babbles away, almost but not quite getting it. I've been able to slip into a role I never thought I wanted like it's a well-worn shirt. Fits me in all the right places.

My life is fuller and richer than it has ever been. But sometimes I look at Ember when we're talking about a real estate deal, or when she's at her sewing machine, lip between her teeth, or when we're sitting on the couch wading through reality TV options, and I can't help thinking, *I wish…* And I don't even know what I'm wishing for. It's not a sentence I'm capable of finishing because if Dirk Churchill isn't good enough for her, there's no chance I am either. Cut from similar cloth. Incapable of being consistently faithful. I wasn't built for long-term, monogamous relationships. She deserves so much better than the crumbs I could offer. Sure, I could take care of her financially, but I'd never be able to be everything she needs. Ember is nothing like Abby. I'd break Ember's heart with my restlessness, which is the last thing I'd ever want to do.

But god, what I wouldn't give, what I wouldn't do for a taste. Our bachata nights are absolute torture. She's so close it would be nothing to kiss her or to touch her in all the ways that I want, to drag her up the coded staircase and take her on that double bed, to fuck her until she cries out my name and she digs her nails into my shoulders with her own release. There's no doubt in my mind that sex with her would be phenomenal, especially after weeks of dance foreplay. We move so fluidly together on the dance floor now that I can't help thinking about how easily it would translate to the bedroom.

I want her more than I've ever wanted another woman, but I also can't imagine giving in to that desire. Too many things would crumble around us. I can't *just* sleep with her, and that's all we'd ever be able to be—fuck buddies. Given that she's only slept with one person, I can't see casual sex working for her, even if the thought is such a pleasurable mess to consider. I'd pat myself on the back if Ember said yes, while also wanting to drive a knife into my chest for giving into my basest instincts.

"Gage!" Ember calls, drawing me out of my circling thoughts.

I pop my head out of my bedroom with the tie I just picked out in my hand. My dress shirt is still open. In the hallway, she's in her knee-length teal silk robe, and I swallow. Her hair and makeup are done, but I can only guess what's under that robe. One tug on the belt, and I wouldn't have to wonder anymore. *Don't think about her naked. Don't think about her naked.*

"Yeah?" I ask, my voice strangled.

"I don't know what to wear. I'm freaking out. Are you sure you want me to go? I can just—I'll stay here and look after Nova. We can cancel Michelle."

"We're not canceling," I say. I'm paying triple time on a Saturday night because Ember didn't want me to hire anyone she didn't know, and asking my siblings to watch Nova each Tuesday wasn't a good long-term solution. Enter Michelle—the housekeeper-and-chef-turned-sometimes-nanny who has been happily picking up the slack and the extra cash. She's out in the living room with Nova right now while we get ready. The time for canceling was hours ago.

I grab her hand and lead her back into her bedroom. There are clothes strewn all over the bed, which isn't like her. She doesn't like a mess, and since she moved in, I've realized that I'm actually quite messy.

"Is the problem really the clothes?" I ask with a frown.

"No," she admits. "I won't know anyone, and I won't fit in. This quarter high profit celebration thing isn't meant for me. It's for you and all the other people who know how to sell stuff. I can't even figure out how to set up a basic website to sell my bags."

"I told you I could hire someone to do that."

"I'll figure it out," she says, a stubborn set to her chin.

"You've been my key person," I say. "You're the reason I've been able to sell houses no one else wants quickly and for good prices. You belong at this party more than lots of other people."

"Your cousin doesn't employ me."

"People are bringing guests. I asked."

She stares at me, and she worries her lip.

"What?" I ask.

"A guest... Like?"

"I don't know. A husband or wife or partner or whatever." I riffle through the clothes still in her closet and take out a red dress. It's a one-shouldered, floor-length, high-slit masterpiece that looks both classy and sexy. Every time I look at her tonight, I'll regret picking this out. I flip the hanger around for her to see.

"That doesn't seem like too much?"

"No such thing." I glance at her over my shoulder. "Hugh said *formal*."

"Okay," she says, seeming to gather herself up. "Okay." She runs her hands along her body, as though she's mentally figuring out how to put on the dress.

I need to get out of here before this gets awkward and really fucking hot. Every fiber of my being is into the idea of viewing what's under her robe, having the privilege of seeing her drop it to the floor and step into this red dress with confidence.

The night we spent above Wino Wine Bar and our Tuesday dance sessions have given me a sample of what her body feels like under my hands, but I'd really like to see the proof with my eyes.

"I'll meet you at the front entrance when you're ready," I say, unable to disguise the gruffness of my voice while I pass her the hanger before heading for the door.

"Gage," she says, stopping me in my tracks.

I turn back and the uncertainty on her face almost makes me tell her she doesn't have to go, that she doesn't have to push herself this far out of her comfort zone just because I want her there. Maybe it's selfish, but I really feel like she's the reason I'm not just surviving but thriving.

"You'll stick with me, right? At the party. You won't wander off and leave me?"

"With you in that dress? I'll be like your second skin." I flash her my wolfish smile before remembering that I shouldn't use that one with her.

"Good." She flushes. "I just... I'm more comfortable on Tuesdays at the palace, but I'm not one of you. There are so many things I have no experience with, and I get tripped up when people assume I do."

"I won't leave you alone," I say, "but I also want you to know that if anyone makes you uncomfortable or is an outright asshole to you, tell me. I can't fix what I don't know about."

"No one has done it on purpose, at least not at the palace. It just happens. They talk about some exotic vacation or some expensive wine or a hotel they assume I've stayed at or know about. Because I live here with you, they think I'm rich. Before I came here, the craziest place I'd ever been was Denver."

"Denver?" I ask with a hint of amusement that I can't hide.

"Yeah," she says with a bit of a laugh. "So you can imagine how those conversations go."

"If you could go anywhere, where would you go?"

"You're going to think I'm a cliché."

"Try me."

"Paris." She gives me an impish smile. "Fashion." She shrugs.

Makes sense. She's been shopping with Ava a few times, and each time she comes home with more clothes that fit her in ways I'd rather they didn't. A walking temptation.

Lately, the two of them have been conspiring over the bags Ember makes. Last week, Ava said she'd put her own hunt for investors on hold in order to make Ember famous. My sister is half bullshit and half wishful thinking, so it's hard to know whether her lofty ideas are even remotely possible. From what I've seen, Ember has a good eye for detail, and I can understand how that would translate to making her bags, even if I don't follow that market.

"What about you?" she asks, the change in subject making her noticeably more relaxed and happier.

"My favorite place to go?" There isn't anywhere I've really wanted to travel to that I haven't been. The luxury of a lot of time, little supervision, and an endless well of cash.

"Sure," she says, and a broad smile blooms.

"Switzerland. Skiing. There's a chalet I've rented there with some friends. Worth the cost. I'll take you there sometime."

"I actually know how to ski," she says, preening a little with surprising confidence. "My parents lived in Breckenridge when I was a kid. Skiing was one of the few things my parents did with us. Any of my happy memories happened in the winter."

I lean against the doorframe and assess her, wondering if she'll tell me the truth. "You any good?"

"Maybe you'll find out someday," she says, and there's a glint in her eyes that tells me she's likely very good. That hint of confidence is rare, but I love catching glimpses of it, as though there's another version of her living inside the one who is perpetually uncertain. What I've found as we've transformed more houses together is that Ember's confidence escalates substantially with experience. When she walks into a house now, she's already three steps ahead of me, mentally tearing the place apart and rebuilding a better version in her head.

Each week on the dance floor at Wino Wine Bar is the same. A flirty brashness is emerging that makes me a little nervous I'll be on my knees begging her for *something* by the end of these four months.

Witnessing the changes in her makes me want to give her every opportunity, every experience, and watch her confidence unfurl. She's become one of the greatest blessings of my life.

"I have no doubt I'll find out all kinds of things about you someday," I say, and this time when I give her my wolfish grin, it's intentional. Every once in a while, I can't help flirting with the line between us. Concrete or sand? A stupid subconscious compulsion whenever she flashes her self-assurance.

"Your default setting is flirty." Her cheeks turn a pretty pink.

"Does that bother you?"

"No, I know you don't mean any of it." She turns away from me, and she presses the dress I picked out to her middle.

I mean every word, but it's better if I let her believe I don't. If she thought I was serious, things would get out of control pretty quickly. The attraction is there, and I'm sure she feels it too.

"I'll let you finish getting ready." I push off the doorframe, and I leave before I say something I shouldn't.

Chapter Twenty-One

EMBER

One of the things I love about Gage is that when he makes a promise, he keeps it. From the minute we arrive at the swanky, upscale ballroom, Gage's hand is on the small of my back, and he takes me with him everywhere. He introduces me to everyone as a member of his team, and he doesn't once mention that I'm Nova's aunt or that I'm also his nanny. His claim elevates my status in a way I don't expect, and it's strange to have his colleagues give me an appraising glance that has nothing to do with what I'm wearing. Though I am aware that my red dress isn't exactly wallflower attire, and I have received a few leering glances from men Gage hasn't taken me to meet.

Like the dark blond man who is staring at me from across the ballroom. He's a perfect example of someone I'd like to avoid. Whenever our gazes catch, he trails his eyes along my figure in a way that makes me uncomfortable. The male gaze isn't new to me. From working in bars and restaurants at sixteen when Athena and I ran away, I know what it's like to be objectified, and it's why I eventually started working at the fabric store. A lot less money and no tips, but at least I felt safe there. The older women who tended to frequent the store were kind, almost motherly. I never worried that some guy's hands would land in places I didn't want. The guy across the room, whoever he is, is a predator. A wolf, and he's got no use for the sheep's clothing.

"Who's that?" I whisper in Gage's ear when there's a break in the conversation.

"Who?" Gage asks, glancing around.

"Across the room. Dark blond. Tall. Kind of intimidating," I say.

"That guy?" Gage tips his head in the man's direction.

"Yeah."

"That's Hugh," Gage says, taking my hand. "I should introduce you."

A protest forms on my lips, but I don't voice it. We've talked about Hugh enough that I know Gage respects him and aims to be like him. As we get closer, I pray my instincts are wrong, but I can't bring myself to meet Hugh's gaze, just in case I'm right. I grip Gage's hand a little tighter, and he leans close to me, his lips skimming my ear. "You don't need to be nervous. He's not as scary as he seems."

Spoken like a man who's never been afraid of anyone, who's never cowered in the corner of a room, or tried to make themselves small so they'd go unnoticed. Most of those experiences came courtesy of my father, but not all of them.

"Hugh," Gage says as we approach. "This is Ember. She's the one who's been working some magic on those hard-to-move properties."

Under my lashes, I glance up, and Hugh's hand is extended. I take it without making eye contact. There's already an air around him that's setting me on edge, causing something inside me to want to flee. My fight, flight, or freeze instinct is on high alert, the one I haven't felt creeping along my spine since the incident at the department store that first week. There, I could flee, but when the fear is strong enough, I know that fleeing isn't my first instinct.

"Gage's secret weapon," Hugh says dryly.

"Oh, I..." I shake my head, letting my dark hair partially obscure my face.

"False modesty," Hugh says with a scoff. "I've got no time for that. He tells people you're the reason he's made any sales."

When Gage encourages me to accept a compliment or stand up for myself, it feels supportive. It's amazing what tone and circumstance can do. Hugh is dismissive, patronizing.

"Perhaps I should be luring you over to my team," Hugh says, and I catch the glint of his teeth out of the corner of my eye. "I could teach you a few new things."

Gage tenses beside me, and his hand on the small of my back circles my waist, landing on my hip. "Maybe she'd be the one teaching you," he says. "After all, we've sold properties your best agents couldn't move."

"Women are exceptional at optical illusions," Hugh says, and his tone suggests there's a private joke between him and Gage. "Window dressing is their specialty."

When I glance up at Gage, he doesn't seem to be in on whatever Hugh is implying, in fact, he seems annoyed.

"You know what I've got no time for?" Gage asks, the arrogant tone that makes me want to throw up my hands with a *hell yes* and also hide my face with an *oh my god, what are you going to say?* is out in full force.

"This should be good," Hugh says, trying to make eye contact with me, as though we're suddenly on the same side.

I inch closer to Gage.

"People who don't have the stones to say what they mean."

"I said exactly what I meant," Hugh says. "I rely on the intelligence of the people around me to be able to keep up."

"Where's the bathroom?" I ask.

Gage has had a couple of drinks since we arrived, and my impression of Hugh is that he wouldn't let Gage win anything, especially an argument, if it didn't benefit him to do so. It's pretty clear that Hugh is a misogynistic asshole, and I can't help feeling a little sad that he's someone Gage respects. Hugh might be a great businessman, but he's clearly a shit person.

"That way," Hugh says with a brief finger point across the crowded space.

I weave through the crowd in the middle of the room and then the tables on the outskirts that are set for dinner. Hopefully, by the time I get back, Gage will have decided that getting into a tit-for-tat with Hugh isn't the best use of his time.

As I'm nearing the bathroom, someone comes over the announcements telling people to take their seats for dinner. I slip down the hallway and into the bathroom where other women are fixing their makeup in the mirror.

When I come out of the stall, the bathroom is deserted. I take my time washing my hands, and I check my phone to see if Gage sent me the table number. I breathe a sigh of relief when I see he has. I text him back to let him know I'll be at the table in a minute. Then I stare at myself in the mirror, wishing I felt more comfortable, more confident in this type of atmosphere.

At least Nova will grow up in these rooms with these people. She won't feel like she doesn't belong or can't fit in.

As I approach the table, a shiver of unease races through me. Gage is at the same table as Hugh, and the only empty seat is between the two of them. Gage on one side of me and Hugh on the other. I slide into my seat, and Gage introduces me to Hugh's wife, Alice, a bubbly, busty blond who seems like an odd fit for the real estate mogul.

The waiters and waitresses come around to pour wine, and when I choose the red, Hugh leans into me, his hand sliding along my thigh.

"You have good taste in wine," he murmurs.

I try to shift away from him, but the chair doesn't move, and I don't want to make a scene. "Thank you," I say, avoiding eye contact.

Gage is next to me, but the man on his right is monopolizing his attention, constantly drawing him into conversations about everything from real estate trends to sports to going to college in California. Through the soup, salad, and main course, Gage checks in with me occasionally, but he's focused elsewhere, not really paying attention.

Meanwhile, every chance Hugh gets, he leans into me to make some throwaway comment, and his hand creeps along my thigh. At one point as the main course is being delivered, I try to brush him off, but he squeezes my leg so hard in response that I wonder if I'll have a mark. His message is clear—unless I want to make a scene, force Gage into an awkward position, I have to put up with his behavior.

"You know," Hugh says, his fingers sliding under the slit in my dress, "when you're ready for a real man, I can give you things he can't."

"You're married," I say, my lips barely moving. There's so much conversation happening around us at the table that no one seems to have noticed how Hugh is behaving. Or maybe he always behaves this way, and they're used to it. No one has clocked how uncomfortable he's making me.

"Whatever you do for him, I'll pay you triple if you fulfill my needs instead."

"Your wife is right there."

"Alice and I have an arrangement. When I want something, I take it," he says, and his fingers try to wiggle their way into places they shouldn't. "And I know you could use the money."

I grab Gage's hand, and I squeeze it. He immediately shifts toward me, full focus. Hugh withdraws his hand from my leg and picks up his wineglass as though he wasn't just propositioning me at the table, treating me like an object to be bought and sold.

"You okay?" he asks.

"No," I say, and I'm struggling to hold in my rage or my tears or both. "I might leave early."

He searches my face for a beat. "You not feeling well?"

I can't tell him here at the table, and I'm not sure if I should tell him at all. As long as I can avoid Hugh for the next couple of months, it'll be fine. There's no need for me to ruin things for Gage.

"I just want to go home," I whisper.

"Then we'll go home," he says without hesitation. He pushes his chair back, and he shakes hands with the guy next to him.

"That was a genuine offer, Ember," Hugh says, but his smile is playful, as though the last hour was all a joke. "Whenever you're ready for a real job, let me know."

"You trying to steal her away?" Gage goes along with the joking tone, and I hate how easy it is for me to second-guess what happened, how Hugh made me feel.

"Giving her a better offer," Hugh says with a laugh. "Competition is good, right?"

Gage glances at me, and I flash him a tight smile, unable to relax. He doesn't respond directly to Hugh, but instead leads me out of the ballroom and toward the parking garage.

In the elevator, he keeps scanning me, as though he knows something isn't right but he isn't sure where to start.

In the car, we're quiet for most of the ride until Gage says, "You didn't have a good time?"

I hesitate to answer because up until we were at the table with Hugh, it wasn't so bad. It was nice to meet the people I'd heard Gage talk about, and I enjoyed being the center of his attention. But I also know I never want to be in that position again, where Hugh feels entitled to my body.

"No," I say, staring out the window. "I didn't."

"Sorry," he says, and he runs a quick hand along my leg. "I won't ask you to go again."

At the house, Nova is already in bed, and while Gage makes small talk with Michelle, I get changed into my sleep shorts and a tank top. Too wound up to sleep, I riffle through the freezer for any leftover desserts that Michelle sometimes makes.

"Hey," Gage says from behind me, and I jump, more on edge than I realized.

I whirl around, my hand pressed over my racing heart.

"What's going on with you?" he asks.

I shake my head and turn back to the freezer. Even if I told him, he wouldn't believe me. Why would he? Hugh made the whole thing sound like a joke, a playful exchange between us instead of the sexual harassment happening under the table, the implication that I'd prostitute myself for money.

"Em," Gage says, coming closer.

He's in sleep pants that hang low on his hips, but all I want to do is curl into him, feel that safety and security I did the night we slept above Wino Wine Bar.

He points to my thigh, and I shift away from him quickly, closing the freezer door.

"Why do you have a red mark there?" He crouches down to examine my leg, and his touch is so gentle it causes tears to spring to my eyes. "Did you bang it on something?" But his hand seems to find the finger imprints without me having to say anything. "Did someone do this to you? What the fuck?" He rises to his full height, and his gaze bores into mine. "Tell me who did that."

Instead of answering, I bite my lip and hold his gaze. If I tell him, I can't take it back. What can he even do? Hugh is his boss, owns the company, and he's Gage's ticket to the career he wants.

"You don't want to know," I say.

His eyebrows fly up. "I don't want to know? Yeah, I fucking do. Nobody, and I mean nobody, lays a hand on you. Not on my watch."

Telling him is pointless.

"It's fine," I say. "I'm just not going to any more of your work events, okay?"

"Em," he says, his voice rough as he slides his hands into my hair, and his forehead brushes mine. His eyes are closed. "Who did it?"

"You *know*," I say, because it feels like he does, as though he's slotted the pieces together, and he just wants me to confirm it.

"Hugh."

"At the table," I say. "All through dinner, he kept putting his hand wherever he wanted under the table. When I tried to brush him off, he did that. Squeezed my leg. A warning, or proving a point, I guess." My voice is thick with tears. "Unless I wanted to make a scene, what was I going to do?"

He presses a kiss to my forehead, and then he draws me into his chest, wrapped up tight in his embrace. Anger vibrates off him, barely contained.

"I know there's nothing you can do," I say, "and it's okay."

He lets out a chuckle that has no humor. "I don't know what I'm going to do, but *nothing* isn't an option."

"I can avoid him," I say, but I burrow deeper into Gage's embrace. Other than our Tuesday dance sessions and when he grabs my hand to lead me from place to place, we don't touch for any length of time, and I like it a little too much when we linger.

In one swift movement, Gage sweeps me into his arms, so I'm cradled against his chest.

"What are you doing?" I ask, breathless. Heat pools in my belly. An unwanted touch is a slow freeze of fear and confusion, but a wanted one is a forest fire fueled by desire.

"Taking care of you," he says, and he carries me to the couch. "He did this shit right in front of me, Em. And I just…" He shakes his head as he sets me down, and he leans over me, one arm on either side of my head.

For the billionth time, I scan his concerned expression, and I can't get over how handsome he is. Chiseled features, deep blue eyes, and hair like midnight. It's truly unfair for anyone to be this attractive on top of so many other good qualities.

"One way or another, he'll feel the pain he inflicted on you." He eases a strand of my hair behind my ear. "Anyone goes after you, they go after me. Always."

A tingly sensation sprouts in my chest and blooms outward. I run my thumb along his cheek, and the moment charges between us. It would be so easy to draw him down, mold my body to his. I'm aching to solidify the connection between us. Never in my life have I felt such a strong physical and emotional pull to a man. There's nothing I wouldn't do for him, and that's a bit terrifying.

He edges closer, slowly, as though testing the waters, and I slide my fingers along the fine strands at the back of his head. He rubs his nose against mine, ever so gently.

"Nobody hurts you and gets away with it," he says, his voice gruff but hushed. He shifts slightly, and his lips graze my forehead again. "I'll get you some ice."

Ice seems like overkill for a red mark on my leg, but being taken care of sends another thrill down my spine. Most of my days are spent caring for Nova while juggling my handbag designs and my realty commitments with Gage. We don't usually take care of each other so much as we take care of ourselves.

He comes back with a soft ice pack and presses it against my leg. When I shiver, he scoops a blanket off the back of the couch, lays it over me, and then sits near the end, taking my feet and setting them on his lap. He passes me the remote, and while I search for something on the TV, he's on his phone.

In moments like this, I'm always surprised at how easy things are between us. He's being abnormally affectionate and attentive, but none of it feels weird or forced. He wants to do all of this, and I want to let him.

His fingers are flying so quickly over the keys that my curiosity piques. "What are you doing?"

"Plotting," he says, and when his intense gaze meets mine a little frisson of fear snakes down my spine.

I don't know what he's planning, but from the intensity of his expression, it's possible Hugh may come to regret the bruise he left on my leg.

Chapter Twenty-Two

GAGE

Nathaniel rubs his face and takes another swig of the coffee I brought him when I woke him up at the crack of dawn. I couldn't sleep, but when I peeked into Ember's room, she was still out cold. So, I brought Nova to Nathaniel's house so Ember could keep sleeping. That bruise on her leg haunts me.

"He did it right in front of me," I say, sitting forward in my seat on the couch. "I was right beside her, and he squeezed her leg hard enough to leave a bruise."

"Call Stephen. File charges," Nathaniel suggests, crossing a foot over his knee in the armchair across from me. "It's assault."

"He'll pay someone off and he'll get a slap on the wrist, and it'll be done." Nova is on the play mat to the left, rocking back and forth on her hands and knees. She's close to crawling, but not there yet. She's babbling away to herself, and my chest heats. The idea of anyone hurting her or Ember sets fire to my veins. When I brought them here, I thought I was offering a better life, a safer existence.

"If you want to hit him where it hurts, that's his company," Nathaniel says. "Tucker-Smith Realty is his baby."

I suck in a deep breath. While I've sold quite a few properties in the last two months, most of them have been lower end. Hugh has kept me away from the big deals—the farms, the businesses, the multimillion-dollar properties.

"Like slander him?" I ask.

"I wouldn't suggest *that*," Nathaniel says with a chuckle. "A lawsuit isn't what you're after. You want revenge, not to fuck yourself over."

"I don't get it," I admit.

"There are lots of people in Bellerive who don't like Hugh. A lot. Probably more than you realize. But he has a monopoly on the real estate market because he makes deals happen."

"He has good people," I say.

"Cut him off at the knees." Nathaniel slides his cup onto the small table beside him and leans forward. "Did you sign an employment contract when you started?"

"Yeah, I signed something," I say. "It was only a page or two. Caitlin said it was surprisingly simple."

"Here's hoping he underestimated you," Nathaniel says with a hint of a smile.

"What would he have put in the contract?"

"I bet everyone else has a noncompete clause. You'll have to call Caitlin and see if yours has one. If not, you're in the clear."

"You think I should set up my own company?"

"You'll need cash, probably more than you have. And you can't use the family trust. The start-up will be tricky, but if you really want to fuck him, steal his top sales agents right out from underneath him."

"I don't have that kind of money—not without the trust."

"You've been paying Ember, right?" Nathaniel says. "Funnel more money in her direction in the next week while you get organized—back pay, bonuses, whatever you want to call it. The trust won't question you paying your nanny."

"Millions of dollars?" I laugh. "Someone is going to question millions of dollars."

"Setting up the company won't be easy, but I think it's doable, whether you funnel the money or not."

Nathaniel isn't usually my first choice as a teammate for revenge plots—that's Ava—but I think I've underestimated him. Maybe I assumed his good nature meant he wasn't even capable of coloring outside the lines to get the desired result. I came to him this morning because I knew he'd be awake, and I knew what happened to Ember would bother him like it bothered me. That's the kind of guy he is—one who wouldn't sit down to watch an injustice.

"If I'm doing this," I say, "I can't have Ember leaving in two months. She's probably the only reason I sold anything in the first place."

"One of Caitlin's partners is an immigration lawyer. Make an appointment. Find out your options. I will warn you that Bellerive's work visas are notoriously difficult to obtain and keep."

"I don't know if I can handle this." I say it before I can think through how it'll sound. I can handle it, and I will... If I have to.

"Here are your options—go to the police or kick him in the proverbial nuts. Which fight would you rather have?"

"Or I could put a hit on him," I say.

"Yeah, sure. Hugh's definitely worth going to jail forever for." Nathaniel points at Nova. "Is that really the life you want for her?"

"I was joking." *Mostly*. I'm not used to feeling helpless, as though nothing I can do will be enough. At least not in terms of helping or defending someone else. Lots of times in my life I've felt like I wasn't good enough or smart enough for whatever task was in front of me, but I've always been able to compensate for that feeling with money. Throw enough money at those situations and you're suddenly just fine for most people. In this case, Hugh has the financial advantage. I've never been the underdog, and it's a really fucking uncomfortable place to exist.

"If you want to take him down," Nathaniel says, "I'll help you."

"Yeah," I say, "I want to take him down. Leave my fingerprints all over his life."

Nova is strapped to me, asleep. The diaper bag is in the corner of Caitlin's office, and I'm pacing, trying to think everything through.

"I don't have a noncompete?"

"No, you don't. His employees do, but the clause prevents them from starting their *own* company, not from defecting to someone else's. Bellerive law is very specific on the limits of a noncompete, if an employer chooses to include it."

"He really thought there was no way I would or could go against him."

"He didn't consider you a threat, no." Caitlin leans back in her chair. "If I'm being honest, that's the side of the bet I would have taken a few months ago too. I don't know if it was becoming a father, or if it's Ember's influence, or what's happened to you, but you're a lot more like Nathaniel than I ever would have suspected."

It's not a compliment that I ever would have thought I'd want, but her words warm my chest. When I was younger, Nathaniel was a thorn in my side, the good angel on my shoulder scolding me, and while I'm still not sure we have exactly the same values, it means a lot that Caitlin notices a change in me. What she sees, I feel, but I don't know how deep this new Gage runs. I haven't tested it by going anywhere without Nova or Ember as a stabilizing force. In a lot of ways, it feels like the two of them are the ones keeping me grounded.

"If I really want to fuck over your brother, what's the best way to do it?"

"I'm in family law," Caitlin says, "not corporate. I only know his contracts because he showed them to me."

"Give me your educated guess, based on what you do know."

"I'd say you need capital. Provide bonuses or financial incentives for the best agents to jump ship."

"Okay," I say, nodding as I think through who I'll approach. "What if I want Ember in the country longer?"

"Definitely *not* my area of expertise." Caitlin drums her fingers on the table. "One of the partners, here at the firm, deals with immigration. It's a spiderweb of rules, though. And if you get caught trying to cheat the system, the government will shut down your business or send you to jail."

"My sister is marrying into the royal family."

"You think that means the rules don't apply to you? I'd bet Maren would say that means the rules apply to you doubly so. You're a reflection of her and the royal family. She can't step in to help you or ask anyone else to do that without some media outlet decrying unfair or elitist treatment."

I hold up a hand. "Can we hit pause on the lecture? I haven't even suggested something illegal yet. I don't know what my options are."

"As soon as you do, you'll be searching for a way to skirt the rules." She picks up the phone on her desk and dials a number.

"No faith," I mutter.

"Robert?" she says into the receiver. "My cousin, Gage Tucker, was hoping to get a consult this week." She listens for a minute, and a tiny line appears between her brows. "Possibly, yeah. Okay, I'll tell him." She rattles off my phone number and hangs up before she stares at me for a beat. "Tomorrow afternoon. He'll come to your cottage."

There's something about the way the room has shifted that makes me curious. "How much of a rule follower is Robert?"

"He gets the job done, and he's maintained his license."

Not exactly a glowing endorsement for the rule of law, but I'll take that in a heartbeat. Someone who understands the needs of their clients and makes things happen is exactly what I want in a lawyer.

"Perfect," I say with a grin.

"I'm sure you two will get along very well. Make sure you're home after lunch tomorrow. He's dropping by between clients, so he doesn't have a firm time yet. He said he'd text you."

"Yeah," I say, glancing down at Nova as she stirs in the carrier. "We'll be there."

She releases a deep sigh. "It won't just be you who goes to jail if anything goes sideways." She gives me a pointed look. "It'll be Ember too."

That gives me a moment of pause, but we don't even know if we have to do anything illegal. There could be perfectly reasonable, rational ways to keep her in the country.

"Don't get so hung up on what you want that you put her future at risk," she says.

"We have two months. There has to be some way to keep her in Bellerive when we've got two whole months to figure it out."

"Spoken like someone who's never had to wrestle with immigration's rules and policies before. Good luck, Gage. You're about to learn that Ava's model of 'Tuckers make the rules' isn't true for everything on the island."

Of all the times to learn that lesson, this isn't when I would have chosen.

"You want to transfer a bunch of money into my Bellerive bank account and pretend like I earned it?"

"You did earn it," I say, taking a bottle of beer out of the fridge. "I was underpaying you. Probation or something. Now I'm back paying you and giving you a bonus for good work."

"How much money are we talking about?" Ember leans against the island and follows my movements.

I had to wait for Nova to be in bed before I had the mental capacity for this conversation. My brain has been stuck on Ember going to jail if I fuck anything up.

"I don't know. I'm going to find out from the accountant tomorrow."

"Then I'll transfer the money out to somewhere else, and you'll use that to start your business? This doesn't sound... Is this legal?"

"It might go against the rules of the trust, but it's not like my parents are going to come after me." I don't think so, anyway. Who knows with Celia and Jonathan, but I highly doubt it. "It was Nathaniel's idea, and he's very by-the-book."

"You're sure?" She bites her lip. "I want to help you. Of course I'll help you. But I don't want to get in trouble."

"The best way to get to Hugh, to show him he can't do whatever the fuck he wants to whoever he wants, is to go after his company. We need the capital to do that. I have some money from the sales I closed, but it's not quite enough." I spent the hours while Nova napped going over my finances. With the amount already in my personal bank account, I can make the company work by funneling a bit out of the trust via Ember. Not as much as I feared, but it is a gamble. "We'll draw up an agreement. Call it you giving me the money as a business loan. And I'll say I'll repay you in X number of years."

"Which will just be for appearances, right? I don't need money I haven't earned. Especially if you're talking about almost a million dollars."

More like *two* million, but I didn't want to freak her out. "We need the contract, but the details between you and me can be worked out later. If we get you a visa, the contract really can say however many years in the future." She hadn't balked at the idea of staying in Bellerive longer, especially when I framed it as her helping me get the company off the ground and making sure Nova isn't neglected. I mean, I didn't use that word—*neglected*—that would be terrible, but I heavily implied it. Beating Hugh will take a lot of time and energy, but I've learned I like being a father, so I'd never sacrifice my bond with Nova for a buck.

"This really won't get us in trouble?" she asks.

"That's why I'm meeting with the accountant tomorrow and the immigration lawyer. We won't do it if it puts you at risk."

"Or you," she says. "I don't want you at risk either. You don't have to go after Hugh. I'm a big girl who's had to deal with a lot of men who think they can do whatever they want. Except for my sister, I've been on my own since I was sixteen."

Each time she's made that argument in the last twenty-four hours, that she can just deal with it because she's experienced it before, I become more determined to ensure she never faces a situation like that again.

"One way or another, I'm starting my own company, and I'm making his life miserable."

"Revenge isn't very sweet if you also make your own life miserable," she says, toying with the beer cap on the counter.

"There is zero chance of that happening."

She comes around the island, and she slides her hands around me, hugging me close. The move takes me by surprise. Of the two of us, I'm the one who's more likely to seek her out.

"Thank you for trying," she says, "even if it doesn't work out. I've never had... No man has ever tried to stand up for me before."

Something in my chest roars to life, and I draw her closer, squeeze her a little tighter. With my chin resting on the top of her head, I vow that I'll never stop protecting her and defending her. She'll never again wonder whether someone has her back because I'll be right there behind her.

Chapter Twenty-Three

EMBER

Robert, the immigration lawyer, is a short man, but he makes up for it with his piercing stare and his air of confidence. His brown eyes are sharp with intelligence as he takes stock of Gage and me across the dining room table. A recording device sits on the table between us.

Nova is on my lap, playing with a plastic set of keys.

The accountant this morning was Mr. Sunny compared to the intensity of Robert. Gage's money plan is technically a loophole within the trust, and the accountant confirmed that we're okay to exploit it as long as it exists. Gage immediately had money transferred into my account, an amount that made my mouth drop open. It wasn't at all what we discussed, and I'm really hoping whatever is going to happen with the immigration lawyer won't be repeated.

Gage is set on a work visa. Since he's already paying me, he explains to Robert, it'll be easiest to go that route.

"You're paying her?" Robert points to me.

"She's already my nanny," Gage says.

"On a tourist entry?" Robert raises his eyebrows. "How many hours is she working per week?" He has a pad of paper in front of him, but he's not writing anything down. That seems like a bad sign. Or maybe he's just relying on the recording.

"We don't keep track," I say, and when Nova drops the keys on the floor, I swoop down to get them back.

"More than ten hours in a month on a tourist visa is illegal. You're allowed pocket money, basically, that's it."

Before I can reply, Gage says, "She's definitely worked less than ten hours each month."

A boldfaced lie, and it's pretty clear from Robert's expression that he knows it. I work more than ten hours in one *day*. We don't have a set schedule or anything in writing, so I'm guessing that's why Gage thinks he can get away with the fabrication. This is something I've discovered about Gage—he'll say whatever he has to in order to get what he wants. Whereas I value truth and honesty more.

Robert releases a sigh and drops his pen on the pad of paper. "Here's how this will go—I'll apply for a visa for a nanny for the Tucker family. You'll be required to run an ad for two weeks in the papers, online, and on social media. If even *one* Bellerivian applies with the same or similar qualifications, Ember is denied her visa." He scans me. "Do you have an early childhood education diploma or anything else childcare related as far as education or experience?"

"No, my first baby experience was becoming Nova's aunt and then her guardian," I admit, and then I take a deep breath. "I didn't even graduate high school."

"Yeah, you're probably fucked for the work visa. You have no discernable employable skills that could compete with a Bellerivian."

"Can we just pretend no one applied?" Gage suggests, and he extends his hand for Nova to take. She grasps his finger and draws it toward her mouth.

"When the posting is tied to a visa, the government gets a copy of any applicants. It's an automatic part of the application process. The government then looks at who applied and the qualifications of the person you want to hire. They either grant the visa or deny it based on that. Not much wiggle room."

"What's our other option?" Gage asks, taking back his hand and giving Nova another toy from the basket beside him.

"There is no other option." Robert reaches for his recording device. "Bellerivian visa laws are very clear. We can certainly advertise any job you wish and see how it shakes out. It's possible there aren't enough nannies or real estate assistants in Bellerive and no one will apply."

"Okay," Gage says, glancing at me. "We gamble and hope for the best."

"Send me the job specs, and I'll start the paperwork. I have another meeting, so I should get going." He doesn't rise from the table, but he switches off the recording.

I glance at Gage, trying to figure out what's happening. He's not leaving, but he just said he was.

"What aren't you telling us?" Gage asks, reading the situation far better than me.

"Make the job criteria as specific to Ember as you can, especially if she's gathered any experience the last couple of months." Robert slips the device into the bag that was slung over his shoulder when he arrived.

"Is that really our only option?" Gage asks.

"I'm not suggesting this or advocating for it," Robert says, making eye contact with both of us. "Tourists who legitimately fall in love with a Bellerivian are able to stay on the island if they marry. After five years, the spouse of the Bellerivian citizen gains Bellerivian status. Those relationships are highly scrutinized by immigration—especially if they are abnormally quick—and so it's not a path I recommend to anyone."

But the way he says it makes me think he *is* suggesting it's an option.

"Marriage," Gage says, and it feels like he's rolling the word around in his head.

"What happens if something like that is proven to be..." Fake doesn't seem like the right word, but it's the only one I can come up with. "If they lied?"

"Deportation is the best-case scenario," Robert says. "Worst case is jail."

"Jail?" I say, and I shoot Gage a panicked glance, but he doesn't seem fazed. "Did you know this?"

"Not specifically, no," he says. "But I'm not shocked."

"We'll make up the job ads," I say. "I'll figure out what makes me special."

"Yeah," Gage agrees, but he seems distracted, like he's still puzzling over the option that would put us in jail. "We appreciate your time." He rises and shakes Robert's hand. "We'll be in touch."

"With only two months until she needs to leave, you'll have to move fast. The third option is that she leaves the country for the three months Bellerive requires for an extended tourist stay, and then she can return for four months again. Rinse and repeat. But she won't legally be able to work for you."

"Oh," I say, immediately grasping at his suggestion. "That's not so bad."

"Not ideal," Gage says.

I'm really getting the impression that jail isn't even a deterrent for him. He's been raised to be so sure of himself, so convinced that his path and ideas are the right one, that not even the idea of jail gives him a moment of pause.

"Having you come and go like that wouldn't be the best situation for my daughter," Gage says nodding toward Nova in my lap. He then searches my expression that probably looks like a stricken, paralyzed deer staring down a transport truck. "To kids, time moves so much slower than for adults. Months will feel like years."

"I'll leave you two to discuss your options," Robert says, heading for the front entrance.

Gage follows him, leaving me still sitting there, thinking. When he returns, we stare at each other across the table.

"You don't want to marry me," I say.

"I don't particularly want to marry *anyone*, but if I had to marry someone, you wouldn't be a bad choice."

"Wow," I say with a laugh. "That's probably the most romantic thing I have ever heard. I've always wanted to be described as '*not a bad choice*' when discussing forever."

"You want romance?"

"I'm pretty sure that's what Robert just told us," I say. "If we pretend to get married, there can't be much pretending involved. They aren't going to make it easy for anyone to cheat the system."

"Five years is not forever." Gage slides into the chair Robert left, and Nova makes a whining noise, trying to get to Gage. She likes him within arms' reach. He stretches across the table and takes her from me, setting her on his lap. "Nova will be almost six by the end. You'll have citizenship, so you'll be able to stay on the island or go back to America, whatever you want."

"No," I say, my cheeks heating because I can't help thinking about what else we'd need to do in order to keep up appearances. "Five years is a long time. We can't pretend for years. It doesn't make sense. What if we hated each other by the end? What if we're both miserable and only holding on for Nova and the status card?"

"I just..." He shrugs. "I don't think we discount it. But we also can't tell anyone we're considering marriage to let you stay in the country. If we end up having to fake it, everyone who knows us has to believe our relationship is real."

"I don't want to fake anything," I say. "I don't want to live a lie."

"We'll do the job ads, and if none of them work, then we'll come back to this, draw up some marriage rules or something." He turns Nova around and she stands on his legs before drawing his face to hers to plant a sloppy kiss. "We're already living together, Em. It wouldn't be that much of a stretch."

Except living together is not *living together* in all the ways we'd need, and I don't know if my heart could take becoming more invested knowing we're just killing time, crossing days off on a calendar until we can cross out our marriage vows.

Chapter Twenty-Four

GAGE

Marriage should scare me. In the past, that's been the case. With Abby, I never wanted it, couldn't truly imagine it, fluffed off her suggestion that we might get there one day any time she mentioned it. The benefits of marriage—consistent sex—were outweighed by the cons—with the same person.

But a week later, when I'm sitting at a conference room table in Robert's office trying to craft multiple job advertisements that can accurately describe Ember's value to my life, while also making it impossible for anyone else to fill the role, I'm starting to see the biggest benefits to marriage. Specifically, that I no longer have to make shit up for bogus employment opportunities.

"The thing is," I say to Robert, "no one who applies will be *her*."

"That's the point of you being so specific," Robert says. "The job is completely tailored to her skill set."

Other than the fact that she makes, according to Ava, amazing handbags, I'm not sure anything Ember does qualifies her as better than anyone else, at least by the government's standards. If they'd just accept my word that she's irreplaceable, this whole process would be a hell of a lot easier.

"She's Nova's aunt. Can I make it that specific?"

"No," Robert says, and he doesn't even crack a smile. "As I said, had you gotten legal advice before she entered the country, you could have filed relative paperwork that *might* have given her permission to stay longer, given the circumstances. Once you're in the country, they don't let you do that anymore, circumstances be damned."

To be fair, Pamela, my fixer, asked me several times if I was sure Ember would only stay for four months. At the time, I couldn't imagine wanting her to stay longer. She was a stranger. Living with a woman and being good together for that length of time didn't seem possible. I thought I liked my own space, enjoyed making my own schedule too much to slot another person into the mix easily.

The truth is, I crave her company, and we're not even having sex. She's the first person I call when something goes right or when my life goes off the rails.

I can't decide if crossing the friend line would increase my level of happiness or make things in the house unbearably complicated. Uncomplicated is generally where I've preferred to live my life.

"Yeah, I get it," I say. "We fucked this whole visa thing up."

"I'll get these ads posted. You'll have to hire for at least one of these jobs, or the government will know you're throwing spaghetti at the wall. If you end up going in a *different direction*, it'll look bad."

"Ember is a rule follower," I say. "This is the only direction she'll accept."

Every time I've tried to nudge her into reconsidering, she's been adamant that she's not willing to put either of us into legal hot water. To be in trouble, we'd have to get caught, so from my perspective, the risk is minimal. It would be easy enough to pretend to be in love with Ember. Seems she doesn't feel the same way about that. Can't say I blame her. Money and sex are all I bring to a relationship. I can pay for shit, and I can fuck. For some women, either of those things would be enough to put a ring on it, and I know because they've told me. Whatever criteria Ember requires to fake some feelings, I don't possess enough of it, maybe not even a drop of it.

The one time in my life I'd actually be okay with a woman catching some feelings—not big feelings but something at least—and it turns out she's been vaccinated against guys like me.

"I'll submit the job specs then, and you hire or don't as you see fit," Robert says. "You'll know within the next two weeks whether you've got any applicants."

I take a deep breath and rise from my seat at the conference room table. This moment feels bigger than I'd like, mostly because the result is completely out of my control. How many times has that been the case in my life? I can't think of another time where I couldn't somehow influence an outcome in the direction I wanted.

"For the record," I say as we shake hands, "the Bellerivian immigration system is bullshit."

Robert chuckles and leads me toward the elevator. "We're an island. If we allowed everyone who wanted to live here to come in with open arms, we'd become severely imbalanced in terms of housing, employment, and cost of living. I'm not going to tell you that the system is perfect—no system ever is—but when you understand how to play by the rules, the regulations aren't terrible."

"They're pretty terrible," I reiterate.

"When you assume the system should bend to your will instead of *you* bending to *its* will, I guess it would seem like that."

Privileged. Spoiled. Nepo baby. I've heard it all. My life has consisted of every-one but my parents bending over backward to make me happy. They never denied us material things either—just the other stuff, the things that can't be bought. Our family pays a lot of money in taxes and charitable donations on the island, so there's a part of me that thinks Bellerivian laws *should* bend to my will. We *are* special.

"Could Maren do anything for me? She's part of the royal family."

"Not yet, she isn't," Robert says as the elevator dings. "The only thing your sister could do is get King Alexander involved, and he's a notorious hard-ass, even about immigration. Considering his wife is a foreigner, I wondered if that might change. But it hasn't." He holds the elevator doors for me to step in.

"Good to know." Another bout of terrible news. Alex married a Canadian, and there were rumors he was on the cusp of abdicating the throne in order to be with her. If anyone would understand desperation, he should be the one.

At my car, I slide into the driver's seat, and I check my messages. For the last week, I've been working remotely. If I set foot in the office and I saw Hugh, I think I'd fucking kill him. Jail is not enough of a deterrent every time I see the fading bruise on Ember's leg.

Tonight at the house, I'm hosting an exclusive, secret event for Hugh's top sales agents. I don't know if I can trust them all, but when I showed up at each person's house this week to see if they were open to hearing me out, they all said yes. If they were going to fuck me over from the get-go, I think I'd have heard some kind of rumbling by now.

If most of them don't agree to jump ship by the time I'm done presenting, I might have to go with beating the shit out of Hugh or hiring someone to do it and living with the consequences. No matter what, he can't get away with what he did. He'll answer for it.

When I get to the house, the catering truck is already in the driveway unloading. Staff who will be working the dinner party are buzzing around the living room, dining room, and kitchen, carrying things in and out, setting up the bar, putting alcohol on ice. I scan the place for Ember and Nova, but I don't see either of them. Then I hear a squeal of delight from outside.

At the sliding door, I take a moment to soak up the happiness radiating off Ember and reflected in Nova. Every time Nova slaps the water, splashing Ember, Ember pretends to be surprised, and Nova is loving her reaction. Their shared laughter puts a vise around my chest. I'd protect both of them with my life—not a single doubt in my mind.

Just over two months ago, I didn't know either of them, and now they're the most important people in my life.

Ember spots me when I open the sliding door, and her already broad grin widens and she turns Nova to see me. Immediately, Nova holds out her arms for me, and although I'll get absolutely soaked, I don't hesitate to take her.

"How's my girl?" I ask, nuzzling her nose.

Nova's tiny hands frame my face, and she gives me a slobbery open-mouthed kiss. When I chuckle, she stares at me for a beat before trying it again with the same saliva heavy result.

"I don't know if that's what a kiss looks like to her," Ember says, "or she doesn't have the coordination to do it without buckets of spit."

Most of the time, we're kissing her, so I'm not sure she *has* seen people kiss—at least not in real life. That comment would be too loaded to make considering I'm trying to not-so-subtly convince Ember that marrying me wouldn't be a hardship.

Should we practice kissing in front of Nova? Show her how it's done?

That would not fall under the *Positives of Marrying Gage* column, though it really should.

"Did you and Robert get the job descriptions made up?"

"We did. He's submitting them today or tomorrow. The easier solution still feels really obvious to me."

"There is nothing *easy* about pretending to be married and in love." Ember laughs as though my suggestion is a joke. "One of us would crack at the first hint of interrogation."

I would not, but she probably would. Not a deceptive bone in her body. She's not an open book per say, but whenever she's being evasive, it's obvious. Anything regarding her sister or her family makes her squirm, and if she can skirt around a firm answer, she will.

"The offer is there," I say. "I'd marry you."

"Whenever I thought about getting engaged, that statement right there was how I pictured it. Me, makeup-free in a pool, my future husband holding my niece, and a very casual could-care-less delivery."

"Oh, come on," I say, throwing out the hand that isn't cradling Nova. "Would you really want me to make a big deal about our fake whatever?"

She glances behind me at what's happening with the catering staff, but I don't turn around. I'd actually like her to answer. On the slim chance she'll agree to this, I need to understand where the bar is. I can do casual, or I can do over-the-top. Not sure I'm capable of whatever the happy medium would be. Is anyone ever happy with medium anything? Go big or go home is my motto. Or don't show up at all—that's the other option.

"All of it would have to look like we meant it," she says. "Which is part of the reason I don't think we can do it. Neither of us is that kind of actor."

"It's not like they'd actually put either of us in jail," I say.

"Excuse me, sir," the head caterer appears at the sliding door. "I wanted to confirm the numbers haven't changed before we start place settings and food prep."

I tug my phone out of my pocket, and there are no new emails or texts from anyone canceling. Here's hoping they all show up. "No changes," I say as Ember hoists herself out of the pool, water cascading along her trim figure. The desire to use my mouth to catch and remove the droplets left behind steals my focus from the caterer for a beat. "Anything else?" I ask without taking my eyes off Ember while she runs a towel along her body. Pretending to be into her isn't even a thing—I'm into her. Would give a whole lot to be much *deeper* into her.

"No, sir," she says, slipping back into the house, and she leaves the door the way she found it, cracked open.

"I should start getting ready, I guess," Ember says, meeting my gaze, completely oblivious to how the sight of her in a teeny-tiny patterned bikini is threatening to undo the little willpower I normally have around her. If I wasn't holding Nova, I'm not sure what I'd do. Something, probably. Wreck everything.

For me, *this* is pretending. Acting like I don't want her, and she's right. It's really fucking hard... In so many ways. Every inch of me wants to devour every inch of her, but if she doesn't feel the same, then I can see how pretending to want me, want *anything* with me, would be the same kind of torture I'm currently experiencing.

And the thing is, if one of us has to suffer, I'd prefer it to be me. Life has already handed Ember far too many hard knocks.

Chapter Twenty-Five

EMBER

As the evening with Gage's colleagues winds down, pride is rushing through me, a river flooding the banks of any rational thought. Throughout the evening, he answered every question someone lobbed at him with ease. He showed off NGE Realty and its branding with confidence, convinced that if he runs a company equitably everyone will benefit. His argument that he doesn't need to be a billionaire off his real estate gig because he already is one seemed like a surprise to most of them. His cut of every sale will be miniscule compared to Hugh—enough to keep the lights on and the customers happy with the level of service.

Even I felt inspired by the time he was done presenting, and apart from the name, which was a surprise, I already knew it all. He'd talked through all the details with me, despite the fact that I have very little experience running a business or developing a marketing plan or establishing cohesive branding. Obviously, he was a bit nervous and stressed leading up to such a huge change, and since I live here, I was an easy person to turn to.

None of the realtors have agreed to join him so far, but they all took the contract to have a lawyer look over. Martin told Gage that he wasn't interested in getting fucked over by another Tucker family member who pretended to have good intentions and ended up letting greed rule their company.

From the little I know about Hugh, that seems like an accurate assessment. Take, take, take.

To his credit, Gage's charm didn't waver in the face of Martin's undisguised anger. He reminded him that Hugh is technically a *Smith* first, and then he doubled down on his commitment to being honest and transparent about the company's finances. On Gage's watch, no one would feel taken advantage of.

"I don't know much," I say after the last real estate agent has left, "but that seemed like it went well."

"Who knows?" Gage rubs a hand along the back of his neck. "I thought they'd all just sign, so it doesn't feel like a win. The honeypot is full. Why wouldn't they want to drink it dry?"

"Sounds a bit like Hugh might have screwed them over a time or two," I say with a shrug. "Trust is earned, right?"

He stares at me for a beat, the wheels clearly turning behind his blue eyes. "I don't want to do any of this without you."

"Maybe we'll get lucky with the visa." Behind Gage, the caterers are cleaning the table, picking up abandoned drinks, flipping tablecloths into neat piles.

"I've never been good at leaving something to chance when the sure thing is staring me in the face."

"You're so sure getting married is the easier solution," I say, keeping my voice low. "It's not."

"I just think you need to keep an open mind, in case this doesn't go the way we want."

The way *he* wants, is actually what he means. Part of me wants to stay, would love to witness Nova growing up, but the closer I get to Gage, the more I worry about having to leave. *We* aren't forever or endgame or anything, and the way he treats me is addictive. No man has ever given me so much tender but fierce protection, and the reality is that we're two people who love the same person—Nova. That's it. We're housemates who have a single common interest.

Staying in Bellerive blurs the lines, but marrying him would obliterate them. Poof. No lines or limits. Whatever commonalities we had or didn't have wouldn't matter. I'd fall so deep I'd never find my way out, and with men, you *always* need a way out.

"If the visas don't work out," I say, "then our plan B is me leaving and coming back every few months."

"That's not plan B if I can get what I want, *exactly* what I want, another way." There's a stubborn set to his jaw.

"I'm not fighting with you about this," I say, holding up my hands.

"We're not fighting," he says, his tone exasperated. "You're being stubborn for no reason."

I can think of so many reasons that marriage is a bad idea that I'm momentarily speechless. Once I recover, I open my mouth to give him the list when I remember that I said I was done fighting about it. If I respond, he's not going to listen. In his mind, the only solution is the one he wants.

"I cannot think of any set of circumstances that would make me believe marrying you was the *best* idea."

"I love when people throw things out into the universe like a karmic dare. Guess we'll see, won't we?"

He's so confident and unbothered, it amazes me. "You can hire people, people who are probably better than me, to do all the things I do for you and Nova," I say.

"No, I can't," he says, and his jaw tightens.

"Name one thing someone else can't do for you that I do. Just one, and I'll *consider* your proposal."

He stares at me for a long beat, scanning my face. "Just one?"

"Just one."

The air grows heavy around us, and a cold sweat breaks out across my lower back. Whatever he's thinking, it's almost palpable in the room, thick with something unnamed, but I can't quite grasp the message. I need him to say it, whatever it is. Anticipation prickles my skin. What could I possibly possess that no one else does?

Nova cries from her bedroom, and he grimaces before shaking his head, and then he leaves me without saying a word.

Disappointment settles over me. He couldn't come up with a single thing, not one, that I can do for him that someone else can't. It's what I expected, what I knew to be true, but I can't help the pinch of sadness.

At least I know, without a doubt, that his offer to marry me is tied directly to Nova and her happiness. If someone asked me, I'd say that what I wanted, what I needed, was for both of us to stay focused solely on Nova. That doesn't change the little nub of dejection threatening to bud inside me. It would have been nice to be important, too, to be irreplaceable in some way to someone.

But that's never been me.

The next week crawls along, and Gage doesn't bring up marriage again, as though my one challenge was enough to make him finally see reason. I'm not special, and we both know it.

Nova has been restless all morning, and I think she might be coming down with something. Normally, she's pretty even-tempered, but every time I tried to set her down this morning, she cried and reached for me.

Ava arrives just as I'm in the middle of mixing a bottle, hopeful that the warm formula might lull Nova into a much-needed sleep.

"I do not do screaming," Ava says when I try to pass her Nova so I can mix the bottle quicker.

"Can you mix the bottle then?" I ask, feeling harried and a bit frantic. Whatever is going on with her doesn't feel like teething, or at least not like when her other teeth came in. But she doesn't have a fever.

Ava takes over mixing the bottle from me, and I take Nova to the rocker in the living room that Gage bought a few weeks ago while she was cutting a particularly painful tooth. I try to lay her on my chest, but she won't settle, and it's not until Ava comes with the bottle that she calms down. In the crook of my arm, she lies, sucking the bottle while making noises that seem to alternate between soothed and discontent.

"What's wrong with her?" Ava asks, falling into one of the couches opposite.

"A tooth, maybe? There's no fever." I stare down at her, pushing down the anxiety that's threatening to surface. Every other time she's been cranky, there's been a logical explanation for it. "Constipated?"

"I could never be a mom," Ava says, scrolling through her phone. "Keeping track of how often someone shits, what it looks like, and then cleaning all of it up? Just—no."

"Maybe she's just tired." Nova didn't sleep well last night while I was on baby duty. She was up every couple of hours wanting a cuddle and generally discontent. "Growing pains?" Every reasonable answer is on a loop in my head, but none of them quite fit.

She finishes the bottle, and when I get up to go put her down for her nap, she starts to whimper. As soon as I sit down in the rocker again, she snuggles into the crook of my neck, her tiny fist kneading the material of my shirt.

"How do you know when to take a baby to a doctor?" Ava asks.

I don't. Other than her wellness checkups, I haven't had to take her to the hospital or schedule an unexpected doctor's appointment.

"Do you think I should take her?" I ask.

"I don't know. My knowledge of babies is zero. I just wondered."

Nova's breathing has evened out, and she's sound asleep. Rather than waking her up and taking her to her crib, I keep the chair gently swaying.

"I can't go anywhere today," I say, gesturing to Nova.

"I didn't come here to drag you shopping—not that I have to drag you into much of anything anymore." She flashes me a satisfied grin. "I came to say that I have a few friends who want to see more of your bags. What have you got that I haven't seen?"

"Back bedroom," I say. "Are you just taking photos or..."

"Samples. I'll have them transfer you the money and then I'll return whatever doesn't sell." Ava stands up, slinging one of my bags over her forearm. "You need to keep your website updated better."

"I don't have time," I say, motioning to Nova. "I get the hours she sleeps or the hours that Gage is home, and he's trying to launch his real estate company. The bags... I mean, that's just a hobby."

Ava's eyes narrow. "Do not put my brother's hopes and dreams above yours. Don't be one of those girls."

"I'm not." Defensiveness skitters up my spine. "But I did come here under an agreement with him. An agreement to look after Nova, to take on her care. I can't change the rules just because I feel like it." As soon as the word 'rules' leaves my mouth, I realize my mistake. It's not even really what I meant.

"You can change the rules whenever you want, and if Gage doesn't understand, that's his problem. I could sell these bags a lot faster if you were producing more or hired help or any of the other thousand things I've told you to do."

I don't say anything, but instead I stare down at Nova who is sleeping, but there's a crease in her forehead as though her sleep isn't as peaceful as normal. Much like arguing with Gage, Ava's only interested in her own opinion. She wants what she wants, and when she can't get it, she looks for ways to force her desired outcome.

"It's stupid that you're putting your dreams on hold for his," she says over her shoulder as she heads for the bedroom hallway.

She would see it that way because she has no idea the life I was leading before Gage turned up. On the knife's edge of being homeless, I've never had the luxury of pursuing a dream. Every day I survived, and that was an accomplishment. It was enough.

When Ava calls my name from the back bedroom and asks me to go back there, I release a sigh. Everything is either really easy or really hard with her.

Gingerly, I get to my feet, careful not to disturb Nova too much, and I practically glide across the floor to Nova's bedroom. Once I'm there, I peel Nova off me, her baby drool having soaked the collar of my shirt.

Maybe the restlessness is just her teeth.

I set her in the crib, and she doesn't wake or stir. For a moment, I watch her, and then Ava calls my name again. With a sigh, I leave Nova's room to go down the hall and stand at the entrance to the spare bedroom. Gage has a desk in here, and I have all my sewing stuff. Any time we're not watching TV together at night as a way to unwind, we're in here—him working out how to establish his new company and me trying to let the creative bud bloom.

"What?" I ask, unable to keep the edge of impatience out of my voice.

"This piece," Ava says, holding up a leather bag I finished last night. "I *love* it."

It's one I was quite proud of, too, because the design felt classic with a twist. "Thanks," I say.

"If I could get this bag in front of someone important—someone career mak-ing—would you take an opportunity if you got it?" Ava puts a hand on her hip.

"What do you mean?"

"A job interview or an apprenticeship or something."

"With a designer?" I ask, my heart thumping. Ava's choice in bags and designers aligned perfectly with mine. If she knew someone, the opportunity would be beyond any dream I ever would have been capable of dreaming, so outside the realm of possibilities in my life, that it's hard to even fathom it.

"Yeah." She doesn't elaborate, just watches me for a reaction.

I bite my lip, and part of me is desperate to say yes, another part of me is terrified to say yes, and a third part of me is anxious at the thought of letting Gage down after everything he's done for me. Now isn't the time to pursue my personal projects—it just isn't.

"I can't let your brother down," I say. "He says he needs me."

"Well," she says, raising the leather bag from the table, "this is a career-making product. If you were capable of mass producing, of doing *any* of the things I told you, then I'd make you do it yourself. Keep the money. Keep the glory. Since you won't take the path I've shown you, approaching the right designer with this bag could change your life. When you're ready to make a life for yourself—not for anyone else—you let me know."

Then she flicks her hair and leaves the room in a huff of annoyance and a cloud of floral perfume. I run my hands down my face and massage my temples.

A job with a designer. A famous designer. My heart thuds with longing. An incredible opportunity, something I never knew I could consider. But since Ava's offer wouldn't exist without Gage and without Nova, it seems wrong to toss both of them aside to pursue it. I want that life—designing bags and doing what I love—but I don't want to give up this one to get it.

So for now, making a few bags in the spare bedroom and selling them sporadically is the best I can do. I'm not unhappy, and after the last few months, that feels like an accomplishment in itself.

Chapter Twenty-Six

EMBER

The time Nova normally wakes up passes, and I check the baby monitor, uneasiness nibbling at the edges of my consciousness. I zoom into the crib to make sure her chest is still rising and falling regularly. Nova's earlier behavior set me on edge, and then Ava's offer only seemed to push me deeper into a weird sort of worry.

I shake my head to clear the negativity, and I adjust the cloth under the sewing machine and press down on the pedal.

The opportunity Ava dangled in front of me feels like a once-in-a-lifetime offer, and I want it. But I can't let myself dwell on what *could* be for me. Athena left Nova in my care, and my niece is the last piece of Athena I have left. Gage is a good dad, but he didn't know my sister, not in any way that matters. I'm her only chance to know our side of the family—not that there's much that's good to know.

Still, I do need a job, and I'm not qualified for any of the ones Gage thinks I can do. But I might actually stand a chance of getting a fashion design visa.

I stop sewing and grab my phone from beside me, firing off a text to Ava to see whether the designer is based in Bellerive.

Within seconds she's responded that everyone she knows who is any good is American, like me.

Taking Ava up on the opportunity would mean I'd have to leave Bellerive, abandon Nova and Gage.

You in? she texts back.

My fingers hover over the buttons, but I can't bring myself to make a decision. Slowly, I type out the words, *I can't*, but I don't hit Send. I just stare at them.

Nova stirs, crying and thrashing back and forth on the monitor. I drop my phone beside my sewing machine, and I rush into her bedroom.

At the edge of her crib, I rub her stomach as she stares up at me, tears pooling in her eyes. I lift her gently into my arms, and she burrows into the crook of my neck. I lay her on the changing table, and I'm talking nonsense to her as I unzip her damp onesie. She must have peed through her diaper. But when I go to tug the material off one her of hands, I notice how swollen her hand is.

With a frown, I take her hand between mine and tip it back and forth. It's not discolored, but it's huge. So much bigger than it should be. I check her other hand, finding the same thing, then I'm examining her body, checking for other signs of swelling. Her face looks normal, but when I draw the onesie off her legs, I find her feet are also at least twice their normal size.

"Oh my god," I mutter, and I lay the back of my hand across her forehead. The other times she's had a fever, I could feel the heat emanating off her, and she's definitely warmer than usual. "What is this?" I whisper.

I peel off her soaked diaper, but I don't find anything unusual in there, and I quickly put on a new one. Lifting her into my arms, I grab my phone from beside the sewing machine and type in a search about unusual swelling.

The first result is congestive heart failure, and bile rises into my throat. That can't be right. Yesterday she was fine. Stupid internet searches always give the worst-case scenario. Panic slithers around my chest, threatening to tighten. With a shaking hand, I manage to scroll to Gage's number and hit the dial button.

It rings and rings, and I bite my lip and pace. When he doesn't answer, I end the call and immediately call again.

"Ember?" he asks on the second ring. "What's wrong?"

"Nova," my voice catches, and I have to take a moment to swallow down the lump in my throat. "Something's wrong."

"Okay," he says, and I can hear my own panic reflected back. "Should you be calling an ambulance?"

"I don't know," I say, and my voice catches on a sob.

"She's breathing?"

"Yes."

"She's conscious?"

"Yes."

His sigh of relief is audible. "Fever?"

"I think so."

"What else?"

"Her hands and feet," I say, forcing the words out. "They're at least twice their normal size."

There's a long pause, and then Gage says, "Well, that internet search wasn't helpful. Jesus." He huffs out a breath. "I'm calling Bill to drive you to the children's hospital in Tucker's Town. Sawyer's physiotherapy clinic is close to there. I'll have her meet you, so you're not alone. I'm in Rockdown, but I'll get there as fast as I can."

"Okay," I say, my voice thick with tears.

"It'll be okay, Em," he says, his voice gentle. "Money fixes everything."

Except, I think we both know that money might not be able to fix whatever this is.

Bill made it to the hospital in record time, and we've already been triaged and delivered to our own private room. Maybe money can't solve whatever is wrong with Nova, but the Tucker name guaranteed a nice room, at least. Gage called ahead to the hospital to make sure we were well-looked-after when we arrived. Privilege with a capital P, but I'm not mad about it.

From the windowed room, I watch doctors and nurses hustling from one place to another, conferring in the hallway, and then Sawyer is outside the door, a hesitant smile. I wave her in, and she slips into the room.

Nova has her face buried in my neck, and she peeks out when Sawyer slides into the armchair beside me.

Sawyer peers at Nova's hands and feet, gently inspecting them with her fingers. "They tell you anything yet?"

"She had a fever when we arrived, so they gave her something for that. Someone is supposed to be coming to start an IV. They're going to take blood, run some tests. No one seems as freaked out as I am."

"From personal experience," Sawyer says, "medical professionals tend to stay calm no matter how mild or serious something is. No one's brain functions well under intense stress, so compartmentalizing is a real thing."

That's not comforting, and I'm not sure if she realizes it. Up until now, I assumed their unhurried and careful steps meant Nova probably wasn't really sick, that maybe I'd overreacted. Now I'm second-guessing everything. The idea that something might be terribly wrong is a thought I'm barely holding at bay.

"Gage must be freaking out," Sawyer says, running her hand along Nova's back. "Being so far away when you're here. Whenever I travel, that's always my biggest fear—being far away if someone in my family needs me. When Maren had her accident in Chile, it was the worst feeling to have her seriously injured and none of us close by."

Every word ignites inside me, each one a firecracker illuminating the truth I haven't wanted to consider. Why hadn't I thought of that?

There's a knock on the doorframe and a nurse pops her head in. "The doctor should be with you shortly. It's been a busy afternoon."

"Okay," I say to her with a nod, and then I look at Sawyer. "Do you think I should be worried? I don't know how worried to be."

Sawyer sucks in a deep breath. "If it was really, really serious, when they triaged you, you'd already be with a doctor. So, it could be serious, but it could also be okay. But whatever this is, they haven't deemed it immediately life-threatening."

That's sort of comforting, but I'm still not sure how I should be acting. If Gage was here, I'm sure he'd be in full Tucker mode, demanding a doctor see Nova immediately. He's the bull in the china shop, whereas I'd tiptoe through, trying not to let any of the cups rattle.

"Kids get sick. When Ava and Gage were little, they were in and out of the emergency department for a few things—ear infections, pneumonia, swimmer's ear, a chest infection. It happens."

And I can't believe this reality didn't cross my mind before. Nova has been incredibly healthy in her short life. Fevers. Colds. Nothing that some medicine at home didn't help us to ride out. The things she might face, the illnesses she might get in the future, have never occurred to me. But the odds are that she'll get something, and as things stand, there's a chance I won't be the one sitting here in the future, with her little face pressed into my neck. Someone else could be in my place. If my visa doesn't get approved for any of the jobs Gage invented, I could be in America when she's ill, maybe even if something is seriously wrong. I might not be able to get here, be here.

She's the last piece of Athena that I'll ever have, and as she's getting older, I see hints of my sister in her that makes the ache of Athena's loss bittersweet. When I was barely holding our life together in Colorado, I knew I'd do anything to keep Nova safe and happy. Even when we first got here, Nova was at the forefront of my mind. But somehow, over the last couple of months, I've stopped worrying as much about whether Nova will have a good life. She will. I have no doubt about that.

Instead, I've been preoccupied with what happens if I become too close with Gage, so I haven't carefully considered what happens when I get too far from Nova. Maybe Nova could cope without me, maybe even thrive without me, but I'd never forgive myself if something dire happened and I wasn't close by.

And if that's my reality, if that's my truth, I need to be honest about exactly what I'm willing to do to ensure I am here for her, in every way that matters, for as long as I can.

Chapter Twenty-Seven

GAGE

Traffic and speed limits can go fuck themselves as I follow Stephen's cruiser down the central highway at full speed. He's clearing traffic, and I'm basically drafting him. As soon as I got off the phone with Ember I called him to see if he was on duty, and after I offered him a date with Ava and five thousand dollars, he made his way to the highway to clear a path for me.

Nova is sick. Ember is alone trying to figure it out. Those thoughts keep circling in my head as I rush down the highway to them.

Well, they're not alone, because Sawyer agreed to go over there, like I knew she would when I called. For most of my life, I've resented the hovering Sawyer and Nathaniel did. Their check-ins and lectures went unheard, unappreciated. But there have been a few times where I've been really grateful for their levelheaded support. Actually, that's been happening a lot lately.

The advantage of having an older sister who has been more like a mother is that there was no way that Sawyer would let her niece and Ember sit in the emergency department alone and afraid. When I call either Sawyer or Nathaniel, I know they'll answer, and I know they'll show up in whatever way I need. Ava and Maren do, too, but their help has always been more conditional, like the help *I* used to offer my family. If it was convenient for me or something I wanted to do, I had no problem pitching in. Otherwise? Maybe not. I can't say I blame at least two of my siblings for treating me the same way.

Fucking embarrassing to realize I've been *that guy* for years. The one they couldn't necessarily rely on. But I've vowed to do better with Ember and Nova, and I think I am. If there was a way to subtly ask Ember if I've been living up to the standard I've tried to set without seeming like a needy bitch, I might nudge her to tell me the truth. Maybe I'm still a shitty human being. I don't know how much I believe that people can change—really change in fundamental ways—and the change hasn't felt hard with Ember or Nova, which makes me wonder if I've even been doing it right. Isn't change, big change, supposed to be hard?

Getting this real estate company off the ground has been really fucking hard, just as a comparison. Some days I question what the hell I'm thinking, but then I remember Ember's bruise, and how she was so resigned to letting Hugh get away with it, and I feel so much rage that I want to tear his company apart, one branch at a time. No one, but especially her, should ever have to accept that kind of treatment.

My company's launch is next week. I have three of Hugh's top agents signed with me, and I'm still hoping to lure away two or three others once I'm up and running. Once they see that I meant what I said, they might have the confidence to make the jump.

Stephen signals off the highway, and I'm on his ass, drifting off the main road with him. We take the corner at high speed, and he drives through the hospital's emergency entrance and through to the valet parking.

I leave the car running and signal to the valet girl that I'm heading in. She chases me with a ticket for the car, and I snatch it from her hand, rushing to the reception.

"Gage Tucker. My daughter Nova is here somewhere." I scan the emergency waiting room, but I don't see them. At least they likely got the room I organized.

"They're in a private room," she says after typing into the computer. "Elevator to the left. Third floor. Ask at the desk there, and they can direct you to the room."

When the doors open on the third floor, a woman I went to high school with is at the desk. She rounds it and signals for me to follow her. She takes me to Nova's door where Ember and Sawyer are waiting.

I open the door, and I stride in, grabbing a third chair and sliding it across the floor until I'm beside Ember. Nova is still tucked into Ember's shoulder, and I run my hand along Nova's back before planting a kiss on her head.

"How's my little peanut?" I ask, keeping my voice gentle and quiet.

Nova emerges to peek up at me, and then she wiggles away from Ember, keen for me to take her.

Ember lets her go to me and then releases a deep sigh. "They're supposed to be coming for an IV and blood work. No news yet."

I check my watch and frown. "Someone should have been in by now, shouldn't they?" Sawyer is on the other side of Ember, and I peer over at her.

Just then there's a knock on the door, and the nurse who showed me the room pops her head in followed by a second nurse. "I'm here to take blood and start the IV." She tows a cart behind her. "Can you sit on the bed behind Nova but keep her sitting up. I need to see the best place to put this."

I get on the hospital bed, but when I try to detach Nova to let the nurse see her, she clings on tight. She's normally an easygoing baby, so I shoot Ember a questioning look.

"She's been like that since we got here," Ember says.

"I'll see what I can do with her like that," the nurse says, examining Nova's arms and hands. Her colleague comes over, and they turn the parts of Nova they can clearly see until they both seem to agree on the best placement. "There's a vein here."

"What do you want me to do?" I ask.

"Just hold her close and tight. My colleague is going to keep the area stable, and I'm going to run the line. She may cry—tolerance varies."

"Nancy is a pro," her colleague says. "She'll be in and out fast."

"You're going to jinx me," Nancy says as she quickly assembles everything she needs.

The two of them work together, talking gently to Nova who doesn't look at them, just keeps herself pressed against me as though I can somehow make it all go away. When the IV goes in, she lets out one wail, and finally looks in their direction, but she doesn't struggle.

They're drawing blood, and they're talking to her as they do it. A frown lays between Nova's brows, and one tear streaks down her cheek, but she doesn't seem to be in obvious pain, either from what they're doing or whatever has caused the swelling.

"That seems like a lot of blood," I say as they insert another vial.

"We don't want to have to do it again, if we can avoid it. Lots of tests ordered to rule out everything we can," Nancy says, popping the vial out once it's full and inserting another. "Has she been in any discomfort? We can give her some more medicine."

Since I haven't been here, I nod toward Ember, and she shakes her head. "She's been okay," she says. "Just clingy."

"That's normal when we're not well," the other nurse says.

"Has she ever been in the hospital before?" I ask Ember.

"Not since she was born," Ember says, and there's a catch in her voice. If I wasn't busy keeping Nova soothed, I'd offer Ember my hand to cling onto. She seems like she needs reassurance, but I'm not sure what to give her.

"The first visit to the hospital can be scary, especially when the reason is unknown like this," Nancy says. "The doctors on rotation tonight are very thorough. If there's something to be found, they'll find it."

She's finished filling the tubes of blood, and now she and her colleague are working on setting up the IV.

"The doctor will be in once we have some results to share," Nancy says. "It's busy tonight, so you may have to sit tight a while."

"Okay," Ember says before I can respond.

Once Nancy and her colleague are gone, I say, "Can't I offer a donation or a pay raise to hurry this up? Everyone likes money."

"Gage," Sawyer admonishes.

"Hey, can you text Ava and let her know she owes Stephen a date?" I ask Sawyer before peering down at Nova who is examining her hand, the frown still present.

"That's how you got here so fast? I wondered."

"That and five thousand bucks," I say.

"If you and Ava keep asking Stephen to abuse his police privileges, you won't have a friend on the force anymore," Sawyer says.

"Bullshit," I say. "I'll just make a new friend."

"Someday, your penchant for sidestepping the rules is going to get you in trouble."

"History tells me any repercussions are a slap on the wrist." Any time I've gotten into a tight spot on the island, the Tucker name or money has saved me. One of the advantages of having a well-connected mother who hates a scandal is that scandals never seem to have a chance to emerge. She's exceptional at burying information so deep that no one can be bothered to hunt for it. "Consequences aren't a thing for me."

Sawyer stares pointedly at Nova.

"*Negative* consequences aren't a thing," I amend.

"Where did I go wrong?" Sawyer laments, staring up at the ceiling.

"To be fair," I say, "it wasn't your job to steer me toward right *or* wrong."

"If it makes you feel any better," Ember says, talking to Sawyer but glancing in my direction, "I don't think anyone went wrong at all. He's a great dad, and he's been really, really good to me. So good."

Something inside my chest bubbles, like the Pop Rocks I used to eat as a kid, the *crackle*, *pop*, and *fizz* on my tongue making me feel strangely joyous. I'm pretty sure it's pride, that I'm proud of myself, but this is a sensation that's been reserved for sporting achievements, not for relationships with people.

Maybe I'm not the massive fuckup I consider myself to be—at least not with her, and that's not nothing. It's a very important something—one of the most important somethings in my life.

"That just gave me a warm fuzzy," Sawyer says, her hand splayed across her chest. "You too?" she asks me.

"The warmest," I admit. "Thanks, Em." My voice is rough with emotion, and Ember's cheeks bloom a pretty pink.

"I will confess," Sawyer says, patting my leg, "it has been a pleasure watching you grow up these past couple of months."

"Thanks?" I say it like a question, but her acknowledgement that something has shifted in me mirrors Caitlin's comment. I just wish I could trust this new me, that I was sure these changes would stick, that if Ember leaves the country, I won't fall back into bad habits, things that'll ruin my relationship with Nova, eventually. Some days I can't imagine going backward, and other days, I'm convinced I'll fuck up. Most of my big life decisions have been, in hindsight, thoughtless or selfish, and it still feels like I could backslide. Under the right circumstances, I might fold for myself when I need to stay in the game for someone else.

Hours later, I'm lying on the hospital bed, and Nova is asleep on my chest. Sawyer is still here, chatting with both me and Ember about whatever comes to mind. Every once in a while, Nancy pops her head in and promises results soon. If Nova wasn't totally wiped out and clingy, I'd be storming the halls demanding answers. But she seems comfortable, and the anxiety that practically vibrated off Ember when I arrived seems to have subsided.

Someone knocks on the door before entering, and when the woman comes in, both Ember and Sawyer sit straighter, which is my only clue that she's likely the doctor.

"We've got the results back," she says, riffling through the pages on the clipboard. "Everything has come back normal that would be extremely worrying. While the swelling is a cause for concern, we don't believe it's tied to anything serious. Likely, it's a virus she picked up somewhere, and it's presenting in her as a fever and swollen feet and hands."

"A virus?" I say with a frown. "It'll just run its course and be done?"

"We suspect the swelling will be gone by morning, but we'd like to keep her overnight, just to be sure. She's quite young, and it's impossible for her to verbalize any other aches or pains or complaints she might be feeling. The stay is precautionary, and you can refuse it."

I shift toward Ember, and our gazes meet in wordless communication. Of the two of us, she's the cautious one, but I don't want to take any chances with Nova's health.

"Stay?" I suggest.

"You're her dad," she whispers.

"They'll stay," Sawyer says.

"I'll ask a nurse to make sure there are enough beds in here," the doctor says.

"That's it?" I ask when the doctor turns to leave.

"We're still monitoring. Hydrating. We'll provide additional pain relief if she needs it, but all the tests that would have indicated something serious came back conclusive and clear."

"Thank you," Ember says. "I'm really relieved."

Sawyer runs her hand along Ember's back, and I feel my own uncertainty seeping out of me. Nova will be okay. Tonight is a precaution.

"At the risk of Nova screaming bloody murder," Sawyer says, "why don't you let me take her for a while? You and Ember can go get some dinner and maybe get whatever you need from home for the overnight stay. When you two get back, I'll leave."

Ember bites her lip, and I can tell she'd rather not leave, but Sawyer's suggestion is sensible.

Then Ember surprises me when she says, "There is actually something I wanted to talk to Gage about, so if you really mean that…"

"I really mean it," Sawyer says with a smile.

As I pass a sleeping Nova over to Sawyer, I wonder what's worrying Ember, because that's definitely what it feels like. Nova is going to be fine, so what else could it be?

Chapter Twenty-Eight

EMBER

Nerves zip up and down my spine as Gage and I wait for his car to be delivered by the valet driver. He's asked me once already what I want to talk about, but I can't make the words come out. They're there, but I know once I say them, they'll set off a series of events that'll change my life forever. That's not an exaggeration, even though part of me wishes it was.

He takes the keys from the valet driver and slides into the driver seat while I buckle myself into the passenger seat.

We drive back to the house, both of us lost in our own thoughts. Once we're in the door, I head to Nova's room to gather some things for her. A change of clothes. Another pacifier. Her blankie. A couple of her favorite books. I shove everything into the spare diaper bag next to the crib.

"Em?"

When I turn, Gage is leaning against the door in the way that always makes my heart trip, like there's a part of me that still can't believe I live with someone this handsome. He's changed out of his suit into gray sweats and a butter-soft T-shirt that makes his eyes look violet rather than blue.

I sling the bag over my shoulder and head toward him. "You should get whatever you need."

"Hey," he says, and his hand comes to rest on the top of my bicep, stalling my escape. "You wanted to talk?"

I bite the inside of my cheek and stare at him. "I'm still working out what I want to say in my head."

His eyebrows lift almost comically high. "*That* can't be good." But his expression quickly morphs from surprise to concern. "Did I fuck up?"

"No." I shake my head for added emphasis, but I still can't figure out how I want this to go.

"And we're *not* going to talk about whatever is worrying you?"

"How do you know I'm worried?"

"I pay attention," he says.

The bag on my shoulder starts to slip, and Gage eases it off, clenching the strap in his hand. We're close enough that if I took one more step, I could be in his arms. Like always, the thought is both thrilling and terrifying. I want him, so much more than I should, but being with him might destroy me and everything else.

"Today, when Nova was sick, I couldn't help thinking about how I might not be here next time. If she's sick or injured or anything—I won't be *here* for it."

"We don't know that for sure," Gage says. "The job ads are new. One of them might work."

"What would it look like," I say, "if we got married?" I let the words come out in a rush so I don't have time to take them back.

He goes completely still, and he searches my face for a long beat. "Whatever you want it to look like. Exactly as things are now or something else."

"We have separate rooms and separate lives..."

"You help me with the real estate, we go to Wino every week, and we watch shitty reality TV together all the time. Our lives aren't that separate."

"We have to be married for five years," I say.

"That doesn't bother me."

"Five years is a long time to, you know, not do certain things." *Like have sex.* For me, it's no big deal. Sex hasn't been a priority for me at any point in my life. But I'm pretty sure Gage is the opposite.

"Like what?" He cocks an eyebrow and grins, clearly trying to make me say it.

"You know."

"Do I?"

We stare at each other, and I refuse to rise to the bait. His amusement at my discomfort slowly evaporates, and his knuckles brush my cheek.

"I'll follow your lead. It can be just us…" He sucks in what seems to be a deep, reluctant breath. "Or we can be with other people. I'd never force you into anything you didn't want, Em."

My heart thrums in my chest at the barest suggestion that we could ever be together like that. The safest option is clear.

"Other people," I say with a conviction I don't feel. "People who aren't from the island, just to be safe. Tourists or we leave the island for a weekend or whatever." Which I'll never do, and at least then, the women Gage is with won't be shoved in my face. I won't have to wonder if I'm sitting across from them at some charity event or business dinner. "You can just tell me you're going out with an old friend or something and then you can fly off to whoever to do whatever."

What looks like sadness floats across his face, but I don't understand why. By all accounts, he broke up with Abby over and over so he could sleep with other people. Ava has told me the stories—some of them more than once. She's stunned he hasn't been sleeping his way through Bellerive since I've been here. My suggestion to be with other people should be a relief. While it's been nice of him to hit pause on his sex drive while I've been living with him, it's not realistic to make him go without for five years. We don't have to break up, and he doesn't have to hide it.

Even though I'm sure I'll wish he did.

"'Old friend?' Is this like the verbal equivalent of a sock on the door?" he asks, no trace of amusement or teasing.

"If you want," I say.

"I don't want that," he says. "I have zero desire to know who you're hooking up with or when."

"I guess I won't be using the *hanging out with an old friend* line on you then," I say, trying to joke away the sudden tension, but Gage's jaw tics in response to my teasing. He is not amused. "Should we call Robert? Talk about what this arrangement should look like to make sure it appears real?"

"No," Gage says, his tone still more clipped than I'm used to. "He'll be pissy with me since he just posted those jobs."

"Is that a problem?" I ask.

"No," he says, leaving the doorway and heading for the front entrance, "I can take care of it."

"I feel like you're mad at me or something," I say, trailing behind him. "You just wish I'd agreed sooner?"

"Something like that," he calls over his shoulder, his tone still not quite right. He grabs his toiletry bag off the table at the front. "I'll meet you in the car."

I stop following him when I realize I haven't gotten my own things ready. Maybe he just needs a minute to process? Maybe he's regretting suggesting it in the first place? Oh, god. I assumed he still meant it, but maybe he hates the idea now.

As I gather my own things into a small bag, I decide I'll just speak to him in the car, let him know that he doesn't have to go through with it if he doesn't want to.

After I've locked the door, I slide into the passenger seat, and without facing him, I say, "We don't have to get married. If you've changed your mind, that's okay."

"I haven't changed my mind," he says, but the tension is still there as he pulls away from the house. "Have you changed yours in the last five minutes?" There's a bit of bite to his words, as though that's what he expects.

"No, I haven't. I want something that guarantees that I'll be here for all the important things for Nova. I just... I don't think I really understood how much I wanted that until today." I take a quick peek at his tense outline. "I can't imagine not having been there today. Having you call me when I'm too far away to be there to see her with my own eyes. She's all I have left." My voice cracks.

Gage abruptly steers the car onto the shoulder of the road, throws it into park, and he turns in his seat to face me. "She might be all you have left of Athena, but she's not all the family you have. You've got me, and you've got all my brothers and sisters. And I know it's not the same—that's impossible—but you're not alone."

"You might feel differently in five years." I give him a watery smile.

"I won't." He scoops up one of my tears with his thumb. "But maybe you will. You'll be tired of all the Tucker drama. Fed up with my idiocy." He leans forward and places a soft, gentle kiss on my cheek, and for a second, I swear he's breathing me in the same way I always do with him. "I'll never be the one closing the door to you, Em. If you want a door shut, you shut it yourself."

A tingling sensation spreads across my body, and when he withdraws a little, we're so close I can see the various flecks of blue in his eyes that make it hard to say exactly what shade they are.

"I don't want you to be miserable just to help me." As much as I'm worried about how deep I'll fall into this pit of feelings that I've already developed, Ava's words from weeks ago are at the back of my mind. Gage never had any intention of getting married so young, and for this to be a fake relationship seems so much worse than if we'd fallen in love and couldn't help ourselves. That the idea of being without each other would be the worst thing in the world. But we don't have that. We just have this agreement to look after each other, in whatever ways we can.

"Me? Miserable? That's categorically impossible," he says.

But he doesn't elaborate about why, so I suspect it has something to do with him being a Tucker or him having money or something like it, just by the gleam in his eyes.

"Once Nova is in the clear tomorrow," he says, "we'll start planning."

"You don't think we should talk to Robert? You could go to jail. I could get kicked out of the country forever. Those aren't small things."

"You worry too much," he says as he puts the car back into gear. "How would anyone be able to prove we haven't actually fallen in love? We live together. We're out in public weekly grinding against each other on the dance floor." He shrugs. "They won't be able to touch us."

Heat creeps into my cheeks at his casual mention of our dance sessions. It's not an inaccurate description, but it's not like we're making out on the dance floor.

"Maybe I do worry too much," I say, "but consequences, *negative* consequences, are a real thing in my life. You might skate through any questions or problems, but what if I don't?"

He glances at me and holds eye contact for a beat before focusing on the road again. "You know I'd never let anyone hurt you, right?"

"It's not about that," I say. "It's not that I don't trust you. My motto is '*better safe than sorry*,' and yours is probably the opposite. '*Don't ask for permission; beg for forgiveness.*' That's just never worked for me."

"You're close, but I don't *beg* for anything."

"Right. Right. Of course. You'd probably demand it."

"Maybe," he concedes. "I've never thought about what my motto might be."

We ride in silence for a few minutes, and I'm not sure if I should press my point again, or if I'll have to go behind Gage's back for the first, and hopefully only, time.

"I hear you," Gage says, just before we pull into the valet parking again. "We'll plan, but I'll also get us an appointment with Robert. Happy?"

"Relieved," I say.

"It's a start," he says with a hint of a smile as he gets out of the car and tosses the keys to the valet driver.

Chapter Twenty-Nine

GAGE

Our night at the hospital, sleeping in substandard cots next to Nova, is undercut with a trickle of grumpiness that I can't seem to stop. It started when Ember said we should fuck other people outside our marriage—not at all what I want—even if she thinks it's the safer choice. And my frustration was compounded when she seemed to believe I'd let her take the fall for the both of us if we got caught in this sham. And then the third thing, the one I've tried to pretend isn't true, is my low-level anxiety over having to be married for five years, but I can't figure out what's making me anxious. So many years. So many unknowns. Maybe that's all it is.

By the time we're cleared to go home the next morning, Nova's hands and feet are back to their normal size, her fever has broken, and Ember and I are barely talking.

Rather than staying at the house, I leave to go line up some properties that I intend to register under my brand, which officially launches in less than a week. I'm also hoping the distance will make me less impatient with her.

After I've signed a few new listings, I drive past the courthouse, and I stop in on impulse to ask about a marriage license. Turns out, we both have to sign it, so

I grab the paperwork. It can take up to fifteen days to process the license, so we need to get on the application.

When I get home, Ember is on the couch and Nova is already in bed.

"There's a plate in the fridge," Ember says as she turns a page in her book.

"What are you reading?" I ask as I grab the plate of food. Bill took her to a bookstore last week, and she came home with an armful of colorful paperbacks that I've ignored as they've become strewn around the living room.

"This one is a sports romance."

"What sport?"

"Hockey."

"You should read about a real sport, like surfing." I hit the timer on the microwave and turn to face her, finally feeling like we're on some even footing again. "I could teach you, but you always say no."

She stares at her book for a beat, and then she glances at me over the back of the couch. "I don't know how to swim."

"What? But you go in the pool with Nova all the time."

"The shallow end. I'm fine if I can touch, obviously."

"Then I'll teach you to swim," I say. "If you're going to live in Bellerive for years, you need to know how to swim." It's sound reasoning. "Speaking of which." I fish the marriage certificate paperwork out of my bag. "It takes fifteen days to process the marriage certificate. We both have to sign. Sooner the better. Time's ticking." I've already filled out all my details, and I slide the sheets toward the middle of the island while Ember closes her book and comes over to join me.

She opens a drawer, probably looking for a pen, and I pass her one of mine. Her brow is furrowed as she fills in all the details.

"Did you call Robert?" she asks as she scribbles her answers.

"Yeah. Left a message. His secretary will call back with an appointment, I'm sure."

"Thank you," she says.

"I aim to please." But the reminder of our conversation yesterday is enough to sour my mood slightly. "I'll drop this off tomorrow. Get that part rolling."

She signs her name and slides them back to me. "What should I do?"

"Shop for engagement and wedding rings."

"Budget?" she asks while I'm taking my food out of the microwave.

"There's no budget," I scoff, but as I turn toward her, I see her smile and realize she already knew. "Buy what you like."

"You want me to buy everything?"

"Should go on your card with no issues. I'll drop more money into your bank account from the trust." As I take a forkful of my food, I catch her expression and realize I've said something that bothers her. I'm tempted to leave it because I'm just not in the mood, but I've decided that if I have a personal motto, it's '*Do Better*,' and so I have to ask. With Abby, I would have sulked and let things fester and not recognized how she was feeling or even acknowledged how I was feeling. While I can't pinpoint the exact source of my bad attitude, I know I've got one. That's progress.

"Okay," she says quietly, and she goes to the couch picking up her book again and thumbing through the pages.

"What aren't you saying?" I ask with a sigh. *Be Better.* Maybe that's it too.

She flips through her pages in rapid succession, the book making a *thwapping* noise as the pages fly by. "This is supposed to look real, right?"

"You want me to buy the ring?"

"Or at least be with me. This might be a… a… an agreement between us, but it's not supposed to look like that."

"Fine," I say. "I'll make some time tomorrow for us to go to Spencer's in Tucker's Town. We can pick something out together. Next week is going to be too busy with the company launch."

"Okay," Ember says with a nod. "Yeah, I get that. Just text me when you know what time you'll be here." Then she takes her book and goes to her room.

Fuck.

We're spending the next five years together, and I'm already unbearable company.

Robert enters our house in a cloud of tension. "What did my secretary tell me you two were doing?"

"We're getting married," I say as I take a bite of my apple. He's arrived after regular business hours on a Friday, so I had a feeling when he texted me to hold off on any additional plans that this conversation wasn't going to be pleasant.

"And what did I tell you before you gave the okay for those job ads?"

"Yeah, I know." I sigh. "But this makes more sense."

"It does *not* make more sense when you've already filed ads with the government. You now have to hire some of those people."

"I'll find something for them to do." I shrug.

Robert rubs his face and drags out one of the chairs at the island. "Where's Ember?"

"Putting Nova to bed. She'll be out in a minute."

"If you're hiring people, that aspect might be salvageable. But you have to sell this relationship."

"What's to sell?" I ask. "She comes to work events with me. She lives here."

Ember walks quickly back into the room and takes a seat at the island near Robert. "Sorry," she says, glancing at Robert. "She was fussy tonight."

"I just got here," Robert says, and he gives her a tight smile. "I was just telling Gage that you have to sell this relationship. Not just outside the house but inside it too. Photos. Shared sleeping accommodations."

"What?" The color drains from Ember's face.

"If the government even suspects this marriage is a fraud, they can ask to visit your house. Conduct interviews with friends and family. It can get very personal, very quickly. Intimate questions can be, and often are, asked."

"Like what her vagina looks like?" I ask, not at all put off by this latest development. In fact, I can feel my bad mood dissipating like a long-forgotten fog. Not that I would ever want Ember to feel forced into anything, but...

"Gage!" Ember turns bright red, and then I remember she's not quite as comfortable with all this as I am.

"Tattoos, shapes, sizes. I've heard a lot in my years sitting in on those conversations. Emails and text messages exchanged." He closes his eyes. "Please tell me you haven't emailed or texted each other about *any* of these details."

"We talk mostly in person," Ember says.

"The two of you need to be out there, in public, obviously in love or lust or whatever you want to label it. But very much, no questions asked, together."

If it's possible, Ember goes even paler.

"I filed the marriage license this morning," I say. "So at least that's done."

Robert gives me a horrified look and slams his palm into his face. "Fucking amateurs. Remember when I told you if you'd called me before Ember came to the island that I could have made all this much smoother? You should have remembered *that* before you did *this*."

"We need a marriage license," I say.

"Before you get engaged? Before people believe you're a couple? The government will look at the timeline. They're very good with timelines."

Ember lets out a squeak of distress.

"It's done now," I say. "What do you suggest?"

"The next few weeks. You two"—he flicks his finger between both of us—"out in public, all loved up. Go places lots of people will see you. Any chance you have to provide a united front, do that."

"Her first initial is in my company's name, which launches on Monday. That's pretty permanent. Very united."

"That's good," he says. "Lends a bit of credibility. Maybe you weren't ready to go public before, but now you are because you're getting married." He holds up a finger. "The actual engagement can be a private affair, but you need to come up with a romantic, over-the-top scenario that seems fitting for a Tucker. Everything, absolutely everything, needs to seem real. Keep asking yourself, '*If this was real, what would I do?*' Or in this case, "*What would I have done?*" and then you keep doing that until you don't have to ask yourself that anymore."

"I'll be asking that the whole time. No one is falling in love for real here," I say, holding up my hands.

"I don't give a shit what's in your heart," Robert says. "I only care what other people see and perceive." He looks at both of us, making eye contact. "What you're doing, what *we're* doing is highly illegal. You don't text or email me anything in relation to this arrangement. You need advice, we meet in person somewhere private. We can't be seen in public together."

"I don't know, Gage," Ember says, wringing her hands.

"Too late now," Robert says.

Between the jobs we filed and the marriage license application, we're locked into this arrangement. Granted, neither of us thought this through quite as well as we should have, but I'm confident it'll all work out fine.

In five years, we'll look back at this uncertainty and laugh because we pulled it off. Everyone got what they wanted, and no one got hurt. But even as I think it, there's a nagging doubt at the back of my brain, Ember and Sawyer whispering, *Consequences*, so loud that it almost drowns out everything else.

Chapter Thirty

EMBER

I'm so stupid. Epically stupid. I knew all the reasons marrying Gage was a bad idea—can somewhat remember laying them out for him when he kept suggesting marriage was the logical option—but when confronted with the reality of not being in Nova's life, I skipped over the realities of being Gage's wife.

Robert leaves, and I stay rooted to my seat at the island, staring at my hands, unable to make eye contact with Gage. Though, he seems unbothered, mixing himself a shake and whistling a tune I vaguely recognize, *actually whistling*, as though this isn't a complete disaster.

I don't know why I convinced myself this would be the easier option, the one guaranteed to keep me on the island. Instead, it might leave me permanently barred from here. Not that long ago, I knew this. It was one of the reasons I wanted some guarantee that I could be in Nova's life, beyond just being her aunt, and Gage gave me that. Legally, I'm entitled to see her at specific intervals throughout the year. No matter what happens, I have that.

But when I held Nova in the emergency room, the thought of anyone else comforting her, being there, became impossible to accept. If I was a plane ride away, who'd be holding her? So, if I couldn't accept someone else in my place, I had to accept something else.

Turns out, I might just be an idiot.

"You're way overthinking this," Gage says just before he hits the button on the blender.

"You're *under*thinking it," I say once the blender stops.

He pours some of the liquid into a glass and slides it toward me. "A celebratory daiquiri," he says. "We just got engaged." He fills a second glass with the red slushy mix and then lifts it as though we're going to toast.

"None of this is funny." I shoot him a glare.

"I'm not laughing," he says. "I will admit to being slightly amused at how appalled you are by this whole thing. Our pretending can go as far as you're comfortable with. No one is going to ask me what your vagina looks like."

I sputter on a sip of the daiquiri. I really wish he'd stop talking about getting up close and personal with what's under my clothes.

"They'd have to examine you to know if I was telling the truth," he muses, "and that seems a bit too far, even for the government."

"The government must have ways of proving couples are frauds."

"Probably, yeah." He takes another long drink of his daiquiri before setting down the glass on the island. "I'm just saying, they aren't going to ask you to take your pants off. We should take basic precautions."

Robert's ideas didn't seem so basic considering we're trying to commit fraud against the government. "We have to pretend to be in love." My stomach rolls at the thought, but I'm not sure if it's pretending or realizing I may not have to pretend all that hard that causes my seasickness.

"That's easy. I'll channel Brice when he's with my sister."

"What were you like... with Abby?" The last words get stuck in my throat, almost don't come out. The more I get to know him, the stranger it is that he was with her for so long, even if it was off and on. "What are you like when you love someone?"

He winces. "The love part, I'm not sure I can answer. Abby and I had a great time, and I might have labeled it love once or twice, but I've never been sure. Abby and I wanted the same things, and that made our relationship easy. That's what I wanted." He fiddles with his glass, sliding it across the surface between his hands.

"I've always been fine with any level of public display. I doubt love would change that. What about you?" He lifts his glass to his lips again.

"With love?"

He nods, and he maintains eye contact while he takes a sip.

"Not my thing," I say.

"You've slept with one guy."

He says that as though it automatically means something significant. My cheeks blaze. But the experience was nothing like what he's probably been imagining. "My sister was always chasing love. She needed it. Wanted it. Took it from whoever would give it to her. But for me, love has never looked safe. Not with my mom and dad, not with Athena and any of her boyfriends, and not with me and any of mine."

"Not safe?" Gage scowls. "Were you..." He hesitates for a beat. "Assaulted?"

"No, no," I shake my head. "It wasn't like that."

"If it was even close to that," Gage says, holding up his phone, "I have a hit person on speed dial. Give me a name, and it'll all be taken care of." There's not even a hint of his normal teasing in his tone. "In fact, if you make a list of every person who has ever caused you a moment of pain, I'll make sure they suffer twice as much. I'll turn someone's side hustle into a full-time gig."

"No one is a hit person as a side hustle," I say.

"I guess we'll see. Names?" He has his phone open, clearly ready to type.

"I don't need an eye-for-an-eye kind of justice, Gage."

"Good, because that sounds like the cheap way to do it. I'm going after both eyes. Their world can be completely dark if they ever made yours dim even a little."

Him offering to blind someone shouldn't be a turn-on, and even as heat begins to pool in my lower half, I know my attraction to him isn't about *what* he's offered but rather what it signifies.

"My first and only time just wasn't a great experience." I can't decide if I'm underplaying my feelings or not.

He sets down his phone, and he leaves his glass resting in a puddle of condensation to circle the island. He leans against the island in front of me, slouching down to make eye contact that's so deep and intimate that I'd be squirming if he was anyone else. But I like seeing myself reflected in his eyes because he seems to genuinely care.

"Will you tell me sometime?" His voice is gentle.

"Probably," I say because it's true.

We're so close, I can smell the rum on his breath, and he's searching my expression for something while I try to determine what's going on in his head too.

"Since we're going to be selling us as a couple in public, can you show me what you're comfortable with?"

"Show you?" My voice is scratchy with sudden uncertainty.

"On me," he says, and he runs his index finger along the back of my hand and fingers. "You can do anything to me. But what would *you* be okay to have me do in public?"

"This." I lace my fingers with his without hesitation. Most of the time, we already hold hands at various points, but it's casual. Unplanned. Usually as a way for Gage to make sure I get from point A to point B safely and with him.

"What else?" he asks.

I only pause for a brief second before running my free hand along his cheek. He's done that to me before, too, and I like it. Nothing about the gesture makes me feel unsure or unsafe. "This," I say.

"What else?" he asks, his voice rough.

I urge him to come a little closer, and he shifts nearer, then I rise on the stool to kiss his forehead. Another Gage move that always makes me feel taken care of, and if we were in a real relationship, maybe even more than that.

He closes his eyes, but we're so close, his breath stirs my hair. Without waiting for his prompt, I place careful kisses along the edge of his face and then his cheek. "All of this too." My voice is breathy.

His eyes flutter open when I draw back a little, and he scans my expression. His nearness, coupled with the crackle of sexual tension in the air, causes me to shift, and my chair wobbles. I almost fall into him, and he drops my hand that he's still holding to steady me, his arm looping around my back, drawing me close. Everything in me ignites with anticipation.

"Anything else?" he asks, his voice barely audible. His knuckles graze my cheek.

"You can kiss me," I say, surprised at my own bravery.

"Right now?"

"In public."

"I don't want to kiss you for the first time as some kind of performance, Em." The intense eye contact is back, making my heart thump in my chest. "I want the first one to be real, at least." But he doesn't close the space between us, seems to have understood in the little I told him that I need to feel in control in order to trust him. He's stated what he wants, but I don't feel pressured to give in.

All the things he's given me without any expectation of receiving anything in return cause me to close the distance between us. At his core, he's a good man. Maybe we're not a love match and will never be in love, but it might be nice to have this, to have him, for a little while. Safety. Control. Protection. Things I never thought any man would offer.

I skim my lips across his, ever so lightly, and his hand digs into my hair, but he doesn't deepen the kiss, doesn't do anything that might make me want to back off, change my mind. So instead of easing away like I should, I angle my head, and I slide my hands along his face, and I deepen the kiss.

Then we're kissing for real, and it's like nothing I've ever experienced before. His lips are both firm and tender, sliding against mine in a smooth rhythm. He dips his tongue in, still cool from the daiquiri, gentle, testing, and I meet the advance with my own.

A sigh slips between us, and I don't know if it's him or me, but it feels right. All of this feels right. Underneath all of our casual touches and tension-filled dance sessions, I've wondered what kissing him would be like, whether it would feel as natural as everything else has. The feel of his hard body and soft lips against me is so much better than I imagined.

"Em," he says between kisses, "I'm going to need to do this all the time."

"Okay," I whisper. The kisses are making me brave and stupid, but I can't bring myself to care as he lifts me off the stool, carrying me toward the couch.

Instead of laying me down and climbing on top of me, he sits in the middle of the couch, easing me down over his lap, one of my legs on either side, and then one of his hands is back in my hair, the other on my ass. I'm grinding against him, and he's kissing me. Soft noises of pleasure are all around us, and some of them are him and some are me and all of them are making me unbelievably turned on. His hands aren't all over me like an octopus, grasping anything they can squeeze, and the fact that he seems completely content just to kiss me senseless makes my heart do funny things in my chest.

I frame his face, break the kiss, and I pant along with him, our foreheads pressed together.

"Too much?" he asks.

"For public? Yes."

He chuckles. "For *any* time. I want you to know you can trust me. Whatever you want, I'll do, and whatever you don't want, I won't do. Was that too much?"

I shake my head, easing my hands along his shoulders. I can't make the words leave my lips.

"I need you to say it," Gage says.

"It wasn't too much."

He tilts my head to plant a kiss on my forehead, and his lips linger for a beat.

"I like it," I add, even though that's an understatement. No man has made me feel like that from a kiss, as though my whole body was a flame, burning just for him.

"So I can do it again?"

"Yeah," I say, and I fight the urge to bury my face, to hide.

"Do you want me to ask you first when it's just us?" He draws back, and he holds my face, as though sensing that this conversation is making me want to fold into myself.

"No," I say.

"Em." His blue eyes are bright with frustration. "If this is going to work, I need you to have the courage to be completely honest with me. It would *gut* me if I found out I did something you didn't want or like."

"I know," I whisper. "I trust you, and I know if I told you no, that you'd be okay."

A crease forms between his brows, and I can almost see him turning over my words. "Why wouldn't I be okay?"

"Just some guys, you know…"

"I *don't* know, but I'm feeling like I'm going to need that list."

"No one has really hurt me, Gage."

"The '*really*' there implies discomfort at least."

I shrug. My taste in guys to kiss or make out with or sleep with has been historically bad. Athena said not all men were assholes, but all the ones she picked seemed to be, and I had the same luck.

Still have the same taste, apparently, considering who I just kissed.

Gage is the exception to my string of back luck or bad choices; I was never sure which it was. And, although I try not to think about it, I often wonder how differently things might have gone for Athena if she'd reached out to Gage. She knew who he was, so it seems unlike her to leave that stone unturned when we were struggling.

"I just want to smooth over the world for you," he says, his fingers toying with a strand of my hair. "Get rid of any bumps and potholes."

"Bulldoze over anyone who dares to make life difficult?" I suggest.

"Exactly," he says with a wide grin that reminds me for the billionth time that he's the most attractive man I've ever met in real life.

He's never met a problem he couldn't make disappear, and I wonder if, the longer I spend with him, the more I'll be able to buy into the dream he's selling. At the moment, all of this still feels too good to be true.

Chapter Thirty-One

GAGE

Robert won't be happy with me, but I needed marriage reinforcements. None of my friends can know the truth—most of them would sell me out if the government came knocking. Two people who'd never let me down? Sawyer and Nathaniel, which is why I have them meet me in Tucker's Town at Spencer's to help me pick a ring for Ember. At least I'm taking some part of Robert's warning seriously, right? Ember isn't down here getting her own ring as though this isn't important and official.

We're ushered to a back room for a private ring viewing. Ember's ring size is in my phone, and she told me not to pick anything too outrageous. Though she's becoming a Tucker, so whatever I pick can't be *too* small. If we have to make this believable, the ring is important.

When the sales agent leaves to get the first set of rings based on my criteria, Nathaniel runs a hand down his face.

"You realize this is fraud," he says.

"Of course," I say. "Robert explained it all to us."

"Please tell me you haven't told anyone else or spoken about any of this around other people," Sawyer says, glancing at the door.

"We're not stupid." I let out a noise of exasperation. "Neither of you are going to sell me out, and I need help. I don't know what the fuck I'm doing."

"Clearly," Nathaniel says dryly.

"I meant the ring," I grit out. "You've picked one out before, but I've never even thought about it."

Sawyer goes very still beside me, and I glance at her.

"What?" I ask. "It's been years. I'm not allowed to mention that?"

"It's fine," Nathaniel says, his voice taking on the same annoyed, gritty texture as my own. "Hopefully, your luck is better than mine."

"She's going to say yes," I say.

"You've been honest with Ember?" Sawyer says. "She knows the risks?"

"Yes," I say.

The door pops open and the sales agent comes in with rings nestled in a felt board. "I pulled anything that met your criteria," he says.

The three of us scan them, and I turn to each of them. "What do you think?"

"They all have rubies," Sawyer says, stating the obvious.

"It's Ember's favorite gemstone." A ruby isn't my personal taste, but I'm not supposed to be buying something *I'll* like—which is also why Sawyer and Nathaniel are here. Left to my own opinions, I might forget that Ember is the one who has to wear it.

Nathaniel starts plucking some out and putting them in the top row. "None of these."

Sawyer's finger goes along the ones left, and she stops at the same one I've been eyeing. It's an oval ruby with a diamond halo in white gold. Classy. Expensive. Large enough to be believable, but not so extravagant that Ember will hate me for it.

"That's the one I was looking at too," I say when Sawyer plucks it out of the felt cushion.

"You're sure about this?" Nathaniel asks, and I can hear the unease in his voice.

"I know what I want," I say. "We'll take that one." I pull up Ember's ring size and pass it to the salesclerk. "How soon can you have it ready?"

"For an expedited service fee, we can have it ready by this afternoon." The clerk sets the ring in the top corner of the board and picks it up, ready to leave.

"Suits me," I say, passing him my credit card.

Once he's left with the rings and my card, Nathaniel rises. "Not sure I was really needed."

"I appreciate you coming down on the weekend," I say. "I just needed a second opinion."

"If you wanted a second opinion on what you're doing—" Nathaniel says.

"I don't." My tone is clipped with annoyance. "It's happening."

Nathaniel shakes his head and slips out the door without another word.

"When are you proposing?" Sawyer asks.

All morning, my brain has been spinning, stuck on whether I make a big deal about the proposal or I just give her the ring when I get home. Our conversation by the pool comes back to me.

"I'm not sure," I hedge. "Soon. Very soon. It has to be."

"If you want to decorate the house, I can take Ember out for a drink tonight. Candles, mood music. Simple, but thoughtful."

That sounds perfect. It's the sort of low-key thing Ember would like, but it gives both of us a memory to tell if anyone asks.

"My friend, Rhonda, is a photographer. She can help you document the moment."

On one hand, having the photos would be good proof of our relationship. On the other hand, I already filed the marriage certificate and having engagement photos after that seems like a red flag. Robert said to ask myself what I'd do if this was real, and I imagine I'd have a photographer and splash the evidence of our engagement all over my socials. Why wouldn't I, right?

"Does your friend do videos too?" I ask. That's me—capture every moment and angle.

"I'm sure she does," Sawyer says, "but then you'd need something meaningful for her to record. What would you say to Ember?" She searches my expression. "Are you *actually* in love with her?"

"No." My answer comes quickly and instinctually, and I think it's honest. I like her—a lot—and our chemistry last night when we kissed was exactly what I expected. For whatever reason, I just seem to get Em, understand what she needs, without her having to say a word. The five years we'll have to be married doesn't worry me as much as I thought it would. We're very different, but our differences don't seem to signal conflict—at least not yet.

But love? At this point, I'm probably a lost cause for love. Whatever trait is necessary for romantic love, I don't seem to possess it. I care, and maybe that's enough. I can fake whatever else might be needed.

At least I'm acing the parental love. I have zero doubts about how I feel about my kid.

"Forget the video," I say. "Photos are fine." I don't have a clue what I'm going to say to Ember, and it's probably better not to have proof of any hint of uncertainty.

"Tonight?" Sawyer asks, taking out her phone. "I'll see if she's free at eight for a half hour or so?" She's already typing.

"Tonight," I agree.

Now I just need to figure out how to organize a proposal that'll make Ember happy without promising things I'll never deliver.

Nova is asleep. Ember is out with Sawyer for a late dinner and a drink. The house is dark, and there are candles laid out in a path to the pool house where the doors are thrown wide open and soft music is playing. It's not the most over-the-top arrangement I could have come up with, but I was really torn about what any of this should look like. Sawyer's suggestion felt like a lifeline and a compromise that both Ember and I could live with.

But as I put this together, I began to wonder whether my over-the-top sentiments of the past have been designed to avoid just the scenario I'm creating tonight. When the flash-bangs are happening in something extravagant, there's not much room for something intimate or meaningful. It's shock and awe and crowds. Light. Easy. Fun. No substance or subtext. What you see is what you get.

It's not two people standing in front of each other, vowing to play pretend for five years. Tonight, it all felt a bit *too* real, too important as I laid down the candles, checked the flower arrangements I had delivered, and picked the music. For Nova's sake, I don't want to fuck up what I've got with Ember. We have a good thing going in this house, and if I screw up, Ember's not going to care how much money I offer her.

The doorbell rings, and I check my phone to see a woman with a camera bag standing at the door. I clear my troubled thoughts to let her in, and we discuss my vague plan before she goes out to the pool area. She assures me that I'll probably forget she's even there.

Before I have a chance to let nerves creep in, the front door beeps after the entry code is punched in. The front door closes, and her heels pause their clicking almost immediately.

"Gage?" she calls. "Is the power out?"

"Leave the lights off and come back here," I say, feeling for the ring box in my pocket.

The *click, click, click* of her heels comes through the house of flowers and candles. The sliding door is already open, and so is the gate to the pool area. The doors for the pool house are thrown wide, and there's champagne and two glasses sitting on the bar inside. Everything is set, but I can feel the hum of uncertainty in me, even though the outcome *is* certain.

Her pale-blue dress swishes around her thighs, and I trail my gaze along the same path I wish my hands could follow.

Confusion mars her face, and she has one hand on her chest, like her heart might be beating too fast. I've seen her do it before when she's in a situation that's made her unsure or nervous, and now I wonder if I should have warned her.

"What's going on?" she whispers.

I take the ring box out of my pocket, and I give it a little waggle to help take the edge off whatever she's feeling.

Her eyes light with understanding, and she breathes, "Oh, Gage. You did this for me?"

"For you. For us." I pop open the box and take a knee in front of her. "I will protect you and care for you with everything I have. Ember Joycelyn Whitten, will you marry me?"

Tears are in her eyes, and she swallows several times before she says, "Yes," in a voice that's so low I barely hear her. "Yes, I'll marry you."

I take the ring out of where it's nestled, and I slide it onto her finger, a perfect fit. Then I rise to my feet, draw her into my arms, and I hesitate for a second before sliding my hand along her cheek and pressing my lips to hers. It's chaste, but despite her saying I didn't have to ask to kiss her again last night, I'm aware that we aren't at a high heat level. But god, I want to be. So fucking badly.

A tear hits my hand, and I ease back to make sure I haven't done something she didn't want. "You okay?"

She nods. "I'm just..." She takes my hand but steps away, turning in a half circle. "You did this? On your own?"

"Just me," I say with a hint of a smile.

Her free hand presses to her chest, and I know I've hit the mark. My chest swells with that fizzy popping feeling, the same as before, as though I couldn't be prouder of myself. But it's tinged with something else. When I scan her happy profile, an emotion I can't place is seeping in at the edges of my pride. Whatever it is, it's linked to her, to this moment.

It's strange to think something performative can still feel so real, so authentic. I've never had something I knew I had to do feel so much like something I want to do too.

Ember's gaze comes back to mine, and the tears are gone, replaced with something that looks a lot like longing. She doesn't say anything, she just closes the distance between us, and there's nothing hesitant or pure about the way her lips seek mine, slide against mine, her tongue slipping into my mouth.

Fuck, yes.

I tighten my hold on her with one hand while the other is in her hair, keeping her lips from leaving mine for too long.

"You are way too good at this," she murmurs as she kisses me again and again and again.

The sliding door shuts, and it causes me to break the kiss. Over Ember's head, I spot Rhonda moving through the dimly lit living room toward the front entrance. She was right; I didn't even remember she was taking photos.

Ember glances over her shoulder, and when she turns back, she raises her eyebrows. "Who was that?"

"Photographer to immortalize the moment forever. Figured we needed some social proof."

The interruption was probably for the best, but I'm tempted to restart what was picking up steam between me and Em. But she was pretty clear that sleeping with me wasn't on her marriage agenda, and pushing her or making her feel like it has to be isn't something I can stomach. I want her to want me as much as I want her.

"Sawyer mentioned that I should clean out my apartment in Colorado," Ember says, but there's nothing in her tone that suggests she wants to.

"That's not necessary."

"She made a good point. If I still have the place, someone might wonder why. I should probably..." She sucks air through her teeth, her chest rising as though it's taking a lot out of her. "I should probably clear out my things, at least. If you can leave it unrented..."

"The rent is nothing," I say.

"How did you buy it with the trust rules?"

"Properties for personal use don't count, and I claimed it as Nova's childhood home. Your unit is remaining unrented for your use, so it's technically a personal property."

"A loophole."

"So many of them," I say with a grin. "I can have someone box up the apartment, if you want." I don't like the idea of her being back there without me, and with the company launch on Monday, I know I won't have the time to go. Only four of Hugh's top employees signed with me, and thankfully Martin was one of them, but we're going to need to hustle to stay afloat and then hustle harder to wrestle the big clients out of Hugh's grasp. A trip to Colorado is probably months away.

"Sawyer said she could watch Nova next weekend, if you have to work, and then I can do it myself."

"I'll organize your flight." As long as no one else is using the company jet, I can avoid sending her commercial by herself, which will make me feel a bit better. "And I'll get Rusty to drive you wherever you need to go once you're there."

"Is it okay if I ship the stuff here?" She bites her lip and seems uncertain.

"Of course. We can put it in an NGE Realty storage facility or one of the rooms here. Whatever you want."

She hugs me tight, but she doesn't seem happy about anything anymore, more resigned. If she hadn't been the one to return to the marriage idea, I'd be worried I've cornered her into something she doesn't want.

We're bound to have some bumps in the next five years, but I won't let her old apartment be one of them.

Chapter Thirty-Two

GAGE

A link to the photos Rhonda took hits my email the next day. When I open them, I'm surprised at how good they are. Ember looks luminous, as though lit from inside, and I'm fixated on her, as if she's the center of my universe. My expression is surprising and not.

"Em," I call to her on Sunday once I've gotten out my work computer. "Come pick some of these for us to post."

"Us?" Em picks up Nova to bring her to the island. "Post where? My socials are a graveyard."

"Don't you think we should both put something out?" Though, I've been debating whether I should tell my friends and family first. I haven't been able to decide what I'd do if this was real. Tell them or be so swept up in it all that I'd forgotten to say a word.

"Which ones do you like?" She presses against my arm, peering at the photos as I flip through them. "She must have photoshopped these. I don't look like that."

"Bullshit modesty. You do look like that," I say with a chuckle. "You are that beautiful. Don't tell me you don't know."

She glances up at me, and then she rises on her toes to plant a quick kiss on my lips. We've been trying out these casual touches today because we both reasoned that we need to seem completely comfortable in public. As soon as news of our engagement breaks, the gossip rags on the island will be jockeying for more photos. Taking photos of children without parental permission isn't allowed in Bellerive, which has meant Nova and Ember have been mostly left alone since they arrived on the island. Once Ember also becomes news and my company launches, the game changes, which I tried to explain to her. But I've been told before that the scrutiny isn't something you can understand until it's happening to you. I've never known anything different.

"With your company kicking off and me leaving the island, is it a good idea to post these today?" She sets the hand she's not using to hold Nova on the small of my back, and she rests her cheek against my arm.

"I haven't told my parents yet either." Or Ava or Maren, and if the sibling grapevine was at work, Ava would have already texted me for not looping her in earlier.

"You don't know how Hugh's going to take the big reveal tomorrow, right? The five of you quitting, NGE Realty going live everywhere with advertising. Our announcement can probably wait, right? We don't even have a date."

"The date needs to be soon." I rub the back of my neck. "And I'll probably need you to plan most of it."

"That's fine." She reaches past me to press the favorite button on a couple of the photos. "When things feel calm enough to announce anything, those are the ones I like."

I drop a kiss on the top of her head, and she smiles up at me. "Pretending isn't so hard," she says.

Oh, something is definitely frequently hard, but giving her affection isn't the difficult part. The lack of follow-through might kill me. It's like hours and hours of foreplay. Every touch, caress, and kiss inches me closer to the begging Ava's already suggested I should do. I've never been so turned on by so little. Every other woman I've been able to take or leave, but with Ember, all I want to do is *take, take, take.*

"Are you worried about Hugh's reaction tomorrow?" she asks.

"He can't do anything about it," I say. "I had lawyers look at what we're doing from every angle, and we're okay that way. I'm sure he'll be angry." Part of me hopes he'll be fucking pissed, and I'd love it even more if he was afraid. NGE Realty is coming for his crown, and I'm not stopping until Tucker-Smith Realty is a shadow of what it is today. Hugh will feel my wrath, and he'll know he brought it on himself the minute his hand touched my future wife.

My wife. Thinking of Ember with that title gives me a moment of pause, but I also like that she'll be mine. That in a few short weeks, she'll be *my* wife, and this intense protectiveness I've felt almost from the moment I met her will be justified. She won't just be a Tucker because she's Nova's aunt; she'll be a Tucker because she's truly and legally mine. As I let myself really absorb that reality, I realize I love everything about it.

The NGE Realty announcement drops in thirty minutes, and I'm sitting in the underground parking garage under Tucker-Smith Realty trying to decide whether I should even go in.

Three of the four realtors I've stolen from Hugh opted to take today as a vacation day. They cleaned out their office over the weekend to avoid a confrontation. I'm glad they had the guts to jump to my team, but I'm a little worried they aren't properly prepared for the fight we're starting if they can't even face him. Martin, however, is in the office right now waiting for the announcement to go live so he can drop his resignation on Hugh's desk himself. I would not be at all surprised if he follows it by whipping out his dick and pissing everywhere.

As for me, I want to see Hugh's face when it all hits his inbox. Since the company dinner, I've been avoiding him or else I'd end up in jail. That's still a real possibility if he says even *one word* about Ember.

If I'm leading these Realtors into a fight, I have to be at the head of the charge, and that means facing Hugh, even if I end up doing something stupid and impulsive while I'm there. Once I'm out of the car, I lock it and head for the elevators.

At the top floor, the elevator door pings, and Martin is standing there with two security guards. I raise my eyebrows.

"Hugh knows," Martin says, "and I didn't get the pleasure of being the one to tell him."

"He's waiting for you," Buster, my favorite guard, says.

That sounds ominous, but I know everything I've done has been on the up-and-up. Apart from stealing four of his best, but even that's not illegal.

I head down the hallway, and everyone turns to look at me as I make my way to Hugh's office. He doesn't stand up when I get to the door but merely smirks at me.

"Big day for you," Hugh says.

"For you too," I say, matching his arrogant tone. "Losing four of your best."

"Not my best if they follow you into poverty. No risk for you. You've got the trust. But for them? Foolish. And when your little side project goes belly-up, I told them I wouldn't take them back, even if they begged. They're fucked, and you fucked them."

"Nah," I say, leaning against his doorway. "It'll be Tucker-Smith Realty bent over begging for mercy. When you're on the verge of bankruptcy, with no one in Bellerive willing to work with you anymore, remember you brought this on yourself."

"I'm not even a little worried." He chuckles. "You were a fuckup coming out of the womb. I took you on here out of pity. Who'd hire you after all the scrapes you've gotten yourself into over the years? No one. No one looks at you and thinks *success story*. A pretty boy who skates by on his wealth. I even offered that poor woman you've been keeping at your house an escape from your ineptitude. A chance to feel fully appreciated and satisfied."

Every one of his comments hits all the pressure points I try to hide, the things I have often thought about myself, the ones my parents have outright said to me in the past. But it's his final comment about Ember that sends me storming into his office, has me lifting him out of his chair and pressing him against his wall like I've grown some superhuman strength.

"You don't fucking talk about her," I grit out.

"Hit me," he says. "I dare you."

"If you ever lay another finger on her, I will fucking kill you." And if I wasn't so angry, I'd probably be shocked to discover I mean every word. I wouldn't hire someone; I'd take pleasure in doing it myself.

"Uttering threats is a crime," Hugh says with a smirk. "Not sure how well you'll do in jail, pretty boy. Your money won't buy me off."

I grind my teeth and push off him, anger still racing through my veins, hot and feral.

Hugh straightens his suit and tie. "Women lie, Gage. Did she tell you she didn't want it? Didn't welcome my advances? If you hadn't been there, I'm sure she'd have been on her knees under the table suc—"

I hit him so hard he falls to the ground, but it's not enough, so I climb on top of him, and I hit him again. His fingerprints bruised her body. A memory of how utterly defeated she was by how he violated her plays at the edges of each punch. The only liar here is him.

Buster hauls me off him, saying something in my ear that isn't registering. My mind is still a cloud of black rage, and if he lets me go, I'm hitting Hugh again.

"Gage, you cannot be fucking doing this here," he says louder in my ear.

Another guard has come in and is helping Hugh to his feet, and Buster turns me so I can't see them and then he starts escorting me out.

"He's a vindictive fucker," Buster says, low enough that only I can hear. "He'll press charges. Get your lawyer ready. He's got cameras in his office. You're not the first to take a swing, not the first person who's wanted revenge."

My hand is aching, and when I look down, my knuckles are raw and red.

Not exactly the start to my new company I'd been hoping for, but it isn't dread circulating in my chest, it's satisfaction. Whether my new company succeeds or not, Hugh will always remember how I beat him to the ground.

Chapter Thirty-Three

EMBER

The NGE news hits the local radio stations, newspapers, TV stations, and social media right at the time Gage told me to check. Shortly following it is a vague story about several altercations at Tucker-Smith Realty with no concrete details. When I text Gage, I don't get a reply.

It's not until noon when I'm littering Nova's high chair with easy-to-eat foods that Ava lets herself into the house, her heels clicking fast on the floor.

"Why would Gage hit Hugh?" she asks the minute I can see her.

"What?" A chill races across my skin at the question and goose bumps surface.

"Gage wouldn't care about anything business-related. Not with his company coming in hot. Probably wouldn't even care if Hugh made fun of or threatened *him*. So, the only thing I can think is that Hugh would have said or done something that involved *you* or Nova. But Nova's too little for anything to matter that much."

"Gage hit Hugh?" I swallow down the lump of anxiety that immediately rises. "Is he in trouble?"

"Not yet, but Hugh is a vindictive prick. It's definitely not a great start." Ava scans my face, and then her gaze zeroes in on the ring on my finger. "No fucking way." She snatches my hand. "Are you marrying my brother?"

"Yes?" It shouldn't be a question, and I realize that the moment my response is out of my mouth.

Ava narrows her eyes and searches my face. "Did he talk you into this? Is he trying to turn you into some sort of obedient wife?"

"No." I shake my head. "It's not like that. I want to marry him." And that part is true now, but I don't know what it means that I want this life with him. It feels dangerous to want any of it with the ticking clock at a low level in the background. He'll be mine, in some ways at least, but at the end of five years, he won't be anymore. The best worst thing in the world.

"Did he beat Hugh up because of you?"

"Probably." I run a hand through my hair, and then I play with the ends, twisting them and flicking them around my fingers. There's a little spark of happiness inside me that I'm trying to pretend I don't feel. While I never would have asked him, wouldn't have wanted him to do what he did, no one but Athena has ever defended me before. "At the company dinner, Hugh said some things to me, and when I didn't respond how he wanted, he squeezed my leg so hard it left a mark."

"Good for Gage," Ava says with a satisfied nod.

"No," I say. "Not good for Gage. He shouldn't go to jail because Hugh is an asshole. That's not how the world should work."

"You'll be happy to know that isn't how the world works. Gage won't go to jail. Tuckers don't do time." Ava waves me off.

"How do you know?"

"Hugh is vindictive, but he's not stupid. Going after his cousin with the law? No. He'll be a lot sneakier than that. Amongst ourselves, we fight quiet and dirty."

Great. That sounds so much better.

Nova bangs the top of the high chair and makes the sign for more. With a sigh, I break up the food I have left, and I scatter it across the high chair for her to fist into her mouth.

Ava takes my hand with the engagement ring and turns it back and forth in the light, and then she meets my gaze. "Why are you and Gage getting married?"

The words I should say—that we're in love—get stuck in my throat. I really need to practice saying this line in front of the mirror or something.

Ava must see my panic or uncertainty because she drops my hand. "My mom is going to lose her mind. I hope Gage is prepared for her wrath. She's not going to be happy."

I don't think Gage will care how his mother feels, but we didn't discuss his family's reaction in detail. We were more concerned about coming up with realistic engagement and marriage scenarios, talking to Robert, trying to make sure both of us stay in the country and out of trouble.

"Gage wants to get married quickly," I say, not meeting her eyes.

"I bet he does," she says with a smirk. "You making him wait until you're married?"

"What? No."

"So, you're sleeping with him now?"

Oh, god. This has gone sideways fast. How did we ever think we could fool the government? I can't even form decent lies to tell his sister.

Her gaze narrows. "None of this feels right to me. You don't seem happy or excited about getting married. You can't give me a straight answer about whether you're having sex with him." She waves her hand around. "Is this some sort of financial thing?"

"Immigration," I mutter, and I hope Gage doesn't murder me for telling Ava.

Ava's eyes widen. "You're going into a marriage of convenience? Oh, this is amazing." Ava takes a seat at the island and stares at me expectantly. "Tell me everything."

I hesitate for the briefest moment, but if there's anyone I can trust, it must be Ava. She's Gage's sister, and I don't have anyone else to confide in. He's already roped Sawyer and Nathaniel into this, what's one more sibling?

"You can't tell anyone. No one. I'm serious. I could get deported. Gage could go to jail, and I know you don't think those are real things, but they are. They really are."

"Sure. Yeah. Whatever. Spill the tea." She leans her elbows on the island, her face cupped in her hands, clearly ready for my story.

After taking a deep breath, I tell her everything while I finish feeding Nova and getting her a bottle. It's only once I'm done and getting Nova ready for her nap that I realize Ava has hardly said anything since I started talking.

"You need to get a lot better at lying," she says. "A lot better. I clocked that there was something wrong with this arrangement right away. Within five seconds of seeing the ring. If a government person comes to this house, they'll see it too. Guaranteed."

"I'm *not* a good liar," I say. "Which I knew when Gage first suggested this plan. I knew I couldn't pull it off, but then… I don't know. I guess I talked myself into thinking I could."

"Actually, you know what, screw the government. If *my mother* suspects this is fake, she'll turn you in herself. Make some sort of deal to spare Gage and have you deported. It's like… a certainty. I don't understand how Gage didn't consider that. She was never great as a mother—really protective of the Tucker '*brand*'—but I feel like she's gotten worse since the Maren and Enzo mess, and now that Maren is tied to the royal family, Mom is even more paranoid. No one can tarnish the Tucker name. Heaven forbid." Ava mocks fainting, but nothing about what she's saying is funny to me.

"Your mother has been really nice to me so far," I say, almost to myself.

"To your face? Sure. She's like that. That's her. Who knows what she's been doing behind your back. Maybe just biding her time until your tourist trip was over. More likely, she was setting up some voodoo shit to subconsciously force Gage to go back to Abby."

"Abby?" My stomach is rolling with dread.

"Abby is more Celia Tucker's speed. Rich *enough*. Maren really bucked against Mom to marry Enzo, and then that didn't work out. He tried to take Maren for a financial ride, but Brice put a stop to that. So, guess who now believes she knows everything?"

I rub my temples and try to keep myself from spiraling. "Maybe we can just never talk to her again."

"Might not be *that* hard for a while. She's not super involved in our lives." Ava laughs. "But five years? You need to get a lot more comfortable with this lie and quickly. Otherwise, you and Gage are sunk."

Chapter Thirty-Four

EMBER

Once Ava finally leaves, I sit at my sewing machine, trying to keep busy so my mind doesn't self-destruct. When it was just the nameless, faceless government I had to worry about, that was bad enough. But now Gage has committed an assault against Hugh, and his cousin will be out for blood, and apparently Celia Tucker will want my head on a platter for marrying her youngest son too. My life has never been a pebble of bad news; it's always been an avalanche, and I don't know why I thought being in Bellerive, being with Gage, might make that less so.

One thing I know for sure—I am so glad Gage didn't post an engagement announcement. We need to be on our A game when that happens. I'll have to crawl my way up from my current F-level game, where I can't even fool his sister Ava.

Gage doesn't get home until so late in the day that I've already put Nova down for the night, and I'm curled up in a chair in the living room rereading the same page over and over again while watching the clock. I only heard from Gage once today, when he told me he'd tell me everything when he got home. Normally, he's more likely to give me a blow-by-blow of his day in texts and phone calls than he is to shut down communication. But he did warn me that today would be chaotic for him, and I'm sure getting into a fistfight with Hugh didn't help the chaos.

When the front door opens, I slide my bookmark into my book, and I don't even pretend to be interested in anything other than him. I get off the couch and grab a beer from the fridge for him. The knuckles of his right hand have gauze over them as he makes his way toward me. I try to pass him the beer, and he takes it from me, but only to set it gently on the island before drawing me into a tight hug.

"Fuck, I missed you today," he murmurs into my shoulder.

"I heard about what happened with Hugh. I feel like all of this is my fault."

He splays his hands on my body, and he kisses my shoulder. "He makes his choices, and I make mine. You aren't responsible for any of the decisions either of us make. For weeks, I've tried to pretend that starting the company was enough, taking him down financially would be just as satisfying as smashing in his face." He lets me go enough to make eye contact, and a smirk plays at the edges of his lips. "Maybe you didn't want me to meet violence with violence, but it felt pretty fucking good."

I frame his face with my hands, and I debate the wisdom of admitting how I felt when I heard. "Today," I say, "it feels pretty good to me too."

He searches my face for a beat, and I understand what he's doing, which is another reason I know we're not good enough actors yet. He's giving me a chance to tell him I don't want him to kiss me, to step away, or throw up some other signal of protest. When I stay relaxed and in his embrace, he brushes his lips against mine, but it's not enough for me, and I run my fingers through the silky short strands at the back of his head and deepen the kiss.

His hands slide under my ass, and he picks me up, carrying me to the couch where he sits down and settles me on top of him, and whether he's giving me the control on purpose or he just prefers me straddling him, I like the move. I can stay or go, and I don't feel caged in by what he wants.

While we kiss, he puts both his hands on my hips, and he tugs me flush against him, so every time I move or shift, I'm rubbing against him. The friction is surprisingly delicious. This is definitely one step further than we took things last time we were on this couch together, but I'm not stopping anything. After my conversation with his sister earlier today, it's clear we need a higher comfort level with each other. We have to seem sure of each other in every aspect.

As we kiss, he urges me to grind against him, and with each press of our bodies, I'm becoming more and more turned on. In other relationships with guys, I've struggled to switch my brain off enough to even come close to getting off. While I might have only had sex with one guy, I've had make-out sessions with quite a few, and in every instance, the guy I was with would achieve his orgasm, and I'd be left wondering whether it was even possible for me to have one, unless I was by myself. The few guys who tried to get me there made me feel like I was performing, and a few times I did pretend to get to the finish line, just so they'd stop. In every instance, it was impossible to get caught up in the sensations, to enjoy what was happening.

But as I grip Gage's face and kiss him, his hand on my hip guides the brush of our bodies into a consistent rhythm. Each kiss and grind brings me closer to the edge of insanity. There's a part of me that's becoming desperate to take off my shorts, undo his suit pants, and release him to see if it's possible for this to feel even better skin to skin. I want him more than I've ever wanted anyone, and if I wasn't so turned on, that would be terrifying. Feeling that way for him has disaster written all over it.

I press my forehead against his, and I'm panting, not able to think coherently about anything but the feel of him against me, even through our clothes. The long, hard length of him is driving me wild with need. The pressure inside of me is curling, curling, threatening to unfurl at any second.

"Gage," I whimper.

"Come for me, Em. I want to watch you get off."

"Are you…" Words are hard to form, hard to consider. "Are you close?"

"Don't worry about me, baby." He nuzzles my neck and kisses behind my ear. His teeth graze my earlobe, and I wrap my arms around his neck, my fingers tangled in his hair.

"Oh my god," I say, unable to stop the words from tumbling out. "Oh my god."

"Look at me," Gage says, and one of his hands is on my chin, forcing me to meet his gaze. His eyes are dark with the same desire I feel coursing through me, uncontrollable, raging so far out of control I couldn't stop now, even if I wanted to. He bites his lip, and the hand on my hip urges me into a harder grind.

My legs begin to shake, and then whatever has coiled inside me springs open, and I let out a deep moan, throwing my head back, my hair tumbling down my back.

Gage keeps the rhythm going, prolonging the end of my orgasm, and then he's clutching my back, both hands splayed against me.

"Fuck, Em." He lets out a guttural groan, and I can feel him pulsing underneath me as I'm starting to come back to earth.

When both of us have our breathing under control, Gage says, "That was a better ending to my day than I expected."

I bury my face in his neck to hide my embarrassment. "I can't believe we just did that."

His hands that had been rubbing my back go still. "Was that too far? Shit. Did I go too far?"

"No, no." I shake my head, but I don't meet his gaze. If he'd stopped, I would have been beyond disappointed. I would have had to flee to my room to finish the job myself. And I can't even say with any certainty whether that would have been the smarter idea. To sell us, we need to be close, but I worry about getting *too* close. How do I even balance any of this? But we're too far down this road for me to back out now, and I'd regret not seeing this through if anything happened to Nova and I wasn't on the island.

"Ava was here today. She knows." I draw back and stare at my ring. "She didn't think I was very convincing about our engagement, and she warned me that your mom will be mad."

He smooths my hair down and kisses my forehead. "I'll handle Celia."

"Gage—Ava said your mom might turn us in. That she would turn us in if she thought she could protect you *and* get rid of me."

"You told Ava about the immigration deal?"

"She thought I was marrying you for money." I twist my hands. "Besides, she's the only person on the island that I can talk to."

He seems to absorb this and then nods. "You're right. Ava's a loose cannon, but she's usually firing beside me, not at me." He rubs his forehead. "We can't tell Maren. With her being so connected to the royal family, I think it's better to give her deniability in all directions."

"And your parents?"

"Tell me your biggest worry."

"That I won't seem happy enough or in love enough when we tell them we're engaged."

"Easy. I'll invite them here this weekend while you're in Colorado cleaning out the apartment. I'll tell them all together. My siblings can be the actors."

"Your parents won't think it's weird you're telling them by yourself?"

"I'll tell them I'm protecting you from their hurtful comments." He kisses my temple. "Which, unfortunately, will be the truth." He glances around the living room. "But, if I'm doing that, before we go *very* public, we need the house to feel more like ours and less like you have a single room. Other than your smutty books being everywhere, there's not much evidence of you outside your room."

Ava got me back reading when she loaned me a sports romance I could barely put down to look after Nova, and then it spiraled from there. The first time Gage picked one of them up and flipped to a random page, he teased me unendingly for a few days about my book porn. Whatever. I'm sure he watches actual porn, and when I finally said that to him, he stopped teasing me.

"You should probably move your stuff into the main suite with me. It's a king bed. We'll never have to touch." He takes my hands in his, and he stares at them between us. "I heard what you want when we talked about our marriage earlier, and I respect that. Discreet relationships with old friends who aren't from Bellerive or people just passing through the country."

When he says it like that, I feel stupid for even suggesting it. We just dry fucked on his couch, and at one point, I was considering abandoning my clothes and his to make that connection much more solid. It's not that I don't want to be with him. In a lot of ways, I trust him more than I've ever trusted any other man.

In an ideal world, we'd agree on a marriage with benefits scenario. No feelings, but enough sex to keep us both satisfied. That might work for me because my sex drive has never been high, but I wouldn't want to pen him in like that. I don't want him to resent me or this situation.

But part of me feels ill at the thought of him being with anyone else, even if I never know, even if he's really good at hiding it. In the five years we'll be married, it'll happen. Might even happen a lot.

"How was your company launch?" I ask to distract myself. "Other than you literally knocking out the competition."

The heaviness in the air dissipates, and he chuckles. "A lot of running around. Interviews. People calling to switch to us. A slew of appraisals. I think Nathaniel was right—people in Bellerive were ready for a change, a chance to give someone else their business. Hugh has burned a lot of bridges, particularly in the wealthier circles. Lots of high-end clients who were pissed at Tucker-Smith Realty for one reason or another. Martin was over the fucking moon."

"So, overall, it was…"

"Good. Exhausting, but good." He rubs his thumb against my cheek, and I lean into his hand. "Honestly, even if it had been fucking awful, coming home to this and to you would have made it a billion times better."

"A billion, huh? I see what you did there," I whisper, and my heart beats a heavy staccato in my chest. Sometimes, he says the sweetest things, things that make me wish I wasn't just a proximity comfort to him but maybe a bit more than that. Magical, dangerous thinking. The more neutral we can stay about each other, at least in private, the easier it'll be at the end of five years.

"It used to make me feel better just to remember I have a lot of money," he says. "Now, you and Nova have the same impact on my mood. I've got you and I've got her, and I could fucking care less about anything else." He hesitates for a beat. "Once I ruin Hugh, that is."

I like the idea a lot—of being important to Gage, of making Hugh pay. But at the back of my mind is Ava's warning about how the Tuckers play quiet and dirty. Hugh won't go down without a fight.

Chapter Thirty-Five

GAGE

The next night when I get home late, the house looks different. At the threshold to the open concept area, I try to categorize the subtle changes. A small bookshelf full of Ember's growing collection of word porn is tucked into a corner near the sliding doors for the pool. There are framed photos from our engagement in a patchwork collage on the wall. A few other framed photos litter the space, and as I walk around, I gaze at each one. Some of them are selfies Ember and I have taken over the weeks since she's been here—me and her, me and Nova, her and Nova. But then I spot one I've never seen before.

"Is it too much?" Ember asks from the hallway to the bedrooms.

"No," I say, and I mean that. It's more than I expected, but the photos she picked are exactly the ones I would have selected. "Where did this one come from?" It's Nova and Ember, and they're outside. They're grinning at each other, and it makes my heart do funny things in my chest.

"Rory took it, at one of the palace playdates, and then she sent it to me."

"Can you send it to me? I want it for my office."

"I'll get you a copy and bring it to your office tomorrow," she says.

"I want it big," I say. "Obnoxiously big."

"For your wall?"

"Yeah," I say, thinking of where I'll hang it. They're my reason for doing all this, and every time I even glance at the photo, I feel a strange energization, like I'd take a hail of bullets for either one of them. The swell of emotion often hits me out of nowhere, and I'm still getting used to it. "And one of the engagement ones too—for my desk."

"I was just..." She gestures toward the bedrooms. "Wondering about moving my stuff to your room? I think we could explain not doing it, if you want to keep your own space until we're married."

"There is no reality in which my family would think I'd agree to wait until marriage." Maybe that sounds harsh, but my family knows me too well to believe I'd agree to that. Besides, it would give my mother more 'manipulation' fodder. She'd assume I was only marrying Ember to get in her pants.

I *would* marry Ember to get in her pants, that much I know for sure after last night. Part of me had hoped that after bringing her to orgasm on the couch, she'd abandon the plan to have us fuck other people outside our marriage. But she skimmed over my comment like us grinding to release changed nothing.

"Ava joked about waiting for marriage, and so I thought maybe that could work." She tucks her hair behind her ears and glances toward the bedrooms.

I set down the photo I'm still holding and head toward her. "What worries you about putting your stuff in my—in the main suite?"

"Do you really want me to sleep in there with you?"

"Why wouldn't I?"

"What side of the bed do you even sleep on?"

I purse my lips as I take her hand and draw her into the bedroom. "Would you be surprised to hear that I normally sleep in the middle?" When I glance at her, she has a small smile of amusement.

"That's not all that surprising." She sighs. "I don't want you to feel like you're being forced into anything."

"I feel exactly the same way," I say. "Maybe we can agree that we'll each state our truth when we're negotiating. Side of the bed? I can go either way."

"I like the right."

"It's yours. So just bring your stuff in and scatter it around. Put all your girly things in the en suite bathroom too."

"Okay," Ember agrees with obvious uncertainty.

As she goes to her room to get the rest of her things, Nova wakes up, and I head to her bedroom to look after whatever she needs. After a diaper change, new pajamas, and a long cuddle in the rocking chair, she's back in her crib, asleep. Work has been so busy since the launch that I haven't been home before she's gone to bed for the night. I linger by her crib, watching her sleep, and I try not to let myself get caught up in who'll be in my bed when I leave here.

Ember doesn't want to complicate our relationship by sleeping with each other, but if anything, what happened between us on the couch just proves that we're both capable of compartmentalizing that aspect of our relationship. We can fool around, have some fun, and not have it turn into something dramatic.

But it feels like a fine line to walk between pointing out the obvious and trying to persuade her to have sex with me.

When I get to my room, the bedside light is on, and Ember is reading. She must have watched all the reality TV she could stomach because she's been single-handedly rejuvenating the physical book market for the last couple of weeks. If I had to guess, I'd bet she's reading a book a day or maybe a book every two days.

"Nova was okay? You were in there a while?"

"New jamas. New diaper. Long rock and talk."

"Rock and talks are my favorite."

"Mine too. I've been too busy lately to get many of them." I go into the en suite and start getting ready for bed.

Once I'm done, I cross the expansive room to crawl under the covers on my side. I flick off my light, and Ember slides a bookmark into her book and turns out the light on her side too. The darkness settles around us, and I can barely make out her outline from the light-canceling drapes. The air feels charged, but I can't tell if it's all coming from me, or if she's just as aware.

"Are you a cuddler?" I ask, turned to face her silhouette.

"Sometimes," Ember whispers back.

"Well, if you ever want to cuddle with me, you're welcome on my half of the bed."

"Good to know," she says, and I sense her turn to face me too. "You can cuddle with me, too, if you want."

"Come here." I reach out, and I loop my arm around her waist, dragging her across the mattress and into my embrace. She lets out a little giggle, the most adorable sound. She has on a barely there tank top and shorts made of the softest material.

When we're flush against each other, I nuzzle my nose against the crook of her neck, and I breathe in the smell of pineapples. "God, I love touching you, being close to you."

Her hands are in my hair, and she kisses my neck and along my jaw until her lips find mine. I tug her half underneath me, slanting one of my legs between hers while I deepen the kiss. "Is this okay?" I murmur against her lips. The other times I've pushed the boundaries between us, she's been on top, in charge, able to easily walk away if it became too much.

"Yes," she breathes out, clutching onto me. "I trust you."

Just like the last time, her words make my chest swell. I've never thought a lot about what it means to be trusted by someone else, but I've spent enough time with Ember the last couple of months that I understand how much weight that statement carries, particularly for her. She trusts me to take care of her, to stop if she asks, to pay attention to what she's telling me both verbally and nonverbally. It's a responsibility that I take seriously.

But that doesn't stop me from scooping her underneath me more and settling between her legs. She's in her pajamas, and I'm in my boxers, and those pieces of clothing won't be coming off. She drew the line between us, and until she asks me to erase it, I'm treating its existence as permanent. Past experience tells me that what we're doing now—grinding and kissing—is a slippery slope. Two scraps of fabric are the only things that differentiate this make-out session from sex.

Each sweep of my hips elicits a moan from Ember, and her knees squeeze my sides. I cup her ass in one of my hands, adjusting the slide of our bodies together, and Ember's breathing hitches.

"Do you like that?" I ask.

"Yes," she says, and her nails dig into my back.

I trail a line of open-mouthed kisses along her neck and collarbone, and then I take her pebbled nipple into my mouth through the cloth of her tank top. She arches into the contact, and I graze the bud with my teeth. Her hands tangle in my hair, urging me to do it again, so I do. The things I'd do to her, if I didn't think they'd alarm her...

"You should be illegal."

"*I* should be?" I let out a throaty chuckle as I seek out the sensitive spot on her neck that makes goose bumps race across her skin. "Why?"

"It all feels too good," she says.

"No such thing as too good." I turn my attention to her other breast, keeping the brush of our bodies steady and tight. Each little noise of pleasure she emits is like a gift, just for me. If I can get her to come again, I'll feel like a fucking god. I so badly want to slip my fingers between us, to seek out the heat of her body. She's so wet that the front of my boxers feel damp and slick with her need. My body wants to be five steps ahead of where we are.

As much as I want her, I'm holding back, unsure of what'll be too far. Her experience level is lower than mine, and at the back of my brain is the *don't scare her* mantra meant to keep my own desire in check. Slow, gentle steps. I've got five years to get from this to where I want to be. And honestly, if this is all I can have for five years, it's not the worst thing in the world.

I've got Em, cradled in my arms, her body pressed tight against mine, evidence of her desire coating me. That's probably a lot more than someone like me has a right to get. If I end up coming in my underwear for the length of our marriage, so be it.

"Gage," she says, clinging onto me, her voice strained with desperation and tension. "Oh, god."

She must be close, and I silently curse the lack of lighting in here. The other night on the couch, watching her come undone, was the highlight of my life. I'm going to do my best to burn her expression into my brain for as long as she'll let me see it, and I'll hold it tight forever.

"I love the sound of my name when you're about to come," I murmur against her neck.

She whimpers, and her legs are shaking. God, I'd give anything to be inside her right now, and the sounds she's making are threatening to send me into oblivion before she makes it there.

"Oh," she cries, "oh, Gage. Don't stop."

She doesn't need to worry about that. I'm fully committed to seeing this through for the both of us. She's warm and soft and so fucking wet that we're both soaked. These classic make-out sessions are like going back in time by ten years, but I'll take anything I can get with her. I'd rather have *this* with her than anything with anyone else.

Her nails dig into my back, and she arches into the contact.

"I want to be with you like this every night," I say.

"Yes," she says without hesitation. "God, yes."

Then I squeeze her ass and rock against her one more time. She cries out, and I seek her lips, swallowing the rest of her soft sounds as I push myself toward my own release.

Afterward, we both lie there, breathing hard in the darkness. Part of me is tempted to push the issue, to get her to commit to having this happen between us again and again because I crave this closeness with her. But I'm really trying to be an actual partner who takes her feelings into consideration, not a fuckboy who only thinks of himself. I've been the latter, and though I didn't recognize it at the time, that persona has never made me particularly happy. He never felt like someone anyone would want to be around if it wasn't for the money.

Gage Tucker was a certified good time, making it rain for everyone, but none of those experiences made me feel like a decent human being. Often, it was the opposite. People liked the money, and they tolerated me.

With Em, I think she likes me, and she tolerates my lifestyle. I've become a fucking cliché, and I'm not even mad about it. I'm absolutely falling for a woman who doesn't give a shit about my money, and I've never been happier.

"Gage?" she whispers in the dark.

"Yeah?"

"Can you do that thing—you know, like you did above the wine bar—where you held me?"

"Come here," I say, scooping her into the middle of the bed where I curl myself around her, caging her in. "Like this?"

"Yeah," she says, releasing a deep sigh. "Just like that."

I nuzzle her neck and then plant a kiss on her temple. Maybe if I treat her really well, do everything I can to make her happy, she won't want to leave me. How badly I want that scares me, but I can't deny it's true. After drifting so aimlessly for most of my life, I finally have something—someone—worth holding onto.

Chapter Thirty-Six

GAGE

Somehow, the kiss-and-grind gods operate in my favor for the rest of the week. No matter how late I get home, I find Ember in the living room reading. We go to bed together, and within minutes, we're all over each other.

We don't talk about any of it outside of the bedroom, and I don't know if I should bring up our unspoken agreement or just be really fucking glad it's happening. I'm really hoping this isn't all we end up doing or being to each other, but I'm also not going to imply with even a single word that it's not enough. As long as she's seeking satisfaction with me, she's not out there looking for it with anyone else. And really, at this point, that's the most important thing. If she wants to get off, she's getting off with me.

Now I just have to endure this long weekend on my own as a single parent, and somehow break the news of my quick engagement to my parents at Saturday's family dinner. Which would be fine if part of me wasn't suddenly worried about sending Ember to Colorado alone to clean out the apartment.

As we drive toward the private airstrip, I try to keep my cool. But it's a losing battle. "Just one security guard," I say.

"No," she says with a laugh. "I'm going back to the apartment building I've lived in since I was sixteen. I'll be there for two days. Security of any sort is unnecessary."

"I've already contacted Rusty to drive you. You've got his number in your phone?"

She slides her hand along my leg, and I catch it, lacing our fingers together.

"I'm a big girl, Gage. I'll be fine."

"You're *my* girl," I say with more force than I probably need. "I should just cancel the open houses on Saturday and the dinner with my family and come with you."

"Gage," she says with a little laugh. "What's wrong with you?"

My emotional landscape is battling a hurricane at the thought of her leaving. Until she's back on the island, I don't know if I'll be able to breathe properly. Which is, obviously, a problem. I have a company to run and a daughter to raise, but Ember is a constant, burning thought.

I haven't quite figured out why anyone would willingly seek out this chest-tightening ache. Who'd opt to have something so volatile and unstable living inside them?

By contrast, what I feel for Nova is scary big but rock-solid, and I don't worry about whether she'll love me back. I worry a little about whether she'll *like* me down the road, but I feel as though father-daughter love is a given. She's got no choice.

Ember, on the other hand, she's got options. I haven't had the balls to ask her again if this marriage is just going to be the two of us, or if she's sticking to her fly-by-night tourists and old friends idea. Before we started screwing around, I didn't like what she wanted, but now I *hate* it. Thankfully, she doesn't seem like the type to be with someone else while we're together, and I'm clinging onto that for all it's worth. It's just us, at least for now.

"I'm just saying that if you need me for anything, just ask. If you need me, I'll get there."

She squeezes my hand, and she leans into my shoulder as I steer the SUV into a parking spot in front of my family's private hanger.

"You have a plane?" she asks, surprised.

"The family does, yeah."

"Why didn't you take it when you came to Colorado?"

"I took it to get there, but I stayed longer than expected, and my parents needed it. I could have gotten one of the helicopters instead, but I figured that would have freaked you out."

"Accurate," she says as she climbs out of the vehicle.

I get Nova from the back, plant a kiss on her forehead, and pop her into the wearable carrier before taking Ember's bag from her and heading toward the waiting jet.

"I suppose you also have a massive yacht stashed somewhere you haven't told me about?"

"Monaco," I say without missing a beat. "You want to take it for a spin? With one phone call I can have it ordered here."

"No," she says with a little laugh. "The person who can't swim doesn't want to take a spin on the Titanic."

"Ah, right. We need to remedy that swimming situation." I tap the side of my head. "When you get back, we'll do that."

"You're in the middle of getting the company off the ground, I don't expect you to take time off to teach me to swim."

"I don't know when I'll teach you, but I'll find the time," I say as we get close enough to the plane for me to introduce Ember to the crew. "Ember, this is the pilot, Deepti, the copilot, Joe, and the flight attendants are Hanako and Archie."

Ember shakes hands with everyone and says their name back to them, a trick she discovered from the queen to help her remember names.

I lead the way up the plane steps, and I set her bag in the luggage bin before showing Ember the spacious seats, the oversized bathroom, and the bar area. The plane was custom-made several years ago and feels old to me now, but Ember's clearly impressed.

"Sometimes," she says before sliding her hand into mine, "I feel like I'm waiting to wake up. Like one day, this will all be gone. Poof. And I'll realize that you and this was a dream, and I'm still in Colorado."

She doesn't say *alone*, but the word echoes in her tone, and not for the first time I feel the sharp pinch of guilt for how long it took me to go to her.

"After this weekend, you'll never have to be there again," I say.

For some reason, my comment doesn't seem to make her happy. Instead, she seems almost sadder. Whenever science gets around to inventing the machine that reads minds, I'm buying one. I'll be the first in line so that I never again say something to Ember that I shouldn't.

"Unless you want to be there," I amend.

"I guess we'll see, right?" She gives a little shrug. "If this all sticks."

Even if I have to Gorilla Glue it together myself, we're going to stick out the five years, minimum. There's too much at stake not to make it work. Not the least of which is rapidly becoming *my* fucking out of control emotions.

Deepti reminds me that there's a schedule they need to stick to, and Nova starts to fuss in the carrier, too used to having more freedom now that she's bigger.

I take Em's hand, and I kiss her palm before pressing it to my cheek. We stare at each other for a long beat, and I'm reluctant to let her go. "You'll be back before I know it, right?"

She rises on her toes and gives me a quick peck around Nova's carrier, and then she plants a kiss on Nova's head. "I love you, you little peanut," she says to Nova, and although I've heard her say it a million times, the words cause my stomach to flip as I make my way out of the plane.

Outside, I lean against the SUV, Nova out of the carrier and in my arms. Through one of the small plane windows, I can make out Ember's form, and I wave. As the plane turns toward the runway, the ache in my chest that is easy to keep at bay when Ember is within touching distance spreads.

If we weren't already doing everything we could to keep her in the country, watching her leave right now would have convinced me that she needed to stay. One thing I know beyond a doubt is that I never want this view with any level of uncertainty. I want to know that when Ember leaves the island she's always coming back, coming home, to us.

I kiss the top of Nova's head as the plane streaks down the runway and rises into the air, temporarily taking half my sanity with it.

Chapter Thirty-Seven

EMBER

Being on a private jet alone with not one but two people waiting on me and eager to deliver anything I can dream up, is a bit surreal. I wasn't joking when I told Gage I'm waiting for the other shoe to drop. When it's just the two of us in his, relatively, modest house, I can almost pretend all of this wealth doesn't exist. Of course I know it does—it lived in my bank account for a hot minute—but other than there being no purchasing limits on anything I could possibly want, and Michelle, who is maid, cook, and babysitter, and all the beach equipment, and the massive pool house with an incredible entertainment center inside...

Okay, actually, maybe I've just gotten *too* used to the other luxuries, and when I'm confronted with a new one, it reminds me of the excess I have begun to ignore. I don't know. But Gage's sheer wealth sometimes freaks me out.

Or maybe I'm focusing on that right now to avoid thinking about why I'm going to Colorado. Agreeing to clean out the apartment seemed like a small thing when I was tucked inside Gage's house playing pretend with him. But now, when I consider what I'm going to have to do, this doesn't feel like a small thing at all.

Maybe I should have told Gage, warned him that I might not be able to do this, that I might get there, open the door to her bedroom, and the threads that have been holding me together all these months since she died might snap. I don't have to keep myself wound tight, carefully upright for someone else when all I wanted to do back then was collapse under the weight of our loss. No one needs me to put them first. There's just me and that room and all those memories—the good and the bad—swirling around me, fragments of a life never quite whole again.

At the airport, Rusty is waiting, and he seems to remember the way to my apartment without me having to say a word. When we get to the building, I expect him to drop me off out front, but instead, he parks in a visitor slot, grabs my small suitcase from the trunk, and gestures for me to lead the way to my apartment.

"You don't have to—" I say.

"Mr. Tucker's instructions were very clear." Rusty follows me up the stairs and to the door of my apartment. "I'm to stay on site in case you need anything at all."

"Like, in the car?"

"In the apartment."

"No," I say as I dig out my key. "You can stick around the neighborhood, if you want. Grab a coffee down the street or whatever. But you don't need to be in here with me."

"He mentioned you might need help."

The last thing I want is someone in the apartment with me while I'm clearing out my sister's things. No one, but especially not a stranger, should have to figure out what to say to me or how to act. Tears are inevitable. I've been holding them in for months, and the closer I've gotten to the apartment, the more I've started to feel the cracks in my composure.

"I have your number," I say. "If I need help, I will text or call you. You can stay close by, but I really don't want a babysitter." Or a bodyguard, which I thought I made clear to Gage.

Rusty deposits my suitcase inside the apartment, and he glances around, clearly torn about whether to follow Gage's instructions or respect my wishes. "There's not much here..."

"Exactly," I say. "Memories and some clothes. I really don't need help. He's just being overprotective." Which is a vibe I normally live for.

Rusty has just closed the apartment door when my phone pings with a message from Gage not asking but *telling* me I've landed, and I wonder if he's tracking me. With a different man, that might feel like too much. But I'm smiling when I type back a response.

Stalker.

It's a valuable plane carrying even more valuable cargo.

My chest warms, the way it always does when he lays on the charm, which seems to be second nature with him. Half the things he says, he probably doesn't even realize I could interpret as meaning more than they do. But when I mull over his words, the truth clicks.

You're tracking the plane, not me?

Correct. But I'll happily track you, if you'll consent.

Why would you want to track me? I'm boring. Shopping. Bookstores. Baby play-dates.

The three dots appear and disappear, appear and disappear.

To me, nothing about you is boring. I find you endlessly interesting.

You should save all your good lines for when someone is around to hear them.

The person I want to hear them seems to be getting the message just fine.

God, he's good. The pretend just flows out of him like water, and I keep having to remind myself that none of this is real. Even over text, he's covering our asses with an incredible smoothness. I just wish my body would get the memo that nothing he's saying is true, or at least not as true as it could be.

When I don't write back immediately, he sends one last text.

Got a property I'm showing. Call me later. I need to hear your voice.

I stare at the text for longer than I should, but I'm torn between being honest and telling him what he wants to hear. After I've gone through some of the things left in the apartment, I'm not sure I'll want to talk to anyone.

Call me when you're done with work. I'm just clearing stuff out, so I can talk whenever.

The truth and probably a lie, all rolled into one. Then I set my phone on the counter and take a deep breath. The kitchen and living room are pretty much empty. The important rooms are the one I shared with Nova, which still has some baby things, and Athena's room at the end of the hall.

I decide to go easy on myself, and I head into the room I shared with Nova. In there, I sort through baby clothes she's now outgrown that I didn't take with us—mostly secondhand stuff that I cobbled together from thrift stores in the first place. But when I get to the bottom of the drawer, there's a onesie folded neatly that stops my heart.

Mommy's Little Princess is scrawled across the tiny surface area of the chest. It's the onesie that Athena brought Nova home in, and I almost can't even bring myself to touch it, as though whatever darkness gripped Athena and wouldn't let her go might get a foothold in me too.

Instead of picking it up, I gather everything else into a bag, and I head out of the apartment and down the stairs toward the baby-and-children thrift shop around the corner. Whatever that feeling was that hit me when I saw the onesie, I can't let it settle, or maybe I don't want it to settle. The pressure in my chest is almost unbearable.

"Ember?" a male voice calls my name just before I open the door to the thrift store.

"Esteban?" I shift the large shopping bag in my hand when he moves in for a hug. We embrace for a few beats, and I remember how he was a constant presence in our apartment for a while when we first moved here. As the bartender at the bar where Athena got her first job, he often came back to our place after the bar, slept on the couch, cooked us breakfast in the morning. Back then, he felt so much older than me, and he's still probably got ten years on me, but in this moment, the gap doesn't feel so huge anymore.

"I heard about Athena, but I've been outta the city for a bit. I should have come around to check on you, but you look..." He shakes his head. "Landed on your feet, huh?"

"Working on it," I say.

"Doesn't look like you're still in the neighborhood," he says, clearly fishing for details.

"Just in the city clearing out the apartment."

"We should catch up. You here all weekend? I'll stop by the apartment. Maybe take you to dinner?"

I bite my lip and second-guess whether meeting with him is a good idea. But it feels nice to see a familiar face after months of struggling either alone or in a new country. There's no harm in a friendly meetup.

"Okay," I say, my smile not quite natural. At the back of my mind is always my engagement to Gage and how it needs to look should anyone care to pry.

"I'll swing by the apartment tomorrow, and we'll make a plan."

"Great!" I say, not completely sure whether my enthusiasm is real or fake.

Chapter Thirty-Eight

EMBER

When I can't avoid it anymore, I crack open the door to Athena's room. Pictures of us and baby Nova are still strewn around the room—in cheap frames or tacked to the wall. There are ticket stubs and posters of events. A work schedule is pinned next to the mirror. Her bed is made. There's still dirty laundry in the bin by the closet.

Time stopped in here, and a few months ago, that's what I needed. To pretend she wasn't really gone, to somehow cling onto the useless hope that she'd miraculously return. To avoid, avoid, avoid as much of the truth as I could possibly turn away from. I needed that to survive, to be of any use to Nova, to keep living in the face of a loss I couldn't process.

But here, alone, now, I scan the room, and I can't put a finger on exactly what I feel. Sadness for sure. The edges of the sweeping, all-consuming grief that threatened to drag me under when she died, are still there. With that though, is a thread of curiosity.

Other than coming into my sister's room to lie on the bed and gossip, or knocking on her door to share some of my own news, this room was off-limits to me. Every inch of it was hers and most of it a mystery to me.

While I clean this out, I get one last chance to know my sister in a way that I never would have chosen, but since this moment is where we're at, I'm done turning away from our reality too.

I can't bring myself to touch her clothes, so instead I drag a shipping box into the room and a garbage bag. I start with the photos and other things pinned to the wall. Quite a few of the pictures I already have, but I take these ones anyway, tucking them gently into the bottom of the box. The flyers and other mementos, after reading them over, I put them in the garbage bag.

And so it goes, around the room, in the drawers. On top of her dresser, I sniff her perfume, and I close my eyes. I can almost sense her in the room, standing behind me, telling me I shouldn't be poking through her stuff.

In the nightstand, I find a journal, and I'm tempted to tuck it into the shipping box, not even open it at all. Even with her gone, cracking the front cover feels like a violation. On the first page is a date from almost two years ago with a dash after it. The dash is where she lived her life, the in-between, the place with no ending. The dash should have gone on for so much longer than it did.

I sink onto the bed, and I trace my finger over the date and the dash. Maybe it's right that it's unfinished.

With a deep breath, I turn to the last entry, and as I read, a horrible understanding dawns. She's talking about Gage, or about his family, at least. It turns out that while I was blissfully unaware, she knew she was drowning, sinking deeper into something she couldn't seem to pull herself out of. She tried to contact him to see if he'd take the baby for a while or even offer some sort of financial help. But it doesn't seem like she spoke directly to him. A housekeeper answered and said they'd leave a message for Gage to return the call. The last line she ever wrote says she hopes he calls back soon, that she doesn't know how much longer she can go on like this.

Tears well up in my eyes and blur the page. He said he didn't know about Nova, and I can't believe he'd lie. Gage is a lot of things, so many things, but he's not a liar. Not to me.

I rub my face and try to think through who Athena might have spoken to. Michelle makes the most sense, but I can't see her keeping the call from Gage. If

Athena spoke to Michelle, Michelle would have left Gage a note or called him or texted him or something. He would have been told.

Beside me, almost as though he knows I'm thinking about him, my phone buzzes with Gage's name across the screen. I feel so lost and sad and just... not myself, that I can't speak to him. Instead of answering, I send the call to voicemail.

I glance at the clock. It's getting late, but with the diary sitting in my lap, I can't help wondering what else she wrote. Did she only try to contact him once? She never told me any of this, but after she died, I suspected there was a lot she didn't tell me. The stoic older sister, my protector, never wanted to burden me with some of the harsh realities of our situation. We were snowed under with bills, and she just kept telling me that we'd be fine, but we *weren't* fine. Not even close.

My phone buzzes again, and I send it to voicemail again. But I know he won't give up, so I pick up my phone to text him.

Sorry. Really busy. Lots to do. Tight timeline. We'll talk tomorrow.

The three dots appear, and he simply writes, *Everything okay? You okay? Do you need me?*

All good, yeah. Just busy.

It's not the same here without you.

Nova's okay? I don't want to dwell on the charming things he says. In the back of my mind, I'm wondering if he *did* know about her earlier, if *my* persistence was the tipping point.

Misses you. Just like me.

If the government ever tries to look at our phone records, we'll seem like a normal couple. The words roll off Gage, effortless. Whereas I second-guess every letter.

I plug my phone in, and then I grab Athena's diary, and I crawl under her covers, pulling them up to my chin. I run my nose along the edge, taking a small whiff, and I discover that the bed doesn't smell like my sister anymore. My chest tightens at the realization. When did she disappear from the room?

Climbing out, I go to her closet, flipping through her clothes, holding them to my nose, but nothing, nothing smells like her anymore. Even that's gone now.

And for some reason, it's that unearthed reality that breaks me, and I fall to my knees in the closet, weeping, with my sister's favorite sweater clutched in my hand.

The next day after sleeping in Athena's bed, I'm feeling a little better. Not completely stable, but my grief is manageable. As long as I don't let myself dwell on what I've lost, and I force myself to be analytical while I sort through her clothes, I can keep myself from breaking down.

Rusty drives me to the Goodwill a few blocks away where I give most of Athena's clothes away. I kept a few pieces with the view of making a quilt or a blanket or something for Nova that symbolizes her mother. At least then she'll have something tangible from Athena. No memories, but she'll still have some part of her mother's history.

Every movement, every choice feels heavy, like someone has piled weights on my shoulders. It takes me several trips to Goodwill and longer than it should to have her room cleaned out.

"Do you want me to book you a hotel room for tonight? Or contact Mr. Tucker about going to the house in Colorado Springs?" Rusty asks when he surveys the almost empty apartment.

"No," I say. The apartment has been cleared out of almost everything, but it's still bursting with memories, and I want to spend one more night steeped in them. Once I leave, it'll never be the same again. "I'm going to spend one last night here." As an afterthought I add, "And don't... Don't tell Gage any of this." What I actually mean is that I don't want him to tell Gage that I'm lonely and sad and sort of wishing I had told him to come. I don't know if it would have made any of this easier, but it would have felt less lonely, of that, I'm sure.

"He wouldn't be very happy with me either," Rusty says, "if he knew I was going along with you sleeping here like this."

"Our secret then," I say.

Then I catch sight of the time and can't believe it's only ten in the morning. Rusty offers to look into places where I can drop off or get rid of the last of the things in the apartment, and after he leaves, I take a deep breath and dial Gage's number.

He has the family dinner tonight, so he probably can't talk long, but I'm finally feeling a bit more like myself, better able to pretend to be more okay than I feel.

"You prepared for battle?" I ask when he answers.

"Much more prepared after hearing your voice." There's a smile in his voice, and I can't help the answering one that spreads across my face.

In the background, I can hear Nova giggling at something.

"What's so funny over there?" I ask.

"I'm playing peekaboo while I talk to you. I've discovered she doesn't need the actual words unless she's the one trying to do it. Just cover yourself and uncover and *voila*. Happy, giggly, baby girl. God, she's so fucking awesome."

"You're nailing the dad thing," I admit.

"And people say it's hard," he says with a teasing tone.

His comment is a reminder of what I found in Athena's diary last night, and I'm tempted to ask him, but I don't know how to broach it without being accusatory. The revelation that she did try to contact him, and she did make contact with someone, is a bit too raw. This whole time I've thought how much different our lives might have been had she reached out to him, only to find that she *did*, and it didn't matter. It's a gut punch I didn't see coming.

"Can I call you later?" I ask.

"You still don't have the apartment cleaned out? I told you to use Rusty. I told *him* to help."

"No, it's..." And I hesitate, guilt pinching at me for a reason I can't explain. "I actually ran into an old friend yesterday. When Athena and I first moved here, she worked with him, and he spent a lot of time with us. I always thought he was so much older, and he is, but... It's different now, I guess."

"You're going out with an old friend?"

The way he says it is weird, and I suddenly worry that I *am* crossing a line, somehow. All of his friends are guys, so maybe it's weird for him to think of me having a guy for a friend.

"Yeah," I say, and I bite the inside of my cheek before continuing, "is that a problem?"

"Em—" A doorbell peels in the background at his house, and he curses under his breath. "Is this really what you want?" he asks, but he sounds distant and distracted.

"I don't under—" My doorbell rings, and I rush to the door to check the peephole. Esteban has dropped by, and I can't help feeling like his timing is terrible. I haven't showered yet, and this conversation with Gage has turned weird.

In the background, I can hear his brother and his sisters entering the house. "I thought you were having your family for dinner?"

"Changed it to brunch. I have a property to show later. Keep Rusty with you, okay?" Gage says, but his voice is weird, strained. Maybe his parents have arrived. We both know the engagement news isn't going to go over well.

"I will," I say. "Good luck with brunch." I open the door, and Esteban grins at me from the other side, and some of the tension that accumulated during my talk with Gage eases out of me. We're old friends. There's nothing weird about seeing him when I'm in the city.

"You're definitely not the little kid you were when we first met," Esteban says.

I laugh at his teasing tone and point to the phone. "Gage, I gotta go."

"Em—" he tries to say again.

"No phones," Ava says in the background. "We need time to strategize since you moved this family bomb to before lunch. Bye, Ember, have a good day." Then the phone goes dead in my ear.

I leave the door open for Esteban, and he enters, taking in the space.

"Not much left, huh?" he says.

"Just the memories," I say, running my hands along the sides of my face.

"You still need help with anything?"

"I've got a bed frame, box spring, and mattress that Goodwill won't take."

"Post it on the community buy and sell." He draws his phone out of his pocket. "If you just want rid of it, someone will come claim it from the curb."

"I'm not on any of those groups anymore." It had been a relief to delete those, to no longer have to search them desperately for things I needed for Nova.

"I'll post it for you. Then I can help you move this stuff down."

"You don't mind?"

"Nah. I'll blast it out for you."

"Rusty can come help move the stuff," I say. "He's just downstairs."

"Who's that?" Esteban asks, glancing up from his phone.

"My driver," I say, and I can feel a blush creeping across my cheeks. It sounds so pretentious, even if it's true.

"Fancy," he says with a smile. "You've gotten so fucking fancy, Ember. Looks good on you, though." He uses his phone to take pictures of the items that are left. "We'll move this outta here, and then you and I can see what kind of trouble we can get up to today."

"I'll get Rusty," I say, and I head down the apartment stairs to finish the job I came here to do.

Chapter Thirty-Eight

GAGE

The good news about having the sudden and irreversible realization that you're desperately in love with your soon-to-be fake wife is that nothing feels like pretend anymore. The bad news is *also* that nothing feels like pretend anymore. Any chill I might have possessed about our impending marriage is gone.

When Ava snatches the phone out of my hand, ending my call with Ember, I'm on the verge of going nuclear. Watching her get on the plane the other day was a gut punch, but then spending yesterday completely cut off from her only solidified my sense that I was in *way* over my head with this girl. I'm fucking drowning in unrequited feelings, which has *never* happened to me. Rational thought has left the building, might even have left the island.

Ember is spending the day with an "old friend," an old friend who claimed she's "not the little kid" she once was. My blood is fucking boiling.

"I can't do this," I say to my sisters, my brother, and Brice.

Nathaniel shoots me a warning glance. "Can't do what?"

"I can't be here. I need to be in Colorado with Ember."

"No," Ava says. "You need to be here, convincing Mom not to do crazy, insane things to keep you from marrying Ember."

"Marrying Ember?" Maren says, shooting a confused glance at Brice. "Since when are you marrying Ember?"

"Surprise!" I say, shifting Nova to my other arm. "That's what this brunch is about. I'm engaged. *Happily* engaged." *Not* so fucking happy *right now*, but as soon as I get to Ember, it'll be better. Maybe. Possibly. Or she might think I've lost the plot and decide she doesn't want to marry me after all. Turns out one-sided love coupled with jealousy is a lethal combination.

"Why wouldn't you be happy?" Maren asks, her eyes narrowing. "What's going on? Something is going on, and I'm not in the loop."

"I'm engaged, and Ember is in Colorado cleaning out the apartment she used to share with her sister, and I think I should be there."

Caterers are milling around us, getting the table set, putting out small starters, and I'm barely able to keep myself from bolting out of the room. With my free hand, I check the status of the family jet and the crew. Then I order the plane.

Fuck telling my parents. Fuck this whole fiasco. The only place I want to be is in Colorado, cockblocking Ember from doing whatever it is she thinks she's going to do with her lecherous "old friend." She can't kiss and grind with me all week and then go fuck someone else. No. No way. Not happening. Not on my very expensive watch.

"I don't know what's going on in your brain," Ava says, pretending to draw her open hand down my face, "but none of it seems good. What are you spiraling over?"

"Can any of you watch Nova for about forty-eight hours?" I ask.

"Absolutely not," Ava says.

"We can," Maren says quickly. "Right, Brice?"

"Perfect," I say. "You're in." As soon as Mom and Dad are here, I'll drop the marriage bomb and by then the plane should be almost ready. None of that is preventing this really tight sensation in my chest from getting worse, but at least I don't feel like I'm doing nothing.

Part of me, naively, thought Ember and I had come to a silent agreement about other people. I'm not fucking around with anyone else, and neither is she.

But she was the one who floated the 'old friend' idea, and maybe she had this guy in mind the whole time. Maybe she just needed a bit more experience and confidence before going for the older guy she's always had a crush on. Now that she's gone from the girl next door to a perfect eleven, she's going to shoot her fucking shot. Her 'old friend' comment is making more and more sense, and I'm becoming more and more agitated at the thought of her in Colorado with him.

"I don't know if I've ever seen you with zero chill," Sawyer says. "What's going on?"

"Nothing," I say. "I just need to get to Ember in Colorado, that's all."

"I never thought I would see the day where you were head over heels in love with someone," Maren says.

Ava examines me, a question in her gaze, but I don't meet her look. *I've* barely come to grips with being in love with my future wife. It's not a radical idea. Unexpected. Maybe a bit unwanted. But it's not like I can snap my fingers and go back in time to somehow prevent this from happening.

The doorbell rings, and my parents enter, decked out like this isn't a family event but something much grander—a ball or charity appearance requiring suits and floor-length gowns. So typical for them to misread a family gathering. It's amazing we all grew up somewhat normal.

Although Ava and I used to consider ourselves the apples that didn't fall far from the tree. Unlike Nathaniel, Sawyer, and Maren, I never felt like I had enough devotion to those I cared about, never enough drive to be better than how I was raised. Ava and I have always been fickle in relationships, unreliable with our family. I'm not sure how Ava feels anymore, but I know how I'm beginning to feel.

"Where's Ember?" my mother asks as she comes forward to take Nova from me.

"In Colorado," I say.

"She's gone back already? That's a relief." She lets out a little chuckle. "I thought for sure she'd—"

"She's gone to Colorado to clean out the apartment she shared with her sister. Then she's coming back here, and we're getting married." I don't rush my explanation, but I also don't give her a chance to interrupt. Might as well drop the bomb, watch it detonate, and then leave the scene of the crime.

"What?" My mother almost roars the word, and I'm tempted to take Nova back from her. "I told you! I said this would happen. I *knew* it. From the minute I laid eyes on her—"

"I asked her. All of it was my idea."

"Of course you'd believe that," my mother scoffs. "The good ones always make you think it's your idea, isn't that right, Jonathan?"

"You did," he says without a trace of irony.

Ava snorts behind me, and if we were talking about anyone other than Ember, I might find his comment funny too. But his claim will only fuel my mother, make her believe she's some kind of expert.

"I'm not defending my choice, and I won't have you saying a single bad word about her—either to her face *or* behind her back to your gossip queens."

My mother stares at me, eyes narrowed. "I don't know what's going on here, but I don't believe this arrangement is in your best interest. Hers? Yes. Yours? No. So I'll say whatever I want to whomever I want whenever I want."

"Then consider your lack of contact with this grandchild and any future babies to be the consequence of that." I shrug. "My age and the family trust mean that we're not dependent on each other, Mother. If you want to talk trash, the only one who ends up in the bin is you." I give a fake salute to everyone. "Enjoy your dinner. I'm heading to Colorado to be with my wife."

Without waiting for a response, I head down the hall to the bedrooms and pack myself a bag as quickly as I can. While I'm there, I text Martin to look after my property showing tonight. Then I throw together things for Nova into the diaper bag and scoop up the portable crib for Brice and Maren to take with them.

My father is at the door to Nova's room, and I glance at him, waiting for whatever wisdom he thinks he's going to impart.

"Son," he says, "whatever has led to this decision, I'd seriously reconsider. At the very least, let me get Caitlin to do up an airtight prenup. You might think you love her now, but marriage is not an easy road."

"Seems easy enough when you take all those detours," I say pointedly. "Stella, Miranda, Claudette... Want to hear the other names Mom screamed about over the years?"

"Tuckers weren't built for monogamy. It's one of the things I thought you understood. Your relationship with Abby certainly seemed to suggest you did."

"I'm not you," I say. Though inside, a twinge of uncertainty strikes. I can't imagine wanting to be with anyone else, ever. Did I ever feel that way about Abby? Maybe. I can't remember, and if I can't remember, I can't be certain that my father isn't right, that I won't develop a wandering eye at some point, just like him. The thought of ever hurting Ember the way he hurt my mother is soul-crushing.

"No," he says with a sigh. "I thought you were, perhaps, smarter when it comes to these matters. Turns out I was wrong. You're getting sucked into the same trap I did. Have the open relationship conversation now, before it's too late. Save you both the screaming later."

I sling my bag and all Nova's stuff over my shoulder. "I'm not you," I say again, firmer this time.

At the junction to the hallway and the open plan, my father holds his hands up in surrender. "Obviously, with all your years of experience, you know best."

My blood was already boiling from earlier, and coupled with my anxiety over what's happening in Colorado right now, I'm in no mood to hear anything my father might have to say. His advice has always been largely selfish, one-sided, and generally unhelpful.

When I set the things by the front door, everyone is taking their seats at the table. No need to waste a catered meal. Sawyer is wheeling Nova's high chair over, and my mother still looks like her head is about to pop off her shoulders.

While I considered the wrath of the government falling on our heads as unlikely, I can't say the same about my mother's. She's tenacious, and normally that's benefitted me. This time, I fear it might ruin the one thing I hold most dear.

Chapter Thirty-Nine

EMBER

Much later that night at the Mexican restaurant, Esteban orders for both of us, making a big show of telling me what's good here, as though we hadn't been here with him dozens of times when we first moved to the city.

After he helped me with the last of the furniture in the apartment, we agreed to meet for dinner, and since things were so easy, so natural between us as we sorted out the last few household items, I never questioned his offer for dinner. Friends, real friends, have been in short supply since my sister died. Meeting him here once he finished work had felt like a good way to cap off my trip home, my time in the apartment. One last dinner with someone who understood where I came from, who my sister was.

But his attitude since we've arrived is leading me to think this is a "date" and not a catch up, as I previously hoped. I'm not wearing my ring, so I guess it wouldn't be obvious that I'm not available or even interested.

But I don't have time to gently set him straight before he's launched into every possible story I might have missed the last few years. None of his claims of moderate wealth or bartender fame feel quite honest though, as if he's trying to make his life seem more exciting and successful than it probably is. And he talks about money a lot, which is a strange thing for me to notice when I've been surrounded by so much the last few months.

Except it's dawned on me that the one thing Gage and I rarely talk about *is* money. When you have a lot, some might even say too much, there's no need to mention how much you have. The cash sitting in your bank account is a given, an indisputable fact that isn't worth discussing. We never talk about how much things cost or whether we can afford something. Gage's motto is that if I want something, I get it, and I've learned to take that to heart.

Esteban has been talking a lot about his bank account, his salary, and how he's on the cusp of purchasing a house in the area. Some might call it bragging, but it feels insecure to me, which is something I never noticed in him when I was younger. Back then he seemed worldly.

"Where are you at now?" he asks as our food arrives.

"I'm living in Bellerive, actually. Not too far from Tucker's Town," I say, gingerly picking up my first soft taco. I send up a silent prayer that I don't spill all the contents down my dress, which cost more than every amount Esteban has mentioned.

"Oh yeah? That's down by Bahamas, right?"

"No, it's actually between Bermuda and Europe, sort of. More north than most people expect."

"Right, right," he says with a nod as though that's information he knew and simply forgot. "Always thought Bermuda was down south too. It's not?"

"No," I say with a small smile.

Honestly, I didn't even know where Bellerive was until I looked it up as part of getting Gage's family's contact information. The only thing I can say for sure, after having been there, is that it's a magical place. Returning to my old neighborhood has made me realize that I don't want to be here, not if I can help it. Bellerive is my home now. So, I might be marrying Gage for Nova's sake, but it's for mine too. After five years, I can live on the island forever... assuming I can afford it.

"Have any plans to come back to the neighborhood? I'll have a place you can stay, even if you've gotten all fancy on that island."

"She won't need it," a deep, familiar voice grits out behind me. "My wife has a place to live on the island."

I startle and whip around, surprised to see Gage there, seething in a way I've never seen before. He looks angry, and I wrack my brain, trying to think of what I could have possibly done to make him so angry. We haven't spoken since this morning. He's never, ever been mad at me.

"Wife?" Esteban says with a confused chuckle, and he scans my hands. "Don't see no ring."

Gage cocks his eyebrows at me.

"I was doing a lot of moving," I say, "and I didn't want to damage it?" It comes out like a question, but that really *is* why I took it off. The thing is worth a fortune, and losing the stones in it seemed all too easy with the work I was doing.

"See," he says, staring down Esteban. "She's not available. For anything."

Esteban peers at me across the table, eyes squinted. "This guy?" But the words aren't accusatory, more questioning, and then I remember how protective Esteban was of my sister and me at the bar. While he was working there, it was one of the safest places either of us were employed. He's big and tough, and he didn't take shit from any customers, which is probably why he eventually had to move on. I forgot all that until this moment, the expression on his face silently asking if I'm okay with what's happening is so familiar.

"Yeah," I say, reaching across the table to quickly squeeze his hand. "This guy." I don't know what's going on with Gage, but I know without a doubt that I'm safe with him. He'd never hurt me, even if he seems inexplicably furious right now.

"Ready to go?" Gage asks, holding out his hand to me, his jaw tight.

"Is everything okay?" I ask, a sliver of panic wedging into my stomach.

"No," Gage says, his voice tight.

"Is it Nova?" I ask, wiping my mouth with my napkin before dropping it on the table and standing beside him.

"No," he says, and his tone softens a little, as though he knows that would send me into a full-on panic. "She's fine. I took care of the bill. Let's go."

"You want my number?" Esteban asks, rising behind me.

"No, she doesn't," Gage says, taking my hand and leading me out of the booth.

"It was nice to see you," I call to him before focusing on the man practically dragging me out of the restaurant. "Gage," I hiss, frustration overtaking my initial worry. "What's wrong with you?"

"Get in the car," he says, holding open the back door, Rusty at the wheel.

I slide in without arguing, but I cross my arms in the back seat, waiting for him to explain himself. But he doesn't say a word, and then we pass the turn to the apartment building.

"Where are we going?" I ask.

"Colorado Springs, ma'am," Rusty says from the front seat. "Mr. Tucker's wishes."

"This isn't going to work for me," I say, turning to Gage. "The silent treatment? Not cool. Like, at all."

"I'll speak to you when we're at the house," Gage says, his tone brimming with warning as he gazes pointedly at Rusty.

Maybe something has gone wrong with the fake engagement? Maybe his mother has already turned us in? Oh, god. It would make sense for Gage to be upset if that was the case. Maybe I can't even go back to the island, after I just came to the realization I never want to leave there. That's completely my luck.

"All of my stuff is at the apartment," I say, carefully.

"We'll get it tomorrow," Gage says. "There's spare everything at the house."

We pull up to the sprawling estate, and Rusty jumps out to get the door to the back seat, and then he grabs Gage's suitcase from the trunk. I follow Gage into the mansion, a dull, almost seasickness threatening to blossom in me. I'm jumping to conclusions, but it's the only thing that would make Gage this upset. His mother must have caused problems already.

Gage waits for Rusty to leave and for the front door lock to click before he turns on his heel and makes his way to the kitchen.

"Drink?" he asks.

"Are you going to tell me what's going on? I take it your mother didn't take the announcement well?"

"About as well as I expected," he says, his reply uncharacteristically curt.

"What is going on with you?" I exclaim, circling the island to grab his hand. "What's wrong?"

"I thought I sent you here to clean out your apartment, not to meet with an *old friend.*" He says the last two words as though they have additional weight, and I stare at him blankly.

"I can't meet up with someone I used to know? I've been in Bellerive, alone, for months, and I can't meet with one friend?"

"Come on, Em. At least be honest with me. I don't need the fucking code word, okay?" He pours himself a healthy glass of vodka and takes a gulp.

"Code word?"

"*Old friend*? That was your suggestion, wasn't it?"

Then it hits me as though I've run into a brick wall. "Oh my god. Gage, you thought I was going to sleep with him?"

"Pretty clear he'd sleep with you," he says, his jaw tight. "I thought we had an understanding—unspoken, sure—but I'm not fucking around with anyone else. It's you. Just you. You're all I want."

He's said the words, but it feels like they've been ripped out of him against his will, and I grip his face, forcing him to make eye contact with me. "You're all I want too."

"Not the way I want you," he says, his expression pained. "Not even close to the way I want you."

I swallow down my instinctual denial because these waters feel new and rough. "Are you... Are you talking about sex?"

He doesn't say anything and breaks eye contact to take another gulp from his glass.

"I don't know how you can question whether I want you that way. It's pretty clear I do," I say.

"But you'd rather be with other people, that's what you said." His voice is rough with emotion, and I realize I must have hurt his feelings when I said that. I didn't know him well enough to notice, or maybe he hid it, but I can see it now.

"Gage," I say, feeling bravery settle over me like a cloak, and I turn him to face me, "the only person I want right now is you."

He scans my face for a beat, and something heavy and indefinable clings to the air around us. I can't decide if I want to sink into this feeling or run from it, but I couldn't make my feet move even if I wanted to.

"Me too, Em," he says, setting down his glass and nuzzling my nose. "Me too." Then his hands slide along my cheeks and into my hair, drawing me into a kiss that's so fierce, I have to rise onto my tiptoes to meet it. "Tell me when you want me to stop," he says between kisses.

It takes me a few more breathless kissing beats before I have the nerve to say, "I don't want you to stop at all."

That's enough for him, and he sweeps me into his arms, carrying me toward the stairs. When we get to the main suite where Gage sleeps, I expect the frantic nature from downstairs to continue, but instead, I'm met with something bordering on worship.

With every piece of my clothing he discards, he kisses a line across my skin, murmuring how beautiful I am, how much he wants me. No one has ever cared for me like this or made me feel like it wasn't just my body or their own release that they were seeking.

Once I'm naked, he falls to his knees, and he prods my legs apart before his tongue makes contact with my most sensitive bundle of nerves, and I gasp. One of his fingers toys with my entrance, and he groans.

"You're so fucking wet for me, baby. I need to taste you," he says before lifting me up and setting me on the bed.

Then he's back between my legs, my knees slung over his shoulders and back as he works me with his tongue. I thread my fingers through his hair, arching my back, unable to believe how good this feels. Shockingly good. Everywhere he touches, it's as though he's flicking on light switches in rooms that were only dimly lit before.

"Tell me how to make you come," he mutters against me. "I want you to come on my tongue, and then I'll make you come again as I fuck you."

My body feels almost painfully aware of every move he makes, slow and deliberate, setting a pace that's making it impossible to concentrate on anything but the feel of his tongue sliding and swirling against me.

Then he dips a finger inside me, and I moan. "More," I say, unable to keep the word from escaping.

He pushes a second finger in, and I clutch at his head, feeling the tightness inside of me ratcheting up another level.

"More," I say, because I feel so close but not yet close enough.

He slides another finger in and pumps in time with his tongue, and the spring inside me cranks another notch.

"Oh my god," I cry. "Oh god, Gage."

He swirls his tongue with a little more pressure, pushes his fingers in a little harder, and my hips buck as my orgasm rockets through me, and I cry out his name, over and over as wave after wave of my orgasm surges through me.

"That was even better than before," I say, when I can finally speak. And what I really mean, but don't say, is that it's better than anything that's happened in my life.

"Thank fuck," Gage says with a chuckle. He places gentle kisses on my body as he works his way up. "If you're too sensitive, we can stop there."

"No," I say with a shake of my head, even though everything feels a little tender. "I want to be with you." I stroke his cheek, and he searches my face for a beat before nodding.

Out of the nightstand, he takes out a foil package, and he rips off the top, rolling it on with a smoothness that reminds me of the vast experience he has. It's only then that I realize how much bigger he is compared to the limited number of men I've seen in the past. Either Gage is huge, or the other guys were less than average.

"I'm a little nervous," I admit before I can claw back the words.

Gage crawls up my body until we're face-to-face. "I don't give a fuck about getting off, Em. You're in charge. You say when we're done, okay?"

"Okay," I whisper, and then I kiss him, and he hitches my leg onto his hip. His tip is at my entrance, and he eases in, slow and careful.

"That's it, baby," he says. "Breathe for me. We're almost there. You're taking it so good. So fucking good."

I bring my other leg around his other hip, hooking it on, urging him deeper, faster. In this moment, there's nothing I want more than to be completely connected to him. He groans and presses his forehead against mine.

"Fuck, Em. You feel so good. So so good."

"I was worried it might hurt," I say, overcome with how full I feel, but it isn't painful.

"Does it?" he asks, going still.

"No," I say. "It feels good. You feel good."

He slides his hand along my leg as he eases out and back in. "I could do this all fucking night. You're so fucking perfect. I could bury myself inside you over and over again." He shifts us slightly, and he sinks deeper inside me, and it feels even better than it did before.

Then he sets a slow, steady rhythm, making sure our bodies brush together with each thrust, and I'm surprised to find the coil inside me winding again. The one other time I had sex was nothing like this. Gage and I are both breathing heavy, murmuring soft words of pleasure to each other as he brings me closer and closer to another climax.

My legs begin to shake, and Gage nuzzles my neck. "That's it, baby. I want you to come for me again while I'm deep inside you. I want to feel every second of the pleasure I give you."

Coherent thought is impossible as I get closer and closer to coming undone. "Don't stop," I say, arching against him, and I know he's watching me, but I can't bring myself to care or feel self-conscious. I'm chasing that sensation that's just slightly out of reach, and I've almost caught it. "Faster," I say, desperate to latch onto the euphoria at the edges of my vision.

He grips my ass and drives harder and faster into me, his own breathing becoming more labored. "Fuck, Em, I don't know..." He sucks in a sharp breath. "I don't know..."

And then the dam inside me breaks, and the rush of my orgasm sweeps over me, lifting me up and over. I close my eyes, moaning as Gage increases his pace, chasing his own release before he lets out a satisfied groan, burying his face in my neck.

We're both still breathing hard, when without warning, I burst into tears. Huge, wracking sobs that I can't stop, even though I don't want to be crying.

Gage stares down at me in alarm, and I sling an arm over my face. He removes it gently, and there's panic in his expression. "Em? This doesn't seem good."

"No, it's—it's—it's..." I choke on the words. "Not you."

He shifts to my side, and he drags me into his arms, holding me tight. "Okay," he says, and I can almost hear him puzzling out my behavior with that one word. "Okay." He squeezes me tight and kisses the top of my head.

"It's just been—it's just been—a hard weekend." I manage to get the words out between sobs.

"I should have come with you," he says, his voice rough. "*Of course* I should have come with you." The second claim is accusatory, as though he should have been able to read my mind, understand how hard it would be here for me, alone.

I bury my face in his chest, and I cry while he rubs my back in circles, not saying anything, just letting me get it all out.

"Do you need to stay here longer?" he murmurs against the top of my head. "I can give Martin all my listings and clients. He'll be delighted."

I muffle an unexpected laugh against his chest because Martin *would* be delighted to take Gage's high-profile clients, the ones who value the Tucker name above all else. From my perspective, it's been an unexpected perk to starting his own company, but Gage seemed like he expected it, as though it was always obvious that the Tucker name held that much weight.

"I don't want to stay longer," I manage to get out. "I just want to go home with you."

He squeezes me tighter for a brief beat before releasing me. "I'll be back in a second." He leaves me and heads into the en suite, and then he returns a few minutes later with a washcloth and a box of tissues. He passes me the warm washcloth for my face, and I press it against my swollen eyelids, happy for the heat. While I'm doing that, he sets the tissue box on my bedside. The whole time, he's still naked and completely unselfconscious, whereas I'm tempted to jump under the blankets to cover myself up.

He tugs the blankets out and slides underneath, helping me to get under when I struggle a little. Once I'm under, he tugs me flush against him, my back pressed into his chest the way I like, the position that makes me feel safe.

"Going through your old stuff was hard?" he asks, gently.

"Yeah," I say. "Most of it was Athena's and Nova's."

"Ah, right. Jesus. I should have thought of that. Here I was, picturing just your stuff, but of course it was more than that." There's a heavy pause, and then he says, "The room that was still put together when I got there, that was Athena's?"

"It was," I say, my voice thick with tears.

He sucks in a sharp breath. "Fuck. I should have come. Do you still need help with that?"

"No," I say, fighting tears, "it's done."

There's another long pause, and then Gage says, "Was it really an accident, Em?"

I tense in his arms, not sure I can get the words out, even if I want to. "What do you mean?"

"Celia sent me a police report on my flight here," he says, his voice gentle. "You could have told me."

"I couldn't even tell myself," I say, my voice catching on a sob. "She must have been so miserable, and I didn't see it. I couldn't see it. I was a terrible sister. She was always so good to me, and I wasn't good to her."

"We can only see what people let us see. From what you've told me, she was big on protecting you, maybe even from herself."

"I should have seen it," I say, the tears coming fast. "We lived together. I should have seen it."

He tugs me around so I'm facing him. "You know what I know? You've got the biggest heart, and if she'd given you any indication of how she was feeling, I know you would have stepped in. *I* know it."

"She tried to contact you," I say, my vision of him blurred by tears. "I found her diary. She knew she was drowning, and she reached out for you." She thought he was her lifeline, and maybe she would have been right because he's certainly been mine.

A crease forms between his brows, and he scans my face like he's trying to figure out if I'm being honest, so it's no surprise when he says, "I never heard from her. I swear that if I'd known, I'd have done something. I won't lie and tell you it would have been *exactly* the right something, but I wouldn't have ignored her."

"A housekeeper answered."

"If you want me to get to the bottom of this, I will."

I stare at him for a beat, and I'm sure he never got her message, had no idea Nova existed. Part of me wants to dig for the person who didn't do their job, for what led to Athena taking her own life, but the truth is that none of it matters anymore. Nothing I find will bring her back, and it doesn't change how she sought help. One opportunity missed. So many lives changed.

"I don't think anything good would come from that," I admit. "Best to let those sleeping dogs lie."

He draws me tight against him, and I breathe him in, part of me feeling so guilty to be so happy when it feels like my happiness came at my sister's expense, both back then and now. I don't have any right to be this content, so I remind myself that it's all temporary, and that eases the sting from Athena's death but leaves a different sharpness in its wake.

For now, he's mine and this life is mine, but like everything else has in my life, this happiness could vanish at any moment too.

Chapter Forty

GAGE

After having breakfast delivered, we're back at Ember and Athena's ratty apartment. It needs a fresh coat of paint, and the windows need to be replaced. I'm noticing things I didn't yet have the skill set to see the first time around. While I could, and did, tell people the place was a dump, I couldn't pinpoint why. Now, I can, and I'd even know how to fix it, if Ember ever did want to come back.

I'm really hoping she never wants to come back here again.

I carry the last box we'll bring on the plane down to Rusty, and I take the stairs up to the apartment two at a time. Everything that happened last night is still swirling around my brain like a fog that won't dissipate.

Seeing Ember at the table with her old friend had sent the most violent rush of jealousy through me that I've ever felt. Abby used to try to make me jealous, and I always used to find it funny. There was nothing funny about how I felt last night.

On the flight, my mother sent the text message with the police report attached that she'd been holding onto in case she *needed it,* which was somehow supposed to prove Athena was a drug addict. She'd overdosed on pills, but that didn't make her an addict. Desperate. Probably pretty fucking lonely and definitely depressed. But an addict? Celia Tucker was grasping at straws as far as I was concerned.

Knowing my mother, it was a move designed to make me second-guess marrying Ember, as though Athena's choices might reflect badly on Ember. But since she really doesn't know Ember, it's only solidified my desire to give Ember everything she could ever want. The most important person in Ember's life left her, and she somehow held herself together enough to provide for Nova. I honestly can't say I'd have been able to do the same.

But the text certainly tells me that my mother doesn't intend to play nice, and that Ember and I need to get pretty fucking good at playing pretend. Maybe I'm no longer faking my feelings, but I can't say the same for Ember. I might have managed to secure a spot in her bed, but I doubt I've wedged myself into her heart yet. Fair enough. People she's loved haven't exactly done right by her in the past.

When I open the apartment door, Ember is standing at the counter, a slightly lost look on her face.

"What's up?" I ask, running a hand down her back.

"Do you think I'll be able to afford to stay in Bellerive after our five years together?"

"I can make sure you do, if that's what you want." Honestly, I'm hoping I've so thoroughly won her over in five years that the only place she wants to stay is in our house, our bed. This morning wasn't awkward, like I'd somewhat feared as I'd fallen asleep last night. I wasn't sure how Ember would respond to what *I* feel is a new closeness.

"Okay, yeah," she says, glancing at me. "I don't know what I want, but I don't think I want to come back here."

"We can figure something out." The place, even with paint and windows, would be a huge step down to what Ember will be used to in five years' time. But again, I'm really hoping this isn't a serious conversation we ever, ever have. "Rusty has the boxes stacked in the back, so if you're ready to go, he'll mail them tomorrow when the post office is open. I've got the jet on standby."

"The jet on standby," Ember repeats, clearly amused. "That is not a phrase I ever thought someone would say with any seriousness in my life." She lingers for a beat and releases a deep sigh. "I'll meet you down there in a minute. I just need one more walk down memory lane."

"You sure you don't want me to stay? You don't have to do the hard stuff alone, you know."

"I know." She gives me a half smile. "But it feels like I should do this one alone."

I press a kiss to her temple, and then I leave her alone to get whatever closure she needs.

Ember has been quiet since she slid into the back of the car after her solo tour through the empty apartment. While the jet taxis down the runway, I'm tempted to push, but I don't want to end up consoling her while she sobs again. I was surprised I was capable of handling her tears without doing something stupid, but I wouldn't want to chance it a second time. She cries, and I want to hand her the world on a platter.

"How did your parents really take the news about us being engaged?" Ember asks, breaking the silence.

"I wasn't being flippant yesterday. They both took it about how I expected. Nothing to worry about." I'll do all the worrying for both of us when it comes to my mother. No need to saddle her with that unpleasantness. "A better use of our time is wedding planning," I say. "Martin is taking care of the business today, so you've got my undivided attention."

"How big do you want to go?"

"Bigger the better."

"Seriously? We have to pull this together quickly. Our time is limited."

"But our budget isn't," I say with a chuckle. "Whatever we want, I guarantee I can make it happen if I open my big, fat wallet wide enough."

"Oh yeah?" Ember says, stifling a laugh. "You got anything else tucked in there that's big and fat?"

"This is likely to be the only time in my life where I'll be happy to have any part of my body described as fat." I waggle my eyebrows. "Mile High Club?"

She leans forward and kisses me, and at first I take that as a yes, but when I slide my hand up her leg, she draws away.

"I've been thinking," she says, and she's wringing her hands, which is never a good sign.

"About?"

"Well, I mean, if we're going to keep doing this..." She gestures between the two of us.

"Having sex?"

"Yes."

"Okay?"

"That maybe we should agree that it's just sex. That we're both committed to keeping any personal feeling out of this."

"Out of our marriage?" I say it slowly, hoping she'll see how ridiculous that sounds. We'll be married, and we'll be having a lot of sex, and neither of us is supposed to feel anything for the other? Like, really? She's delusional. "You want to keep feelings out of our *marriage*?"

"And the bedroom." She meets my gaze, and her expression is serious.

Jesus. I might have a rougher road to winning her over than I thought. Do multiple orgasms not hook a woman anymore? Unlimited funds and lots of orgasms. It feels like she should already be in love with me.

"I might need you to explain this to me," I say.

"Obviously, you have needs, and I get that." She swallows. "And I'm... I can take care of those."

So clinical. Maybe I don't want her to explain.

"But for Nova's sake, I think it would be easier, in the longer term, if we remained friendly, but nothing else. Just, like, good friends. Best friends, even."

I'm sure there's some adage about the best long-term partners being your best friend. That's a thing, isn't it? But I keep my lips sealed because if she needs to convince herself that we can do this no-feelings plan when I'm already desperately in love with her, I'll let her do that. This way, I can keep being in love with her and somehow convince her that being in love with me is also a better plan than the nonsense she's spouting. Nova would be better served with two parents who loved her *and* each other.

"Right," I say. "Just so we're clear. We'd be best friends who are married and have a lot of sex, but we cannot fall in love. Is that your proposal?"

"Y-yes," she says, not at all convincing.

"Yeah," I say, keeping my tone casual. "I can go along with that."

"Really?" She perks up, clearly surprised.

I'm already completely fucked, but I might as well pretend I'm not. Secret agent my way into her heart. "To be clear, if I say yes, we're mile highing it, right?"

"Gage." She slaps my bicep. "This is serious."

"Trust me, babe. Nothing is more serious to me right now." I wink at her. "Am I hitting this privacy button or not?"

"Will they know what we're doing?"

"I mean, I'm sure they could guess." I let out a chuckle. "We're getting married. It's believable we'd be fucking every chance we had. We're selling the lie." Or the truth, if you're me. Maybe part of her truth too. There's no doubt she wanted me last night.

She reaches past me and hits the button. "I don't know what's happening to me." She lets out a little giggle. "I've never been like this."

"You've been Gageified, baby." I get out of my chair, and I haul her with me, sliding my hand into her hair and kissing her.

"Gageified?" Ember laughs as I kiss a line down her neck. "Please tell me that's not a line you use."

"Only on my wife," I say, sliding my hand up her leg and under the hem of her sundress. She changed into it when we got on the plane, and if she's not wearing underwear, I'll know I completely corrupted her after just one night. But when I get to her ass, there's still lacy material.

"Your wife," she says with a sigh.

Yeah, I'm winning her over. One orgasm, one caress, one sighed 'wife' comment at a time. She's mine, and once she's legally mine, I won't be letting her go without a fight.

I walk her over to the wall, and with the touch of a button, the seating area starts flipping and sliding to convert into a bed. Ember watches, her expression stunned.

"You just turned the seats into a bed," she says, pushing down on them with one finger. "That's not even that hard. And there's sheets?"

"Which are changed after every flight, regardless of who has been using it and for what."

"Right," she says, slowly. Then she turns, rising on her toes, and she kisses me. "I would have done it anywhere," she says, "because I can't stop thinking about you."

Music to my ears.

"I want to take you from behind," I murmur against her lips.

"I haven't... I've never..." She flushes. "That's not a code word for my ass, right?"

I can't help my laugh, and I run a soothing hand up her body for a moment while I gather myself. "I mean, we can certainly do that at some point, if you want, but no, that's not what I meant."

"I don't think I'm quite *there* yet," she says, blushing and then she draws me into a kiss again.

We're peeling off clothes. Each piece hitting the floor, easily discarded. Whatever inhibitions she had for a brief moment seem to be gone. Since I clarified I would not be taking the dirt road, she's been all in, hands and lips all over me.

Once we're both naked, I say, "On the bed, on all fours. Ass toward me."

Ember gets on the bed, and she glances at me over her shoulder, I run my hand along her ass and her leg, savoring the contact, the anticipation. "You're such a good fucking girl."

Then I spread her cheeks, and I worship her with my tongue from her clit, all the way back, loving how turned on she already is, how she moans my name and grips the sheets. When her legs start to shake, I pull back, grabbing a condom from nearby and rolling it on.

"I'm going to love watching my cock slide in and out of your warm pussy, knowing that you're this wet just for me." Just the thought of it has made me rock-hard.

"Yes," she breathes. "Yes."

Then I ease into her, nice and slow, conscious that she might be sore from last night. "You're so sweet and tight. Fucking perfect."

"Gage, I need more," she cries, trying to push back against me. "I was so close before."

"Not this time," I say, giving her ass a light tap. "I set the pace today, and when I finally let you come, I'm going to be buried to the hilt inside you." I take her hips, and I tug her back, sliding deeper into her. As I thrust, I lean forward, my hand rounding her hip to rotate my fingers over the bundle of nerves, sure to drive her wild. In her ear, I say, "And when we get home, I'm going to keep fucking you every chance we get. We're going to fuck so often that you'll crave my dick like candy, seeking the sugar high so badly that you'll dream about being fucked. Wake me up in the middle of the night to have that craving satisfied. Want me and this feeling so badly, you'll barely be able to think of anything else." God knows, that's exactly what's going to happen to me.

And then I ease back, her labored breathing to my satisfaction, and I watch her take every inch of me over and over again. "Look at how well you take me. How perfectly we fit together."

"Gage, please" she says, my name garbled by her desire. And I know what she needs. Harder, faster.

"No," I say, keeping the steady pace. "You'll come when I tell you to."

"Oh, god," she pants, and when she gazes at me over her shoulder, her long dark hair a heavy curtain, partially obscuring the intense desire coating her expression, I almost lose it. It seems impossible to love someone this much, to want to be even closer, deeper, than I already am. That Ember trusts me enough to take her to the brink, to know when to propel her over, is pretty heady stuff.

"Tell me you love it," I say. "Tell me you love having me inside you, and I'll give you what you need."

"I love it," she pants, and a hint of a smirk touches her lips when we make eye contact. "I love having your big, fat dick inside me."

"That's my girl," I say, with a strained chuckle. "Now hold on, I'm going to tip you over the edge." Then with one hand gripping her hip and another causing havoc with her clit, I drive us both over the cliff of sanity.

Chapter Forty-One

GAGE

This morning, after posting our engagement announcement all over my socials, I headed to meet some potential clients and their listings. At each stop, I become more aware of something Hugh predicted, which irritates the fuck out of me. Getting engaged seems to have given me a more reputable edge, at least with the older, more established clients. More than one mentions how much more mature I seem than the last time they met with me, and how they're pleased to see how stable and focused I am on making my real estate company the best in Bellerive. If Nova didn't make me stable, a wife sure as shit wasn't gonna do it, but who am I to argue with a client when they're telling me I look better, more appealing, than I did before? I'd have to be insane to open my mouth and contradict them.

So that's who I am now—Gage Tucker—real estate mogul, father, engaged man, and as stable as the earthquake-proof foundation in your office tower.

Their comments rub me the wrong way, and when I come into the office to a flurry of congratulatory exclamations, I try to conceal my annoyance. For Hugh to be right about anything is a thorn in my side.

When I get to my desk, my secretary puts through a call from Robert, and I brace myself for criticism about the engagement announcement. Too soon or too late or too something, I'm sure.

"I just wanted to let you know," he says, getting to the point, "that all your job applications for Ember received Bellerivian candidates. I'll send their information over to you, and you can decide who you're going to hire to fill those positions."

"Any of them happen to moonlight as a wedding planner?" I ask, rocking back in my chair, poking at Robert in a way that I know I shouldn't.

"I don't know. You can ask them. During the interviews you conduct for the jobs you posted."

His tone isn't lost on me, but I'm choosing to gloss over it. "I'll hire someone to do something."

He releases a deep sigh and hangs up without saying another word. Somehow it makes me feel better that he hasn't equated this engagement as an improvement in my character.

I'm staring at the dead receiver in my hand when my secretary's raised voice hits my ears, and I rise from behind my desk just as Abby storms in, slamming the door in my secretary's face.

"Did we have an appointment?" I ask, picking up my phone to check my calendar.

"Do I need to show you my tits to get one?" She mocks lifting the hem of her shirt.

"Been there. Done that. Not interested in doing it again." I toss my phone back on my desk. "What do you want?" Every time we've run into each other the last few months, our encounters have become less and less civil. Whatever patience we normally afford each other has evaporated, and I'm braced for an argument.

"You're *engaged*?"

There's so much venom in the word that I fight a flinch. As I stare at her, neither confirming nor denying what she clearly believes to be an accusation of some sort, I wonder whether I could have circumvented this confrontation by giving her a heads-up.

Probably would have resulted in the same reaction, but at least I would have been initiating it, aware it was going to happen.

Then she does something I never would have expected. She bursts into tears. "We were together for five years. Five *years*! You haven't even known her for five *months*."

Her tears should probably move me in some way because she's right—we spent a lot of time together. Too much, in hindsight. I was wasting both of our time by keeping the pattern going. It was never going to go where she wanted it to, and I think I knew that deep down. But I'm still sort of surprised she's crying. Other than the first time we broke up, we've both been dry-eyed and clearheaded. We break up and make up, but none of those ever felt filled with emotion.

I would fucking die if Ember walked out my door and never came back.

"When you know, you know," I say, splaying my hands wide.

She picks up the globe sitting on the side table near the door, and she throws it at my head. I manage to duck just in time.

"That's such trite, clichéd bullshit!" she yells. "God, you can't even tell me the truth?"

"It *is* the truth." I keep my voice even despite her hysterics. "I understand why you might be skeptical, but it doesn't mean it's not true."

"Is she pregnant now too? Trap you with a second baby?"

"What the fuck are you talking about? No one is trapped."

"There's no way this relationship is real. She's brainwashed you or something."

"Brainwashed me? Okay, Celia Tucker."

"So your mom doesn't believe this is real either? Ember Whitten is a gold digger, and she's somehow made you pity her enough to marry her."

"I don't pity her." I can't keep the disdain from my voice. "I'm marrying her because I want to." *Because I love her.* But I can't quite get the words out. They feel rusty and ill-used, and now that those words are real, it doesn't feel right to be giving them out to anyone but Ember. Fuck if I know when I'll actually have the courage to tell her that I'm not faking anything.

"For five years, I gave you whatever you wanted," she says, wiping away her tears as they fall. "You want to break up to fuck other people. Fine, we do. You want a threesome, we do that. Whatever you wanted, I agreed to it. I gave you *everything*."

I run a hand through my hair, trying to gather my thoughts. Five years encompasses a lot of growing up, and near the end, if I'm honest, it all started to feel a bit empty. "That's just sex." The words leave my mouth, and I can't even believe I've said them. Now that they're out there, I realize it's true. My relationship with Abby was based almost purely on sex—it was always the reason we broke up, and it was also the reason we'd end up back together.

Abby gapes at me, and then she closes her mouth, her jaw tight with frustration or anger or maybe even rage.

What I have with Ember, the closeness, the fact that I can rely on her for anything, that's so much more than anything I ever shared with Abby. Even if Ember and I weren't sleeping together, she'd still be my choice.

"She is the opposite of *everything* you ever said you wanted. I'm not buying what you're selling."

"I've grown up, Abby. Had to happen at some point."

"Not that fast. Not in a matter of a couple of months. She's trapped you somehow. And there's no way I'm letting some trailer trash weasel her way—"

"Shut up," I say, my voice as hard as steel. "You do not fucking talk about my wife that way. Ever. If I hear you've been speaking badly of her, I'll do everything I can to make your life fucking miserable. Do you understand? I'm not playing around, Abby."

"I understand you got some random woman pregnant by accident, and that her sister is taking advantage of your good nature. That's what I understand, and if you can't save yourself, I'll figure out a way to save you." Then she storms out the door before I can say another word.

Fuuucccckkk.

The last thing I need is another person peering into my marriage with Ember in disbelief. While I'm no longer lying, Ember certainly is.

Chapter Forty-Two

EMBER

Over the last week, wedding planning has gone into full swing. Ava has been the point person for everything, since I don't really understand the scope of a Tucker wedding. Both Gage and Ava have told me that it needs to feel grand, almost larger than life, but I have no idea what that means. It's one thing to see something on TV, but it's another thing to be the one trying to plan it.

Instead of leaving the house to do our wedding things, Ava calls and has people come to us. It's another blatant display of power, but it makes my life with Nova easier. I don't have to worry about gathering all her things or wrangling her to stay near me now that she's crawling everywhere.

The whole experience has been strange, though, because every person who comes to the house from cake decorators to caterers to professional designers are falling all over themselves to do something, *anything* in the wedding. Ava told me that it's an opportunity for many of the people we hire to level up, become more visible to the ultrawealthy on the island. I get it, but it also doesn't sit right with me.

In the end, I ask Posey to take over decorations. As an interior designer, I trust her eye, and we've spent some time together. She understands how to somehow blend what Gage wants with what I'll be comfortable having. Rory, the queen of

Bellerive, offers to let us get married on the palace grounds, which Ava assures me is quite a coup. I'm not sure I could have said no, even if I wanted to.

So it feels like everything has fallen into place, and quickly, when Ava arrives to bundle Nova and me up and into the waiting SUV to go dress shopping. Ava said the lighting is critical for proper dress evaluations, and no lighting in the two thousand square foot house Gage and I are occupying would do justice to the fashion masterpieces I'm meant to be trying on. It's probably the one experience I really want to have anyway, so I don't argue.

Up until now, none of the preparations have felt overwhelming. During the day, Ava walks me through everything I could possibly need to know about getting married to a Tucker, and at night, Gage shows me what it'll be like to be actually married. And that, at least, is addictive, just as he predicted. Every night I wait for him to come home, and we go at each other like we're starved for touch, completely insatiable. Being with him is like nothing I've ever experienced before, and I can't imagine I'll ever have whatever this is between us again.

We arrive at the exclusive wedding dress store without incident, but all the windows have coverings on them, and we're ushered through to a back room as though my dress is top secret information.

Ava sits in a comfortable chair, and I place Nova in the spinning play chair they have nearby with various things she can pull and bang and move around. She's immediately entranced, and the clerk takes me back to the dresses she pulled after I described what I wanted. A very fitted top down to the waist and a very full skirt. Since I'm living a fairy tale, I figured I might as well embrace it.

When I come out in the first one, Ava wrinkles her nose. "Don't you want something sexier?"

"No," I say with a little laugh. "If I did, I'd have asked for that."

"I think I liked it better when you were quiet and meek," Ava says with a pouty half smile.

She has a point. I can't remember the last time I hesitated to tell either her or Gage how I really feel about something. Whatever I'm thinking or feeling flows out easily, even in the bedroom, somewhere I never thought I'd be comfortable with a man, I'm more confident of what I want and how I want it. The best part is that I know Gage will listen, or if he doesn't listen, it's because he has some way to make what I'm feeling even better. He is a certified sex god.

"They're all like this," I say, gesturing to the flowing, full dress. "You just need to tell me which one you like best. This is the style I want."

"Does he call you *'princess'* in bed?" Ava asks with a smirk. "Is that what this is about?"

"No," I say, blushing. "I'm living a fairy tale, and I'm getting married. This is what I want. Full fantasy." I stare at myself in the mirror, and while the dress doesn't feel quite right, the style does.

"Next," Ava says, waving her hand. "I'll tell you which one looks best."

Ten dresses later, I'm back in the second one I tried on, the one I was sure was "the one," but Ava said it was best to test drive as many as possible before committing. Somehow, I suspect that's her motto for everything in life.

Once I've said yes, there's a flurry of measurements and tittering over dress fittings and timing. Ava takes my phone and starts scheduling things into my calendar. All the other fittings are happening at the house, and when I try to question Ava, she merely tells me to trust her.

When we're finally ready to leave, Nova is cranky and in desperate need of a nap. The salesclerk goes to the front door and then hustles back to us.

"Too many people there," she says. "I'll check the back."

"Too many people?" I ask.

"Welcome to the life of a high-profile Tucker," Ava says.

"What does that mean?" I ask, glancing around.

"The back is packed too," the clerk says. "Neither is ideal. It's a straighter, less narrow shot to your car from the front."

"Right," Ava says with decisiveness, "front it is. I'll lead us out. There will be a lot of flashes, so shield Nova's head with your hand or the diaper bag. Whatever you've got."

"What are you…" I trail behind Ava as she struts out the door, and as soon as the blacked out door pushes open, I hear the *click-click-click* of cameras. I hesitate for a beat.

"You'd better go," the clerk says. "Won't get any easier if you wait."

I draw Nova into my chest, pressing her face into my neck, even though she's not entirely sure about it, and I follow Ava out. As soon as I'm visible, people are shouting my name, flashes are going off, and the rapid-fire clicks of the camera are my soundtrack all the way to the car. When I won't look up, a camera is shoved in my face, and I stutter to a stop. Then it's like a mob, circling me, cameras going off, and Nova is crying now, screaming.

Ava has waded back into the fray, and there's Bill, too, pushing people out of the way, urging me toward the open door of the SUV. But I have to buckle Nova in, and the whole time I'm doing it, there are picture after picture and question after question being lobbed my way. I try to block them out, but the few I hear are intrusive and some are downright vulgar, as though trying to get a knee-jerk response from me.

My heart is in my throat, and I'm going as quickly as I can to get Nova secured. Then I round the car with Bill on my outside edge keeping everyone back, and then I slide into the back seat, and I let out a whoosh of breath.

"That was awful," I breathe out. "Why is this happening?"

"Blame Gage," Ava says. "His big, splashy announcement told people they should care. They've also uncovered the link with your sister, which is news now too. It's all very scandalous, very juicy." Ava shrugs. "If your handbags take off like they should, this will be your life. Fame. Fame. More fame. If not, you'll become a boring married woman within a year, and this will all, mostly, stop."

"We've been on the island for months now," I say, but then I half remember Gage's warning about the engagement creating interest. I just had no idea *this* would be what that would look like.

"Yeah, but Bellerivian laws dictate that you can't take unapproved photos of minors. Nova wasn't news because she wasn't worth anything in terms of pictures or a story. And you weren't news because Gage told everyone you were the nanny. But now? *You're* news. They'll blur out Nova's face and run some think piece on how you won the heart of the youngest Tucker. All bullshit, but it'll be fun to read. I always love to see how wrong they get it."

Ava is clearly delighted by the whole experience, and I think I might be traumatized. My heart rate hasn't yet returned to normal, and I'm still seeing spots at the edges of my vision from the flashes.

"I am never leaving the house again," I whisper.

"Yeah, I figured that'd be your reaction. Hence the dress fittings at the house. One swarm would be enough for you."

"But you *like* it?" I ask, bewildered.

"I want this to be my life forever," Ava says with a wistful sigh. "I want everyone to love me."

From what I've seen, that's never how fame works. Once you get high enough, the number of people trying to tear you down seems to also rise exponentially.

Ava has only just left the house when Gage comes storming in.

"You're home early," I say, pointing at the hallway to the bedrooms, where Nova has just fallen asleep and putting my finger to my lips.

"Of course I am," he says, a touch of irritation in his tone. "I was getting tagged all over social media after those jackasses swarmed you. I already have a complaint registered with the police department and Stephen. I also called the store and told them that scene was unacceptable for a high-profile client. Also, Ava should know better."

"She did seem well-aware of the chaos we'd cause," I admit.

He's in front of me now, and his gaze travels over my face, the back of his hand skimming my cheek. "Are you okay? You looked terrified, and I wanted to murder every single one of them."

"I'm okay now," I say, stepping into his embrace. "They weren't going to hurt me, but it just felt so sudden and frantic and loud. So much shouting. And I was trying not to panic for Nova, but she'd already missed her nap..."

"She was cranky. You were stressed." He rubs slow circles along my back, and my core begins to heat at the contact.

As soon as Gage touches me, something inside of me lights up. Before we started having sex, I knew I was attracted to him, considered him almost surreally handsome, but now that we've been intimate, it's a whole other level of attraction.

"I've already hired security," he says, "at least until after the wedding. You can't be trapped in this house, and that scene today was completely unacceptable for you and for Nova. Should never have happened, and I'll be telling Ava that too."

"I don't think she'll listen."

"Maybe not," he says with a sigh. "Either way, I'm not dropping it." He gazes outside, a pensive look on his face. "Since I'm home early..." he says, focusing on me.

"Uh-huh." I give him a small suggestive smile, and heat is already surging to my core.

"Yes, that, but also no," he says, placing a quick kiss on my nose. "I still need to teach you how to swim. You can't live on an island, in a home beside the beach, and not know how to swim."

"In a house with a pool no less," I say, drawing away from him. "I'll get my suit."

"No suit needed," he says, his gaze darkening.

"But it's the middle of the day. Anyone could show up."

He doesn't back down from his statement, and I gaze at him for a beat. "You're serious?"

"If you're not comfortable, it's fine."

"You're going to be naked too?"

"Of course." He's already shedding his suit jacket, undoing the buttons on his shirt.

The area around the pool is heavily treed, but there's a direct line of sight to the vast, well used expanse of beach below.

"I'm getting my suit," I say, disappearing down the hallway, my pulse in my ears. The idea of being watched is both thrilling and terrifying. It's not surprising that someone who looks like Gage wouldn't care, but me? That's a step too far.

Gage is already in the pool when I get back, and I think he's naked, but I'm trying not to stare.

"Are you getting shy on me?" he teases. "I thought we were over the shyness."

"You're naked—in public."

"I'm naked at my home," he says, stretching his arms across the edge of the pool, giving me a world-class view. "Which just happens to overlook a very public, and often busy, beach."

"I could never," I say.

"I think you could," he says with a sly grin. "With the right motivation." Then he claps his hands. "Right—do you know how to float at least?"

"On my front, yes. On my back, not really." I descend the stairs to join him in the waist-high water.

"We'll start with the basics today. Floating—front and back, and treading water."

"Which is?"

"Holding your head above water in an upright, stable position. Lots of different ways to do it."

I do my front float with my face in and out of the water, and then he shows me some simple kicking and sculling to keep my head above water. He leads me by the hand into water where I can barely touch on my tiptoes and gets me to practice. When I get tired, I bounce off the bottom and then keep going.

Once he's satisfied that I can keep myself up for at least a minute, he leads us back to the shallow end.

"All right," he says. "For the back float, I'm going to get you to lie back, and I'll gently support your lower back. You'll rest your head on my shoulder. Pretend you're lying on a bed or a cloud, if a bed seems too suggestive." He winks.

I laugh a little and turn my back to him before starting to lie back. His hands slide along my body, helping me stay near the top of the water, and my head rests just above his shoulder. Then his voice is in my ear, and a shiver runs down my spine. There is nothing I love better than being close to him.

"You're doing great," he murmurs. "Pretend like there's a string from your belly button to the sky, forcing your stomach to stay near the surface."

"Okay," I say, my voice breathy and turned on.

"Arms out nice and wide. That's right. Just like that. Now open your legs a little more."

God, I love it when he tells me I'm doing a good job, in or out of bed. It's like fuel that goes straight to my core, making each nerve stand in anticipation of being stroked.

"Now I'm going to ease my hands away. Keep your stomach up. Keep it up. Yes! Good!"

And then I'm floating, staring up at the clouds, and I hear Gage's whoop of excitement, but when I laugh, I sink, and I scramble for my footing before standing up. He immediately engulfs me in a hug.

"Oh, babe. That was *so good*," he whispers in my ear.

The euphoria of getting it right, coupled with his proximity and lack of clothing send me straight into a lust spiral. When he loosens the hug, I thread my fingers through the back of his hair, and I kiss him.

He meets my kiss with the same intensity I feel, and then he's discarding my top, tossing it toward the edge of the pool, and he lays me back on the stairs, peeling off my bottoms. His lips barely leave mine. I don't even care that the concrete is digging into my back a little, that anyone close enough might hear my moans of pleasure because all I can think about is him.

With his mouth, he gives attention to each of my nipples, one at a time, teeth grazing against the sensitive skin, sucking and licking, driving me absolutely fucking wild, and his fingers and thumb work magic on my core.

"Gage, I need you," I gasp, feeling myself climbing higher and higher. "I need you inside me now."

"Fuck," he says, his forehead pressed against mine. "I don't have a condom near. I'll just take care of you, baby."

"I'm okay with leaving it out if you're okay with it," I say, giving him an open-mouthed kiss, my hand finding his hard length and gliding up and down. We talked about how I was on the pill, but we never talked about losing the condoms. In this moment, I want him so badly I'd probably let him do anything he wanted. Every time it's like this—he remembers protection when I'd likely forget because, unlike with anyone else, I'm so in-the-moment with him.

"You're sure?" he asks, gazing down at me for a beat.

"Yes," I say, kissing him again. "Please. Please."

"I fucking love it when you beg," he says, and he hitches me more securely onto the stair, and then he eases into me. "Holy shit," he says, his voice strained. "Bare is really fucking different. God, babe. I want you so badly I'm only going to last two seconds."

"Make it three, and take me with you," I say, urging him forward.

He chuckles and begins to move. "Deal." His breathing is more labored than normal as he fights for control, but he keeps us locked tight together, a steady rhythm. "You're so tight. So wet. I'm barely keeping it together."

"Please, Gage," I say, arching into the movement, watching the clouds pass overhead while I chase the sensation building between us. It's so close. "Harder, please."

"Fuuccckkk," Gage groans out, but he does as I ask, and after three or four hard thrusts, I've caught the wave, crying out as I ride it, and he follows right behind, groaning into my ear. "Jesus," he pants into my neck, keeping me locked tight against him as we pulse in unison. "That was..."

"Yeah," I agree, barely able to speak.

"Looks like I got you naked in the pool after all," he says with a chuckle.

"You played dirty. You know I can't resist you."

"One of my favorite things about you," he says, placing a gentle kiss on my lips.

It's become one of my favorite things too—that we can't seem to get enough of each other, and I'm so glad I don't have to worry about it coming to an end anytime soon.

The wedding is only a week away, and despite Robert's claims that Gage and I would raise red flags everywhere with our quickie engagement and wedding and weird circumstances, everyone seems to be buying that we're happy.

Honestly, it helps that we are. Wildly, probably borderline inappropriately, happy. Everywhere. All the time. I don't know if he's acting, but I'm not. I *cannot* get enough of him.

From surprise lunch dates, to our Tuesday night dancing, to dinners at restaurants across Bellerive, to our flirty texts—we've popped the cork on our relationship, and giddy happiness is spewing everywhere. The only downside is the intense interest from the press, but Gage says it's good to legitimize us.

So when the doorbell rings, I assume it must be my final dress fitting. Whoever it is has to be vetted by Gage's security detail before they even get close to the door. And no one has the door key anymore. After one too many close calls with Ava almost catching us in a very compromising situation, Gage changed the door code.

When I throw back the door, it's not Sarah the seamstress, though. It's Celia, and she sweeps into the house, plucking Nova from my arms with an authority she really doesn't have. The woman never comes here unless Gage is home, and I don't know if that's because that's how he wants it or how she wants it. I've never asked.

"Celia," I say, following her and Nova into the living room. "What a nice surprise."

"I was missing my favorite granddaughter, and I realized that I could visit with her while you signed some pesky papers."

"Papers?" I ask as she tugs a sheaf out of her oversized purse.

"Since you're becoming a Tucker, it's just a few family things to take care of," she says, passing me the pages as though they're nothing.

And I may not have graduated high school, but as I start reading through them, it dawns on me what these pages likely are. "If you'll excuse me," I say, "I need to use the bathroom."

"Here's a pen, if you want to sign before you go." Celia clicks open the pen in her hand and tries to pass it to me.

"I'll sign when I come out," I say, offering her a strained smile, but instead of going to the closest two piece, I head to the main bedroom and the en suite I share with Gage. Before I've even closed the bedroom door, I'm dialing Gage's number.

"What's up, babe?" he asks, a hint of a smile in his voice.

"Your mother is here with some paperwork for me to sign."

"Paperwork? What paperwork?"

"I'm no lawyer, but it looked like maybe something to do with me not getting anything if we divorce."

"A prenup," Gage says, his voice tinged with frustration. "Don't sign anything. I'll take a look when I get home."

"Your mom will lose it on me."

"Just kick her out," he says easily.

"I'm not kicking your mother out. We have to play nice with her, remember?"

There's a heavy pause on the other end of the line, as though the reminder that we're faking this marriage has landed harder than I intended. I mean, we're not *really* faking most of it anymore, but it's not as though we're getting married out of love.

"Blame me," he says with a sigh. "Tell her I said you can't sign it until I've read it. I've gotta go. But if you need me to come home, send me an SOS text, and I'll cancel my day and be there."

"No," I say. "No, that's too much. It's just your mom." Though the *just* part doesn't feel accurate. "I'll see you tonight."

"Can't wait," he says before clicking off.

I hold the phone in my hand for a beat, savoring the feeling in my chest. It's become our new routine—I say that I'll see him later or tonight or whenever, and he always, always says that he can't wait. I've never felt like I was someone's Christmas present before, but that's how he makes me feel. As though I'm precious and special. Amazing acting on his part. I can see why he was so sure he could pull this off. He oozes charm without even trying too hard.

Then a little twinge of sadness snakes in to steal a bite of my happiness, like it always does. Sometimes I really wish it was real, that it could be real. But letting go of my grip on my feelings is too risky—what if he doesn't return them, what if we're not right together, what if he gets bored of the poor girl who never even graduated high school?

Pretending is so much safer than letting anything get *too* real.

The nice part is that I know, no matter what, Gage has my back. So I sail out into the living room, and I ignore Celia's pen offering for a second time.

"I'm sorry. I can't sign that. Not right now." I cross my arms and face her.

"Why not?"

"Gage asked me not to."

"Right, well, my son seems to be having trouble understanding what's best for him lately."

"I won't go against him."

"I find it strange that you wouldn't want what's best for him. Don't you?"

"I find it strange that you believe he's not capable of knowing what's in his best interests. He's not a child anymore." I didn't mean to go toe to toe with her, but that seems to be what's happening. Pissing her off isn't what's in our best interests. Our impending marriage isn't real, and making her angry is still a risky situation. "Look," I say, changing tactics. "I think Gage just wants to look it over himself. If he wants me to sign it, I will."

Celia offers Nova back to me, and she lets out a pained sigh. "Here's the thing, Ember. If you were really *only* interested in my son for who he is and not his bank account, signing this legal document"—she taps the papers on the table—"is a no-brainer. What do you care about the money if you've got him?"

It's a compelling argument, and it almost makes me snatch the pen that's still in her hand and scrawl my signature across it. Because I don't care about the money, at all. If she knew how much was already in my personal account, she'd probably have a coronary. Gage is incredibly generous and thoughtful and a thousand other things I would gladly shout from the rooftop.

But it's because he's all those things that I don't take the pen. He asked me not to, and I owe him far more loyalty than I owe his mother.

"Thanks so much for stopping by, Celia. I'm sure Gage will be sad to have missed you."

She purses her lips and the hard click of her heels resounds throughout the house as she makes her exit.

Chapter Forty-Three

GAGE

It's been a shit day, and when I get home, for the first time in a long time, I'm not thrilled to see Ember is still awake. I haven't had a chance to wrap my head around what to tell her about the prenup. My mother was being sneaky and underhanded, but if I remove my own feelings of outrage, she's probably not wrong. With anyone else, I'd never go into a marriage without a prenup.

What message does it send if I don't get her to sign it? Romantic or foolish? Everything would be so much easier if I didn't have the shadow of my mother and the government peering over my shoulder, if I didn't have to wonder how things appear. It would be so much better if I didn't have to care because we were real. But we aren't—at least not on her part—and I don't want Ember to ever have to stand up in a courtroom and try to lie to me or for me.

"You okay?" she asks, the minute she sees me.

She reads me impeccably well. It makes me wonder if I have a poker face, even though I've played the game long enough to know I do.

"Hugh's managed to scrape back some high-profile clients by lowering his commission percentages. We're still outperforming Tucker-Smith Realty, but it left me with a sour taste in my mouth."

"If he gets back a few, maybe that'll make him less likely to be a dick?"

"Hugh was born a dick," I say, taking the beer she offers me. "But you're right. Maybe if he feels like he's had a few big wins he won't try something underhanded. Well, more underhanded than what he did to get those clients, anyway." In that sense, Hugh and I have been very tit for tat, but I'm not getting into that with Ember. It's better if she doesn't understand how dirty the business side of things has gotten a few times. I'm winning, that's all she needs to know.

"What do I do about that?" she asks, gesturing toward the papers strewn across the coffee table before wringing her hands.

I pick up the pages and flip through them, scanning them quickly. Nothing jumps out to my untrained eye as a massive red flag, but I don't know if saying that will make her think she has to sign it. And I haven't even decided if she *should* sign it.

"Should we call Robert?"

"We can," I hedge, unsure of what sort of advice he might give.

But she doesn't hesitate. She takes my proffered phone and searches through my contacts until she finds him.

"Can I call him this late?" she asks, biting her lip.

"He'll just bill me about five times his rate, but he'll answer. You can call." I slouch into the couch, and she hits Dial, putting it on speaker phone and setting it on the coffee table.

"Gage," Robert says, his tone wary. "I thought we had an agreement."

"Quick family law question for you. Let's say my mother dropped off a prenup, would you ask your soon-to-be wife to sign that, or no?"

Robert sighs. "Scan the prenup and email it to me. Give me ten minutes and then call me back."

"Excellent," I say. Then I tip back the rest of my beer, use my phone to scan each of the pages, email them to Robert, and sit on the couch, feeling, for the first time in a long time, a little depressed. I'm not even sure I knew that's what I felt back then, but after riding this emotional high with Ember for a few weeks, it's hard to crash back to earth, even a little bit.

Ember leaves her spot on the chair across from me, and she pushes my knees apart so she's kneeling on the floor between my legs.

God, she's beautiful. Absolutely stunning. The most perfect woman I've ever laid eyes on. I love her so much it's almost physically painful, and the urge to admit my feelings to her sits on the edge of my tongue. Might even be part of the reason I feel a twinge of sadness right now. I'd love to say them, to be able to tell everyone I really mean them, that I'm going into this marriage with intentions even my soon-to-be wife doesn't know about. But if I say those words, I break our deal, and I'm so close to getting what I want. Once I've got her for five years, I can take my time winning her over. There's no rush once we're married.

She says she trusts me, but I don't think we're completely there yet. I don't know what I need to do to get us there, but I'll have years to do it. Maybe, with any luck, she'll look at me one day and realize I'm someone she can love back.

"You're the best part of my day, you know that?" I say, smoothing her hair and pressing my lips to her forehead.

She lies along my body, her ear to my chest, and she releases a deep sigh. "Everything in the world seems better once you're home."

We stay like that, comfortable and quiet, and I love that we can have these moments too. Things between us don't have to be frantic or hard or brimming with sexual tension; they can be filled with an easy contentment to share the same space without talking.

Before the ten minutes is up, my phone peals on the coffee table. I hit Answer and then immediately put Robert on speaker.

"What's the verdict?" I ask.

"Prenup is standard. No Celia Tucker surprises buried in it."

"Do we sign it?" I ask.

"I have two questions. One for you. One for Ember. Are you ready?"

"Fire away," I say.

"If she was anyone else, would you expect her to sign it?"

He doesn't pull any punches. "Yes," I say, but I want to qualify it with the fact I never expected to actually be in love with any wife I had. Nothing about this situation is what I imagined in my head during all those hypothetical situations. Yes, I'd have asked them to sign a prenup, but this doesn't feel remotely the same.

"Ember, do you trust that he'll look after you, regardless of what this legal document says?"

"Yes," she says, and it's emphatic. "I know he will."

"Then I think you've got your answer. I wouldn't trust Celia as far as I can throw her. Sign the last page, and then both of you initial each and every page. Gage, you drop it off with Carlos, the Tucker family lawyer, tomorrow. Don't let Celia near those pages. I know what I read just now, but I can't guarantee that would be the version delivered to Carlos, if it was left to her."

"Right," I say, my voice tight. "Makes sense." Who can't trust their own mother?

"I've given you my family law perspective. Enjoy your evening. You'll be billed appropriately."

"Never doubted it," I say with a chuckle.

He hangs up first, and then Ember leaves me to grab a pen. We sign the end and initial each page. Once we're done, Ember gets an envelope and drops all the pages in, slipping it inside the computer bag I use for work.

She takes my hand and leads me back toward our bedroom, and my initial contentment at how sure she was that I wouldn't screw her over when our relationship ended has transitioned into a melancholy awareness of the ticking clock between us. Since when did *years* not feel like enough time?

Just before we go into our room, Nova cries out from her bedroom.

"I'll get her," I say, when Ember turns toward the sound.

"You sure?"

"Yeah. A little rock and talk might do me some good."

She runs her hand along the side of my face and places a gentle kiss on my lips, as though she senses how fragile and not myself I feel tonight. The air between us hums, but neither of us says a word.

In Nova's room, I scoop her out of her crib, change her diaper, and then I settle into the rocking chair. She babbles away to me, and I can feel every drop of stress seep out. What I've somehow managed to build in this house is pretty fucking special. I release a deep sigh and let my head rest against the back of the chair.

Nova pulls herself up my chest, and she frames my face, placing a sloppy, wet kiss almost on my lips. A chuckle escapes me, and I give her an amused grin.

"You want a kiss, my love?" I press my lips to her cheek, and I savor the tinge of lavender that still clings to her skin from her bath. "I love you, Nova. You're the best damn thing that ever happened to me."

Between Ember and Nova, I've got the most powerful one-two love combo when I walk into this house, and I'll tell any lie or admit any truth I have to in order to keep them both here.

Chapter Forty-Four

GAGE

Today has been chaotic, but not in the way I always anticipated my wedding day would be. Whenever I was forced to consider getting married, I figured I'd be having a full-on panic attack over committing to sex with the same person for the rest of my life.

But that hasn't been my biggest stressor in the run-up to standing here, at the altar, waiting for Ember to emerge out of the castle doors, already thrown wide.

No, my stress came from being forced to spend a night away from Ember and Nova. In what felt like something insanely archaic, my sisters talked Ember into sleeping at the palace with all of them, taking Nova with her.

Since I absolutely refused to participate in a bachelor party or anything resembling it, the only people who came to my house last night were Seth and Nathaniel to have a few drinks and reminisce about times I'd prefer to forget. There's only looking ahead for me now.

Once they left, I walked around the house, stunned at how empty everything felt without my two girls. It made me realize I might be begging Ember to consider a sibling for Nova in the next five years. Never, not in my wildest dreams or worst nightmares, did I anticipate enjoying being a father, relishing this quieter life

Ember and I have established in our house. Life is never boring, but not in any way I could have predicted.

Bellerive Blue carpet lines a route from the side of the castle, through lines and rows of well-padded chairs, to a small pergola lined with flowers and gauzy fabric. Nathaniel, Seth, and Brent are standing with me. Our wedding party discussion ended in tears when Ember admitted she was having a hard time asking Ava to be her maid of honor because she'd always pictured Athena in that role. I'd told her she didn't have to give anyone that title if she didn't want to, or we could create a new one. When tears fell down her cheeks at the suggestion, I held her while she cried, mentally going through every option I could think of to soothe her hurt, even though I knew I couldn't.

Athena's death brought Ember and I together, but it crushed something in Ember that I'd do anything to repair. It's a hard line to walk when I let myself consider it—being grateful I get to be all these things to and with Ember while also being conscious of the loss Nova and Ember have suffered.

Sawyer comes through the double doors, carrying Nova in her arms. Nova is in a frilly white dress that almost engulfs her, and all the bridesmaids are wearing violet. Behind Sawyer is Maren, and then Ava comes strutting out like she's the true star of the show. I can't help rising on my toes, glancing around her, trying to catch a glimpse of Em.

And then she's standing in the doorway, my father on her arm after offering to walk her down the aisle. We opted to take the suggestion as a peace offering from my parents, but it still seems weird to see her there with him. As the music starts, and she begins to walk toward me, it's easy to block out my dad.

She looks amazing in a ball gown with her long dark hair in gentle waves framing her face and falling down her back. If I wasn't already completely and utterly sure about this marriage, seeing her coming toward me would have done it. After not being with her for twenty-four hours, I'm eating her up with my gaze. There's a heavy contentment in my chest, like a deeper part of me that knows Ember is my person, the one I was meant to end up with, even if the circumstances have been less than ideal.

Fuck the five years. She might not know it yet, but she's mine forever.

When she reaches me, and my father and I do the exchange, I lean into her ear and whisper, "Marrying you is better than any dream I've ever dared to have."

She meets my gaze with such tenderness, I can almost convince myself she might feel for me a sliver of the love I feel for her.

Then we're standing in front of the officiant, reciting standardized vows, and sliding wedding rings we purchased together onto each other's fingers. The part I've been anticipating comes last, when I'm finally allowed to kiss her.

"You're the most beautiful wife in the world," I murmur before I slide one hand around her waist, another on her cheek, and draw her into a long, heartfelt kiss that promises so much more to come.

Then we're both swept into a whirlwind of pictures and dinner and dancing at the reception. There are family and business associates and royalty mingling around, and it's hours before I have a chance to take a deep breath. When I do, Ava sidles up to me, clearly already a little drunk.

"I was just talking to Abby's brother," she says, swaying to the music. "Abby is a Bitter Betty."

"Jarod?" Even though we've drifted apart, it didn't feel right to leave Jarod off of the invite list. We had a lot of good years together. "What'd he tell you?"

"Abby keeps talking about getting evidence that you and Ember aren't legit. She's obsessed, according to him."

"Let her be obsessed," I say, glancing around to see if anyone might be trying to overhear our conversation. "She's not going to find anything. We're the real deal."

Ava throws a drunk arm around me. "Well, I believe *you* think that."

"Thank you, Ava, for the reality check." Not that I needed it. While something hums between me and Em whenever we're alone together, I'm sure it doesn't mean to Em what it means to me. Right this minute, that doesn't bother me, though. Today just guaranteed me five years to hook Ember as deep as she's hooked me. It'll be enough—it has to be.

"Just keeping it real," she says with a smirk before taking a few steps away from me and then turning to point her finger in my general direction. "Watch your wife's back or Abby will be sticking a knife in it."

Like hell I'll let that happen. If I even catch a whiff of Abby planning anything, I'll find a hammer to drop on her life before she even gets a chance to raise hers.

Then I spot Ember across the room, talking with animation to Posey and gesturing to the hanging lights, which really elevate the outdoor tent. Hiring Posey was a good decision—she nailed the lower-key desires of my wife with the high-end necessity of becoming a Tucker.

My wife. The only other two words that give me that same rush of love are *my daughter*.

Part of me can't believe Ember and I even made it here. Between Robert's claims about the wedding or my mother's threats or Abby's vicious anger, I half expected someone to object when the officiant paused to see if anyone was going to come forward. When no one burst into the wedding to out us as imposters, I released the breath I'd been holding in a rush.

"She didn't blow the budget," my mother says grudgingly as she appears at my side.

"I can't tell if that's a compliment or a criticism," I say, and I peer down at her, taking note of her flushed cheeks. She's clearly had a few glasses of the very expensive champagne circulating. Half the nonexistent budget must have gone to alcohol.

"She signed the prenup," Celia says.

"She did."

"If I'd known she was going to sign it, I would have led with a better one."

"Always lead with your best offer," I say, stifling a laugh at her disgruntled grumbles. "You should know that by now."

"I didn't think she'd sign it. I thought I'd have to come back with another offer."

"To be clear, '*a better one*' would have meant?"

"Protecting more Tucker assets. Locking everything down."

"She gets *nothing* if we divorce."

"You've become too kindhearted to let that be true," she says, sliding me a sly look. "I have no doubt some under-the-table negotiations happened before she signed."

"Doesn't change the legal papers she signed," I say. "Based on who you are, I get that you think you know her type, but you really don't. I'm happy, Mom. Genuinely, completely happy. Please don't ruin this for me. I can only forgive so much, and I'd *never* forgive you for that."

She stares at me for a long beat, and then she nods her head. "I hear you, Gage."

But that doesn't mean she's listening.

The evening winds to a close, and thankfully enough people have left that Ember's been able to glue herself to my side as we work the crowd.

We're in the middle of talking to Posey and Brent when the sound of a chopper echoes over the palace grounds.

"That's our cue," I whisper in Ember's ear as Brent and Posey excuse themselves, leaving us alone.

"Our cue?" She glances up at me, bewildered.

"Our ride is here."

"The helicopter is ours?"

"Figured it might be more of an experience than the jet again. But if you're not on board, I can get the jet prepared."

"No, no." She lets out a little laugh. "I just never thought I'd leave my wedding by helicopter." On her toes, she grazes my cheek with her lips. "This whole day has been a fairy tale, an experience I never knew a person in real life could have."

"If anyone deserves to be treated like a princess," I say, "it's you."

"You are the most charming man I've ever met."

"Want to hear the good news?"

"Hit me with it."

"Not only am I the most charming man you've ever met, but I am now your husband. You're stuck with me forever."

She grins. "Forever, huh? I guess we'll see."

The fact that she didn't contradict me feels like a step in the right direction. Maybe that's all I need to do. A few gentle nudges, guide her to where I want her to end up. If I keep acting like it's going to happen, maybe it will. Positive thinking or something.

"Where are we going?" she asks. "We never talked about going somewhere."

"This is my gift to you," I say.

"Gage," she cries. "I didn't know we were giving each other gifts. I've got nothing to give you."

"Sure you do," I say, running my index finger along the sweetheart neckline of her dress. "You're my gift, and I intend to unwrap you later."

"That's not a gift. You unwrap *me* all the time," she says with a little laugh.

"On the contrary, I feel privileged each and every time that I'm the man who gets to do it. Maybe it's not special to *you* anymore, but every single time I'm amazed that you're letting me so close to you."

She stares up at me, like she's trying to parse out what's real from what I've said and what's for show. "Such a charmer," she whispers, "and you're all mine."

The chopper touches down on the pad on the other side of the estate, and I grab Em's hand, leading her toward the lit path that'll take us there. People cheer as we leave the reception tent, the MC announcing us as Mr. and Mrs. Tucker one more time.

"Is Nova coming?" she asks, keeping pace with me.

"No, my sisters and Michelle are watching her for a few days. We won't be gone long, but I thought it was important that we do it."

"Right, for appearances," she says. "I don't have any stuff, though."

"Ava packed for you."

"Oh, lord. I can only imagine."

I chuckle at Ember's reaction, but despite what she said, Ava and Ember have been shopping together often enough that I know Ava would know what she'd want, even if Ava didn't personally agree with each selection.

We reach the chopper, and I help Ember in first, wrestling her dress into submission. As we're adjusting our headsets and getting buckled in, Ember says, "Are you going to tell me where we're going?"

"Switzerland," I say. "I'm interested to see whether you really can school me in skiing."

A slow smile spreads across her face, and I know I picked wisely. "We're skiing?"

"We are."

"Oh, this will be fun." She lets out a delighted laugh, and the sound injects euphoria into my veins. Making her happy is its own kind of addiction.

Chapter Forty-Five

EMBER

The best part of my short honeymoon with Gage, other than getting uninterrupted alone time and a whole lot of attention from my husband—husband!? How weird is that?—is that I didn't know it was coming. I didn't have time to stress or worry about leaving Nova, and it turns out that the separation doesn't really agree with me. Thankfully, it hasn't agreed all that much with Gage either. If we aren't skiing or having sex, we're bothering whoever has Nova with endless FaceTime calls. We are terrible at being on vacation without her. Michelle told us she thought Nova might be close to walking, and Gage and I stared at each other in horror, and then Gage actually suggested that maybe Michelle should not be encouraging Nova to walk without us there. And of course, I completely seconded his very rational opinion by telling Michelle that walking was overrated. Nova was too young to walk. Crawling was clearly the superior choice.

We took a helicopter ride to become helicopter co-parents.

But also, I'd be heartbroken if we missed her first steps. Absolutely gutted. Once we got off the FaceTime call, we debated cutting the honeymoon short, but we're both so hyperaware of how things might appear to outsiders looking into our marriage that it didn't seem like a good idea to leave early. What newlyweds don't want this alone time? Maybe we could have explained it away by saying that we're more in love with Nova than we are with each other? Would that make our marriage actually less legitimate? Aren't you supposed to love your kids more?

I hate that we have to think about all those factors, but that's our reality. Our marriage isn't real; it's a deception meant to let me stay close to Nova.

Except, the last few days alone with Gage with no distractions, I look at him and I think, *I could love you. I could love you so easily.*

"Should we call Michelle again?" Gage asks as he slides his suit jacket on. "Make sure she's not encouraging any bad behavior?"

"We can't call her again," I say with a laugh. "And if we tell her again not to let Nova walk, she's going to think there's something not right with us."

"I should have postponed the honeymoon. Waited a few weeks until Nova was definitely walking. We knew she was close."

"Yeah, but eight, not quite nine months, is still really young to be walking, so maybe it won't happen yet. Michelle said she'd record it for us if she took a step." Which isn't at all the same thing, but I'm trying not to put a damper on our trip. Only so many things are in our control. "But," I say, walking over to help him with his tie, my A-line dress swishing around my thighs, "I really love that we feel the same way about this."

"Misery loves company," Gage says, peering down at me with a hint of a smile.

"Something like that," I say, grinning up at him. "When I first contacted you, I wasn't even sure you'd care, and look how far we've come."

"I love her. She's got me completely and utterly wrapped around her finger."

"She really does," I say, and when I finish the tie and make eye contact with him again, the air charges around us. It's a sensation that I've become more and more familiar with, as though the air around us is alive with unspoken things.

I could love you. I could love you so easily. The words hang in the air, but I can't voice them, partly because I'm not even sure I want to. They're there, uncontrollable and true. But once they're out in the open, I can't take them back. I can't decide *not* to fall in love with him or even that I haven't. It feels too much like a promise, as though I will. Love isn't inevitable between us. It can't be because it would ruin the little family we've built.

But the thought of being in love with him causes my throat to go dry, and I have to clear it. I'm *not* in love with him. He's not the fuckboy I thought he was when I first met him, and so I've come to love a lot of things about him. Which is good. It's good for our marriage, and it's good for any future relationship we maintain because of Nova.

If I don't love him, it's easy to keep him in my life forever. I'll never have to see him with another woman, whoever replaces me in five years, and feel bitter or angry that it's not me. I'll never have to look at him and wish I was someone he could love in return, that it was possible he could love me. I'll never have to wonder if he'll leave me, too, because he'll have no reason to—we're buddies, best friends, co-parents—the kind of person he'd have no reason to drop from his life.

From everything I saw with my parents and with Athena, romantic love is messy and scary and unpredictable, and I know my heart just can't handle it. I need stable and reliable. Even now, nothing I feel for Gage is either of those—and I must put a cork in those feelings to prevent them from seeping everywhere.

I will *not* fall in love. I refuse.

Gage presses his lips to my temple and murmurs, "You think too much."

"One of us has to."

"That doesn't seem right." Gage says, giving my ass a light slap as he steps around me, on the hunt for something. "Have you seen my shoes? You know, we've got enough money that we could both switch off our brains and we'd still be completely fine. Hire people to do everything for us."

"Money isn't what preoccupies my thoughts."

"I know. You're good like that. You want to reenact another one of your books tonight? Is that what you're thinking about? Those kinds of thoughts are Gage-approved."

"What *are* we doing tonight? Dinner, I know."

"It's a surprise," he says, bending down to dig one shoe out from under the bed. Then he sits on the edge and slides them onto his feet.

"Another surprise?"

"Of course," he says. "It's the last night of our honeymoon, and you've only kicked my ass a little on the slopes. I've got one last hurrah organized as your reward."

A reward is definitely deserved since I kicked his ass on the ski slopes a lot. But I've already rubbed it in repeatedly. He knows the truth.

Being back on the slopes was weird, though. I have so many family memories tied to skiing, most of them positive, most of them anchored to my mom and my sister. It made me feel closer to them, and I told Gage it was probably a gift he never intended to give me, but I appreciated it, nonetheless. A piece of my childhood, however small, that actually made me happy, maybe even a little proud, because I *am* a good skier.

Gage's phone dings, and he checks it, nodding at me. "The car is here. You ready?"

"Just need to grab my coat on the way out."

The views from the rooftop restaurant are incredible. There's a panoramic sweep of mountains in the distance, and the room is all glass. Every table has propane heaters or fireplaces, which keeps the area toasty.

In the far corner, a section of the room is partitioned off, and we're led there. We slip between the black curtains, and it's like we're in our own private world. There's a table for two, set back from the window, and then two plush chairs with a fire table between them, perched near the window to take advantage of the vista ahead. The mountain ranges stretch out in front of us, and I'm not sure a view like this could ever get old. Instead of sitting down at the table, I go to the windows. They've gotten the lighting in the room just right, so it feels as though the glass isn't even there.

"Gorgeous, isn't it?" Gage asks, also ignoring the table and coming to stand beside me. He runs a fingertip along my bare skin, my heavy coat taken at the front desk. He's not looking at the view; he's looking at me.

"If this is what you do for your fake wife," I say, "I can't imagine what you'd do for a real one."

"You are my real one," he says, kissing my shoulder. "In every way that counts."

Except the one that I'd think should count the most—we aren't in love. Sure, there are people who go into arranged marriages without love, but neither of us comes from that tradition. We got married out of necessity, not want. I need to keep reminding myself.

"You trying to win me over with sweet words?" I tease, turning in his arms.

"Yes," he says. "Is it working?"

God, I hope not. "I'll keep you posted."

"I look forward to your updates." He kisses a line up my neck, nuzzling under my ear, and I cling onto him as heat pools in my core. The want is constant, as though I'll never get enough of him.

"What exactly are we eating?" I ask, my voice breathy when I was aiming for a teasing tone.

"Whatever you want," he says with a rough chuckle. "What are you hungry for, wifey?"

"Wifey?" I ask with a laugh.

"I'm trying it out," he says, finding my lips and kissing me deeply. "Just go with it."

The curtain rustles, and we break apart to find the waitress exiting as quickly as she entered. "I think this space needs a door," I say.

"I'm sure they've seen worse." He leads me to the table, and we pick up the menus.

There are no prices, but I've gotten used to that now. We order, and then throughout the meal, we chat. Sometimes it seems impossible that we still have things to say to each other, but it feels like there are no barriers between us. Anything I can think to ask, he answers, and I try to do the same for him.

Once all the dishes are cleared and after dinner drinks have been ordered, Gage leads me to the two armchairs. When I go to take a seat in my own, he tugs me into his lap instead, making me straddle him.

"You were already far enough away for long enough," he says, kissing under my ear and sliding his hands under the hem of my dress, kneading my upper thighs with his strong fingers before cupping my ass. "You should turn around. The show is about to start."

"Show?" I ask, peering over my shoulder, but Gage lifts me up and helps me rotate in his lap, so I'm leaning against his back, facing the view.

"Yeah," he says, his breath feathering my ear. His hands are back under my dress, running along my thighs, skimming across my panties. With him, it never takes much, and I'm already ready and willing.

The first firework streaks into the sky, and as it lights up the mountain range, Gage slips his fingers into my panties, finding the bundle of nerves, circling leisurely.

"We're going to watch the fireworks, and I'm going to make you come."

"Oh, god," I moan, resting my head against his shoulder as he dips a finger into me.

"You're going to have to be quiet, sweetheart," he growls in my ear. "Unless you want the whole restaurant to hear you. Those are curtains, not walls."

"I don't know if this is a good idea," I say, breathy as the next boom goes off, sparkles and glitter dotting the sky. "They're coming back with our drinks. What if the staff sees us?"

"Let them," he mutters, his attention already fully focused on making me lose any sense of time or space. "Do you want me to stop?"

"No," I say, trying to grind against his hand. "Never."

"That's my girl," he says, pushing a second finger in.

It's a struggle to keep quiet as he leads me higher and higher. With each slide and swirl of his hand, I have to bite my lip to hold back my moans. "Gage, I want you inside me when I come."

With one hand, he keeps rotating his fingers on my most sensitive parts while he releases himself with the other. I try to turn in his arms to straddle him, but he stops me.

"I want you to watch the fireworks while I fuck you," he says, tugging my panties to the side and guiding me down on top of him. "Ride me, baby. Ride me as hard as you need."

I brace my hands on his knees, and his hand keeps working my clit while I rise up and down on him, so consumed with bliss that I'm barely aware of what's happening around us.

"Look," Gage says, his voice gritty. It's clear he's barely holding himself in check.

In the sky, my name is written large, and as I watch, the peak of my orgasm just out of reach, our names and wedding date appear in the sky.

"You did that for me?" I ask, amazed that it's even possible.

"I'd do anything for you," he says. "Anything, Em."

The thing is, I'm starting to believe him, and I don't know what to do with that. *I can't fall in love with him. I can't.*

Rather than dwelling on my emotions, I focus on the physical sensations, grateful for the distraction, and I pick up the pace to drive us both right off the cliff together.

Chapter Forty-Six

GAGE

"Whatever my wife wants, she gets," I say into the speaker phone while I try to compile our recent listings and sales. "It's Nova's first birthday party. I don't care how much it costs. If we can't rent a section, then just bill us for the whole goddamned play center."

"I suggested that to Mrs. Tucker, but once I told her the fee, she asked that we call you," Persia says.

"You're clearly robbing us," I say, but I accept that as the cost of getting what Ember wants. "I have things to do. Just bill me." Then I hang up.

Ember still hates okaying anything over a certain dollar value. Once the fee of anything rises too high, she has the person call me to okay it. Secretly, I think she just likes me playing bad cop to her good cop. Around the island, she's developing a reputation as being kind and easy to deal with. I am not. My mother, of all people, told me it was also becoming common knowledge that I was ridiculously protective of Ember, much like the king is about his queen. I told her I was glad—it would mean fewer headaches in the long run—people would expect my reaction. Anyone who tries to hurt Ember or screw her over would suffer my wrath, in any way I saw fit to administer it.

"Knock knock," Ava says at the door to my office.

"I'm busy," I mutter, searching for the latest sale in the pile. My social media manager wants to do a big push to advertise how we're a winning company. We're still beating Hugh, overall, but it's by the skin of our teeth. A *"look at us, we're so great"* socials campaign might keep us ahead.

Ava ignores me and closes the door, taking a seat across the desk from me. I glance up at her and stop what I'm doing. She's not going to leave until I let her say whatever she feels is so important she had to come here instead of the house.

"You've had a few months to settle into this whole marriage thing," she says, releasing a huff of annoyance. "Now I think it's time you considered what will make Ember happy."

"I *always* consider what will make Ember happy."

"That's weird because when I asked her whether you two had talked about her handbag expansion, she told me you've been too busy to hear it."

I lean back in my chair, and my first instinct is to deny it. Technically, it's somewhat accurate. Work takes up a huge percentage of my time, and when I'm at the house, I tend to spend it with Nova in my arms or on my lap. Not exactly prime heart-to-heart moments, there. At night, we're both exhausted, but we always make love. If she'd told me even one of those nights that she'd rather talk about something on her mind, I would have listened.

"I got her the tickets to Paris Fashion Week for Christmas. She's going there *with you*." And leaving me and Nova for almost a week, which I've been glossing over, so I don't freak the fuck out. I've already hired security for the trip. No fucking chances will be taken with my wife.

"Ember is incredibly talented. Beyond the whole wife, pseudomother thing she has going on—the girl has an eye for design. There will be people in Paris that I'll want her to meet."

"So introduce her."

"You are so dense sometimes. If I introduce her, inevitably, she'll be offered some opportunities that might pull her away from Bellerive."

Ah, there's the catch. I run my hands along my face, not saying anything, letting my silence speak for itself.

"She'll never say yes if she thinks you don't support it. She's got this whole martyr thing going on where you're concerned. Thinks you saved her life or something."

Has Ava always been this bad for my ego? Making it seem like my wife is with me out of obligation or gratitude instead of anything resembling love. Fucking brilliant.

"But I think *you* need to think about what her life is going to look like when this marriage is over."

"No," I say, my voice tight. "I don't need to think about that at all."

"It's really unfair for you to pursue your happiness and completely ignore hers." Ava cocks her eyebrows at me, her expression defiant.

"Are you trying to tell me that Ember is unhappy?" My gut twists. Surely I wouldn't have missed *that*.

"No," Ava says, annoyance tingeing her voice. "I'm just telling you she's not as happy as she *could* be."

"What do you want me to say, Ava?"

"If she mentions talking to designers to you, I want you to encourage her. Support her. Be the good, caring partner you claim you want to be. 'Cause right now, from where I'm standing, the only person you're worried about is yourself and your company."

"That's not even remotely true."

Ava holds up her hands, and she rises from her seat. "I'm just telling you what it looks like to me. Vintage Gage Tucker is back in the building."

It's a low fucking blow, the kind only a sibling can deliver. Have I been that caught up in my own bubble that I haven't noticed anything since we got married? Is it possible that Ember isn't as happy as I am? The thought is a knife to my gut.

Rather than sitting around and letting the knife twist, I have my secretary redistribute or cancel my appointments for the day, and I go home to my wife.

When I get home, the house is quiet, and I check my watch. Nova must be down for her afternoon nap, and then I catch the *clack-clack-clack* of the sewing machine. Instead of going back to talk to Ember, I try to gather my thoughts. What am I supposed to say? *When you go to Paris, take any opportunity that comes your way, even if it takes you away from me?* In no way is that what I actually want.

"Hello?" Ember says coming down the hall. "Oh, hey. I thought I heard the security alarm ding. You're home early. Everything okay?"

She crosses the entrance to stand on the other side of the couch, facing me. Her brow is furrowed, and she searches my expression. "Gage?"

"Are you happy, Em?"

"What?" she breathes out the question like I've fired a shot.

"Are you happy?"

"Yes," she says, a hint of panic in her voice. She rounds the couch to sink into a seat, and I sit on the coffee table, taking her hands in mine. "Oh god, are you not happy? You want to be with other people?"

"Oh, fuck no, I don't want that." I let out a strained chuckle and lean forward to kiss her forehead.

"But you're not happy," she whispers.

"No, I'm happy. I'm fine. For me, everything is great. Really." I try to make eye contact with her, but she's clearly in a thought spiral that's going nowhere good. "Em, look at me."

She makes eye contact and then her gaze skitters away.

"Em," I say again, keeping my voice level and patient. I came here, trying to do the right thing, and I've totally fucked up this conversation. She's freaking out, and there's a tiny ball of panic in my stomach at seeing her so distressed. "I am exactly where I want to be, and I'm with exactly who I want to be with. I didn't ask for *me*. I genuinely want to know if you're happy."

"Yeah," she says, tears pooling in her eyes. "I'm happy. Why wouldn't I be happy?"

"Ava said—"

"Ava? Oh my god. Ava made you think I wasn't happy?"

"Not exactly." I wince. "She said you've wanted to talk to me about expanding your handbags, and I've been too caught up in my own bullshit to listen. To be a good fucking husband and partner. She might as well have kicked me in the nuts."

Ember sniffs, fighting her tears, and she lets out a strangled laugh. "I'm so glad she didn't."

"Honestly, it might have stung less. Have I been ignoring you? Ignoring what you need?"

"No," Ember says, scooping up her tears with her fingers. "You're getting your company off the ground. There's nothing that says I have to be trying to get my handbags off the ground right now too."

"But you can," I say. "There's also nothing that says you have to be tied to this house if you don't want to be."

"It's not that I don't want to be." She hesitates for a beat. "It's just that I want this other thing too. If I have a chance to have it, you know?"

"Well, if you have the chance," I say, my voice growing thick with what I know I'm going to say and have to pretend to mean with a conviction I don't quite feel, "then you should take it. Seize it. We can figure out whatever we need to figure out afterward."

She scrambles off the couch and into my arms, straddling me on the coffee table, her small hands framing my face, and she stares at me for a long beat. "When does any of this start to feel real?" she whispers, searching for something in my expression that I can't understand.

"What do you mean?"

"When we met, I almost fell down the stairs, and you saved me, and it feels like you've been saving me every single second of every single day since then."

There's that gratitude that Ava laid on me earlier. Not exactly the emotion I want to inspire, but at least it's one I can give right back.

"You save me too—all the time. Before I met you, I was treading water, didn't have a clue which way to go, but it just feels so obvious now. What I want. What I need to do to get it."

"Yeah?"

"You and Nova are my home. The two of you are everything." I press my lips to her temple. "I want to beat Hugh because of what he did to you, and because I'm fucking competitive. But I'd drop the company, watch it crumble to dust, if I was faced with any kind of choice that involved you or Nova. I wouldn't think twice."

She wraps her arms around my shoulders and buries her face in my neck, squeezing me tight. "She's so lucky to have you," she whispers in my ear. "You're such a good dad."

But it's not just a good dad that I want to be.

Chapter Forty-Seven

EMBER

The last time I left Gage and Nova was hard because I knew what lay ahead of me—cleaning out the apartment, going down the lane of memories with my sister. As the private jet taxis down the runway toward Paris Fashion Week, I'm in tears because of what I'm leaving behind.

"We're gone ten days," Ava says, sipping her martini. "It's not like you're never going to see them again."

"That wasn't even what I was thinking," I say, tears streaming down my face. "But now I am." What if something happens to them? Or happens to me? I replay my kiss with Gage on the tarmac. It wasn't the best because Nova was in his arms, and she kept trying to kiss me, too, and I couldn't get as close to him as I wanted. Fate wouldn't be cruel enough to let that be our last kiss.

"Have you told him yet?" Ava asks, peering at me over the rim of her cup.

"Told him what?" I wipe at my tears, but it's futile because more and more keep coming.

"That you're in love with him."

"I'm *not* in love with him."

"So you're a sobbing wreck every time you leave everyone? I call bullshit on that." I open my mouth, and she holds up a hand. "And do not tell me all of this is over missing a week with Nova. That is *certified* bullshit."

"I'm not in love with him," I say, my voice barely above a whisper, but my fingers stray to the white gold bracelet on my wrist, the one Gage and Nova gave me for Christmas.

"I did sort of believe you before—before you started going all doomsday and '*how will I ever live without him.*'" She mock faints, fanning herself like she's in an old movie. "You've played your cards close to the chest. I'll give you that. I bet he's got no idea that you're head over heels in love with him."

"I'm not in love with him," I repeat, my tears drying up. "I love a lot of things about him, but I'm not *in* love with him. There *is* a difference."

"I know the difference," Ava says with a laugh. "This ain't it."

I cross my arms and stare out the window.

"Look, you're not ready to face your feelings. Fine. I won't say another word, and I won't breathe even a syllable of it to my brother. But you're going to be married to him for years, so I think you need to figure out a way to... You need to tell him."

"Absolutely not," I scoff. "No. Even if I was, that'd be a hard no."

"Why?"

"You wouldn't understand."

"Probably true. Try me anyway."

"Love comes and goes. It's not stable. You can't trust it."

"Every kind of relationship can be volatile, Ember. Romantic love does not have the market completely cornered on that one."

"People tell you they love you, and then they leave you or they hurt you. That's not a life I want Nova to have. Not a life I want to live again."

"Ahh..." She takes a long sip of her martini. "You don't trust him enough yet. Huh. I did not see that coming as the central issue. But I guess it makes sense. What with your fragmented family dynamics. My family is fucked-up, but we're still in one oddly shaped piece."

"He'll get bored of me," I whisper. "And I don't think I'll ever get bored of him."

"Love is a risk. Can't deny that. But what's the alternative for you? And besides that, you're already in love with him." She throws up her hands. "It's a done deal. And maybe it feels okay to deny it right now, what do I know? But I can't see how running away from your feelings, pretending they don't exist, is going to make either you or my brother happy in the long term. You'll both end up miserable and in love—taking poison and stabbing yourselves, each thinking you're doing the other a favor."

"That seems excessive," I mutter.

"Romeo and Juliet *were* excessive," Ava agrees. "Don't be like them."

I don't say anything more because there's nothing more I can say. If I really let myself consider the truth, I know what I'd find, but I've worked exceptionally hard the last few months to avoid drowning in my feelings. Yes, they exist, but I refuse to let them consume the course of my life.

The ten days pass in a blur of introductions and back room discussions and having people I've never met dissect my designs, critiquing them and complimenting them. Between meetings that Ava arranged—because she knows everyone—I've spent as much time as I can FaceTiming Gage or Nova, ideally both of them at the same time.

All these exciting things are happening to me—opportunities I never would have even dared to dream about—but all I can think about are Gage and Nova and what I'm missing. I stare at their faces on the screen, and *that's* where I want to be—with them. It's hit me that maybe I haven't been deferring to Gage's career this whole time. The sacrifices this career path would force upon me aren't ones I'm ready to make.

We're on our last day in Paris when Ava takes me to one last meeting with the Franza siblings, Petra and Paul. There's something about this particular meeting that's making even Ava a little edgy, and she's been cool like ice for all the others. But her anxiety is rubbing off on my already heightened emotions, so when we enter the Franzas' suite for the meeting, I'm worried I'll throw up all over them when I open my mouth.

"I'm not going to be able to talk," I murmur to Ava as we're being led from the front door to a private room within the hotel suite.

"I think they're going to be doing most of the talking," Ava says. "Just make sure you *really* listen."

That sounds ominous. "Do they want my bags?"

But we're entering the room, and there's no time for Ava to answer before Paul and Petra look up from the huge conference room table, designs strewn all over.

Their family origin is well-known—an East Indian mother and an Italian father. Petra takes after her mother with dark skin and midnight-colored waist-length hair, whereas Paul is lighter-skinned but dark-featured. Petra is staring at me with her caramel-colored eyes, and words leave my brain.

I'm used to glamorous people, and I've even met glamorous people I admire on this trip. But there's no way I could have ever predicted that I'd be in the same room as the Franza siblings, much less that they'd have any interest in talking to me. I didn't graduate high school—left in my sophomore year and never returned. It's ridiculous that I'm here, and I grab a hunk of skin on my arm, twisting sharply.

Still here. Not dreaming.

"Petra and Paul, this is Ember Whitten, Bellerive's most famous handbag designer."

I shoot her a look of alarm. She hasn't introduced me to anyone else like that, and quite frankly, I don't think that claim is true. I honestly don't know if people are talking about me that much. I have sold a lot of bags, but *most famous* feels like a lie.

"That's not..."

Ava gives me a sharp look, and I realize I'm going to need to channel Gage to get through this conversation. I'm too nervous, too unsure. How would he handle this? I've heard him schmooze with lots of people since I arrived in Bellerive, especially since he started his real estate business. *Find your inner charm, Em.*

I take a deep, steadying breath. "She's too kind," I say, extending my hand to both of them to shake. "I'm married to her brother, so she's probably trying to win my vote as favorite sister-in-law."

"I already have it," Ava says, flicking her long dark hair back. "Neither Maren or Sawyer are ruthless enough to get you into this room."

Paul lets out an amused chuckle. "I love a woman with confidence." He scans Ava like he'd enjoy devouring more than her confidence. He has to be at least fifty, which gives me the ick factor, but Ava, as always, seems to be lapping up the attention.

"You've already loved me, Paul." Her lips twist with the hint of a smirk.

"I also like women who give second chances," he says, his gaze pointed.

"I don't like second anything," Ava says with a shrug. "Besides, we're here to talk about Ember."

"Yes," Petra says, firing a warning glare at her brother. "We wanted to discuss your handbags, Ember. Ava brought us a few of your clutches, and we were impressed with the design and the quality of the products. Very clean lines, but unique in their construction."

"Thank you," I say, my heart pounding. This feels like it's leading somewhere other than a compliment, and I don't know how I'm going to feel about whatever she'll say. Ava is adamant that she can make me famous, but now that I'm here, I'm not sure that's what I want. I love making and designing bags, and I'm mostly content with the number of clients I have.

"We'd love to have you come out to Los Angeles to bring you under our umbrella of designers. Down the road, there might be an opportunity for you to have your own line. We can't guarantee that, obviously."

"That's an incredible offer." One I would have fought tooth and nail to have had laid at my feet before Athena died, before Nova was born, before Gage walked into my life.

But I don't know if I would have jumped on this opportunity because it was what I truly wanted or if it would have been an escape from my life at the time. My life in Colorado wasn't one I chose so much as one I lived to survive. With Gage and Nova, I have no need to escape anything anymore.

"I would need to speak to my husband," I say, and I can almost sense Ava rolling her eyes. She doesn't understand why Gage is a factor, even after she clocked the fact that this marriage might not be as fake for me as I want to pretend.

"The Los Angeles move wouldn't necessarily be permanent," Petra says. "But we'd need you there long enough to make sure you were part of the team, really dialed into the brand."

"How long do you think that would be?"

"Oh," Petra says, breezily. "I wouldn't want to say. Every person has settled in differently and in their own time. I wouldn't want to mislead you. It'll be a substantial commitment."

"Ava indicated you were open to negotiation, so we hope that's true," Paul says, a twinkle in his eye like he knows Ava enjoys spewing her own bullshit everywhere.

"Oh, yeah, I..." All my Gage coolness has evaporated. "I just need to talk it through with my husband." Or say no, which is my first instinct. Anything that'll take me away from the island, from Gage, from Nova, is a no from me.

"Wonderful," Petra says. "We're really looking forward to working with you."

Wait. Did I say yes? I glance at Ava, alarmed, but she has a deceptively sweet smile on her face as she shakes everyone's hand and she ushers me toward the exit.

As soon as we're out of the suite, she whirls on me. "You couldn't have just said yes? I faced Paul to get you that meeting."

"I didn't know you slept with Paul Franza. How would I know that?" I hiss as we make our way to the elevators.

"He was a terrible fuck. Awful. As brilliant as he is at design is equivalent to how bad he was in bed. Can you wrap your head around that? I could not. It was a struggle. And I still got you a face-to-face with him."

"I really did not need to know all that. How am I supposed to work with him when every time I look at him I'll think about him having sex with you?"

"It was brief and terrible, so there really isn't much to think about." Ava struts out of the elevator on the ground floor and makes her way to the car. "My point is that I did that for you. Not the fucking, the meeting. And then you don't even say yes?"

"You might think my marriage is worthless, but I don't." I huff out a breath as I slide into the back seat of the waiting car.

"I don't think it's worthless, but I think you're worth more. You don't have to tag along behind Gage like a puppet doing his bidding."

"That's not what I do. And honestly, even if that is what I did, if I'm happy doing it, why should it matter to you?"

Before Ava can say anything, her phone rings a shrill tone I've never heard before, and I plug my ears. Ava digs around in her bag before pulling it out and answering it quickly.

"Who's in trouble?" Ava asks instead of saying hello. She listens for a long time, and then she looks at me. "What kind of evidence do they have?" She doesn't say anything as the person on the other end seems to be speaking, but it's quiet enough that I can't hear what's being said. "Right. Okay. I'll call Caitlin and Nathaniel and Mom. Thanks for calling, Stephen. I owe you."

When she hangs up, she reaches over and takes my hand—the bracelet Gage gave me tinkling on my wrist—a serious expression on her face. "I need you to take a deep breath before I tell you this."

Tears pool in my eyes at the expression on her face. Ava is never serious about serious things. If she's already bracing me, whatever she's going to tell me can't be good.

"Gage has been arrested by the government for committing marital fraud. The police have just been to your house. Michelle has Nova, but Gage is on his way to the station. I need to call everyone else, but you need to *keep calm.*"

"Okay," I say, tears falling down my cheeks. Inside my purse, my phone buzzes, and I dig around to frown at the unfamiliar number. "Hello?"

"Thank god," Gage says, his deep voice an immediate comfort in my ear. "I've been arrested. You're my one phone call. I need you to hold it together, Em. Okay? It's going to be fine. Just a misunderstanding, I'm sure."

"Okay," I choke out. "What do you need me to do?"

"Call Robert. Call my brother Nathaniel. One of them will be able to sort this out if I can't from here. And don't come back to the island until I tell you it's safe or one of them does. I don't know if they'd arrest you, too, and I don't want you in here."

"I feel like I should be there," I say.

"Nova is with Michelle. I'm fine. There's no reason for you to drop yourself in this mess too. I'll be out in twenty-four hours."

"Really?"

"Yeah. I'm Teflon, babe. I'll be fine. Enjoy an extra day in Paris."

Someone in the background yells that his time is up, and Gage's voice is muffled for a minute before he comes back.

"I'll see you soon, Em. There's nothing to worry about."

"Okay," I say, drawing in a deep breath. "Ava is already calling Nathaniel, I think. I'll call Robert." I sniff, trying to keep my tears of panic at bay. If Gage thinks this is nothing to worry about, there's no need to be bawling my eyes out. Besides, he's told me some of his more colorful stories, and he's been in jail in the drunk tank before. He'll be fine.

"You and me," he says, his voice heavy with meaning.

"We're a team," I agree, feeling a rod of strength go up my spine. If Gage needs me to be strong, I can make myself do that. It's not the first time I've had to hold myself together when it felt like everything was falling apart.

And then he's gone, and I clutch the phone to my chest. Before bringing it back and scrolling through my contacts for Robert's number.

"Bad news," Ava says, ending whatever call she was making beside me.

"More?" I ask, finally finding Robert's number, my finger hovering over the dial button.

"Robert has also been arrested."

"Oh shit," I whisper. "Gage isn't getting out in twenty-four hours, is he?"

"No," Ava says, her voice edged in a worry I've never heard before, "I don't think he is."

Chapter Forty-Eight

GAGE

It didn't take long for the government to transfer me from the regular police station to some top secret immigration center. From listening to the officers' chatter, it sounds like Robert is here somewhere, too, as part of some big immigration sting. Hearing that was the first indication that whatever is going on here might not go away as easily as I'd like. Attorney-client privilege must count for something. They can't really come for me and Ember through Robert, can they?

The door to the room pops open, and I sit up straighter. A guy in a cheap suit enters, a manila file folder clutched in his hand. Without saying a word, he spreads out various pages, and I peer at them, curious, despite myself.

All the job ads that Robert and I filed are there, and it's then that I remember I didn't actually hire anyone to fill those. I can't help my grimace. Robert warned me, but with all the wedding planning and trying to run Hugh's company into the ground, I lost track of this piece.

I make eye contact with him, and I shrug. The other times I've been in trouble, Caitlin or the family lawyer, Carlos, have always advised me to keep my mouth shut. There's only one thing I'll open it for, and from experience, I know my timing has to be impeccable.

He still hasn't said anything, and I haven't either. He can't question me because I requested a lawyer, and I'm not going to incriminate myself. I'm not an idiot.

Then he sets a device on the table, and he hits Play. Ember's voice fills the room followed by mine, and as I listen intently, I hear us discussing our fake marriage. I work to keep my expression neutral as I try to remember when we'd have been this stupid. A splash of water. Nova's giggles.

Shit. We did. By the pool. While the catering company was there. Someone with the company must have recorded us, either by accident or on purpose. It's hard to believe it was an accident when the guy in front of me looks so smug, but it's been months. *Months.* Why would this surface now?

Then he lays out other sheets of paper, and as I lean forward to peer at them, they're written statements from catering company employees who overheard the conversation, legitimizing it. There are also two other statements from another time that I don't remember at all where Ember and I, apparently, made it clear our future marriage wouldn't be real.

"Does this job pay well?" I ask, cocking my head.

"Well enough," he says with a smirk.

"Most government employees I've talked to really enjoy having some extra cash or holidays or special purchases. A new car. Pay off the mortgage. A luxury vacation. Things like that."

He gives me a mild look, not even a hint of greed or hunger entering his gaze. "Bribing a government employee is a criminal offense—more severe than the one you're currently facing, I might add."

"I can't believe you're suggesting I should bribe you," I say with a scoff. "I was merely passing the time with some idle conversation." He could have lured me into incriminating myself more, but he's clearly a straight shooter. I respect that and it annoys me, all at the same time.

Before he can reply, there's a sharp knock on the door, and Caitlin enters.

"I'm representing Mr. Tucker," she says, sliding into the seat next to me.

"You going to offer me some '*extra*' cash too?" he asks.

"I'm sure you misunderstood my client. He simply enjoys talking about money." She doesn't even glance in my direction.

The government employee snorts, but he pushes the papers toward Caitlin with his index finger. "Your boy is fucked."

"I'd like a moment alone with my client," she says, giving the employee an icy glare.

"Sure thing," he says, lumbering to his feet. "I'm sure you were already briefed on the way in, but he's to have no contact with his wife or anyone associated with her."

"I'm aware," Caitlin says.

This is news to me, and I stare at the side of Caitlin's face. I can't talk to Ember? At all? That's worse than being in here, and I'm suddenly glad I used my only phone call to at least reassure her that I'd be fine.

The door clicks shut behind the government worker, and Caitlin picks up the pages spread out on the table, scanning them.

"Not great, but not terrible," she murmurs.

"They also have a pretty clear recording of Em and I talking about a fake marriage. He played that gem for me," I say.

Caitlin groans, and she takes her phone out of her bag, her fingers flying over the keyboard.

"What's that about?" I nod at what she's doing.

"I'm not an immigration specialist. The only one at our firm is in custody. I'm reaching out to some friends on the island to see who might be able to come help." She breathes a sigh of relief. "Scarlet Sinclair has agreed to come. Five times her normal rate. Her reputation is squeaky clean, and she's tenacious."

"Why didn't I just hire her instead of Robert?" I ask, annoyance seeping in.

"Did you want someone who played by the rules or someone who'd do whatever you wanted?" Caitlin eyes me, and it's clear she knows the answer I'm not going to bother to say.

"I get that you don't know all the legal ins and outs, but when she gets here, can you stay in the room?"

"If you want me to," Caitlin says. "But Scarlet is good. You won't need me."

"It's not that," I say. "I need someone who knows me. I don't know what will be said, and I might need a voice of reason."

Caitlin sits back in her chair, and she maintains eye contact with me for a beat longer than is comfortable.

"It might not have started out as real," I say, "but it's real now. For me, it's real. And I won't give Em up. Not for anything."

Caitlin's expression turns sad. "I fear we might be about to find out how true that is."

I've been in the room, alone, for hours. They've given me water but not much else. I have no idea what's happening beyond this tiny space, but Scarlet popped in to introduce herself and to say she'd be negotiating with the government on my behalf. Before leaving, she reminded me not to speak to anyone without her in the room. That hasn't been a problem because no one has come to see me. I don't even know where Caitlin is.

Patience has never been one of my virtues, and I end up pacing the room, doing some pushups, anything to keep either my mind or body occupied.

There's a sharp knock on the door and Caitlin, Scarlet, and two government workers, also in cheap suits, enter.

"These gentlemen would like an opportunity to frame the deals they've proposed for you. Then we'll have a chance to discuss before moving ahead with a plea," Scarlet says, gesturing to the men across the table.

"Plea?" I ask, eyes narrowed.

Caitlin and Scarlet ignore me, and the original government worker clears his throat.

"Option one," the man says, sliding a piece of paper across the table to me. "You plead guilty. You are sanctioned, not jailed. Your marriage is annulled. Ember Whitten faces no jail time and no sanction, but she is permanently barred from stepping foot on Bellerivian soil."

"Permanently? As in never again?" I ask, glancing at Caitlin with wide eyes. This is exactly what I told her I wouldn't allow to happen.

"Correct," he says.

"What's option two then?" Option one is unacceptable.

"Option two is that you plead innocent, and a court date is set," the second guy says, the one I'd assumed was merely a seat filler.

"A trial?" I ask.

"Yes," Caitlin says. "A full-blown trial."

"And if I do that?" I ask.

"Either you get off," the first guy says, stepping in again, "or you'll go to jail, the marriage will be annulled, and Ms. Whitten won't be legally allowed to enter Bellerive again."

"But if I win, I get to keep everything as it is right now." It's a statement, and it seems to make Caitlin a little jittery to hear me say it with such conviction.

"We need to discuss the options with our client," Scarlet says.

"Sure, sure," the first man says, and the two of them get to their feet, leaving the deal memo on the table.

As soon as the door clicks closed, I say, "Option one is out."

"Option one is the best option," Caitlin says. "It guarantees you won't face jail time."

"It annuls my marriage. It means Ember can never live here, with me, in Bellerive."

"You can live somewhere else," Scarlet says. "Anywhere in the world."

But my marriage will be dead. The five years I thought I'd have to somehow make Ember fall in love with me will be gone. She's not going to want to live with me in some other country. Why would she? All of the incentives and advantages of being married to me would be gone—no citizenship, no guaranteed proximity to Nova.

And as much of a pain in the ass as some members of my family can be, I don't want to live in some other country, and that's what I'd have to do if I wanted to give Ember the access I already legally promised. I wouldn't be able to fly her in for Christmas or a birthday or even if Nova was sick.

"Ember has had a job offer to work for Franza Fashion in Los Angeles," Caitlin says. "If you take the deal, she'll take the job."

"Does she want the job?" I ask, feeling foolish as soon as the words are out of my mouth. Of course she does. Why wouldn't she? Isn't this what Ava warned me about? Holding Em back isn't what I want, but I don't want to let her go either. "I need to speak to her—to Ember."

"You know you can't," Caitlin says.

"Your jail time would be doubled without question," Scarlet says.

My thoughts are swirling around my head, refusing to settle. None of this is an acceptable outcome. I want my marriage. I want my wife. I want my family to stay intact.

"If you go to court," Scarlet says, "there's a chance they could come after NGE Realty too. You filed false jobs with the government, or that's how it appears when you didn't hire for any of them, and they were all slated for Ember to take."

"I just forgot," I say, running a hand through my hair. "I'll hire them all. What the fuck do I care?" I shift my gaze between Caitlin and Scarlet. "How am I supposed to make this decision without talking to Em? I'm not just deciding my own fate—I'm deciding hers too."

"The evidence—" Scarlet starts.

"I don't give a flying fuck about the evidence. I love my wife. I love her. Annulling our marriage, having her permanently banned—neither of those work for me. If Em wants the LA job, she can take it. She can take it. You can tell her that. But I want you to go back to these people with a third option. I'll go to jail—I'll take my sentence—but there's no annulment, and Ember isn't banned."

"Gage," Caitlin says.

"No," I say, holding up my hand. "You're my lawyers. You have to present my deal to them. If they say yes, I'll sign the papers. But only if it's for the third deal—the one where I'm not making a decision for Em. Otherwise, I'll take my chances in court." I rub my face. "If I have to go to jail or go to trial to keep my family together, then so be it."

My chest aches with the weight of the decision because I might not be giving up on Ember and on my marriage, but I'll definitely be sacrificing time with my daughter, and I have no idea yet how much that will be. For the first time in my life, it feels like I'm truly stuck, none of the solutions getting me exactly what I want.

Chapter Forty-Nine

EMBER

To Ava, the solution seems simple. I take the Franza job, move to LA, and Gage brings Nova to live in LA. Sure, I'd never be able to attend any family gatherings in Bellerive, and my marriage would be annulled, but none of those registers on Ava's list of important things.

All of it registers on mine.

Gage's siblings are like my family. They've filled a void that felt deep and vast when Athena died. I don't just have a single person I can count on—I have several.

So while the annulment is nothing to Ava, to me, it's a lot. Gage would no longer have any legal tie to me. None. No reason to be tied to me, either. Why would he? He's only marrying me to help me stay in the country.

The thought of losing him, as much as I don't want it to, terrifies me. I can't imagine watching him with other women and pretending to be okay with it when I thought I'd get him all to myself for five years—maybe more. We wouldn't have wanted our fake relationship to be too obvious. To throw these connections away makes me feel sick to my stomach. I'd never choose to leave any of them.

It's impossible to make decisions this huge without speaking to him, and I'm not allowed to talk to him at all. Caitlin and Scarlet said they even had to be careful about what information they passed between us.

Do I take the job and try to move on? It feels like giving up on the thing I want most in the world—it's not a fashion job or fame—it's a family. With Gage and Nova, I have a family.

"I can't take the job," I say to Ava.

"You're thinking about it as though it's the job or Gage. At the moment, at least according to Caitlin, you can't have Gage. That option is gone."

"It's not gone. He hasn't signed anything, has he?"

"I don't know," Ava admits.

"I just don't understand where all this evidence against us came from, how people even suspected we weren't real. We were happy. Really happy."

"Evidence?" Ava asks, as though this conversation is new and not a regurgitation of one we've had before about how Robert led the government to us. "Abby for one."

"What?"

"She called me last night in tears that she'd somehow fucked Gage over."

"How would she have or get evidence?"

"She's been digging. I did warn Gage, but I guess he didn't take me seriously."

I'm still absorbing that news when there's a knock on the hotel room door, and I glance at Ava to see if she ordered room service again. We've been trying to stick close to the hotel, and her only source of amusement has been ordering things to the room—food, clothes, jewelry, or whatever else catches her eye online.

"Not me," she says.

I'm not sure if she means she didn't order anything or she's not getting the door, but either way, I get up and cross the expansive suite to check the peephole. Outside, a man in a suit is standing with an envelope in his hand.

"Can I help you?" I ask after opening the door. Gage has security somewhere on this floor—sometimes I can see them, and sometimes I can't. But whoever this is wouldn't have made it past some sort of checkpoint.

"You've been summoned back to Bellerive," the suited man says, handing me an envelope.

"Summoned?" I ask. "By who?"

"All the details are in the envelope, Mrs. Tucker." Then he turns on his heel and strides down the hall.

I go back into the room, closing the door with my foot while ripping open the envelope. Quickly, I scan the sheets. "Oh my god," I whisper.

"What?" Ava asks.

"I'm being summoned back to Bellerive to be questioned in the case of Tucker versus Bellerive."

"He's going to trial?" Ava screeches, getting off her chair and snatching the paperwork out of my hand. "He's such an idiot."

"What does this mean?" I ask. "Why wouldn't he take the deal?"

"If I had to guess?" Ava says, searching my face. "He doesn't care if he gets off if it means you'll never be able to be in Bellerive again."

My heart squeezes painfully in my chest. "Can I just tell him to take the deal?" I ask. While it's not what I want, the idea of him going to jail, being ripped away from Nova, is an awful outcome. She loves her dad, and she's too young to understand what's happening.

"I'll order the jet," Ava says, already on her phone. She sucks in a deep breath. "We'll know soon just how bad this is."

Caitlin sits across the table from me with another man—a lawyer—on her right. I don't know him, but she said Scarlet wasn't legally able to represent both Gage and me since Gage is forcing the issue to trial, and there are severe consequences for both of us if we're found guilty.

"It's a messy situation," Caitlin says, carefully. "I'm not technically in the room right now, do you understand?"

"Yeah," I say. If Scarlet is a conflict of interest, then Caitlin's presence here would be too. But I'm grateful for the familiar face.

"This is Bennie. He's going to take you through the evidence the government has."

I watch and listen as Bennie lays out all the times and places either me or Gage slipped up. It's way more than I expected, and I wonder whether it's possible Abby really did all this work just to get rid of me.

"I don't understand," I say. "If all *this* counts, then doesn't it count that we're clearly... happy?" I can't say *in love*, even though this gaping wound in my chest is trying to tell me otherwise.

"Your level of happiness isn't in question," Bennie says. "It's whether you set out to defraud the government."

"Even if they gave you a lie detector test right now, and that test proved that you and Gage are madly in love, it doesn't change the evidence to the contrary. The two of you set out to deceive the immigration department. Your intention was to cheat the system."

She's not wrong, so I don't even know how to respond. But it doesn't feel right that we can get in trouble when nothing about our marriage has felt fake since the moment we got married. Gage might be acting—I don't even know what to think anymore—but I *know* nothing is fake for me.

"Gage can't win," I say. "That's what you're trying to tell me, right? He's going to go to jail."

"And you'll be deported. Your marriage will be annulled," Bennie agrees. "We'll make the moves we're able to make to keep you here—your blood connection to a Bellerive citizen being one of them—but it's likely too late to work that angle with any success. The government will work—not overly hard, given the evidence—to prove that fraud was your intent."

"Caitlin, can you just tell Gage to take the deal?" I ask.

"The government has rescinded the offer," Bennie says quietly. "He lost his window of opportunity there."

"What?" I shift my gaze back and forth between them. "No. No." I shake my head, tears pooling in my eyes. "If he's convicted..." My voice breaks, and I force myself to suck in a shaky breath. "What's the sentence?"

"One to three years," Bennie says.

"There has to be something we can do," I say. "Can I just—can I go to jail instead?"

"No," Bennie says. "That's not the way it works here. You're American, and sending you to jail would be a mess the government doesn't want."

"Oh, god." I clutch my cheeks, trying to avoid freaking out. "There has to be something. There has to be something we can do."

"Celia Tucker is already campaigning behind the scenes for a lighter sentence. She may be doing other things that I'd rather not know about," Caitlin says with a wry smile.

"So there's hope?" I swipe at the tears that are running like rivers down my face.

"I don't know," Caitlin says. "I don't want to give you false hope. He's in a tight spot, and he didn't take the smart choice. He let his emotions lead him."

I don't know exactly what she means, but I'm clinging onto the notion that Celia Tucker can somehow work a miracle. Even a year in prison would be devastating for his relationship with Nova.

"Who'll raise Nova?" I ask, my eyes wide with panic. "I can't leave the island if Gage goes to prison."

"Gage can sign over temporary custody to you, or Maren and Brice have offered to take over her care until one of you is able to resume it." Caitlin leans against the table and grasps my hand.

"I don't understand why he didn't take the deal."

"He's Gage Tucker," Caitlin says, as though that explains everything, and it does, a little. "He thinks he can beat the evidence by sheer force of will."

My stomach is on the verge of revolt. In Paris, I finally realized what I wanted—that nothing was more important to me than Gage and Nova, and now I'm watching that life crumble and seep through my hands, a castle turned to sand.

"I just wish I could talk to him," I say. "When will I get to talk to him?"

"Not before the trial," Bennie says. "And if you're deported, you're on a plane within twelve hours of the sentence being handed down. It's unlikely that you'll speak to him again in person until this is all resolved."

"So if he goes to jail," I say, "I won't speak to him until he gets out?" My voice catches on the last word, and I'm barely holding myself together. I'll lose him, and I might lose Nova. I don't know if it would have felt any better if he'd taken the deal, but at least there might have been a glimmer of hope. Right now, all I see are dark clouds.

"That's the likely scenario," Caitlin says.

She's still gripping my hand, and I slip it out to rise to my feet. As I pace, I try to keep myself from hyperventilating. But I'm not doing a very good job of staying calm. This is so much worse than anything I could have dreamed up. I press my back against the wall, and I stare sightlessly into space. Gage and I are a team, but I don't feel like a very good teammate right now. I don't know how to play these political games.

Trouble has never been a pebble; it's always been an avalanche. And it's fucking crushing me right now—the realization that the consequences Caitlin once warned Gage about are going to bury us both, and there's no shovel to be found anywhere. My chest is so tight I can barely breathe.

I cover my face with my hands, sink to the ground, and I finally let the sob that's been building for days work its way out. I love him. I love him so much, and I might never get to tell him, might never get to be with him again. The happiness I thought I was so close to grasping was just a mirage, and I grip the bracelet on my wrist, desperate to cling onto any aspect of the family I've always longed for.

When there's a sharp knock at the door, I can't even bring myself to look up. More bad news. More evidence. More rocks rushing down the hill.

"Ember." Caitlin's voice penetrates my consciousness enough that I take a few deep breaths, trying to get myself back under control. When I finally look toward the door, I'm stunned for a moment at who is standing there, and then I scramble to my feet.

Chapter Fifty

GAGE

Ember is back in the country, and my gut has been in knots for the last twenty-four hours, knowing she's so close, and yet I can't see her or talk to her. It was the only thing Scarlet told me—that Ember had been summoned back to the island.

I've been led back to one of the interrogation rooms, and I'm half expecting an update from Scarlet or Caitlin when I enter the room, but the person sitting at the table isn't either of them. It's my mother.

"This foolishness stops now," she says, rising to her feet when the government agent who took me to the room slips out the door. Trust my mother to be able to do the one thing I've been dying to have for days—a private meeting with someone other than my lawyer.

"How'd you make this happen?" I ask, sliding into the seat across from the one she just vacated. "Can you get Ember in here too? It'd be a lot easier to know what to do if I could just talk to her."

"I can tell you what to do. Take the fucking deal. She's deadweight. You can't save her, but you can sure as hell save yourself."

"I'm not taking the deal. It's off the table anyway. Waited too long."

"I got it back *on* the table," Celia says. She slides an envelope across the shiny surface toward me. "Sign it, and we'll all be better off."

"No, *we* won't. I want my marriage. I want my wife. I want her in Bellerive. The only person this works out well for is you. An annulment. Ember gone from the island. It's everything you've wanted from the minute she showed up."

"If you'd just let me handle this baby situation from the start—"

"She contacted Caitlin, I don't see how—"

"If she'd just contacted me first, like the other one did…" She turns her back to me.

"Other one?" I rise from my seat, bearing down on my mother. "Did Athena contact you? Are you the one she got in touch with?"

"What? No." She crosses her arms.

"Mother," I say, my tone brimming with warning.

"How was I supposed to know it was real?" She runs a hand along the top of the chair next to her. "When I asked you if you thought you might have little Gages running around the world, you told me it was impossible."

"I had no idea you were trying to tell me someone contacted you." I draw a hand down my face. "A DNA test is all you needed."

"You think your father hasn't had women claiming he fathered their children? I'm very familiar with the shakedown, Gage. Most of them aren't even worth addressing."

God, that makes me wonder how many half-siblings I have all over the world. That's a discussion for another day. "Do you have any idea what your lack of caring did?"

"Oh, yes. It got you into a marriage you didn't want. Into fatherhood you claimed to never desire."

I plant my hands on my hips, prepared to get into this with her when she pivots toward me.

"You need to take this deal."

"No."

"Okay—you're worried about Ember. I understand that." She's taken on a conciliatory tone. "What about your daughter? If you're convicted, you face one to three years in prison. Nova could be four before you ever get to rock her to sleep again—hell, she'll be out of that stage by then."

A vise tightens around my chest, almost unbearable. I've avoided thinking too closely about the choice I'm making, its impact on Nova. She's young, and she needs Ember in her life.

"You've had your last rock. Your last infant cuddle. The minute you walked in here and dug in your heels, you gave all those moments up."

"Stop," I say, my voice hoarse. "You don't understand."

"I understand that you made some really dumb choices and now you're faced with the consequences. I understand that you don't want Ember permanently removed from the island."

And I want her to stay my wife. I want the family we built. I was supposed to get five *years* not five months.

"But if you're choosing Ember, it means you're not choosing Nova. And, truthfully, you're not really picking Ember either. She'll be deported either way. If you take the deal, at least you'll get that time with Nova. You won't miss watching her grow up. You won't have had your last toddler cuddles."

For the first time since I arrived in custody, the enormity of my choice is hitting me. I've been so focused on overcoming the charges, that I haven't truly considered what'll happen if I don't manage it, if I do get convicted. I've been clinging so hard to the idea that I can keep my family intact that I've been blinded to the reality.

"Mom," I say, my voice watery with unshed tears. "Don't make me choose."

She taps the envelope on the table. "I have faith that you'll make the smart choice here, Gage."

"Mom," I say, sinking into my chair again, my head in my hands, the edge of the envelope at the corner of my vision. "I can't let her down." But I don't even know which "her" I mean. My wife. My daughter. I promised I'd protect them both with my life, but right now, I'm not protecting anyone.

"The offer expires again in two hours," my mother says, setting a pen beside the envelope, and then she slips out the door.

I draw the envelope closer, and I wipe the tears that have somehow escaped against my will. Inside, the offer is exactly the same one presented to me days ago, the one I was so confident I'd never sign. I stare at the words, my vision blurred.

I sit back in my chair, and I pick up the pen, twirling it across my knuckles, working up the nerve to sentence myself and Ember to a life of misery and uncertainty. If I could just talk to her... I'd give anything to talk to her.

There's a sharp knock on the door, and I'm so startled I drop the pen, scooping it up as someone enters the room.

"I'm going to sign," I say, with a resigned sigh, half expecting my mother.

"Are you?"

The voice is familiar and not, and I bolt upright in my seat, the pen clutched in my hand. "Queen Aurora," I say, unable to keep the surprise out of my voice.

She slides into the seat across from me, but the warmth I've normally seen in her expression at events, around her family, even when I've seen pictures of her with Ember, is missing.

"I really like your wife," Queen Aurora says.

"Me too," I say, my voice rusty with emotion. "Me too."

"I'm not the politician. That's my husband. I don't get involved in government business because, quite frankly, I didn't grow up here, so I never feel like I have the full scope. But immigration, I understand. The island is small, and the population needs to be one that can be sustained."

I don't say anything, I just stare at her. I'm not sure if she's here to chastise me for trying to skirt the rules, or if she's here to offer some modicum of support.

"I went to see Ember—"

"How is she?" I lean forward on my elbows, eager for any unfiltered news.

"She's..." She shakes her head. "I think it's best if I stick to why I've come here. I want you to tell me the story of you and Ember. If your version matches hers, then I'll ask the king to intervene with immigration on your behalf. I can't guarantee he will, but I rarely ask for anything political, so I think there's a chance."

"You want our story?"

"From start to finish, yes," Queen Aurora says.

"Can anything I tell you be used against me or Ember in court?"

"That's not my intention," she says. "As you pointed out, you've got a deal on the table that prevents either of you from going to jail."

"I just want to be completely clear," I say, fingering the paper in front of me. "If I tell you my story, and that story matches my wife's, there's a chance she can stay on the island, and we can stay married? I'll get to keep my family?" My voice catches on the last word, and I pinch the bridge of my nose, feeling tears threaten again. I can count on one hand the number of times I've cried in my life, and I'm on the verge of doing it again today.

"Yes," Queen Aurora says, and her voice has taken on the softer quality she's known for.

I stare at the page in front of me, aware that the queen's deal is the miracle I've been seeking for days, but there's also a chance Ember will have filtered our story in a way I won't. That she'd tell a truth or leave out a detail that I might add. There's also a chance she'd lie completely to try to protect me, save me from jail.

So, which path do I take? Follow the lie down the rabbit hole, or take a chance that the truth, the whole truth, will be the thing that sets all of us free?

I know what Ember would do. There's really only one option. I open my mouth, and I start to speak.

Chapter Fifty-One

EMBER

Caitlin enters the immigration interrogation room with Bennie, and I get to my feet. Bennie waves me down, but I'm too nervous to sit.

"We don't know anything yet," he says.

"Nothing?" I press my palm to my chest and try to force myself to breathe deeply. It feels like I've been standing on the edge of a cliff for the last few hours. After the queen left here, I knew she was going to speak to Gage. I could only hope whatever he told her was the same thing I'd said, but if he did-—if his story exactly matched mine—I don't know how that reality will settle over me.

"The queen might not be *the* politician, but she's still in a political role. She's not going to make any promises or reveal her feelings unless there's some action behind it," Bennie says.

"But she didn't say she couldn't or wouldn't help," Caitlin clarifies. "So there *is* hope. Any deals or court appearances are on pause right now."

The only version of the queen I really know is Rory—my friend—the person I chat to at playgroup and whose number I have in my phone. To realize she holds my entire life, everything I care about in the world, in the palm of her hand is terrifying.

"We're in limbo until she makes a decision?" I wring my hands over and over. "Do you know what Gage told her?"

"She didn't let anyone in the room with her. No one knows but her and Gage. I don't even know what *you* said," Caitlin reminds me.

I know what I want, what I hope for, but god, I am so afraid to even let myself consider that my story and Gage's matched. My head swims at the thought. Even if a tiny part of me that I don't want to acknowledge thinks it might be possible, that outcome also feels impossible. "When do you think we'll know?" I ask.

"Typically, if King Alexander chooses to interfere, it'll be quick. He doesn't like a lot of debate once he decides," Bennie says.

"Does he interfere?" I ask. "Has this happened before?"

"No," Bennie says with a grimace. "This would be a first. He's very careful with his political moves, and this one would be costly to him. Gage Tucker is a prominent figure in an immigration sting. But it's also why I think he'd move quickly if he does step in. Minimize the gossip. Downplay the rich-poor conversation. Try to figure out a way to play off you and Gage being picked up and detained as a mistake."

My heart is beating erratically in my chest. It's all going to come down to whether Gage's truth matches my truth, and I can't believe fate won't do me dirty. A hot, enormously kind billionaire is not going to fall in love for the first time with someone like me. That's not how my life works. But I can't help wishing that it could be, just this once.

Nerves zip up and down my spine like an electrical current as Bill drives me home—back to the oceanfront cottage I've been sharing with Gage for months. He's already there with Nova, according to what Caitlin told me almost an hour ago, having been released a full day before me. I'm going back to a place I thought I might never see again. To know my time isn't limited, that the clock isn't ticking in the background is a relief. Or it should be...

But if Gage is out and I'm out, that means our stories must have matched, that Rory was able to work a miracle with King Alexander and immigration.

That also means that I know exactly what Gage must have told her, and in all the time I've known him, I don't think I've ever been so nervous to face him.

Has it been obvious that I'm in love with him? That I'd never willingly leave him, even after the five years? Did he know that's what I'd say and so he said it too, or does he love me back? It seems unfathomable that me, a high school dropout with limited sexual experience and two genuine pennies to her name, could be someone Gage could love. While I know how he's treated me, and I can logically see how that treatment might add up to big feelings, it still seems so unbelievable that I might not be alone in this love story. Is it really possible that Gage Tucker—my arrogant playboy who's never loved anyone—could be in love *with me*?

The thought makes my head spin, which makes me a little queasy.

At the door, I key in the code, and I slip inside. Nova should be sleeping, so being quiet is the best idea, and my stealthy entrance has nothing to do with my nerves. Nothing at all. But my heart pounds in my ears, anyway, mocking me.

Maybe he just said what he thought Rory wanted to hear, and it just happened to match what I said? The best kind of coincidence. Realizing that's what happened would be a knife to my heart, and I don't know how we keep this marriage going if he lied.

I set my suitcase from Paris beside the door, and I'm just slipping off my shoes when Gage rounds the corner into the front entrance. He doesn't break his stride as he rotates me around, presses my back against the wall, and kisses me deeply. The minute his lips glide across mine, I let out a moan of contentment, desire, relief. One of his hands is on my hip, the other in my hair, and I clutch at him, desperate to keep this connection. The kiss goes on and on, and I relish the feel of him, the closeness that I get to experience again.

"I love you," he murmurs when we break the kiss. "I love you so fucking much it makes my chest hurt."

Relief rushes through me that I don't have to wonder or tiptoe around how we both ended up free. "I love you too," I say, my voice suddenly watery with tears.

"I was so afraid I'd never be able to say that to you." Because as many signals as he gave me, that his feelings might be real, might run deeper than I'd ever dared to hope, I don't know if I would have been brave enough to admit my equally deep and scary feelings if I hadn't been so forcefully confronted. Loving Gage feels like both the greatest risk and biggest reward of my life.

Gage frames my face and kisses me again, and then we're shedding our clothes, as though neither of us can believe how close we came to being separated, how we almost didn't get to keep this life we've built together. I don't know how I would have survived being in Los Angeles without him and Nova, knowing we might never be together again.

The energy between us is frantic—hurried kisses and desperate caresses. His hands are rough on my skin, but I like it and need more of it. Every brush, every touch, every squeeze reminds me that I almost lost him, almost lost this. And I want to feel it all.

He lifts me up and braces me against the wall in the hallway—any thought of us going to a bedroom or somewhere more sensible doesn't happen. He sinks inside of me, and his gaze travels over my face until our eyes lock.

"I'm never letting you go. You're mine, Em. Mine forever. This isn't fake. It's real. So fucking real."

We both let out a groan of contentment when he presses deep inside me, and I wrap my arms around his shoulders, thread my fingers through his hair. It's impossible to consider I could ever be so close—both in mind and body—to anyone else. He's a dream I never dared to have.

"I don't even have the words to tell you how much I've missed you," Gage says, his forehead pressed to mine as he rotates his hips.

"Should we..." He hits the spot that makes my knees go weak, and I stutter to find a coherent thought. "Talk?"

"Lots to say," Gage murmurs. "Mostly about how much I love you. How much I love fucking you. How you're stuck with me now, wife. There's no end to us."

All of it is music to my ears, and soon we're not talking at all, a chorus of moans and sighs and pleading words as we drive each other deeper into the depths of pleasure. I was so certain I'd never have this again, and it makes me cling tighter, urge him closer, trying desperately to make sure we connect in every way possible.

"I'm not going to let you go, Em. I could never let you go."

And they aren't empty words—I know the lengths he'd go to keep me in his life. Every reservation and bit of uncertainty I've had is gone.

Gage Tucker loves me, and I love him too.

We've landed on the couch, tangled up together and still naked. He keeps staring at me and smoothing my hair, as though he can't quite believe we've made it to this place together. I know how he feels because I feel exactly the same way. If someone had told me months or years ago that this is where my life would lead, there's not a chance I'd have believed them. It's the sort of thing people write stories about—happy ones—unlike the rest of my life, which has been mostly a string of depressing tales.

"If only I could have talked to you..." he says.

"I know," I agree. "I thought that a million times. You're the first person I call about anything, always. To not be able to talk to you was so..." I search for the right word, but it doesn't really come.

"Lonely," he says. "For the first time in my life, I wasn't sure everything I wanted could work out. Every option felt like the wrong one for you or for Nova."

I kiss his cheek and the crook of his neck. "Did Ava tell you who was behind some of the evidence?"

"Yeah," he says, a tightness to his voice. "Abby. But she also said she heard Hugh had a hand in it. Makes sense. Would have taken deep pockets and resources to get all the little scraps that added up to a bigger picture."

"Not the right picture," I say.

"Not an accurate one. They had no idea that the words were fake, not the feelings." Gage kisses my shoulder. "I have a plan for both of them."

"Maybe we should just let it go?"

"No," Gage says, decisively. "They almost cost me the thing I hold most dear—my family. I can't forgive that. I won't. Business is one thing, but anyone who comes after you or Nova can't be given a free pass."

I don't want to argue about it when part of me feels the same way—Gage almost went to jail—so I don't say anything, and the two of us stay locked together, content in the silence.

"Do you want the LA job with Franza Fashion?" he asks, his deep voice rough.

I take a minute to think about it, even though I've thought about it a lot. The context is different now—I'm not being forced into anything. "I want some pieces of the job—the fashion part. Learning from them would be incredible. But I don't want to spend years there, and unlike Ava, I have no desire to be famous. I'm as famous as I'd ever want to be right now."

"You can always tell them your terms and see if they agree. No harm, right? And if they say yes, you might get the best of both worlds."

"I don't want anything that'll take me away from you and Nova."

"I get that, and I don't want that either," he says, "but I also don't want you to look back with any kind of regret. We have to make sure we're looking after each other, so that we both get what we want and what we need. I don't know…" His voice hitches. "I don't know if I've been doing that."

"You have," I say, keeping my voice gentle. "And I guess I need to not be afraid to ask for what I want. It's a learning curve." The men in my life have never been supportive or communicative, but Gage is, and I need to work on talking to him, negotiating this life we're going to live forever.

"If I've somehow managed to be what you need, then I don't want to forget to be that guy. You're one of the two most important people in the world to me. You and Nova. The only job I care about is taking care of the two of you. That's it. Nothing else matters nearly as much."

"I really love you, Gage Tucker."

He grins. "I thought it was going to take me years to hear that. You can say that to me whenever you want."

"I've never said it to a guy before," I admit. "Just my sister and my mom."

He takes my hand and rests it on his heart and then he lays his hand over it. "I'm honored to be the first and only."

"Unless we have a little boy," I say, the words slipping out before I can think them through.

We both freeze and stare at each other. "You want more kids with me?"

"Yeah, I mean... If you do..."

"Without a doubt," he says. "Definitely."

I smile, and he smiles back.

"More kids," I whisper, sort of surprised we're both so on board when Nova is still so little. But he's a good dad, and I love our parenting partnership. We might not always approach problems in the same way, but he cares and he listens, and those aren't qualities to be taken for granted. "I think it's going to take a while for all of this to settle in my brain," I say with a little laugh. "Like when I first came here, it all feels unreal, like it could disappear in a moment."

"I'm not going anywhere, babe. And I've got the rest of our lives to prove to you that what we've got is real and permanent and the most valuable thing I have in my life."

"Gage," I choke out, overwhelmed with emotion. "I love you so much."

"I love you too, Em. Forever."

Epilogue

GAGE

The newest elite catering company on the island buzzes around the house, preparing for the Tucker family dinner tonight. I hesitated in hiring them because Verna Davis works for them in the kitchen. Even though he probably wouldn't see her, being anywhere associated with Hollyn Davis seems to poke a hole in Nathaniel's carefully constructed armor. Makes sense—as far as I can remember, Hollyn was basically raised by her aunt. I'm sure Nathaniel saw her a lot in the time he was with Hollyn, maybe even ate a lot of their cooking.

Ava said I'd become too sensitive to other people's needs if I wasn't going to hire the company because of one kitchen staff and Nathaniel's high school drama. Does she have a point? I guess we'll find out tonight.

Our former catering company has been banished from every Tucker and Tucker-adjacent family across the island. The consequences of them having employees willing to hand over recordings and information to Hugh and Abby while on a job have been felt far and wide. Last I heard, they were on the cusp of bankruptcy, or they'd have to start dropping their prices to appeal to a lower level of clientele. How the mighty do fall.

The list of mighty who have fallen is deeply satisfying at the moment. After Hugh tried to meddle in my marriage, I went after his company harder than I had before. With Nathaniel's savvy business decisions, I was able to snatch some huge clients out from under Hugh, and then his wife finally had enough of his shenanigans and filed for divorce. Even with a prenup, Caitlin said it'll be a significant financial blow to Hugh. Does his misery make me happy? Yes. Does that make me a bad person? Ember tells me it doesn't, and her opinion is the only one that matters.

As for Abby, she fled the island the same day I got out of prison. Any sort of justice will have to be served cold. Though Ava tells me she's heard Abby doesn't intend to return to Bellerive, that there's *"nothing here for her now."* Definitely for the best. The only thing she'd find would be my wrath.

"Gage!" Ember calls from the back bedrooms.

I stop watching the busy hive of activity around the living room, kitchen, and dining room to respond to her call.

"I'm worried I don't have everything," she says, staring into the suitcase she's packing for Nova.

"If you forget anything, we can just buy it." I shrug. "As long as you've got her blanket, pacifier, and her favorite ducky, we're good."

She bites her lip and glances at me. Even after being my wife for more than a year, Ember still hesitates to spend unnecessary money. She'd rather remember to pack something than have to spend money to replace it while we're away somewhere.

"Just think summer in Bellerive and pack accordingly," I suggest. "Los Angeles isn't that different."

She nods while she sorts through the piles in the suitcase. "This is probably good."

"It's six weeks at the LA mansion while you intern with Franza Fashion—we're not moving there permanently."

"Yeah, I know, it's just…"

I wrap my arm around her shoulders and kiss her temple. "I love how thrifty you are."

She laughs and gives me a little shove. "It's probably the one thing I can say with confidence that you find annoying."

"Endearing."

"Same thing."

"Vastly different," I say. "Sometimes I find your preoccupation with not buying things baffling—we're contributing to the global economy—but I'm never annoyed by it. Not even a little."

"The global economy?" Ember asks with a scoff. "More like the global landfill."

"See? I love that you think of these things and that Nova will grow up considering all these angles I missed as a child." Of that, I'm sure. I'm not likely to convert Ember to a life of excess before Nova is old enough to understand that things have value.

"I'm sort of surprised that Petra Franza pursued me so hard, if I'm honest," Ember says, glancing at me. "I thought when I said no initially that'd be the end of it."

"They know talent when they see it," I say. "You don't become the top anything by letting your best people slip through your fingers." And I've taken that advice to heart with my own company, making sure that bonuses are plentiful, and percentages are still higher with my agents than any other agency.

The doorbell sounds, and I scan Ember for a beat. "You okay?"

"Yeah," she says with a little laugh. "I'll stop stressing now and enjoy the evening."

"We leave tomorrow," I say, sliding my hand down her back. "Lots of time for you to worry still."

She smacks my arm playfully, and I swoop in for a quick kiss before heading for the door. There are few things that give me more joy than teasing my wife about anything.

My family arrives in a continuous stream, as though they planned their entrances together. Maren and Brice are first, followed by Sawyer, then Ava, Nathaniel, and finally my parents.

Although I wouldn't claim that my mother and Ember are best friends, the frost between them seems to be thawing. My mother tried, in her own way, to save me when I was being too stubborn to save myself. But she would have happily thrown Ember to the wolves, and that didn't go unnoticed by either of us, even if she was also pushing me to be a good father, to consider the impact of my choices on Nova.

Once we're seated around the table and the various courses are being served, the family gossip runs hot and fast.

"King Alexander will not leave me alone," Sawyer says with an exasperated glance in Brice's direction. "Your brother is far too persistent."

"I actually don't think his idea about having a sports team on the island is a bad one. I don't know that hockey makes sense," Brice says, "but he's got a vision."

"I don't know why I have to be the one to commit to helping with team wellness as part of his bid for anything and everything," Sawyer says.

"He wants to prove the island has top-notch services. We're small but mighty," Maren says. "It's a compliment. He could be hounding other people, but you have the best rep on the island."

It's true. Sawyer charges less than most, has longer work hours, and she makes frequent house calls. There is no one more dedicated to helping people on the island than Sawyer. She probably hates the thought of making any money at all. Bleeding fucking heart.

"How's the documentary going, Nathaniel?" Sawyer asks, always uncomfortable with any sort of accolade or compliment.

"We're in postproduction," Nathaniel says. "I've been approached about helping with a home makeover show, actually."

"A home makeover show?" I scoff. "What do you know about that?"

"Nothing," Nathaniel agrees easily. "But we'd be taking low-income houses and helping to fix them up before the homeowners put them on the market." He swishes his roast beef around in his gravy.

"And those houses should be sold by NGE," I say.

"Posey is already on board as one presenter," Nathaniel says, ignoring me.

"Oh," Maren says. "She'll be great."

"I love her," Ember says from beside me. "She'll be perfect."

"They've been struggling with casting a second person," Nathaniel says. "They've asked me to help in the search and step in as producer. I'm considering it."

Which, in Nathaniel-speak, means he'll likely do it. Anything that's about low-income families in Bellerive, and Nathaniel opens his heart and his wallet.

"You're allergic to money," Ava says from across the table. "You'll do it for sure. If any of your school or famous friends are looking for an investment that'll make them money, you can point them in my direction."

"Back to funding your perfume line?" I ask, amused.

"Yes," she says with a haughty tone. "Maybe other people don't want to be famous, but *I* do."

"I pity the person who has to work with you," my mother says. "You and your wild ideas. Will I live to see the day where you're levelheaded?"

"That's right," Ava says with a grin. "I cannot be tamed. I'll be wild—and rich—until the day I die."

My father reaches for my mother's hand and gives it a squeeze. She gives him a distracted half smile.

"What's going on there?" I ask, nodding at their joined hands. They rarely touch, much less show each other mutual support.

"Your mother has something she needs to tell you all. She wanted to wait until all the tests were back, but with Ember and you leaving for weeks, it's best to tell you all now," my father says.

My mother shakes her head, and when she doesn't speak, my father steps in again. "Her kidneys don't appear to be functioning properly. Tests have been ordered. They've ruled out cancer, but they're not sure what's causing her problems."

"Okay," I say, carefully. "It's good that it's not cancer."

"It's not good that they don't know," Maren says, a crease in her brow. "They have no idea?"

"They're running tests. There are a few rarer forms of disease that they think it might be. She's going to need your support during whatever treatments are suggested, get tested as donors, and so forth."

"A transplant?" The shock I feel is in Sawyer's voice.

"Whatever needs to be done," Nathaniel says, making eye contact with each of us, "we'll all do our part."

All of us nods, even Ava, but the announcement creates an undercurrent of sadness for the rest of the meal. We might all have mixed feelings about Celia Tucker's effectiveness as a mother, but we'd never wish her harm, and we'd circle around her when needed.

As the evening winds to a close, Nathaniel is the last one to leave as we're talking NGE Realty strategy. We've become a lot closer over the last few months as he's guided me—and I've actually listened—to success. I've spent most of my life underestimating his ability to get things done.

We're at the door, Nova and Ember in the bedroom doing a rock and talk, when we overhear some of the servers commenting on a staff shortage.

"Who didn't show up?" I ask the staff, mildly curious as Nathaniel is putting on his shoes.

"Verna Davis," the worker says with a grimace. "Not at all like her. No one has been able to get in touch with her."

"Have the police been informed?" Nathaniel asks, a definite tension to his posture.

"We let Steph know," she says with a shrug. "Verna's an adult. I don't think they do much when it's only been a few hours."

"I know where she lives," Nathaniel says. "I'll swing past to check on her on my way home."

Except I know that's at least an hour outside of his way. Last I heard, she lived in the poor part of Rockdown, and Nathaniel lives in central Tucker's Town. He's never willingly inserted himself in Davis business—actively avoids any mention of Hollyn or her family.

"You sure?" I ask. "Want me to come with you?"

"Call Stephen," Nathaniel says. "Have him meet me there."

"Right," I say. "Of course." I slip my phone out of my pocket as Nathaniel closes the door behind him.

"Everything okay?" Ember asks, coming out of the bedroom hallway. "Nathaniel doesn't normally sound like that."

I'd ask what she means, but I noticed it too. Worried. Voice tight. "Probably just a misunderstanding," I say. "You all set for tomorrow?" I send a quick text to Stephen instead of calling him, and then I focus on Ember.

"I'm really nervous," she says, stepping into my arms. "I'm glad you and Nova are coming with me."

"We Tuckers stick together," I say, my mind straying briefly to my mother. "You don't get off this island without me anymore."

At least not yet. The last time is too fresh in my mind, and Martin jumped at the chance to take the lead of NGE while I was gone. It's a long time to be away, but Nathaniel also agreed to check in with Martin, double-check the books, and ensure everything runs smoothly. Hopefully, the Verna wellness checkup is nothing—a miscommunication over work hours or where to be.

"I like the sound of that," Ember says. "Sticking together."

"Like the strongest, toughest glue. You'll have to have me surgically removed," I say.

That makes Ember laugh—one of my favorite sounds—and she rises on her toes, her lips skimming mine. "I'm the luckiest woman alive."

I don't contradict her, tell her that I'm the lucky one because we have this argument all the time—who's luckier? Hopefully, our luck holds, and Nova and all our future children will be the beneficiaries of the deep, endless well of love we feel for each other.

The future, that mythical thing that once both bored and scared me, doesn't do either, anymore. I'm excited, and I can't wait for it to happen. But I never want to get so caught up in tomorrow that I forget to be thankful for today. As I sweep Ember up into my arms and carry her toward our bedroom, I'm well aware that each day feels like the best day ever, now that I have them.

Bonus Deleted Scene

FIRST CHRISTMAS TOGETHER

Gage

I don't really remember what Christmas was like as a kid—isn't that stupid? Who doesn't remember Christmas? It's one of those topics that's come up with my friends in college or on nights out when we'd rib each other or lament not getting something particularly desired.

I must have felt excited about something or giddy with enthusiasm about some aspect of the season, but I can't remember that. Anytime Christmas came up, I concocted some story that seemed fitting of a Tucker. Outlandish. Over the top. Completely and utterly fake.

For me, Christmas has always been the season of awkward social commitments where my family pretends my parents aren't fucking around on each other or that my mother isn't furious with my dad for some reason. We were dressed up in finely tailored and uncomfortable clothes and paraded around from one rich person's house to another.

So when my mother tried to herd us into a laundry list of parties, I refused. Nova isn't going to grow up dreading this season. We've committed to the Tucker Family Christmas Party, and that's it.

Instead, the highlight of Nova's childhood is going to be the Christmas Festival of Tucker's Town, and when I pull into the lot reserved for Tucker family members, Ember's gasp of surprise is the best sound I've ever heard.

"Snow?" she says, and she laughs. "Are you serious?"

The cool wind is alive with snowflakes when I open my car door, and Ember follows, breathing in the air.

"You miss it?" I ask.

"A little," she says. "Is that weird? Most people would kill for this warmer weather where the worst that happens is a bad thunderstorm and sheets of rain." She pulls her jacket tight around her, and I'm glad I told her to wear her warmest sweater.

"I like winter," I say. "In small doses I control. Which is what makes the Christmas Festival the best kind of experience." I scoop Nova out of her car seat, and I settle her in my arms. When I put her in her warmest clothes and put some old mittens on her, Ember laughed at me. But with the snow machines kicking out cold fluff into the air, I'd rather my two favorite people were warm enough to enjoy the beauty of the false season.

Nova's head turns every which way as she tries to figure out what's floating in the air. I hold out my hand and let some snow land, both of us staring as it melts. She meets my gaze, her greenish eyes alight with amazement.

"Snow," I say. "This is snow."

She grins at me, and my love puddles at her feet. Jesus. Is there anything better than delighting this kid?

Ember appears at my side, and she opens her mouth, sticking out her tongue. A snowflake lands, and she shows Nova, who promptly copies her, giggling at the feeling of the cold wetness on her tongue. Her jiggly belly laugh is a shot of endorphins straight into my veins.

My heart is so fucking full in this moment that I have to bite my own tongue to keep from saying something that'll make Ember think I've lost my mind. And

I have. I've lost my ever-loving mind over this woman and my kid. Never in my wildest dreams did I think that this would be the life that would make me happiest—happier than I've ever been.

None of my happiness has anything to do with money or power or building the Tucker empires. It's a belly laugh and a beautiful smile. It's feeling Ember grab my hand as we wander toward the town center, and it's hearing how excited she is by all these winter activities she recognizes, how happy she is to be able to share them here, with Nova and with me.

I kiss the top of her head while we observe the scene for a moment. Snow machines are coating the air and ground with the white stuff, and there's an outdoor skating rink which must be taking half the power in Bellerive to keep frozen. Ice sculptures are shaped into slides of all sizes and shapes, and kids are going down on pieces of plastic, their laughter filling the air.

At the heart of the town square, King Alexander and Queen Aurora are with their toddler daughter, Grace, watching the scene, waiting for dusk to hit for King Alexander to deliver his speech for the opening ceremonies, just before the Christmas lights spring to life.

Queen Aurora catches sight of us, and she waves us over, enveloping Ember into a hug. The two of them immediately begin talking excitedly about the winter season that's come to life in Bellerive.

In the distance, Nick Summerset and his wife, Julia, are trying to help their infant daughter, Amelia, to paint the snow walls, and I leave Ember talking to wander over to see whether I can get Nova to try her hand at painting too. Seems like an exercise in futility, but it's not long before the three of us adults are grinning while the two girls splatter the finger paint all over.

When Ember's arms circle around my waist, and I feel her cheek press against my back, I lace my fingers with hers for a moment before she comes to my side, and I kiss the top of her head.

She nods at Nova sitting on the ground in front of the wall, covered in finger paints. "Your mom is going to love that."

"Might have to bathe her before the Tucker ball," I agree.

"What time do we have to be there again?" Ember asks.

"Whenever we arrive," I say. "I want these memories."

She takes my hand and squeezes, understanding without me having to go into great detail that I never felt like I had my parents' attention or their time, and that I intend to give both to Nova.

"She's a lucky girl," Ember says, staring at Nova.

But I'm the one who feels lucky in this moment—the woman I love on my arm, the child I adore at my feet. Stunning to think I somehow fell into this much happiness.

Somehow, Ember and I agreed that Santa wouldn't wrap his gifts so that Nova could see the spread the minute she woke up.

The next morning, I'm buzzing and wide-awake long before either Ember or Nova. I've given gifts—lots of them—but I've never put so much thought into what someone might want, labored over exactly what to get with so much intention before.

I'm in the kitchen, coffee already in the pot, a breakfast casserole heating in the oven when Ember wanders out of the bedrooms.

"What are you doing up so early?" Ember asks, coming over to loop her arms around my waist, pressing her sleepy, soft body against me. Fuck, I love the feel of her against me—doesn't matter the context.

"It's our first Christmas together," I say, as though that explains all this nervous energy vibrating off me.

"Do you want me to get Nova up?" Ember asks, leaving me to pour herself a cup of coffee.

I lean against the counter, and I watch her for a beat. The truth is that today is no different for Nova. She's too young to understand the significance, and since we're expected at my parents again tonight for a family dinner, it's probably better to stick to her routine as much as we can. Last night was late due to the Tucker Family Christmas Eve Party.

"We could," I say, stretching my hands along the counter behind me, forcing my nerves to fuck off. "We could exchange our gifts—for each other."

"Okay!" she says with more enthusiasm than I expected. She practically bounces over to the Christmas tree. "Me first." She digs through the presents and finds a rectangle that I've already pegged as some kind of book.

Did I snoop? Yes. Am I proud of it? A little. I've never looked forward to receiving a gift from anyone, and Ember's also been giving off a strange energy in the run-up to today. My curiosity is piqued.

"I wasn't sure what to get the guy who just buys himself everything he could ever want," she says, sitting on the couch with my present in her lap. "So, it's not much, and it wasn't expensive or anything."

I already know I'm going to love it. If she made it or thought of it or bought it, I want it. Instead of taking the seat beside her, I snatch the three things I have for her out from under the tree. Like her, my gifts aren't the most expensive things I could have bought, but I put a lot of brain power into my purchases.

I set my presents on the coffee table, and I sit next to her, our legs touching. I slide my hand along her thigh. Whenever she's within touching distance, I need to have a hand on her.

She passes me her present, and I turn it over in my hands, savoring the anticipation. Then I peel back the first layer of paper and then another until I see the front of a matte book. It's me and Ember and Nova—a snapshot a friend took at one of the kid events in Tucker's Town we've attended together. Emblazoned across the front is *"Our First Christmas Together"*. I pinch the bridge of my nose as I crack open the cover. Inside are all my favorite photos of Nova, Ember, and me with both of them. It's like a walk down memory lane, every highlight I could have thought of on the pages. She's even remembered things I've said or things we've done and written the moment from her point of view—framing me as this great dad, a caring partner.

"This is the best gift," I say, my voice thick with emotion. "Truly." I turn the last page, and then I meet Ember's watery gaze with my own blurry vision. "You're the most amazing woman—even if I lived a thousand perfect lives, I'm not sure I'd ever deserve you."

She frames my face, and she kisses me, and I set the book on the coffee table blindly, drawing her onto my lap, deepening the kiss. I dig my hands up under her sleep shorts, cupping her ass and fitting her tight against me.

"My wife," I murmur against her lips, and it never gets old.

"What'cha got for me, big boy?" she asks, her tone teasing.

"Nothing as great as what you got me," I say. "But I hope you like it anyway." I reach around her and grab the envelope and the wrapped boxes. "These two are from me," I say. "This third one is from Nova, so we can wait until she wakes up if you want."

"Which one first?" Ember asks, wiggling on my lap and making it hard for me to concentrate but also keeping me from being too nervous.

"The box. It's probably less exciting."

She opens the wrapping paper carefully, and when she sees what's inside, she grins. "You get tired of my books scattered all around your house?"

"Our house," I say, gently. "And no. I thought you might like being able to take an unlimited amount of books with you everywhere you go. And I got you one of those monthly reading subscription things too. Read as many books as you want."

Her eyes soften, and she stares at me for a beat before planting a chaste kiss on my lips. "I love it," she says. "It's a really thoughtful gift, Gage."

"The next one is a bit better," I say, nodding at the envelope.

She slides her finger under the seal and opens it to take out the typed pages. Her eyes scan the words, and she presses her hand to her chest. "You got me tickets to Paris Fashion Week?"

"Best seats at every show. Ava is going with you. Hotel is booked. Private jet is booked. A girls' week full of all the things you love." I tuck a strand of hair behind her ear.

She meets my gaze, and the air around us feels heavy with emotion, as though we're both holding back on saying what we really mean, what we really feel. I'd love for that to be true on her part because it's definitely true on mine. I've never been in love with someone like I am with Ember.

"How is this my life?" she whispers.

"I ask myself that all the time," I say. "I got the better end of this deal for sure."

She laughs and shakes her head. "You most definitely did not."

But the moment between us is gone, and I hear Nova making noise from the bedroom. Ember hops off my lap, and then she leans over, rubbing her nose against mine.

"Gage Tucker, you are some kind of wonderful." Then she presses her lips against mine before heading for the bedrooms.

I pick up the only box left, and I rotate it around, hoping she'll like the silver bracelet inlaid with our names and star signs. That way, she'll carry our little family with her wherever she goes.

"Oh my god, Gage!" Ember calls from the bedrooms. "Nova needs a bath. This is disgusting."

I chuckle and get to my feet. "On it," I say, heading for the bathroom to draw a bath. The presents can wait when every day, even the messy ones, feel like a gift.

Bonus Deleted Scene

NOVA'S FIRST CHRISTMAS

Ember

It's been a weird morning. Gage has Nova in the living room, and I've been in her room, staring at pictures of my sister. Most days, she crosses my mind. An expression on Nova's face might trigger it, or I'll look at Gage and wonder what might have happened if my sister got him the first time she reached out. Some thoughts are more helpful than others.

Nova's birthday has triggered an avalanche of memories and emotions tinged with regret and sadness. I hear footsteps behind me, but I don't turn around.

"You okay, babe?" Gage's hand settles on my hip, and I know if I turn around I'll find Nova perched in his arms, a toothy grin on her face. There's nothing she loves more than being carted around the house by her tall father—not even her own wobbly walk, which makes my heart burst with emotion each time I see her toddling from one couch to another. Babyproofing has taken on a whole other level.

And my sister—Nova's mother—has missed it all.

"A bit sad," I admit, picking up a photo of me and Athena.

He draws me into his side, and his lips settle in my hair, a soothing constant. Athena's the one topic Gage never seems to know how to tackle, and I get it. Nova's birth caused Athena to slide down a hill she never recovered from, but Nova's brought so much joy to my life and to his.

"Someday it might feel different," he says.

"I hope so," I say, and I mean that. I'm not sure my grief over losing my sister will ever be completely gone, and I'm sure Nova will have her own challenges when she gets old enough to understand all of it, but I want to be able to celebrate Nova's birth with all the joy she's given me. I don't want this tinge of sadness, but I can't help it this year. It's here whether I want it or not.

"Any time you want to talk about it…" His hand is firm but gentle on my back as he draws small circles.

Gage Tucker is my favorite adult in the entire universe. Every time he offers this unconditional support, I'm surprised, but I'm also so freaking grateful for it. I set the picture on the shelf, and I turn into his arms, burying my face in the part of his chest not taken up by Nova's round belly. I burrow into him, and I whisper my fingers along Nova's side, eliciting her baby giggle that never fails to warm my heart. Her onesie today is just a giant number one emblazoned on her chest.

"Should we start getting ready?" Gage murmurs from above me.

"Probably," I say. "I spent weeks planning her birthday party. It was a wedding-level mission."

"I know women who have spent years planning their weddings," he says with a chuckle. "A few weeks on a birthday party seems about right."

"True," I say, stepping away from him and digging around in Nova's drawers to put together her diaper bag for the day.

"The guest list was half of Bellerive, though. I can see why it might have gotten a little out of hand." His tone is teasing, but I still shoot him a look.

"I can't help that I've met so many people at the palace on Tuesdays who have babies close to Nova's age." It's one of my joys, actually. At any moment, I can get Nova a playdate, which also gives me some adult time when Gage is tied up with clients or has a bazillion showings on a weekend. My life doesn't revolve around him, which makes it all the sweeter when it *can* revolve around him.

"What are you wearing?" he asks, his hand sliding up my leg, dangerously close to my ass.

"Something sensible," I say.

"Boo," he says with a chuckle. "Can I pick it out?"

"You want to dress me?"

"More than that, I want to undress you, but since I doubt you'll give me that option, I'll pick something that'll give me easy access to those gorgeous curves." He squeezes my ass. "Fuck, I love your ass."

"Please don't let Nova repeat that sentence."

He laughs, and he shoots me a grin over his shoulder as he heads into our bedroom. God knows what he's going to try to make me wear. Once I have the diaper bag packed, I head into the main bedroom to find three outfits on the king bed.

"I get to pick?" I ask, eyeing the three options. One is a short, tight dress that is not at all practical. But I know from our Tuesday night dancing sessions that he loves it. I can't crawl around a toddler climbing structure in it without causing a Bellerivian scandal. The other two are rompers—one in a plum color that I love, and the other is in a bright pink. I snatch up the looser plum romper and head for the bathroom.

Once I'm in there, I realize why Gage picked it. I can't get it buttoned up without help. When I come out of the bathroom, he smirks at me.

"Need a hand?" He's set Nova on a play mat with some toys, and his gaze has darkened with obvious interest in more than doing up the buttons on my romper.

"I'll need help getting out of it too," I say. "Like every time I have to use the bathroom."

"That's the plan," he says. "A little alone time in all the chaos is good for us. Those family bathrooms are a godsend." He rises from the bed and comes over to sweep my hair onto my shoulder. His breath skims across my skin as he buttons one, and then he grazes my ear with his teeth before doing up another. His hand sneaks up under the hem at the back, circling around to run his fingers across the lace of my underwear before drawing me back against him, letting me know how much he wants me.

"I'm not having sex with you in the family bathroom at the play place," I say, my breathy voice making me sound less than convincing.

"We'll see," he says. "Sometimes you just can't help yourself."

Which I both love and hate about being with him. I've never wanted someone so much and so quickly in my life. It takes very little convincing on his part to get me begging to have him inside me. The closeness is addictive—as are the orgasms.

"The last button?" I remind him.

"On it," he whispers against the nape of my neck, his lips feathering my skin, leaving goose bumps and damp panties in his wake. He buttons the last one, and then he taps my ass before stepping away. "You're in so much trouble later."

"You think I'm going to be a bad girl, do you?" I glance at him over my shoulder.

"With me? The baddest," he says with a smirk. "Just the way I like it."

A shiver of anticipation races up my spine because I can already picture it, and I should be disgusted at the idea of having him fuck me in the locked family bathroom, bent over the sink, watching me take every inch of him in the mirror ahead of us. But it doesn't seem to matter what he suggests or where—even if I'm initially turned off—I end up coming hard and enthusiastically to his ideas. If it didn't feel so good, I'd think it was a real problem.

"Is that what you're wearing?" I ask, eyeing the jeans that sit perfectly on his hips, the butter-soft T-shirt that stretches across his broad, defined chest. It's unbelievable to me that he's mine and that—at least right now—I'm the only one he wants, the only one who gets to touch him like I do. Makes me want to be very bad right now.

"You don't think I look good, babe?" He runs a hand down his chest before looking up at me with a twinkle in his eyes. He knows. He knows exactly how good-looking he is.

"You'll do," I say, trying to walk past him out of the bedroom, but he catches me around the waist, drawing me back against him, his breath hot in my ear.

"I'll do?" His voice is dangerously soft. "Is that all?"

"Gage," I moan. "We're going to be late."

"Let them wait."

"Nova is on the floor."

"We both know if I pushed even a little, that wouldn't matter. So tell me the truth."

"You look hot, so hot I can't believe I get to sleep with you later."

He nibbles on my ear. "I can't wait to see that pretty little mouth doing all sorts of naughty little things."

I can't help another moan of approval. "We need to go," I say. Because if we stay here any longer very good but very bad things are going to happen.

He chuckles, and his breath fanning across my skin sends another outbreak of goose bumps racing across my body. I am absolutely ruined for anyone else.

"Gage," I breathe out, completely helpless.

"That's how you're going to sound later," he says, "when I'm between your legs, you balanced on the edge of madness—not sure if you're asking for relief or to have the feelings prolonged." He tugs me tight against him so I can feel how turned on he is, and I love it. I love how much he wants me. "But that's later, not now. Now we've got a party to go to." He smacks a loud kiss on my neck and steps away as though he hasn't already driven me to the brink of insanity.

He sweeps Nova into his arms and lifts her over his head, talking gibberish to her. I stand in the middle of the bedroom, sucking in a few deep breaths before grabbing the diaper bag and following him out.

The party passes in a blur of following Nova around the play place, talking to other parents, laughing at the antics of other babies and toddlers, and trying not to drink so much that I need the bathroom multiple times.

So I'm surprised at the end of the afternoon when Gage stands on top of one of the chairs and calls for everyone's attention.

"Before everyone heads in every direction, I just wanted to take a minute to thank my wife for putting this afternoon together. I sometimes ask a lot of her—whether that's organizing dinner parties or birthday parties or weddings..."

This draws a chuckle from the crowd.

"But I am so deeply grateful for her. When I first found out I was a father, I had no idea what I was doing. Didn't know how to change a diaper. How to mix a bottle. How to run a bath. I am not exaggerating when I say that she walked me through every step of my parenting journey from the minute I saved her from falling down a flight of stairs."

This draws another laugh.

"I saved her once, but she's saved me every day since. She's the first person I want to call when something goes well, and the first person I turn to when things go wrong. There's no one else I'd want by my side, and I can't believe that Nova and I get to share this life with her." He lifts his glass. "If you'd all be so kind, I'd love for you to raise your glasses in a toast—to Nova turning one, and to my incredible, incomparable wife. No one tell her that I got the better end of this deal."

A chorus of "To Nova and to Ember" floats around the room, and Gage meets my gaze with a light in his eyes that always makes an answering glow rise in me. He's so good at pretending that it almost feels real.

Acknowledgements

As with any book, I'm thankful for such a supportive partner and my understanding children. Sometimes I'm lost in a book idea or writing a chapter when I'm sure they'd like my attention elsewhere. Hopefully, seeing my pursue my dreams has a net positive impact.

I'm really grateful to Isabella whose keen eyes caught a lot of my Canadianisms during the proofread, and whose ability to pull content and think creatively about it, helped me immensely once the book was finished. She's a dream to work with, folks.

A special thank you to Angela who caught a fairly major continuity error in an early draft. Your thoughtful comments and ability to see what I couldn't was incredibly helpful.

Thanks to my cover designers and illustration team of Luciana Bertot, Shannon Passmore, and Amanda Walker. Covers are probably one of the most stressful parts of this job for me and these people made it infinitely easier.

About W. Million

W. Million is a high school teacher whose award winning contemporary romances about strong women and troubled men have captivated her loyal readers. Writing as Wendy Million, she is also the author of the romantic suspense series *The Donaghey Brothers,* the contemporary second chance romance, *When Stars Fall,* and the NA sports romance *Saving Us.* When not writing, Wendy enjoys spending time in or around the water. She lives in Ontario, Canada with two beautiful daughters, two cute pooches, and one handsome husband (who is grateful she doesn't need two of those).

<h1 style="text-align:center">Also By W. Million</h1>

Bellerive Royals Series – Interconnected standalones

Fake Crown

Scarred Crown

Heavy Crown

Fallen Crown
New Adult Sports

Saving Us

Fake Crown
Donaghey Brothers Series – Romantic suspense

Retribution

Resurrection

Redemption
Adult Contemporary Romance

When Stars Fall

Miss Matched

www.ingramcontent.com/pod-product-compliance
Lightning Source LLC
Chambersburg PA
CBHW061109310726
48974CB00002B/456